MW01681060

# Bel-Air Confidential

## A Futuristic Romance

The Confidential Series

Book One

Jeni Lynn

Bel-Air Confidential,
A Futuristic Romance



Edited by Gina Denny
Proofread by Denoument Editing
Cover art by Imperial Cat Circus (@pann_98) and Sorealee
Cover design by Bookfly Design

Published by Jeni Lynn Books
2337 Roscomare Rd. #2-313
Los Angeles, CA 90077

www.jenilynnbooks.com

Library of Congress Control Number: 2026904589

ISBN 979-8-9939639-0-7 (hardback) | ISBN 979-8-9939639-1-4 (paperback) |
ISBN 979-8-9939639-3-8 (ebook) | ISBN 979-8-9939639-2-1 (audiobook)

Subjects: BISAC: FICTION / Romance / Science Fiction. | FICTION / Romance / Suspense.

Human Authored Reg #: 4778337
https://authorsguild.org/human

First edition: 2026

# Contents

*It takes a village to complete every significant effort.*
*Thank you to mine: my special reader friends who read the early versions (several times)—Audrey, Marsha, and Susie; the friends who believed I'd actually finish the thing, and that it would be great—Ann, Deb, Elaine, and Jenny; my fellow authors who shared their knowledge and cheered me on, and amazingly still answer the phone; Brynn, my brilliant marketing and design manager; and my wonderful husband and children who have supported this dream in every possible way.*
*I'm grateful. My love to you all.*

*A special acknowledgment to NASA. All of the planets and moons mentioned are real. Having the ability to dig deep in NASA's website and uncover the latest thoughts and science about our universe was invaluable.*

# Sunday, February 15, 2172

When the airship landed with a bone-jarring bump at Los Angeles' Intergalactic Port, Alex hoped the nightmare had ended. Even with the meds, Alex's head pounded, and her whole body ached from yesterday's attack. Up the aisle, the flight attendant began mopping up the tray of drinks that had crashed to the floor.

Alex gingerly slipped on her glasses, her body protesting at even that slight motion. She'd lucked out that the seat next to her had been empty. As it was, all she'd had energy for when she boarded was sinking into her seat and digging out a wipe to clean off the nasty-looking goo smeared across the armrest.

Two weeks, she thought, just two more weeks to keep it together. Then she could fall apart. Fortunately, her cousin Emily hadn't been with her in Hawaii. The sound of a dog barking, Emily's comm tone, dragged Alex back to the present.

**General sent you security named Jared. Look for a big guy holding our special tin. The tov's in B42. Welcome home!!!**

Jared? Alex wondered as she sent Emily a thumbs up and carefully stood. Wincing in pain, she bent down to grab her carry-on from the below-deck compartment, ignoring the looks from the two self-assured salesmen who'd been celebrating a row back. Having received her share of propositions and unasked-for comms on her Pocket-Venus figure over the years, it was easy to brush off the two.

Walking off the airship, she spied a well-built man, a round pink tin in his hand, towering above the crowd. Adjusting the filter on her glasses with a twist, she could see the stunner in his shoulder holster and a glowing A on the tin's top.

Alex nodded as she headed toward him. Even though the guy was handsome and built, she'd met enough like him growing up in L.A. to dismiss any allure of good looks and muscle. She was grateful for the extra security though, yesterday's ambush still echoing.

After the attack and her uncle's murder, the General had assigned security to her and her cousin Emily. The General hadn't received a speck of kickback about the cost of a guard. Too much was on the line; too many lives hung in the balance.

Taking a shallow breath to keep from hurting her ribs more, she breathed the city's familiar, sweet woodsy scent. She remembered her grandmother talking about the old days when visitors complained about L.A.'s oily stench. It wasn't until fusion replaced petroleum and the city rebuilt its tree canopy that it shed its rep as a smoggy, concrete metropolis.

"I'm Jared," said the muscled mountain.

"Are those for me?" Alex nodded to the tin the man held.

"I brought your favorite, Mexican wedding cookies." Jared handed her the metal container.

Alex opened the tin and saw that it held the sugar-coated cookies. The tight band around her chest loosened. The letter A on the tin, the code words, and the cookies confirmed that Jared was the protection the General had sent.

"No offense, but why didn't Janice come?" Alex asked him, as a few minutes later, she took control of her blue tov. She directed it to lift out of the spaceport parking lot and turn towards home.

"She couldn't leave her assignment," he replied as he scanned the other tovs for possible threats. "She sends her regards."

Alex could tell Jared wasn't thrilled she'd taken the controls instead of letting the sleek tov navigate home. But she loved slipping in and out of traffic, jumping to the upper lane to see the glistening Santa Monica Bay on her left and Century City and downtown L.A. spread out on the right. A half hour later, she dropped back to the slow lane to exit the 405 and merge onto Sunset.

"Don't look, but a green tov's tailing us," Jared said, drawing his stunner and resting it on his lap.

"I'll lose them," she told the man before telling her household bot to send the tov's signature to Beverly Glen.

"On it," Isobelle replied.

Alex contacted her neighbor friend, Natalie.

"Hi Nat, a paparazzi's hugging my tail. Can I slip in for a sec?" Alex asked as she slid through a yellow signal and turned left into Bel-Air's West Gate. Telling her tov to enter stealth mode, she hugged the next three curves, then sped up the tiny connector street before veering right onto a side street.

"Those guys are the worst. Gate's opening," a smoky voice drawled.

A minute later, Alex slid through a ten-foot-tall wood and iron gate, which immediately closed behind them. She noticed Jared looking around in amazement. He then did a double-take when he spotted the two huge, silver, predatory-looking bots flanking the parking area that led to a multi-winged steel and glass house. As Alex set the tov on the path, the twelve-foot-tall raptomatons turned to stare at them.

"Alexandra, why does it always take some snooping Neanderthals to bring you over?" asked a beautiful, slim woman as she approached the vehicle. "And who do we have here?"

Alex noticed with amusement as her friend artfully draped

her arm over the opening of the passenger side, her hand casually resting on Jared's bicep.

"I'm Natalia," she purred to Jared. "Who are you, handsome, and can you dump Alexandra and stay for a while?"

"Don't paw, Nat. Jared, this is Natalia Commings. Nat, meet Jared, a good friend."

"I bet he's a good friend. You never share your good friends, Alexandra." Natalia pouted as she sized up Jared's muscles. "That's not very neighborly. Though I can see why you wanted to evade the pap, Alexandra. What the hell happened to your face?" She lowered her sunglasses to take a closer look.

"I tripped and fell. It's not as bad as it looks," Alex fibbed, not wanting to worry Natalia. "Thanks for the sanctuary. I need to get home, though. The pap should be gone. I'll comm you later."

"You'd better. And you, handsome, can comm me any time." Natalia patted Jared's arm and flashed the look that made her famous.

"Welcome to Bel-Air," Alex said as she pulled out of her neighbor's driveway. A quick glance at Jared showed Nat's magic had worn off as he scanned for the green tov.

"That wasn't paparazzi following us," he said, still checking the area.

"I know. Right now though, whoever it was should have reached Mulholland, wondering which way we went."

A couple of minutes later, Alex pulled into her driveway right as a large, black, six-legged bot scuttled off the roof and down the front.

"What the heck?" she exclaimed, shutting down the tov and walking up to the front porch.

A familiar, wiry man in coveralls stood near the front door, studying something on his comm.

"You can't put this off any more, Ms. Addington," the man said.

"What happened?"

"Branch punched a hole in the roof right over the inside courtyard."

"It can't be patched?"

Alex had been babying the ancient Spanish tile roof for several years. It was going to cost a fortune to replace. She'd hoped to have at least another six months.

"The last patch was the final one your roof will take. I'm sorry, Ms. Addington. I've put on some Synthpla, which should hold for a couple of weeks. Say, are you alright, Ms. Addington?"

"Yes, I'm fine. I fell down, but I'm okay." Alex mentally crossed her fingers at her second lie of the day. Technically she did fall down. Just because she was helped was beside the point. She promised the roofer she'd call as Jared approached, holding her bag.

Once in her bedroom, Alex stripped off her traveling clothes and slipped on her ancient grey sweats and faded UCLA top. She didn't want to think about the colony that needed saving or if her and her cousin's new network tech would arrive in time to make that happen, not to mention the roof and the money she'd need to fix it.

As the quiet in her room seeped in, memories from yesterday's attack began to surface. Shuddering, Alex heard her comm ping, interrupting her thoughts. She sat at her desk to accept the incoming call, glancing out the window in time to see Isobelle finishing Jared's tour of the backyard. A second later, a holo of the Honolulu Police Department Sergeant assigned to her case appeared, his now-familiar stacks of skimpads teetering on his desk.

"We still haven't been able to find your attackers or their boat. We did find this flag in the water. Does it look familiar?" he asked, showing her a tattered, yellow flag that had a circle with a line drawn through its middle.

"I haven't seen anything like that before," she answered, thinking whoever had made the flag should have drawn a better image of Jupiter, the ends of the line barely exiting each side of the circle.

"Regarding your uncle's murder, the captain received Space Force's request to keep it quiet for the next two weeks. He said he'll honor the request, but will have to add the incident to the blotter after that."

Alex thanked the Sergeant, asking him to relay her appreciation for the blanket order. That would give her and her cousin some much-needed breathing room, as chaos would surely hit the feeds when HPD released that news. After a few more fruitless questions—fruitless because she didn't have any answers—the Sergeant promised to comm her later with any new information.

Thinking about the flag, Alex gingerly spread some of the Erisalve the medic in Kailua had given her. Flipping the cap closed, she felt her pain blessedly cut from a screaming level of 10.9 to a tolerable 3-ish.

The relief made Alex feel she could start looking for a way to make some quick cash for the roof. Pierre's LA reopening was basically ready. Her other work, which involved the new deep-space network, would take some of her time, but not all. Emily, who had written the software for their network device, which they'd named Ola, would be central to the upcoming network tests. Since Alex had created Ola's hardware, she would only be able to resolve basic problems, now that the units were off-planet. A moment later her comm pinged again.

"Have I got a cream-cake assignment for you, not to mention the eye candy of a boss who can rock my boat any time," said a holo of Alex's headhunter friend Janice, her round face, rounder body, and raspy voice appearing in the space across from Alex.

"I could definitely use some easy money. And anyone can rock your boat at the moment. Spill, before I tell your hubby you're drooling over another guy," Alex threatened as she bent to secure her shoes.

"You're never any fun," complained Janice. "You know the Hotel Bel-Air's opening in two weeks, launching with Swan Song's pre-Oscar and after-parties?"

"I'd heard something about it, but I've been busy with Pierre's. Isn't Susan handling that?" Alex searched her memory for details.

"Well, she was. She just had a bad accident. She's alive, but the docs put her in a coma. It happened last night on PCH. Mr.—, oh darn, I can't remember the owner's name.

"Anyway, Mr. Hunk-Hotel-Owner contacted me since I found him Susan. He asked if I knew anyone who could take over for her. I mentioned you. I just got off the phone with him. Wait! It's coming! The little guy hasn't sapped all my marbles yet." Janice stopped to think as she rubbed her belly. "His name is—damn, lost it again.

"Anyway, if you're interested, he'd like to meet you at the hotel tomorrow morning at nine. I know you said you've a lot on your plate, but you mentioned the other day that the club job was ending. Since the hotel's next door and, knowing Susan, everything will be well organized, you should only have to oversee what she's set up to earn your monthly fee for two weeks' work. It should be a piece of cake."

Alex thought for a second, figuring since the job was next door she could fit it in, and the money would top off the new-roof fund. Besides, she owed Susan big-time after she'd helped with a project last year.

"You sure have cake on the brain. But he'll meet my fee? Really? Not that I'm arguing." Alex made a note to send Susan flowers. "What's he need?"

"He's extremely busy with his other business. He has some big contract deadlines coming up, so he's desperate. That's why he's paying a lot. He doesn't want to have to worry about anything." Janice started to get up before deciding it wasn't worth the effort and plopped back down. "Oof. That means you have to be available 24x7. Susan had moved into the hotel. He insisted. Since you live so close, I bet you can talk him out of that. Also, his rep is that he's a player, but Susan said that's not true."

"I don't care if he's a player." Alex had no interest in the rich, entitled, and pretentious. Besides, with her bruises, she didn't look like anyone's arm candy, she thought as she finished her braid, so Mr. Hot-Hotel-Owner wouldn't bother her. If anything, the work would be the distraction she needed for the next two weeks, especially since, with its location, she could be readily available if anything came up during the network tests. "Sounds great. I can be there tomorrow." She'd managed a lot of events as a cover for her real work over the years. This one should be a breeze.

"Pierre's reopens tonight, but besides the nightclub, I don't have any other projects going, so it should be pretty quiet after that."

Fortunately, few knew of her and her cousin's work. Instead, the Sol System accepted her event-planner cover, which she had been using for years when she traveled on and off-planet. She'd worked hard to create the impression she preferred socializing and party planning. Living in a mansion in Bel-Air, one of Los Angeles' more exclusive neighborhoods, further reinforced that image. Still, she felt guilty she'd hidden so much from her friends over the years.

"Send me any information you have and tell him I'll see him tomorrow morning. Thanks. You're the best."

As she ordered flowers for Susan, Alex wished Emily was home so she could talk to her about this morning's network test. Since her cousin wasn't supposed to return for another hour, Alex decided to go for a walk, pushing down the tiny, hidden button on the top of her pendant to activate her cloaker.

She slipped past Jared, who was talking to Isobelle in the kitchen, feeling like a kid sneaking out of the house. She could tell Jared was intrigued by Isobelle since most people only used humanoid bots for manual labor. Besides, the general had said

Jared was there to provide security when she and Emily went out. Technically her walk wouldn't be "out." She'd be linked to the house security, and Isobelle would be scanning. She felt safe enough.

As she stepped outside, Alex spied Harry, their robohawk, circling above and Henry, the latest version of their robot squirrel patrol, waiting on the fence, poised to pace her.

She'd really missed home, she thought, as she walked through the backyard and up the hill. The pink-blossomed tulip trees and budding pink and white camellias reminded her spring had started. Although sore and badly bruised, it felt good to be outside. The crisp, cool air smelled of fresh earth and plants. After passing the vegetable garden, she veered left onto a tiny path.

At the end stood the old wood gate that marked the entrance to the side yard between the hotel and the house. As she closed the gate, she pulled her sweatshirt off, accidentally dislodging her sunglasses and disconnecting the cloaker, almost pulling her top off in the process.

She tugged down her shirt, tied her sweatshirt around her waist, and reconnected the cloaker. As she stood silently, letting the solitude sink in, she looked across the canyon, the hills green from the winter rains. Besides linking her to Isobelle and the house systems, the cloaker broadcast a signal, like the one in the tov, that dampened any nearby electronics, so she wasn't worried anyone would know she'd entered the yard.

Heading downhill, she gazed about the meandering fifty-yard-wide strip of land that separated her home from the hotel. Part of an agreement between Alex's ancestors and the man who had built the luxury hotel in the 1940s, the strip of land had since grown dense with towering California oaks and sycamores.

The only hotel employees who entered the side yard from the hotel were the gardeners. In summer, they assisted in clearing dry brush. Other times they helped clean out the stream that meandered through Stone Canyon to ensure it kept flowing from her property and feeding the hotel's lake.

She wound through the trees until she reached the small clearing and Big Ben, the giant old oak she and her cousin had named when they were kids. She eased down with a sigh, leaning back against the sun-warmed trunk. Finally alone for the first time since the attack, a tear tracked down her face, followed by a growing stream. Removing her sunglasses, she laid her head on her knees and started sobbing.

She'd been so scared in Hawaii. She'd really thought she was going to die. There was no way they would have believed that she and her cousin were the brains behind Ola. She and Emily had hidden their tracks too well. Her heart started racing as she recalled the cold, dead look in the men's eyes. She instinctively knew they wouldn't care that they hurt her, that she was just a job, and from their increasing glances at her bare legs, a job they'd enjoy.

She ruthlessly slammed the door shut on those thoughts, concentrating instead on the sounds around her. Worn out, she wiped her face with her sweatshirt, closed her eyes, and leaned back against the tree, soothed by the warm bark, the birdsong, and being home. She drifted off, confident her squirrel patrol would alert her of any danger.

Life was hopefully starting to improve, Erik thought as he ended the comm. The last couple of weeks had been a shit storm, topped by the horrible accident at Farout Base and near total destruction of the base's life support.

At least their team had aced this morning's network test. Erik pushed back from his desk, wanting to relay the other good news: finding their event planner's replacement. He also wanted to see what Ron, their head of security, had discovered about this morning's vandalism, another piece of craziness. Leaving his office, he headed down the hallway, spotting his partner Linc hovering in the security room entrance.

"Something happening?" Erik asked as he walked up.

"Check this out." Linc shifted to make space so Erik could see into the room. Ron was sitting at the security desk monitoring several large displays on the wall. "Ron, run that again."

A small, curvy woman appeared on the screen, standing near the top of what they'd been calling the side yard. She pulled off a faded UCLA sweatshirt, her sunglasses falling off and top lifting in the process. Erik sucked in a breath as he saw multiple, vivid purple and green bruises circling her ribs, neck, and what looked like a black eye. As the woman tugged down her top and replaced her glasses, she fumbled with her necklace and suddenly disappeared.

"What the heck?" Erik asked, first shocked at the woman's bruises and then stunned at her vanishing. "Run that again, Ron."

The men watched the display, not saying anything as they saw the woman disappear, leaving only trees and grass.

"What do the other cameras show?" Erik leaned closer.

"Nothing, just the normal: trees, squirrels, birds, more trees, more squirrels." Ron tapped his keyboard to bring up other security feeds. "I checked Bellagio, Capello, and Stone Canyon. Nothing. A few tovs, but they all flew up Stone Canyon. Nothing turned onto Capello or Bellagio, and no pedestrians."

"Run it again, only slow it down. Stop," Erik said right after the woman disappeared. "Pull up the feed from when she first appeared. There. Zoom in on the grass." He pointed to the image showing the earlier feed. "Look. The grass is undisturbed. After the woman disappeared, the grass looks like it was stepped on. And check that out — what's moving that branch? It's not windy today."

"I'll have Antonio check it out." Ron tapped his comm to contact one of the guards on duty.

"Wait. I'm heading up there. I wanted to look at the work on the new gates." Erik had already planned on inspecting the new sensors for the stream's gates. "When I return, I want to talk with the both of you."

"I'm heading to look at the new solar array," Linc said, turning to head outside with Erik. "I'll go with you part of the way."

The two men hiked up the hotel property, passing Puck's, the hotel's restaurant, and the upper suites.

"Man, it feels good to get outside after this morning's tests." Erik breathed in the spring air as he looked around, noticing the painters had almost finished the last coat of the building's white trim before telling Linc about the new event planner.

"Good, no one has time to deal with parties with the Farout disaster," Linc said grumpily. "Besides, since we're going to win the contract—I'm not jinxing us," Linc added, holding up his hand to keep Erik from talking. "We need to be ready for the onslaught of new customers."

"Nothing's guaranteed." Erik had a nagging feeling that someone was trying his or her hardest to sabotage them or their company, especially after last night's vandalism and their event planner's crash on PCH.

After Linc headed off to check the solar array, Erik silently disengaged the lock on the wrought iron gate that led to the side yard and stepped inside. The cry of a hawk soaring overhead, hummingbirds buzzing around, and the chittering of squirrels interrupted the quiet. Good thing lizards didn't make noise, or he'd go out of his mind. Growing up in a tiny house surrounded by groves of massive Black Walnut and Toyon trees in East L.A., he'd felt connected to nature as a kid. Now that he lived in high-rise penthouses, he wasn't used to the outdoors anymore.

As he walked up the hill, eyes peeled for the woman or anything else suspicious, a squirrel seemed to run alongside him, chittering loudly before scampering ahead. He definitely needed a break soon if he believed a squirrel was watching him.

Up past the stream, he saw the old wood gate that led to the house next door; rough carvings of sprouting seedlings covered the gate, an image that felt familiar. He shelved that thought, wanting to stay alert to possible danger in the wilds of L.A. While he was a big guy, he knew how to be silent and stealthy, skills he'd learned early in life. With regular practice in the holoroom, he'd kept sharp.

Rounding a tree, he spied the woman he had seen earlier, asleep on the ground beneath a giant tree. A squirrel—damn, there were too many of those furry rats around—looked like it was creeping close to her, maybe to bite her? Did it have Marbola or some other nasty disease? He quickened his pace, determined to protect the woman from the furry, rabid monster.

"Hey! Hey!" Erik yelled, waving his arms, hoping to scare off the furry bastard.

Suddenly, a loud chitter woke Alex. Unsure where she was, she spied a blur of fur and a dark, giant shape of a man looming over her yelling, "Get out of here!"

With a cry, she scrambled up, turning to run for the gate. In her panic, she caught her foot on a tree root and fell hard, a sharp stab of pain knocking the breath out of her.

"I'm not going to hurt you," the silhouette of the man promised as she turned and tried to scoot backwards away from him, the sun too bright to see his features.

"I'm sorry I scared you. I'm from the hotel. I was yelling at the squirrel. I thought he was going to bite you." The man backed up a few steps, holding his hands out, apparently trying to look less menacing.

Alex sucked in her breath, making her grimace at the pain in her ribs. As he stepped out of the sun, his features were no longer hidden. Standing in front of her was one of the most masculine men she'd ever encountered. Muscular, definitely not slim, her gaze rose from solid, long legs, flat stomach, broad chest and shoulders, to rest on full lips and piercing eyes below a head of wavy jet-black hair. Too bad he looked like such a suit. Who walks through nature wearing a dress shirt, slacks, and fancy shoes, she wondered, noticing the spider creeping up the outside of his pant leg.

"I was checking on the stream gates to make sure they're working when I saw that nasty, furry thing about to attack you," the man told her. "What are you doing here?" he asked, hooking his sunglasses in his dress shirt and peering at her closely.

Alex relaxed a bit after he'd said he worked next door. He was probably one of the facility engineers, although he was still dressed a bit too formally. Who else would be checking the stream gates? She attempted to push herself to stand. "I live next door. I should get back."

"Do you know you're on private property?" he asked curtly.

Alex, bristling at his arrogance and ignoring his biceps, launched to her feet, forgetting about her ribs. A piercing pain hit so sharply, her vision blacked around the edges. She would have stumbled again, except a strong hand suddenly gripped her arm, keeping her from falling.

"Are you ok?" Eric asked, concern coloring his voice. "Do you need medical care?"

"I'm fine, thank you." Alex carefully pulled her arm away, trying not to pass out. "I have a right to be here, but I was just going. Besides, only the hotel's maintenance people are allowed here," she added as she turned toward the stream.

"Wait a minute." Erik reached out to grab her arm again. "You're the one trespassing. Also, the stream's cold."

Erik found her defiant, dismissive tone—one he rarely heard from women—refreshing, making him want to shake her and simultaneously protect her. He didn't need any complications, though. No matter how captivating she was with that long ebony braid that he suddenly yearned to unleash and watch spill around her, those bruises and that attitude spelled drama.

Alex stepped back, out of his reach, dismissing the spark she felt when his hand had grasped her arm. The stream, more like a creek at the moment, wasn't that wide or deep. Surely, she could cross without too much pain, as she eyed the water flow slowly down towards the hotel.

If she crossed here, she'd be close to the gate and home free. She stepped off the bank, aiming for the other side. Somehow, she miscalculated, missed the other side by an inch, and slipped into the water.

"Oh my god!" She expected only a couple inches of water; instead, she hissed as freezing cold water reached to her butt.

"I tried to warn you. We've been working on the stream. Do you need help?"

"No, I'm fine, just fine," Alex muttered, embarrassed by her clumsiness in front of this too handsome man and mad she even cared. She clamored up the stream's bank, ribs screaming as wet leaves and mud clung to her sweats and now-soggy shoes. Glancing back as she reached the gate, she'd swear she'd caught a glint in his eyes, the bastard. She then slipped through the gate and slammed it behind her.

"What happened to you?" Isobelle asked as Alex stomped toward her. "I had eyes on you, but then something strange happened after you fell asleep, and I lost visual. Harry's regular vision worked, but not the infrared. I could not see through the tree canopy," the bot added, plucking off a couple wet oak leaves sticking to Alex's clothes.

"I'm fine, besides making a fool of myself." Alex limped toward the house. The last thing she needed was more bruises. "Nothing worth talking about. Some stuffy facilities guy from the hotel was there. Did you know they'd dredged the stream?"

"I was going to tell you." Isobelle picked a leaf out of Alex's braid. "They also installed new gates."

"Yep, found that out," Alex grumped, her waterlogged shoes

squelching as she walked. Alex eyed the bot, daring her to say another word. Isobelle always looked like she had just walked out of a fashion spread, her grey bob sleek, her slacks and blouses always pressed and stain-free. Her only quirks the bright, sometimes garish earrings she wore and the cheeky sayings she embroidered on her blouses.

"How are my cousin and Jared getting along?" Alex asked, determined to change the subject and forget about the too attractive man as she limped along.

"Like two rabid dogs circling and ready for a fight," Isobelle said with a smile. "Jared was really angry when he found out you had gone for a walk. When Emily returned, she said you could not be safer, but he rushed out to look for you, muttering about crazy women and that the General was not paying him enough. Then your cousin walked rather loudly to the lab, talking about something called he-men know-it-alls. I found it quite interesting."

After checking the new stream gates, Erik headed back to his office, thinking about the woman he'd come across, intrigued she hadn't been afraid to stand up to him, even though he was at least a foot taller. Not many people did that these days, partially due to his size, but also because, knowing he was wealthy, they usually wanted something from him.

"Did you find anyone?" Linc asked as Erik entered his office and sat behind his desk. Linc and Ron, both in Erik's office, had turned Erik's guest chairs around to face the display above the fireplace that was showing the now-empty grounds where the woman had been walking.

"I found her. Turns out she's from next door. She was asleep under a tree. She might be one of those students we heard the owner puts up."

He wasn't quite sure, though. She didn't look young enough to be a coed. "I told her she was on private property, which she didn't like me saying. Then she tried crossing the stream." Erik recalled the woman's curves that had become strikingly apparent when the water soaked her sweats. "Did you figure out what's wrong with the cameras?"

"No, I saw you go through the gate, and then nothing; everything went blank," Ron said. "They just came back. It's almost as if there's some kind of interference. I'm checking into it."

"What about the damage to the Camellia suite?" Erik asked the hotel's head of security.

"Fortunately, the cameras worked there. Although why the alarm didn't go off, I'm still trying to figure out. Two masked guys cut the chain-link fence at 2:13 a.m., broke into the suite, and then carried out the monitors, guest comms—only stuff with value. They were pretty sloppy, though. One left a partial print, and the other's mask slipped for a second. It looks like they're your run-of-the-mill burglars. I have pictures of their tov, a brown long-bed, that they loaded the stuff in, but no plates. I've sent everything to the police and am searching some darcom sites to see if I can discover anything."

"How long until the fence's fixed and wired with the new cams?" Linc asked.

"The parts are in, so tomorrow at the latest. Gary's already working on it."

"Let us know when it's live, and add the cams to our feeds, too." Linc stood to turn his chair back towards Erik's desk as Ron left.

"Any news on our hacker?" Erik asked Linc.

"Not yet. Whoever did it is good, but not that good. I can't believe they tried to set up Meg."

Erik could see Linc's frustration as his friend ran his hand through his spiked blond hair.

"You told her?"

"I didn't have a chance before she figured it out."

"She's going to be worse than ever." Erik sighed, thinking of their CFO as he dialed himself a cup of coffee from the old brewer perched next to a brand new, gleaming beverage machine. Meg had worked for Erik and Linc for almost sixteen years now, and her tolerance had lessened over the years.

"Want some?" Erik asked when he saw Linc looking at him and his coffee.

"I'll get it myself." Linc sighed, getting to his feet. "I hate that machine. I can't wait until we get the new Raleigh working. This stuff is sludge."

"I can't figure out why someone would go to all the trouble of breaking into our systems for such a small contract." Erik slightly nudged the chair Ron had sat and then carefully set his cup on the coaster on his desk. "Fuck, it's almost as if someone's trying to make Xtra look bad."

"The hack was sophisticated, which means it wasn't cheap." Linc frowned as he dialed himself a cup of the dank coffee. "You owe the pot. Pay up." Linc tapped the Ceres Crystal bowl half full of antique poker chips that sat on the corner of Erik's desk.

"I can't believe you ever talked me into this." Erik grabbed a yellow chip from the top drawer in his desk and tossed it in the bowl.

"You know we have to clean up our language, at least before your sister's family comes. It wouldn't hurt to be better around our clients, too."

"What about Susan's accident?" Erik asked, agitated at the thought of their event planner being hurt because she worked for them. He reined in his frustration, straightening the skimpads on his desk and placing his litpen diagonally on top. "Any news about her tov?"

"Not yet, but hopefully by end of day."

"I feel like we're under siege. What about you?" Erik looked at his friend.

"I think something's up," Linc agreed. "I think we should put the emergency plan into action, at least until the network contract's awarded. If we're wrong, no harm."

"Agreed."

Someone had sabotaged Erik and Linc's company ten years ago, right after they had won their first big communications contract. They'd finally discovered their receptionist and a competitor had worked together to steal some of their secrets. The two went to jail once Erik and Linc had found the evidence to convict them.

After that, Erik, Linc, and Meg had developed an emergency plan they could immediately launch. It would secure the company's systems while also leave honey pots around to lure and catch any thieves.

"Will you tell Meg, or shall I?" Linc asked as he spun the nine-level holo puzzle Erik kept in his office.

"I'll let her know. I need to tell her Susan's replacement will be here tomorrow at nine. I'll lock the system down. You prepare the traps."

After Linc left, Erik pinged Meg. While waiting to hear from her, he thought about the network contract they hoped to win. Before the Farout disaster, Erik had wanted to win the contract, knowing it would ensure the company's future. Becoming the processor of all of humanity's extraterrestrial network data would guarantee Xtra's place in space for decades.

Now though, people's lives were on the line. In addition to the deaths of the famous astrophysicist Dee Star and ten of the base's twelve systems engineers, the radiation that had hit Farout Base had crashed all of its comms and life support systems. Space Force had two weeks to reach Farout and upload a fix to reboot their systems, or the remaining 187 people on the dwarf planet would die.

At this point, Erik almost wished he hadn't talked Linc into buying the hotel. Before the Farout accident, the two were planning on enjoying the hotel's opening and parties, and then prepping and competing for the network contract. Now Space Force had escalated the timeline due to the accident, and the tests had begun that morning.

"I heard you took a dip," Emily said as she entered Alex's bedroom, munching on macadamia nuts. Their German Shepherd, Fred, followed close on her heels, hoping a nut would drop.

"A dip in my pride if you want to know." Alex thought about the irritating hunk from next door as she changed into dry clothes. "If you value your life, you'll give me some of those." She reached for the bowl of nuts Emily held.

Emily laughed as she swiftly backed out of Alex's reach, clutching her bowl. "Get your own. I'm not sharing. Or, are you wanting these?" She waved around a second small bowl of nuts. "Iso will be mad if we fill up before dinner. She told me she's making a salad with a macadamia vinaigrette, macadamia-encrusted Opah, and macadamia nut pie."

"That sounds real light." Alex thought of all those calories before grabbing the second bowl. She popped a nut in her mouth before slipping on dry shoes. "What's with all the macadamias?"

"Iso discovered February's National Macadamia Nut Month. Be glad you missed the smoothie. Don't try one if she offers." Emily made a sour face. "The muffins, though, are to die for, unfortunately. So, how are you doing?" She took a serious look at Alex, noting the vivid purple and green bruises around her eye and circling her neck. "Besides the pain, are you okay?"

"I'm as okay as I can be." Alex carefully sat down on the edge of her bed. "A bit jumpy and paranoid." She started to pet a sleeping Chutney, who had curled up at the end.

"I wouldn't call it paranoid. I'd call it smart!" Emily paced in front of her cousin, angry at what had happened. "This attack takes things to a new level. Even though Jared's extremely annoying, I'm glad the General sent help."

"I don't get it." Alex looked up, frowning. "Why would anyone want to sabotage the deep-space network? Who would benefit?" Alex noticed Chutney was tiring of the attention. The big tomcat would only stand so much petting before the claws came out.

"Remember last Thanksgiving?" Emily asked as she continued to pace. "When Uncle Wally mentioned that group called the Solars? He said he was hearing some weird rumors. That the group wasn't happy people were planning to explore the Oort Cloud, but he hadn't been able to find out why."

"People have already entered the Oort Cloud, though—at least a few have. Sam and Charlie's ship wasn't the only one lost. The network will just let people communicate when they get out there. Besides, those people on Farout will die if we don't help them."

Alex carefully scooted back on her bed and rested against the padded turquoise headboard. She really didn't want to think about any more deaths, especially their uncle's or the losses of her and Emily's husbands. She hoped that Space Force would be able to find their husbands' lost spaceship after the network tests had finished, but five years had passed since their ship had disappeared—too long for Charlie or Sam to still be alive. Now, though, the lives of people at Farout colony were in jeopardy.

"I think someone wants our new code," Emily said. "Getting that comm yesterday from those thugs who said they had you, and that we had to give it up to get you back. I was freaking out. If you hadn't commed me right then—" Emily started pacing faster across the white-oak plank floor, her breathing quickening and fear evident on her face.

"But I did, and I'm okay," Alex declared, hoping her attack wouldn't trigger Emily's agoraphobia. "We have to assume someone believes we know something about Uncle Wally's inventions. Fortunately, it doesn't seem like they know we're Al and Lee, much less that we developed the new network device."

Alex started petting Fred, who had laid his head on the bed close to her, still hoping for a nut. The contact soothed the panic threatening to erupt as she thought about yesterday's attack.

"I looked again at all the teams competing for the network project. They all seem to want it to work, or why compete? I haven't found anything that points to one of them desperate enough to hurt anyone, much less want people dead. What about you?"

"I didn't find anything either, but it has to be one of them since there aren't any other companies that are Space Force contractors." Emily started pacing again.

Alex wanted to switch subjects, for both her and her cousin's sake.

"It sounds like the first test went okay this morning." She and Emily had thought about running the tests in Kahaluu as usual, but decided they'd rather be in Bel-Air. It was still too raw being in Hawaii after their uncle's murder. Thankfully the network test at Earth's orbiting Gateway space station had been a success. "What was the reason for the delay?"

"All Space Force said this morning was that they needed to delay the Gateway test two hours." Emily finally sat on the chair across from her cousin. "General Watson wouldn't tell me anything. Ola had a few glitches at first when I was linking it to the station, but that string you sent when you were on the airship smoothed the wobble. After that, I was even able to double the input coming from Gateway."

"That's great. Farside's Wednesday, right? I'll be here for sure." Alex was mad that on top of everything else, yesterday's attack made her miss this morning's test at the space station. At least she'd be here for the Moon's Farside Base test. Even more than Gateway, the base on the other side of the moon desperately needed more bandwidth.

"Endeavor will be on the back side by then. Then we'll start seeing how fast Ola can really go." Emily smiled and rubbed her hands together. "Are you up for meeting the General tonight at Pierre's? I can go by myself."

"I'm going. I need to check on the opening anyway." Alex reminded herself to make sure she loaded her checklist in her comm before they left. Pierre was reopening his L.A. club and restaurant after the complete overhaul Alex had helped oversee. She needed to go. Besides, she knew her cousin could use the company. Emily was working hard to manage her agoraphobia. Alex didn't want anything to happen that would make Emily backslide.

Even though she felt somewhat fragile, she could hold it together long enough to go, especially after another dose of that miracle numbing cream. She had opted for the cream over a stronger medpac. While a medpac would heal her faster, the pacs usually made her depressed and sleepy for weeks. She was already sad enough. She needed to stay sharp.

"I hope you can cover that black eye and those bruises, or Pierre and the General are both going to blow a thruster when they see you." Emily looked at Alex, concern in her eyes. "Before I forget, I have something for tonight." Emily pulled a small blue box from her pants' pocket. Opening it, Alex saw a pair of gold dangly earrings. "These babies," Emily said, holding up the earrings, "work with your ring. Let me demonstrate."

Emily double-tapped her ring, an intricate silver band of sprouting seeds, against one of her silver earrings and then touched the remaining macadamia nut in her bowl. When her finger touched the nut, it started smoking. When she lifted her finger, the smoke cleared, leaving what looked like a much smaller, dark brown nut.

"Wow! You figured it out. That's great—a little scary, but great. How's it work?"

"I'm pretty proud of it myself," Emily preened. "If you want to give someone a minor shock, touch your ring to either earring once. If you want something stronger—say you need to disable someone—tap twice. But be careful. At full strength, it can cause some serious damage."

Alex slipped on the earrings. She touched her ring, a gold version of Emily's silver one, against an earring once and then touched the remaining nut in her bowl. The nut jumped at her touch. "Ceres! How do you turn it off?"

"Once you've used it, it shuts down and won't work again until you tap it."

"So, if I touch a person, what happens?" Alex set her bowl on her nightstand. Fred was dismayed he hadn't been offered the nut.

"It depends on their size. One touch—I'm calling it Level One—will feel like a very bad bee sting to someone our size. Someone big like Jared will feel a smaller shock, but still a shock. Two taps, or Level Two, won't kill anyone, but I think it will deliver enough charge to make them pass out. You never know; we might get the opportunity to try Level One tonight." Emily's eyes shone with mischief, Alex knowing she was thinking of some of the handsy jerks they'd encountered at nightclubs.

"This is one of your best inventions yet," Alex said with a smile.

Just like Emily, Alex did not like being touched by strangers, especially after the attack in Hawaii. "How many jolts before it runs dry?"

"Each earring has enough power for two Level Ones or one Level Two. After the network test's done, I'm going to try and bump that. In the meantime, when you put your earrings in the box, they'll recharge."

"Hey man, all work and no play makes someone very dull," chided Linc as he entered Erik's office and saw his friend still working at his desk. "It's Sunday. You know, a day of rest and all that. Just because there aren't any waves, there're other interesting activities available. Pierre L.A. opens tonight. The Stombolers are playing. I was able to snag a couple of invites." Linc turned on the latest Stomboler hit on his comm.

"There." Erik closed down his systems and stashed his skimpad in his top drawer. He checked the satin-smooth top for any rogue materials he'd missed. Satisfied that nothing marred the black walnut surface, he rubbed his face. "Our key data and applications are now separate from the rest of the systems and secure. Only Meg, you, and I have access. How about you? Have you set up the honeypots?"

"All in place." Linc had created several pots of fake data on their contract bid to try and catch possible thieves. "Now get changed. Let's go play."

An hour later, as the two men entered the club, heads turned to take in the extremely attractive testosterone filling the entrance. Even jaded celebrities sucked in stomachs and postured to look more appealing to the men, both dressed in Slayer slacks and Capit tailored shirts. Erik wore black and burgundy, setting off his dark looks. Linc dressed in white pants and a navy shirt that accentuated his deep tan and white blonde hair. While many men in L.A. looked fit, and many had money or brains, Erik and Linc were the complete package—a raw and rare blend few could ignore.

"Welcome, Mr. Wolfe, Mr. Cussler." Pierre, the club's elegant, silver-haired owner, appeared at the entrance and greeted the two. "You have a reserved table upstairs. Mindy will be your server, whichever floor you're on." Pierre signaled to an attractive young waitress in a black mini-dress, who promptly took their drink orders while eyeing them appreciatively.

After a few dances with two long-legged A-list actresses, Erik headed up to the second-floor lounge and sat at their reserved table, leaning back in his chair while Linc continued to flirt with the women downstairs. Sipping his Macallan Oak, he looked over the railing, smiling sardonically at the antics some of the women were using to try and capture Linc's attention and his friend's equally smooth, evasive maneuvers.

Linc and Erik liked to play the field and keep it simple, which meant no strings. Recently, Erik had wondered about having a relationship similar to the one his sister enjoyed. But he'd quickly shoveled those thoughts into a dark hole after a short-lived liaison with a woman who was more interested in his money than him. Returning to the single life, he determined to keep it that way. Both he and Linc only connected with women who understood the rules. Since plenty were willing to play, he saw no reason to change his ways.

As Erik looked across the club, he appreciated the refresh. A tech he'd never seen before made the place feel as if the club sat submerged in the sea. A self-proclaimed water rat, he liked an oceanic environment, either one of Earth's or another planet's. He definitely enjoyed hearing the occasional whale whistles and seabird calls, which he could clearly hear now he'd come upstairs.

A familiar face on the dance floor caught his eye. Leaning against the brass railing, he looked closer at the black-haired beauty dancing below alongside a very muscular, large man and a tiny, curvy woman with long platinum hair. The first woman looked a lot like the one he'd discovered today under the tree. He couldn't tell for sure from the distance, but not many had a lush figure like hers, even though it was now encased in a sleek silver bodysuit that left no skin exposed. It even covered her neck. Intrigued, he continued to watch the woman move seductively to the beat.

He wasn't the only one who had noticed the woman, interested looks filling the room. Suddenly, a too-tanned, mildly handsome man stepped into her circle, attempting to cut in. She shook her head and turned away. The intruder, obviously not used to rejection, grabbed her arm. Suddenly, the man leapt back as if stung, and the woman mouthed something to him. The man, his face contorting in a snarl, started to say something back until he noticed the monster of a man looming behind her. He turned and angrily pushed his way through the crowded dance floor, looking for an easier target.

"May I get you something else, a drink, appetizer or... anything?" Mindy asked, leaning over, exposing her ample cleavage as she wiped the already-clean table.

"I'll take another Macallan," Linc told Mindy as he plopped down, arms around two blonde, long-legged women, their dresses so short that Erik was amazed they didn't reveal more, not that he minded. "So will he. Ladies?"

When Erik glanced back at the dance floor, the woman and her friends had disappeared. As he looked around to see where they'd gone, he saw the flash of a silver bodysuit, a matching stiletto boot, and long ebony hair disappear through a door. On the opposite side of the room, two bouncers were escorting the asshole who'd tried to manhandle the woman out the door.

Erik grabbed the hand of one of the women, who was sitting with them and hauled her up to return to the dance floor. Once downstairs, he made his way over to the door the woman had disappeared through and pushed against it. At that moment, the enormous man who had been dancing with his woodland pixie opened the door, locked eyes with Erik, stepped out, shut the door behind him, folded his arms across his massive chest, and cocked an eye at him as if daring him to get past.

"Sorry, isn't this the way to the men's room?" Erik asked as he held up his hands to show he hadn't meant to get in the way. While Erik was big and built, able to take down just about anyone, this guy loomed like a mountain. He also didn't look dumb, intelligence showing in his dark eyes as they traveled down Erik's body from his head to his feet and back up.

"Men's room's over there." The man nodded across the dance floor, not moving an inch from the door.

"My mistake. I thought it used to be here." Erik turned and headed across the room after telling his dance partner he'd see her back upstairs. Something seemed off, but he couldn't figure out what. Shaking his head, he decided he'd head home. He'd had enough for tonight, feeling strangely uninterested in the women who seemed so eager.

As Alex and Emily entered the private dining room, which Pierre had named the Garibaldi room after the local, bright-orange fish, Alex glanced around, glad to see the room's floor-to-ceiling aquariums she and Emily had created were functioning properly. They had had some problems three weeks ago when several robot fish had stopped moving. Across the room, the General stood looking at a cluster of Garibaldi swimming in front of him, forests of king kelp swaying in the background.

"These fish look absolutely lifelike," the General said as he turned to greet Alex and Emily. "Your uncle would have been so proud of you. He also would have been proud of how well Ola performed this morning. The comms guys were amazed how quickly you two adjusted that string. In fact, they'd really like to talk to you about how you did it. I told them you'd consider it once the contract's in place, but not before then," he added quickly, seeing the panic on Emily's face.

"Everything's still set for Wednesday?" Alex asked as Emily handed the General the mindrive.

"Endeavor should be in place no later than Tuesday night. Plan on starting at 0500 Pacific Earth Time." As the General eyed Alex's pale face, he added, "I still think you should have let Jared bring the drive tonight."

"Too many weird things have been happening lately," Emily said. Alex nodded in agreement.

"It's not that we don't trust Jared—" Alex added.

"We don't trust anyone," Emily completed.

"Especially after the last time when the data got corrupted.

Anyway, I needed to come see how the opening was going, and Emily wanted to get out."

"Pierre and his manager could have handled tonight, and if any of your technology didn't work, so be it. How are you really feeling, my dear?"

Alex could tell the General noticed the faint outlines of the bruises she hadn't completely been able to cover on her face and puffiness around her eye.

"I'm fine, General. Really," she said, wanting to reassure the man she'd known since she was little. "I only have a few bruises, nothing major." Even though that wasn't true, she didn't want to worry him. "Have you discovered anything?"

"Nothing. Definitely professionals," he replied gruffly, his fury at someone hurting Alex bubbling to the surface. "But we haven't stopped looking. They can't hide forever. Honolulu PD is as keen to catch them as we are. If we have to look under every piece of lava and board every boat between here and there, we'll find them.

"Now, how is Jared working out? You girls aren't torturing him too much, are you?" The General brightened at the thought. "Though he did say you gave him the slip today." He looked at Alex and shook his head. "You can't underestimate whoever's behind this or their motivation. You need to keep Jared with you when either of you go out." The General looked sternly at the two women.

"I never really left the property." Alex considered the land between the house and hotel an extension of her property. "You know I'm wired to the house, and we have eyes on the canyon. Also, if Jared hasn't already informed you, I've taken a job next door at the hotel to manage their opening in two weeks. The woman who was handling it was in an accident."

"You do know the hotel's owner, Erik Wolfe, is CEO of Xtra, which is bidding on the network contract?" The General sat down at the long brass-and-glass dining table, motioning the women to take a seat.

"I hadn't had time to check him out completely. I was going to do that tonight when we got home." Alex looked at Emily, who shrugged, letting Alex know she hadn't made the connection either. "The job would actually help with my cover now that Pierre's open. We don't want to expose ourselves just yet."

"The media's going to go nuts," Emily said, taking a deep breath.

"Walter, of all people, would have understood you sticking to your plan and revealing your identities when we announce the contract award," the General said, trying to bolster the women's spirits.

Alex knew Walter's death had also hit him and his wife hard, and he was trying not to get riled at the injustice of his friend's death in front of them. With their uncle dead, the women realized they had to reveal their identities so they could take control of Walter's company, Seed, as well as authorize the search for their husbands' ship.

"If you take the hotel job, you need to be careful. I wish you wouldn't, though. Helping Pierre is one thing—"

"I need to stay busy. You know that. I'd just be stressing, hoping that everything works, and that would drive me crazy."

Alex had discovered long ago that if she didn't stay busy during stressful times, her heart would start acting up. The doctors had never figured out why since her heart beat fine when she wasn't under stress. They had tried drugs, but she couldn't stand the side effects. She'd tried shrinks and meditation. Those had helped, but not enough. After her uncle's murder, the attack on her, and the crazy tight schedule they now faced to save Farout, she knew her heart would start a wild tango if she didn't bury herself in something fun and happy, like the hotel parties. Besides, she needed the new roof. The fact that the job came up at the perfect time almost made her feel as if the universe wasn't completely against her.

"Just because we have no reason to think Wolfe was involved, it doesn't mean there couldn't be others at the hotel who might be a threat. This morning someone broke into one of the hotel suites. It sounds like everyday thieves, but LAPD's still checking it out."

Alex and Emily looked at each other just as Alex stifled a yawn, exhausted from the past couple of days. Once home, they needed to tell Isobelle about the vandalism next door and check last night's logs.

"I won't keep you any longer," the General said, seeing Alex's yawn and rising from the table. "Please promise me you girls will be very careful. You can't leave Jared out of the loop, much less behind. I don't care if you're just going to get the mail. In fact, let him earn his keep and get the mail.

"You two are Sol-System assets. Besides, Mary would string me up if anything happened to you." He patted the two women on the arm. "You know she wanted to come tonight and see for herself that you were alright."

"We love you, too," said Alex.

She and Emily gave the General a tight hug before leaving. Stepping out of the private room, they found Jared waiting in the hall.

"I think it's safer to exit through the garage," Jared said as Pierre appeared to lead everyone towards the private elevator to the garage. "The paparazzi have already gotten their shots. The tov's downstairs."

As they headed to the elevator, Alex realized that once the tests finished and they had revealed their identities, they would probably stop meeting Pierre in secret. While he was technically retired, he still dabbled, his word, not theirs. In the past, when the General was occupied and Pierre available, he would meet with the women to share information too sensitive to send. Once people knew their real identities, people may become suspicious if they met with Pierre.

"By the way, was the men's room on this side of the dance floor before the remodel?" Jared asked Pierre.

"No," Pierre answered, "It's always been on the other side. Why?"

"Just curious. A guy tried to enter the hallway after we came in. He said he was looking for it; that it used to be on this side." Jared shared a look with Pierre before following Alex and Emily into the elevator.

After returning home from Pierre's, Alex, Emily, and Isobelle sat around the lab's worktable and looked at the holos in front of them. Nearby on the pet beds, the cats and dogs snoozed after following the women into the underground lab. The holos, fed by an array of sensors, both static and mobile via robotic animals, showed numerous views of the property, including Jared prowling near the greenhouse in the back.

"I think we should put three squirrels at the hotel and a couple of hummingbirds," Isobelle told Emily and Alex as she placed the robotic creatures on the table.

"Agreed. I don't think Snake's ready to go past our property, and Hawk still can't see through the trees." Emily glanced up before clacking away on her keyboard. "I may have a fix for that, though."

"How was your visit with Eva?" Alex asked Isobelle.

When Space Force shifted the mission from just testing the new deep-space network to a rescue mission, Eva volunteered to go. Humans couldn't perform the network tests fast enough since the ship would be speeding past each test site now that Space Force had accelerated the schedule. Eva, a bot, had worked with Emily and Alex since they were young, when their uncle created her a few years after Isobelle. Alex understood Eva was the perfect choice for the mission—Eva knew how their device, Ola, worked and she understood networks—but Alex felt sad she was going.

She wasn't sure when, or even if, she'd see her again. Losing another being, while she still reeled from her uncle's death, hurt.

"She had everything in order," Isobelle said as she rechecked the robot creatures that sat on the lab table. "I told her I would miss her. She said to tell you both the same."

"If the network works, we'll at least be able to talk to her." Alex hoped that would be true. The way so many humans discounted bots, Isobelle didn't have many friends—bots or human—in her life. In fact, besides Emily and Alex, Eva was the only one Isobelle felt safe enough with to admit her dreams. When Walter created the two bots, he established false identities and accounts so they could buy what they wanted and live how they wanted. At the time, arguments about whether bots should have rights had already begun escalating.

After Walter's death, Emily and Alex had secretly ensured the bots on the company's payroll continued to receive their pay. That was another reason the women needed to reveal they were Al and Lee so quickly. They weren't stupid. The board wouldn't be able to deny them stewardship over the company as CEO and president once they learned they owned all the company's patents.

"I bet you're going to miss her," Alex said.

"People say bots don't have feelings," Isobelle commented stiffly.

"And some people are idiots. We know you have feelings, Iso."

"Yes, especially when we steal any cookies you've been hiding," Emily said, smiling.

"Oh no!" Alex peered at the small display she'd brought up on the table. "I've already met my new boss."

She tapped a key, and a holo of the man she'd met hovered in the center of the table. "Erik Wolfe. He's the guy I met in the side yard—the one I thought was the hotel's facilities engineer." Alex groaned as she dropped her head in her hands. "Great," she muttered, thinking back on how terrible she'd looked—hair messed, no make-up, not to mention her bruises. She hoped in the late afternoon light he hadn't seen them.

"Well, Janice and you were right, he is definitely hot, and so is he," Isobelle said, as Alex flipped through the many pictures of Erik she was finding. She'd stopped on a picture of him and another extremely ripped man standing on a supersized catamaran, both in boardshorts, topless, tan, buff, and glistening.

"He looks familiar, too" Emily mused, inspecting another image of the two men, this time wearing tuxedos. "I remember. The other guy's Linc Cussler, Xtra's president."

"Did you know that this January's *Galactic Style* named them the year's hottest bachelors, dubbing them 'the Space Men'?" Isobelle asked, reading from the *Galactic* article she'd called up on her screen. "The article says it is because of their success in space, intelligence, money, and their supposed ability to send so many women into orbit."

"Well, I won't have to worry about any orbits with them," Alex said, somewhat relieved, yet also irritated and unsure why. Even if Erik liked her, she thought, if he found out just how smart she was, he'd likely dump her. It wouldn't be the first time. "It looks like their type is the blonde, leggy, perfectly sculpted species," she snarked as picture after picture showed the men with long-legged, bronzed, pouty, perky, busty women.

"Either one of them could take me to space anytime," Isobelle said, looking at their images.

"Are you crazy?" Emily exclaimed, surprised by Isobelle's response. "They look like the love-em-and-leave-em-before-even-spoonin' types, even if they are really smart—"

"Let's change the subject," Alex interrupted. "Mr. Wolfe—" Alex stopped and looked sternly at the two when Emily imitated a wolf howling, making Isobelle smile.

"—and I will be working together," she added, absently twisting her long hair into a bun and securing it with a litpen from her desk. "Back to security. I'm going to take Larry with me tomorrow and let him out at the hotel. We can see how well his skin holds up."

Larry, shaped like a lizard, and Sheila, built to look and move like a snake, were the women's most ambitious robotic creations. So far, they'd only let the prototypes maneuver around the property. Even though their motor skills perfectly mimicked the creatures they looked like, their "skin" was still wearing unevenly. Alex had just changed their skin's formula again.

"Sounds like a plan." Emily looked up from her tablet at her cousin. "I'll have Larry ready in the morning. You look beat. Go to bed."

"I'm going. Let me know if you can get Hawk's infrared up." The Erisalve Alex had applied before they left for *Pierre's* had worn off, and the pain in her ribs was screaming.

"I will add another bird and squirrel, too," Isobelle said.

# Monday, February 16, 2172

Erik studied the article on *Pierre's* wondering what he was missing as he sat at his desk in the hotel. He'd chosen to convert the Swan Suite into his offices because he liked its view of the hotel lake and proximity to the entrance. Through the French doors, he saw the crew of gardeners planting the last of the Iceland poppies that Manny, the hotel's head gardener, promised would bloom in time for the opening.

It was still early, and he had been trying to take care of the comms that had come in since yesterday when the story popped up. He zoomed into the accompanying image, taken last night, that showed his next-door pixie dressed to kill in her silver bodysuit, hair loose like black silk spilling all the way to her waist, standing arm-in-arm with Pierre and the other woman from last night, who was as fair as she was dark.

The caption identified her not as the UCLA student he'd thought she was, but Alexandra Addington, the woman he was meeting at 9:00 that morning. She'd supposedly played a key role in *Pierre's* makeover, the reporter had written, gushing about Alex's innate ability to define new trends. The blonde, it turned out, was her cousin, he read as Meg entered the room.

"Ron's sent you a prelim on Addington, said she looks clean.

Did you know she lives next door? Hey, that's her, the new event planner." Meg leaned over Erik's shoulder to look closer at the image. "I like her outfit. She helped with *Pierre's*? I'm impressed. What'd you think when you were there?"

"I was very impressed," Erik said, remembering his pixie's curves, which were striking, although he'd also been taken by the club's new look. The ocean tech Pierre had installed was amazing. He opened the file Ron had sent, finding a professional headshot of Alexandra with the same ice-blue eyes staring back. Swiping through the report, he saw that she'd worked for numerous big names and companies.

There wasn't much in the way of personal information: her parents were dead, Emily—the one he'd seen with Alex at Pierre's —was her cousin, she traveled on and off-planet quite a bit, and owned the old mansion next door.

"I'm surprised you haven't run into her before," Meg said, head cocked as she looked at the pictures of Alex.

Erik also was amazed he hadn't seen her before as he scrolled through the numerous publicity shots of her taken at various hot spots around the system. It seemed Ms. Addington liked to socialize, which not so long ago might have piqued his interest.

"Too bad she's such a clubber." Meg continued to peer over Erik's shoulder, noting his lengthy perusal of the photos. "Although, for the hotel opening, she'll probably be perfect and know most of the celebs coming," she added as Linc strolled in.

"Hey, you left early last night." Linc said, sipping something Erik suspected he'd talked one of the new waitresses into making. "Who's the looker?" He joined Meg examining the holo. "She looks familiar."

"All women look familiar to you," Meg told Linc as Ron walked in.

"That's the girl who was in the side yard yesterday," Erik said. "She was also at *Pierre's* last night. She's Susan's replacement."

Ron glanced at the holo before sitting down in the guest chair across from Erik's desk. "I didn't see any mention of a current boyfriend. If she's nice, I'd definitely ask her out."

"Back off." Erik demanded, eyeing everyone, feeling weirdly protective. "She's going to be working here, so hands off. In fact, she'll be here soon."

"Hey, don't look at me," Meg quipped over her shoulder as she sniffed the coffee in the pot and reluctantly poured herself some. "I don't swing that way. And I'm always nice. By the way, Jenny said to tell you she's told Sally her new boss will be here soon."

"You always get the hot ones," Ron griped to Erik. "Besides, you may change your mind. I just finished the deep dive into her background. Guess who she's related to?"

"No idea. Who?" asked Erik a bit impatiently. He wasn't thrilled his friends were so interested in the woman.

"Dees and Rictor."

"Dees *and* Rictor?" Linc parroted, seeing Ron's sharp nod.

"She's both Walter Dees' niece and Steven Rictor III's niece."

Erik steepled his fingers as he considered Ron's news. "That's one point in her favor and another against. Who'd have thought she's related to one of the best tech inventors of our time and one of our nastiest competitors? How'd she end up connected to both?"

"Luck of the draw?" Linc asked.

"Either way, we need someone now, and her rep's solid." Erik wished they had a door number two.

"She and her cousin started Allee Cats," Meg read over Erik's shoulder. "That's that nonprofit that saves feral cats. I vote let's give her a try and keep a close eye on her."

"You just like cats," Linc said.

"Cats, most times, are better than people," Meg admitted.

"I'll take her cousin." Linc eyed a picture of Emily with Alex before reading the caption underneath. "'Cousins Alexandra Addington and Emily Dees grace Robin Starfire's annual Alphabet Party in London.' Hey, didn't we go to that?" Linc asked Erik. "I don't remember seeing those two, and I'm pretty sure I'd remember them. We went to the party after we met with General Watson."

"Yeah, we were hoping to meet Al and Lee that trip, though I don't know why since they're such recluses," Erik replied. "We arrived at Starfire's late, but I think I'd remember seeing them if they'd been there."

"While you two reminisce, I actually have work to do." Meg headed out the door.

"I need to check on a glitchy sensor in a minute but wanted to let you know that I just heard from George about Susan's tov," Ron said after Meg left. "He said it looks like someone tampered with its controls."

"Damn, are you sure?" Linc asked, sitting down in one of Erik's guest chairs.

"George is a genius," Ron said. "He calibrates the police fleet so they can fly higher."

"Do you think he'd do that for our tovs?"

Erik knew Linc was picturing how much time they could save if they could fly high enough to cut over the local mountains and city's high rises.

"You're kidding, right?" Erik asked, visualizing the huge fine they'd get when LAPD caught them.

"One can dream. What else did George say?"

"He told me Susan wouldn't have noticed anything was off with her tov," Ron said. "It was programmed to power off right when she hit that final curve from Malibu Canyon onto PCH. It was a miracle she didn't die."

"Can George figure out who did it?" Erik was furious someone would hurt one of his employees.

"I asked him to dig deeper," Ron replied.

"Let us know. And Ron, tell everyone to keep their eyes out."

After Ron left, Erik looked over at Linc, his frustration making him straighten his already uber-neat desk.

"Have you seen that someone made another attempt on Xtra's stock?" Linc asked.

"Fortunately our defenses worked." Erik started to heat up again. After the last attempt at a hostile takeover, Erik had developed a program to automatically counter any unusual movement while alerting them to potential threats.

"Have you noticed that these distractions, for want of a better word, are increasing?"

"Yes, and unfortunately, the stakes are getting higher. Susan could have been killed." Erik, visibly agitated, tapped his litpen on his desk.

"Her accident and the break-in both tie to the hotel." Linc looked over his coffee cup at Erik.

"Can you ask Meg to block out thirty minutes for us to talk later? We're missing something. In the meantime, Ms. Addington should be here any minute."

"Alexandra Addington's here to see you," Jenny's voice interrupted. "Shall I send her in?"

"Catch ya later." Linc rose to leave Erik's office. As Alex walked in, he stepped aside, holding the door open, eyeing her head-to-toe as she passed. He then looked at Erik, a wolfish grin spreading across his face, before stepping away.

What a curiosity she is, Erik thought, as Alex entered, a professional smile on her face. She'd looked like a fragile, damaged pixie asleep under the tree when he first saw her. Last night she'd become a red-lipped siren, and now, in her tailored grey suit, she looked like a professional. Her skirt was form-fitting but not too tight; her crisp pink blouse was buttoned appropriately; a lock of hair was the only part out of place. He briefly wondered who the real Alexandra was of the three, then ruthlessly dismissed his curiosity. He didn't need to know.

"We meet again." Erik stood and held out his hand. "Erik Wolfe."

"Alexandra Addington, although most call me Alex." She clasped his hand, having to look up despite her high heels. She instantly felt dwarfed. A jolt of electricity shot up her arm the second Erik's big, calloused hand engulfed hers. *Down, girl. Just because there's a zing, it don't mean a thing*, she chanted silently, trying to tamp down the surprising reaction.

Erik released her hand, sat, and motioned her to sit in one of the dove grey guest chairs facing his desk. "So besides being a neighbor, please tell me a bit about yourself."

For the next ten minutes, as Alex discussed her experience with Erik, she was surprised to discover his quick mind. Several times he asked her about people she'd never work for again, and it was clear they weren't his favorite either.

"I have a project I'm working on," he continued as he sat back in his chair. "A deep space network contract's currently underway as we prepare to open the hotel. Space Force had scheduled the contract competition for later, but circumstances made them push it forward.

"I'll be focused on that, so I expect you to finalize Susan's preparations for the opening parties—both the *Swan Song* Oscar party and the after-party for the movie's crew—and manage the events on those days. I'll also need you to ensure that the celebrities who are staying here receive the personalized swag Susan prepared for them, and that all their needs are met. Susan had moved into the hotel, and, now that you're taking her place, I expect you to do the same so you can take care of any emergencies that may come up."

"I'm afraid that's not possible, Mr. Wolfe," Alex countered, her voice calm. While she could manage working at the hotel, it would be challenging to hide her bruises the whole time, and the last thing she needed was another challenge. She also had to be home for the network tests. "However, I'll be right next door, and when I go out, I'll have my comm."

"I told Janice that was a non-negotiable," Erik said to her, jaw clenching.

"And I told Janice I would be readily available at a moment's notice. If that's not acceptable, then I'm sorry to have wasted your time," she responded, starting to stand. She could tell he was used to getting his way from the surprised look that flashed across his face before he quickly covered it up. While she wanted the job, she refused to live at the hotel. She desperately needed time to feel completely safe and not constantly be on guard.

Erik bit back an oath. Aside from her family, Alexandra was perfect for the job. As they'd talked, he discovered she had the best knowledge of the hotel of anyone he had met, even Susan. Besides, he didn't have time to find anyone else. Janice had already told him he was extremely lucky that Alex was available.

"Fine, Ms. Addington, but make sure your comm is on at all times," he stated, eyes glittering dangerously as if daring her to respond with anything but an affirmative. "Now, you'll have to excuse me. I have another meeting." Erik stood and held out his hand. "Let's meet again at 5:00, once you've settled in and reviewed Susan's notes. Jenny, my admin, will introduce you to Sally, who will be your primary support."

When Alex stood and shook Erik's hand, she felt another zing. Determined to ignore it, she left to find Jenny.

Erik watched Alex leave his office, thinking about the electricity he'd felt sizzle between them and how her pupils had enlarged when he'd shaken her hand. For him, the contact had shot directly to his loins, giving him an insane desire to pull her close and explore that chemistry.

*Bad idea*, he told himself as he rounded his desk. Too much was fucking happening: the contract he and Linc were determined to secure for their company; the lives of the Farout colony's inhabitants hanging by a thread; the suspicious happenings at the hotel, and Susan's crash. He couldn't afford any fallout from a workplace dalliance, which—even if that didn't go against his personal rules—a one-and-done was all it would be. He had to focus, he told himself, as he absently tossed a chip in the chiming bowl and walked out.

So far everything was a-okay, Alex thought as she settled into her office at the hotel. She must have imagined the zing from Erik's touch that she'd felt earlier, as well as yesterday. He'd been extremely professional this morning when asking her about her experience and finally yielded when she said she wouldn't move into the hotel.

Erik was an intriguing package, one that, at another time, she might have wanted to unwrap. Although he was pretty bossy and, she suspected, a bit of a neat freak. Still, she hadn't felt this kind of chemistry since her husband, Charlie. Comparing Erik to the few men she'd tried dating since Charlie's ship disappeared hardly seemed fair, and Gary, her college mistake, didn't count. Charlie, compared to Erik, had been more boy, too, Alex thought, feeling uncomfortable her past love didn't seem to measure up. She'd married Charlie when they were both in their 20s, and when he disappeared, he'd just been coming into his manhood.

Alex had met Charlie, a Space Force engineer, one day when she and Emily had been visiting NASA's Jet Propulsion Laboratory. She had lost her way after visiting the restroom and had literally run into him, who had been getting ready for his first space trip with fellow astronaut and best friend Sam Zara. When the men returned from their two-year trip to upgrade the Samuels telescope, they contacted Alex and Emily, who were both living in Kahaluu with their Uncle Walter and Aunt Lelani.

Alex and her cousin, not long out of college, had fallen for the young astronauts. The men proposed a year later. Before marrying, Alex had told Charlie about her alter ego, "Al." Emily had told Sam about "Lee."

Six years later, Sam and Charlie were flying a routine mission to replace Farout Base's food filters. Only supposed to be gone a month, a malfunction in one of their ship's propulsion engines made their ship miss the planet and instead drift out of the solar system.

That was almost five years ago. Today, Alex had a hard time picturing Charlie, much less remember their connection. It was disconcerting that she felt a spark with Erik. They had only met yesterday.

Maybe it was because Erik oozed masculinity, like the mountain lions roaming the local hills. Sure, she'd met tanned, buff Hawaiians; smart, lean, pale tech heads; and plenty of slick suits. A few had piqued her interest, briefly, but until Erik, she'd never felt this kind of electricity. She sighed.

At least she could freely enjoy her office, looking around again at the freshly painted, white wainscoting and ceiling molding set against the hotel's signature pale-pink walls. A set of French doors opened to the patio and lake beyond, where she could see the swans preening in the sun. Her office had been converted from Swan Suite's second bedroom, located right down the hall from Erik's office. It felt a bit too close to him for her sanity, but for the view of the lake, the money, and only two weeks of work, she decided she could manage her reactions to the oh-so-manly man.

Earlier that morning, after entering the hotel grounds, she'd released Larry under a large camellia bush studded with hot-pink flowers next to the restrooms. Checking her comm, she could see from the lizard's blip that he'd followed her and was now sitting outside the French doors. Blips from the hummingbirds and squirrels showed they roamed near, too. She hadn't activated her stealth capability because Isobelle, having noticed some anomalies when she'd been in the buffer zone, was checking it out today. Besides, she wasn't trying to hide and didn't want to make anyone suspicious. From what she'd read, Erik had a crazy high IQ.

A half hour earlier, Jared had contacted her, letting her know their link was working. With that and the heavy security she'd seen when she arrived, she felt pretty safe. As Jenny handed her a hotel ID chip for her comm, extra guards had been added because a suite had been vandalized along with the growing buzz about the hotel's opening and parties.

Alex suspected another possible reason for the extra security was the network competition. She'd just seen Linc Cussler, Xtra's president, step into Erik's office along with a small group of what looked like engineers.

"Time to get to work," Alex told herself, bringing up Susan's plans on her display. An hour later, worry creased her brow as she made notes. An hour after that, she was softly swearing. What the hell had happened? Every internal order and external invoice she looked at had something wrong: either the date, time, material, color or something. She didn't get it, but at this point, she didn't want to waste time with the why and instead set out to fix the most critical errors first.

Two hours later, she closed her comm and stood, deciding she needed to stretch her legs. She winced at the pain in her broken ribs; the Erisalve she'd applied this morning had dulled it somewhat, but if she moved, her ribs reminded her they were broken. She glanced out the French doors again, relieved to see the swans still swimming placidly on the lake. The birds, extremely protective of their territory, were great watchdogs. If they spotted any strangers, Alex would know it. Leaving her office, she went to find Sally to see if Susan had left any documents with her.

"I sent you everything Susan worked on," Sally stated, then turned back to her display.

After thanking the abrupt woman, Alex headed back to her office, mentally shaking her head at Sally's attitude. Just before noon, Erik stuck his head in Alex's office to tell her that food was part of the package and to head over to the restaurant or call for room service when she was hungry. As he was leaving, he stopped to check what Alex guessed was a blemish at the top of the door frame. Lifting his hand, drawing his shirt tight against his built frame, he ran his fingers over the white paint, making Alex wonder how it would feel to have those fingers skimming across her skin. She shook her head. She had to focus on the party plans and find something to eat.

A free lunch was a nice perk, although most days Alex figured she would bring something from home. Being short, she couldn't eat much without putting on weight, a problem Erik certainly didn't have, his flat stomach evident when he'd been checking the bubble in the paint. She'd decided not to tell him about the problems she'd discovered, partially because she felt she could fix them. She also wanted to talk with Susan first. It seemed odd Susan had made so many errors.

When she asked the vendors about the mistakes, they said they'd occurred when they'd received updates. Someone had called Westwood Florist, but Rachel didn't remember who had changed the date. Someone had messaged Ice Designs to alter the delivery time for the ice sculptures, yet Ricardo couldn't find the email. It was just noted on the order, and the pattern continued with the other vendors.

She hoped she could catch and fix everything before the opening—the list was long. Unfortunately, she hadn't been able to talk with Susan. When she called the hospital, they told her Susan wasn't available. When she called Janice, her headhunter friend told her they'd had to sedate her while her head injury healed. Alex had just about finished reviewing Susan's plans when she noticed Sally standing in the doorway.

"I'm leaving. I have an appointment," Sally said, obviously anxious to go, a slight frown giving her a pinched look.

Smiling and trying to be warm to the cold woman, Alex said, "Thank you for all your help today."

"Good night," Sally responded stiffly before turning and leaving.

"Good—" Alex started to say, but Sally had already left. "Oh well," she muttered as she turned back to her notes.

"Oh well?" Meg asked, knocking and then entering Alex's office.

"Oh, nothing. Sally just left rather abruptly." Alex smiled at Meg, who already had been much more welcoming than Sally.

"Yes, well, if you sense a little hostility, it's because she thought we'd offer her Susan's job after the accident. She's competent, though. Besides a degree in marketing, she has minors in IT and finance. I was actually surprised she accepted the position in the first place. If it were permanent, we'd likely talk to her about her welcoming personality."

As Meg explained Sally's attitude, she walked over to look out the French doors. "Since it's only for a couple more weeks... Let me know if she becomes difficult."

Both Alex and Meg turned to the door as another knock sounded on the doorjamb.

"Who's difficult?" Linc asked. "May I enter?" He had a small black bag in his hand.

"Alex, this is Lincoln Cussler, Erik's partner and Xtra's president. We were just discussing Sally's winning demeanor, although I've noticed she's much warmer to the men around here. Why are you here?"

"Gary and Ron are off-site at a meeting, so I thought I'd stop by and ensure Alex's tech works." Linc strolled over to Alex's desk comm. "May I?" he asked, gesturing towards the machine.

"Of course." Alex rose from her desk, thinking it was strange that the company's president was doing such a simple job. "Everything seems to be working." Wow, she thought, getting a load of Linc up close. He was as good-looking as Erik, equally big, maybe a bit taller even. But where Erik was dark with piercing green eyes, Linc had blue eyes and white-blonde hair, spiky and longish on top and close-cropped on the sides.

She could tell from the slight wear on both their faces – Linc's furrow between his eyes and Erik's slightly lined forehead – that they didn't go for skim treatments. The faint white creases beside their eyes had to mean they spent time outdoors, Alex thought, before chastising herself to stay focused.

After entering some commands on her comm, Linc stood up

from leaning over Alex's desk. "All done. If you need anything, don't hesitate." He smiled at Alex before nodding at Meg and leaving.

"He's such a flirt, but a harmless one," Meg said as she headed towards the door. "He's also nosy. I've got to get back to work. Yell if you have any questions that Jenny or Sally can't answer."

After Linc and Meg left, Alex spied a wadded-up piece of Hydrac paper on the floor next to the door. The paper, which was milled and pressed from a fibrous plant found on Pluto's moon Hydra, had become extremely popular in the past couple of years after Stargear discovered a cheap way to manufacture and ship it. Linc must have accidentally kicked it into her office when he came in. She absently picked it up, thinking of Linc and wondering if everyone at the hotel was extremely athletic and attractive. Meg was also striking—tall, brunette, and slender. Sour Sally, pale and thin to the point of gaunt, didn't count.

Alex examined the paper curiously, checking out its structure. She hadn't seen a lot of Hydrac before, and Earth-based paper had essentially disappeared in the last century during the Heat Years. She realized the paper was covered with calculations that were being used for the test at the Moon's Farside Base. Reading through the numbers, she noticed an error at the bottom. Sitting back down at her desk, she absently corrected it while she waited for a vendor to answer her comm.

*He's my boss; there is no zing. He's my boss; there is no zing,* Alex silently chanted to herself before entering Erik's office at 5:00. He was on the phone but stood when he saw her and motioned her to a high circular table as he finished his conversation.

"I thought the table would be more comfortable. Coffee?" Erik decided she was even prettier now than this morning as a late afternoon ray of sun caught her through the window. She looked a little end-of-day mussed, a few tendrils escaping from the intricate twist of black silk at her nape. He envisioned pulling out the pins from her hair and tousling it even more.

"Do you have coffee?" Alex asked, interrupting Erik's thoughts. She looked around, eyes widening when she spied the new coffeemaker partially hidden behind the cabinet door. "Do you mind?"

"Don't touch—." Erik jumped as Alex practically ran to the machine.

"I've discovered a few tweaks that make this machine sing," she said as she turned and started pushing various buttons on the gleaming paragon.

"I really don't think—." Erik didn't value much, but good coffee was one of the things he truly cared about. Even though he hadn't had the time to figure out how the thing worked yet, the Raleigh was king of the coffeemakers. "It took me a long time to get that machine. You wouldn't believe what I had to go through to get it." He was still annoyed at the manufacturer for essentially blackmailing him before they'd sell him one. "They delivered it this morning. I haven't had the time to figure out how it works."

"It's actually quite easy once you know the logic. You look like an Americano kind of guy," Alex said, eying Erik. At his amused nod, she quickly pushed a series of buttons. "Try this." Alex returned to the table and handed him a cup. He breathed in the aroma. She turned and, pushing a few other buttons, made herself a slightly frothy cup of what he figured was probably a latte as he took a cautious sip of his.

"This is really good," Erik groaned, taking another sip. "How can I make one again, and how come you know so much about the Raleigh?" he asked as she returned to the table with her cup.

"Push the blue button, then green, turn the left knob halfway, then push the yellow button twice." Alex placed her cup on the table before going on tiptoe to maneuver herself up into the tall chair. "I did some work for Veaga Enterprises." She didn't mention that she'd volunteered Al and Lee to figure out why the new Raleigh kept glitching in exchange for a donation to the county's foster kids.

Erik reached out to steady her. "I hadn't realized how tall this table was until you got here," he mused. "You know Emilio Veaga?"

"I helped him on the Raleigh's launch," Alex said, embarrassed she'd almost lost her balance while trying to gracefully plant her butt in the high chair. "Sucks being short," she muttered under her breath, flustered by the electric jolt of his touch again.

"I like short," Erik said, his green eyes focused intently on her. "So how was your day?"

Alex worked to gather her thoughts. When he pinned her with his full attention, she felt he was so finely attuned to her that he could hear her heartbeat, which was skipping madly. Taking a breath, she answered, "I'd like to change a few things. How involved do you want to be?" He was sitting close and smelled good—a bit of musk, earth, and, she was sure, an off-world aroma that wrapped around her senses.

"I want to know about any changes you make and expect you'll continue to keep records as Susan did." Erik decided he wanted to be more involved in the opening than he had been with Susan, whom he'd only met with once a week. "Let's plan on meeting daily at 5:00, unless something comes up. What do you want to change?"

Alex explained that she planned to tweak the menu for the opening party, which she wanted to discuss with him before talking with Chef Leon. "The movie featured a butter lettuce salad throughout. Since it was such a big deal in the movie, I'd like to change the salad to that one."

"Don't waste your time. Susan and Chef tried, but the lettuce's apparently been hit by some kind of disease. There isn't any available."

"I might be able to get it."

"I don't want you wasting your time. It's not important."

"You're kidding, right? Did you see the movie?"

"Parts of it," Erik admitted, feeling a bit uncomfortable about having not seen the whole of his friend's movie.

"Okay," Alex thought, surprised he hadn't watched one of the decade's biggest movies, especially since the hotel was hosting parties that celebrate it. Then she remembered that Space Force had accelerated the network tests. He's probably been swamped.

"Well, so you know, the salad's a big part of the movie. And I think," she said, trying to be diplomatic, "if I can get the lettuce, the hotel should serve that salad." Alex knew some growers, old family friends up the coast in Oxnard, who had farms and, as a special favor, could likely supply what she wanted.

Erik eyed her, once again surprised by her tenacity. "You really think it's that important?" At her nod, he conceded. "Don't spend too much time trying. If you succeed, go ahead." He wondered who she knew and how she might have such pull. Chef and Susan had told him they had tried everything to get that blasted lettuce.

At Erik's concession, she felt another zing. She hadn't seen any of the playboy that article had talked about. So far, he'd been professional, thoughtful, and dang smart. She shoved those thoughts aside. She needed another complication in her life like Saturn needed more moons.

"What about Sally?" he asked.

"Sally?" she parroted, then understanding he was talking about her admin. "She's fine. I appreciate the help."

Alex wasn't going to tell him she thought Sally was a piece of work. Realizing with his nod that the meeting was over, she grabbed her skimpad and tried to gracefully slip off the high seat. She then remembered the paper she'd discovered earlier that she'd brought in to hand him. "I found this on the floor."

Erik took it, not looking at it. Instead, he asked, "Have dinner with me tonight."

Alex's eyes widened; then she chastised herself for thinking he was asking her out. She realized he wanted to talk about the hotel.

"I have some plans unless it's urgent."

"Nothing urgent," he said, unexpectedly frustrated she'd turned him down. "Though I'd like you to eat from the menu occasionally and let me know what you think. Maybe dinner another evening. How about Wednesday?"

Erik didn't care he was putting her on the spot. Besides wanting her opinion, she intrigued him, even though she wasn't his usual type. Usually, people—especially women—wanted to be around him. While Alex's behavior exemplified professionalism, and he was beginning to think she was quite smart, she was almost skittish around him. Which was somewhat strange considering how many clubs and parties she appeared to have attended.

"Wednesday would work," she said, trying to keep it light. She needed to escape. She was feeling hot—either that or the thermostat had broken. Erik was rapidly becoming dangerous to her libido. In fact, it was likely he could be addictive. She already liked how he smelled, for heaven's sake. She had to leave. Besides, she had to talk with Emily about the network tests and their progress on the robots.

"Hey, did you see those—" Linc said as he entered Erik's office, stopping mid-sentence when he saw Alex. "Oh, sorry. I'll come back later."

"I was just leaving." Alex picked up her tablet again and headed for the door. "It was nice meeting you both. Thank you for this opportunity. I'll see you in the morning unless something urgent comes up."

"So?" Linc asked Erik after waiting a minute for him to stop watching Alex leave the hotel on his vid. "I haven't seen you this interested in someone in a while. What gives?"

Erik turned and looked at Linc. "I'm not sure. There's something about her. She's attractive and smart. What's not to like? She's like a puzzle I want to solve."

Erik decided that even though he couldn't date her during the next two weeks while she was working for him, all bets would be off after that. He still wasn't sure about her bruises, which was another good reason to wait these next couple weeks. The thought of waiting was oddly entertaining since he'd never been willing to wait for a woman before. And if he couldn't touch her, he could still work towards that end. He'd already knew he got under her skin. He liked seeing her flustered.

"Puzzles? I like puzzles," Meg said as she entered Erik's office. "Wanna do a puzzle tonight?" she asked the two, who both rolled their eyes. "Spoilsports."

As Alex headed home through the side yard, she lectured herself about letting Erik distract her. She had to keep her eye on the new network system and ensure it would work for the Farout colony. She knew a lot of the people who were stuck at Farout Base, some she considered friends. She couldn't let a hunk distract her from saving their lives or from her and Emily's last chance to locate Charlie and Sam's ship. She had been trying not to think about the possibility of finding their ship, but with the anniversary of their disappearance looming, it was hard to ignore.

They still didn't know who had killed their uncle. It had only been a week, and the pain of his loss was still devastating. The one slip her attackers made had led her, Emily, and the General to suspect that the killers, or person who'd hired the killers, were somehow involved with the new network.

They had kept asking her about the material her uncle's company, Seed, had developed for the new network—material she and Emily actually had created as Al and Lee. Space Force had given each of the seven companies competing for the network contract a sample to incorporate into their data processing solution. No one else had access to that material, which included elements recently brought back from Mars.

Besides, while the General had told her that Space Force had cleared Erik of any involvement in the murder, she'd guarded her heart for so long, she didn't know if she would ever find the key to unlock it. As she entered the kitchen, she tabled that thought. Instead, she happily focused on the group she considered family, watching them prepare for dinner.

"Alex! Yay! You're back." Anita ran over to Alex and gave her a hug.

"Hey freshie." Alex returned her hug, biting back a groan at Anita's too exuberant embrace. Alex then turned to take in Bev's tennis shoes, jeans, t-shirt, and moderate makeup. "And look at you! Are we actually rubbing off on you, or are you sick?" She held her wrist up to Bev's forehead, pretending to check for a fever.

"Stop that," Bev laughed, also hugging Alex. "I decided to, like, not use so much makeup. I've noticed that, like, most of my professors—at least the good ones in the engineering department—don't wear a lot of makeup, like you all."

"Well, I think you look wonderful." Alex smiled at the girl. Bev, a star graduate of the county's premiere foster system, had blossomed since she'd come to live with them as a UCLA freshman three years ago. Alex hoped that Anita, also from the same system, would follow, having only lived with them for a quarter so far. "And you've put on a bit of muscle," Alex said to Anita, seeing that her very slight frame had filled out a bit.

"She has finally joined us for our training sessions," Isobelle said, as she pulled a roast chicken from the autove. The women and Jared started pitching in to get dinner on the table. "Jared has even considered joining the group," Isobelle added, putting the security specialist on the spot.

"Yes, ma'am." Jared eyed the housekeeper, "health nut" embroidered on her lilac blouse's pocket. "I like how you're keeping to the nut theme, Isobelle," he added.

Alex noticed that Jared evaded committing to train with the group. While everyone had accepted him into their circle, she could tell he was still adjusting to her house full of women, evident by the glances the solider kept giving her family as they chatted about their day and passed the biscuits, honey, and butter.

After dinner—during which Isobelle had even served a macadamia nut-based sauce for the chicken—Alex talked with the girls about their classes while they cleaned up. She then headed to her bedroom, realizing she felt safe for the first time since the attack. As she passed the girls' area of the house, with Barney and Fred following her, she could hear Anita on her comm with a classmate. Barney sniffed at the cats lounging in Anita's doorway, while Fred completely ignored the sleeping felines as both dogs padded after Alex into her bedroom.

In the kitchen, Isobelle noted that Jared had returned inside and was in his room after contacting Space Force about the grey tov stopped out front. She had also seen that Jared had planted some of his own sensors around the property.

Three minutes later, a black and white pulled up and shone a light in the tov driver's eyes. After a quick chat with the police bot, the tov driver sped off towards Sunset. If the squirrels had successfully attached the tracers to the tov, it would be interesting to see where it went, Isobelle mused as she turned out the lights and headed for her room.

# Tuesday,
# February 17, 2172

The next morning, Alex wound her way across the damp lawn, the dogs trailing behind her as they explored the morning's fresh scents. A skunk had definitely wandered near, Alex registered, nose wrinkling. Besides the skunk, the dogs likely smelled coyote and possibly raccoon or mountain lion.

Wearing her worn burnt-orange tennies, with her grey stilettos in her old canvas bag, she thought of Emily and Isobelle teasing her about her attire during breakfast. Thank heavens the girls had already left for school, or they would have pitched in on the effort.

She'd donned one of her killer—if she said so herself—tailored Terry Ford suits that her designer friend Juliette had helped her find last year. She'd also selected a new, luxe makeup and hair program advertised as exclusive to today's female executive. She believed that if her fees were high, she had to dress the part. Not into fancy or expensive when at home, Alex walked the walk when she had to, having learned that appearances could be wielded like weapons. Regardless, at breakfast Emily had razzed her as Alex leaned against the counter and finished her bowl of granola, oatmilk, and orgberries.

"Iso, doesn't Alex look nice this morning?" Emily had said innocently, eying Alex from the breakfast table.

"Come to think of it, Emily, why yes, she does."

"Are those new shoes?" Emily spied the Chars peeking out of Alex's bag.

"Yep." Alex handed her bowl to the autowash.

"The ones you said you were saving for a special occasion?" Emily asked. "Perhaps a wolf occasion? Get it, Iso, a wolf occasion? As in Erik Wolfe?"

"You'd better not give up your day job, Emily. Comedy is so not your forte. Everyone over there dresses like they have a designer on call. You should see their CFO, Meg." Alex would rather talk about the weather—sunny again—than Erik. She admitted she felt more in control when she looked her best and would use every tool she had to gain an edge. Instead, she told them about the weirdness with Susan's plans for the hotel opening and following parties.

"That's strange Susan dropped the ball so badly," Emily said. She also knew the woman.

As Alex entered the side yard and headed towards the hotel, she continued to think about the errors. Emily and Isobelle felt she should tell Erik. If only she could talk with Susan—when she'd called the hospital this morning, the doctors still had her sedated.

Eying the two squirrels pacing her, Alex observed how they clambered through the tree canopy, analyzing the fluidity of the latest version of 'skin' she'd created for the little robots. Satisfied, she shifted her attention to the upcoming day. She needed to delve further into the party prep and then review the hotel's guest list.

She also must ask for her advance, something she included in all her contracts after being burned in the past. When she had accepted the hotel job, she had almost felt embarrassed taking her fee for what she had thought would be little more than a babysitting job. Now she figured she would earn that fee. Most of the advance would go for the new roof, while the rest she'd use for some new tech for the girls.

Thinking of new tech, she thought about tomorrow morning's test at the Moon's Farside Base. She figured she would have plenty of time before she needed to report to the hotel. With yesterday's start of the tests, she practically lived with fingers crossed that their device's external material, which she'd created by blending elements from the Earth, Moon, and Mars, would work. She'd learned, like so many before her, that anything could happen in space, which always gave her a thrill and a bit of craziness until her theories proved true. The network device, which she and Emily had named Ola—meaning life in Hawaiian—had successfully operated at the Gateway Space Station. Next stop, the dark side of the Moon. While worried, she also grinned. She loved the rush from pushing the boundaries of the unknown.

As she entered the hotel property, Alex wiped the smile from her face so she didn't look like a lunatic. If anyone saw her bruises, which she continued to disguise as best as possible, that would be bad enough. Looking around, she saw painters finishing the trim on the upper rooms, and gardeners planting baby's breath and poppies. The redwoods, almost lost during the worst of the Heat Years, looked healthy as they towered over Stone Canyon, with clumps of bird of paradise nestling in between.

She loved this old hotel almost as much as her own home. Growing up, she had frequently sneaked onto the grounds to share tea with the swan keeper, Miss Bird, and cajole cookies from the cooks. As she rounded a corner, lost in her memories, she sucked in a breath, stopping short at the sight of Erik's bronzed, wet, chiseled back, then tight butt, then strong thighs. *Oh Lordy me*, she thought as he pulled himself up out of the pool.

She watched Erik reach for a towel and dry off, water droplets gleaming on his taunt, wet skin in the morning sun. OMG. Her heart raced as she imagined being his towel and following the water sliding down his body. She'd like to take a picture to drool over at night. Instead, she began backing up silently to go another way. She suddenly felt uncomfortably hot. When she stepped on a traitorous twig, Erik's head snapped around, and his green gaze zeroed in on her as she stood frozen like a criminal—or a perv, she thought.

*Pull it together, Alexandra.* She took a breath, straightened her shoulders, and began walking forward. She forced a smile, offering a sunny "Good morning" as she approached, doing her best to act as if he was wearing a business suit instead of a not-big-enough-to-hide-the-jewels-OMG aqua speedo. She would not look down. She would not look down. Damn, she wanted to look down.

"Good morning, Alexandra," he answered, a smile on his full lips, a wicked gleam in his eyes. He took a lightning-quick perusal of her, stopping for a double-take on her orange tennis shoes. After his gaze quickly traveled down and back, he met her eyes again, obviously approving the extra time she'd spent this morning, aside from her shoes.

"I forgot to ask if you swim. If so, you're welcome to use the pool anytime." He eyed her intently as he dried his chest and then slung the towel around his neck.

"Thanks, and yes, a little." She wasn't exactly lying. Lately she had little time to swim, and it had been a long time since she'd been a lifeguard. Since she wasn't planning on anything long-term with the man, much less short-term, she didn't want to get into her history.

She'd learned over the years to keep things as general as possible because the minute she said anything about herself, people wanted more details. Then she had to lie. It had just become easier to keep to herself, even though she felt lonely at times. She had become less lonely with Charlie since he knew her secret, but after his ship disappeared, she found the loneliness weighed heavily on her. Once she and Emily revealed themselves, maybe she would try opening up to people more.

Erik wondered at the brief flash of sadness in her eyes. "I give lessons."

"I bet," Alex replied before she could catch herself. "I mean, you look like you'd be a good swimmer and therefore a good teacher." She kicked herself for sounding so lame. A sprinkling of coarse black hair covered his chest before heading down to where she should not look. *Great conversationalist, dodo.* She wished she had changed into her heels. Barely clearing 5'2", Erik towered over her, his dark, flat nipples at eye level.

"I'll be tied up in meetings today. If you have any questions Sally can't answer, Jenny and Meg will be available."

Alex felt stupidly disappointed when she heard she would not see him later. At least, she figured, it would give her more time to try and talk with Susan. Catching herself staring again, she wished him a good day and walked towards her office, overwhelmed by his almost naked, pure and unadulterated manliness too much this early in the day. She needed coffee—that was it, a big cup of high-octane brew.

That was interesting, Erik thought as he finished drying off by the pool. And boy was she hot in that grey and pink suit, the skirt's slit showing a hint of toned thigh. She'd braided her long ebony hair in some intricate design that made him want to grab it and wrap it around his wrist. He almost felt like he was in elementary school because even with those horrible orange shoes, she made something inside him want to paw the ground and yank her braid, impatient to get her attention.

*Whoa boy*, he told himself, working to calm his libido before he shocked the staff with a tent pole in his speedo. Nevertheless, he appreciated the view as she wove through the pink Spanish arches; the splashes of color from the violet bougainvillea added their accent.

He found he was enjoying his pixie, unexpectedly savoring the novel experience of taking things slow, as he walked towards his office to change for work. He didn't want to explore why he was willing to take time with her since he hadn't been willing with other women. Maybe it was her fresh mix of assuredness and vulnerability that did it.

Right now, though, he and Linc had to ensure Xtra was ready for tomorrow's network test. Each test of Ola, Seed's amazing new device, would also allow Space Force to evaluate the competing teams' ability to manage the flood of incoming data Ola was sending.

Presently, Space Force—heck the world—didn't think any company could capture and manage all the telemetry and coms data they expected Ola would eventually generate in real time. However, Linc and Erik believed they'd figured out how to do that and more.

Tomorrow, Ola would arrive at Farside Base, and their system, eXo, would be ready, too. Then, after the Farside test, the ship carrying the device and that bot, Eva, would continue its race to Mars and then Farout. It was just pure luck that the mission included a final test at Farout, he thought as he finished dressing.

He wondered how everyone was holding up on the planet. Living on space rations in an emergency environment was enough to make most people crack. He knew a few of the folks stranded and tried not to add worry about them to his pile of concerns. Fortunately, he'd heard that everyone selected for the Farout mission had been chosen for their solid temperaments as well as their expertise. Now dressed, he entered the hotel conference room precisely at 9 a.m., smiling as he heard a laugh erupt from the team.

"Did you see how Seed—I wonder if it was Al—tweaked Ola during the Gateway test? That was smoking hot," said Debbie, eXo's co-lead and software engineer.

"Here's the man of the hour. Three cheers." Linc stood and raised his mug as Erik entered. "Not only does he make sure we have snacks, he also catches errors that the rest of us dumbasses, ladies not excused, miss."

"Here, here!" the others echoed, raising their coffee and teacups in agreement.

Erik looked at the smiling group sitting around the table, wondering what the heck Linc was referring to. "What are you talking about?"

"Remember that calculation we'd been reworking without success?" Linc rifled through a stack of skimpads and slips of Hydrac paper he'd brought to the meeting. "Here it is," he said, pulling out a sheet and handing it to Erik. "I found this in your office yesterday afternoon."

Erik took the paper, and saw that sure enough it had the calculation, but part of it had been edited. Erik recalled how Alex had handed him a piece of Hydrac. He hadn't looked at it, but wondered who'd made the edit as he sat down at the conference table.

"Which one of you figured out that we'd made a damn typo?" he asked the group after looking more closely at the edits to the formula.

"We thought you did," said Carlos, eXo's other co-lead.

"Well, it wasn't me, though I'd love to take the credit." Erik looked baffled at the paper. "If that was the paper Alex had given me, she said she'd found it on the floor." He looked around. "Where's Jim?"

"Out sick," said Carlos. "It's possible he figured it out and then dropped it by accident. He was here yesterday. Want me to call him?"

"Not if he's sick," Erik said. "But when he's back, tell him I'm going to assign him a babysitter if he keeps losing papers. I'm serious this time. I swear Jim would lose himself if he could," he said, thinking about the kind, brilliant, but very absentminded engineer.

"So, where does that put us? How'd our test go?" he asked Denise.

"Like a dream," Denise answered, practically vibrating. "With the correction, we're humming. The edit's already in place." She clicked open a series of screens on the wall display that showed a long set of rapidly changing numbers. "Based on our simulations, our capture rate's off the charts."

Erik sat back in his chair.

"Our next challenge, besides acing tomorrow's Farside test, will be next week's Mars test. With that one, we'll have to show how well we can manage a tenfold increase in incoming data. It will be quantum processing on steroids. With the actual telemetry from tomorrow's Moon test, we can stress-test eXo more and fine-tune anything we need for Mars."

eXo's ability to manage and store megaloads of data were a result of Erik and Linc's discovery of Marsirium's remarkable storage properties. When they combined the Mars mineral with their innovative coding, they built a data management and storage system that leapfrogged all other existing technologies.

With each successive test, the new network would have to manage exponentially more data. If it couldn't handle the ever-increasing onslaught, the new deep-space network wouldn't work. The further the tests went out, the greater the challenge. Everyone was chafing to move into the Oort Cloud, the system's most distant region, but without communications, it just wasn't safe. That danger became abundantly clear with the disaster at Farout.

Erik, Linc, and Meg had decided to keep the system's full abilities a secret for the time being. They knew that with the data rates they achieved in the initial tests, the team in the conference room, as well as their expanded teams in Playa and those at Space Force, would soon realize they were working with groundbreaking technology. But they didn't know everything. Once Xtra won this contract, the company would announce its even bigger discovery.

The team worked late, breaking only for essential tasks as they fine-tuned the instruments and code. Once they won the contract, companies would be calling. They needed to be ready to rapidly ramp up their business. If their projections were correct, the amount of data they would start managing then would be, pun intended, astronomical. But first things first: tomorrow's test, then Mars, then the Farout test and saving the Farout colony.

As Alex sat in her office, she took a moment to look out the French doors and absorb the beauty of the tulip trees' pink, waxy flowers and the Pear trees' fragile white petals as they shattered, creating the city's version of snow covering the grass. Most L.A. natives—the few that remained—joked that spring in Los Angeles lasted a week. That week you'd carry the one sweater you owned, and maybe, just maybe, if you were really lucky, it would rain a bit more. If it did, spring lasted a few days longer.

Alex watched the petals falling and swirling outside, the hotel's lake in the background. She'd missed hearing the rumble of Erik's voice today as she'd worked, which felt strange to her. She'd only met him yesterday, making it much too soon for missing. Maybe it was because Erik's voice had the same deep, rumbly tone as her uncle's.

Unfortunately, Susan was still sedated, and Alex didn't want to bother her even if she had been awake. She had already called most of the vendors and fixed the errors, an accomplishment helped by some sweet-talking and subtle bribery. She then started diving into the multitude of in-house orders when she glanced at the clock, surprised to see it was almost day's end.

A flash of white disappearing past the patio door caught her eye. She leaned forward to see better, and sure enough, one of the swans was going AWOL. Probably Odette, Alex thought as she rose from her desk.

She had learned long ago how to manage the big swans. She quickly slipped on her tennis shoes and headed out the patio doors onto the grass, spying what she was now certain was Odette waddling towards the entrance.

Walking quietly up to the bird, Alex called her name softly so as not to startle her.

"We need to go back to the water," she told the swan. Alex could tell Odette was thinking about pecking her for being a spoilsport as she started to raise her head and spread her wings. It had been a while since Alex had been around the big birds. Odette obviously had forgotten who was boss. Cautious in case the bird suddenly turned on her, she stood as tall as possible and slowly crowded Odette, shepherding her back to the lake. Finally, Odette turned and started waddling back, giving Alex an occasional side-eye.

"You can't keep letting Hercules push you around," Alex told the bird as they headed back.

Giving Alex another glare, the bird then slid into the water as Hercules slapped his wings on the surface as if to lecture Odette for wandering off where it wasn't safe. As Alex turned back to her office, she spotted Meg waiting in the doorway.

"It looks like you know your way around those birds?" Meg asked, adding, "I was walking by when I saw you out with the swan. I came to see if you needed any help or first aid."

Alex noticed that Meg seemed a bit tense. She had heard that a workman had been attacked while cornering the swans earlier. He nearly lost an eye, which was probably why Meg looked worried.

"After the swans chased and trapped my cousin and me one time, my uncle made us take what we called swan lessons to earn a certification," Alex said. "Miss Bird will vouch for me. I'm always careful around them though," Alex added. "By the way, who do I talk to about getting half my fee?"

As Erik sat in his tov heading back to the hotel, he watched Alex wind her way toward the side yard on his comm. He had been checking the vid at the top of the property where the burglars had broken in when he spotted a flash of orange in the distance. She had on those God-awful burnt orange tennis shoes—the same ones she had been wearing when she walked with that swan earlier.

Ron had alerted him about that. He had held his breath as he watched her walk up to the giant white bird, which was almost as big as her and certainly a hell of a lot more dangerous. For the life of him, he couldn't figure out why women thought they were romantic. They could be lethal. Then, amazingly, she had what looked like a conversation with the swan, which then went with her back to the lake like a giant, white-feathered puppy. He couldn't believe it. When he got within twenty feet of those things, they started flapping their wings, whipping their heads around, and eyeing him like he was a devil coming to kill them.

He shook his head remembering the intent expression on her face as Alex talked to the bird. It had looked at her as if it understood her while they walked side-by-side across the grass, her ass-ugly tennis shoes matching the color of the swan's feet.

Now she smiled and greeted the workmen, who returned her smile like goons. One even tipped his hat. Who does that anymore? The workmen seemed overly attentive to her comings and goings, and fixated on her curves, he thought darkly.

Alex stopped to talk to the head gardener, Manny, who Erik could tell also was happy to see her. She pointed up and across, gesturing toward heaven knows what. The two then walked over to a tree. Alex then squatted down to peer at something at its base. The way her skirt went taut around her butt, the slit in the skirt exposing a few more inches of tan, toned thigh, made Erik's blood thunder in his head. Manny knelt down next to her and poked at the tree's base while she bent close and watched.

A minute later, the two rose. She then hugged Manny—he couldn't believe his eyes. Manny was a decorated Space Force

Defender, one of the deadliest of space soldiers—and walked to the gate, closing it behind her. She was truly a pixie, he thought, camouflaged in a Ford suit and ugly orange sneakers, sprinkling her fairy dust on everyone as squirrels trailed her and hummingbirds buzzed nearby.

Time to get back to reality, he thought, wondering what had come over him as the tov pulled up to the hotel, and he stepped out and entered the lobby.

"Hey, how'd it go?" Meg asked as she rose from one of the sofas in the recently finished lobby.

"General Watson was very pleased with our results. Where's Linc?" Erik looked around the lobby.

"He was mumbling something about coffee, so probably in your office."

"We need to get him a Raleigh for his birthday," Erik muttered. "Yes, I know, you too. How is the order going?"

"Are you kidding? We're still up in the hundred thousands. We've only moved up three, so maybe we'll get another in ten years, if we're lucky. They said that they'd only sell us one more, not two, because we already have one."

The two entered Erik's office as Linc was pouring himself a cup of coffee from the carafe sitting next to the Raleigh.

"Nice of you to join us," Erik snarked to Linc.

"I keep telling you to have the kitchen put a thermos in the hall. Then I'd never be in here, or better yet, in my office." Linc took a cautious sip of his coffee and then sighed in appreciation. "This coffee's amazing. What changed?"

"First, I keep telling you to go get your own thermos. Second, Alex, the one who's taken over for Susan, did something to the Raleigh."

"You let her touch the Raleigh?" Linc exclaimed, clutching his heart in shock.

"She pounced on it before I could say anything," Erik said as if he hadn't just uttered life-altering news. "Apparently she worked for Veaga and learned some tricks with the machine." He nonchalantly straightened some papers on his desk.

Meg and Linc stared at Erik as if an alien had taken over his body. Last year, he had abruptly severed a budding relationship with a beautiful, nice, smart woman just because she had touched the Raleigh without asking.

"What?" Erik eyed the two, ignoring their shock. He knew it was strange he'd let Alex touch the Raleigh, but it had happened so fast. Explaining to his friends what had happened in a way that sounded normal was beyond him.

"Let's move on. The meeting went great. General Watson was extremely pleased after he took a preliminary look at our results. We've been approved for tomorrow's Moon test, as we expected we'd be." Erik grinned, slapping Meg and Linc's hands in celebration before sitting down.

"Did the General say anything about the data rates we achieved?" Linc asked as he settled in one of the guest chairs.

"Not a word. Although his eyebrows lifted a bit when he was looking at the numbers, so I know he noticed, the canny bastard." Erik admired the General. "Do you think the Playa team has observed anything unusual yet?"

"I can tell that a few suspect something's up," Linc said, sipping his coffee. "I think Denise and Lori here are suspicious, too, but they haven't asked me anything. Have they said anything to either of you?"

"They haven't said a word, but I agree with you," Erik said. "I still don't want to reveal anything until after the contract's awarded. How about you two?"

"I think we'll have to say something after the Mars test." Meg stood to get some water. "The rates eXo will be managing at that point will be off the charts. When Mars happens, I doubt we'll be able to keep our results secret. I think we should be ready to release if it leaks.

"In the meantime," she added, "how about revealing to one or two select sources that you've developed a unique circuit board, and that you'll announce its characteristics and properties after the contract awarded? That way, you're providing some information, which should hopefully mollify everyone. What?" Meg caught the two men glancing at each other.

"Yes, mollify is my word for the day. Unlike some people, I didn't have a private school education," she snipped, her attempt to make the men feel bad not working per usual. "Anyway, how about giving the press a nugget? You can bring in that reporter, Tracy Fielding, at the *Times*, and how about someone at *Space*? You can offer them early access when the contract's announced."

"Works for me." Erik turned to Linc. "How about you? Are you ready for a bit of limelight? It's your turn to talk with the media."

The three had grown up seeing countless celebrities crash and burn, Linc's parents being a prime example. As soon as they could afford it, they had all had media training so they could manage their exposure to the press and public. That's when Meg started working on her vocabulary with a word a day, a suggestion from one of the instructors.

"I know, it's my turn." Linc frowned while making notes on his pad. "I'll get back to you two with a draft and revisit the release for when Space Force announces the contract winner. That's not that far away. Less than two weeks."

"I sent the information for tomorrow's Moon test to the Playa team," Erik said. "They should be ready for you to confirm our link whenever you have time."

"I'm going now. I'll see you guys later."

"I saw Alex with one of the swans earlier," Erik casually mentioned to Meg.

"Odette"

"What?"

"The swan's name's Odette," Meg said.

"Okay, I saw Alex walking with Odette. Doesn't she know how dangerous they are? She could have been hurt. Did you see it happen?" Erik didn't like the fear he had felt when he had seen Alex with the swan.

"Whoa, first, yes, and yes, I was worried after the swan attacked Stan last month. By the time I saw Alex heading towards Odette, though, it was too late.

"You should have heard her. She was telling Odette not to be afraid of Hercules, and the swan was looking up at her as if she understood every word." Meg eyed Erik, who returned her gaze with a raised brow, clearly amused by what sounded like a soap opera between two birds.

"Hercules is mean?"

"I'm not sure," Meg said, a small smile on her face before finishing her water. "Anyway, she has a certification in swan husbandry from Stanford. No joke," she said, enjoying Erik's look of surprise. "I confirmed it. There's such a degree.

"Miss Bird also vouched for her. I commed her. Miss Bird even said if something happened and she wasn't around, we should contact Alex or her cousin for help."

"I still don't like it." Erik remembered how Stan had almost lost an eye. "Those birds are as big as Alex."

"Well, you might like this less. Alex asked for half of her pay today. I gave it to her since it's in her contract. No, I didn't ask why," Meg said when Erik started to ask, "but I did overhear her telling someone that she'd have the money tomorrow."

*Susan has everything under control*, Alex muttered to herself as she wound through the trees, Barney keeping pace. What a crock. Served her right for wanting a distraction. Now she definitely had one, especially if, on top of that, she had really seen her old college ex, Gary. If it was him, hopefully she could avoid him. Maybe it wasn't even him, a possibility she doubted after she recovered from her shock. As Alex stopped at the vegetable garden to pick an early snap pea, Emily called out.

"Can you move any slower?" Emily yelled, hands on her hips. "Quick, Al, I've been waiting for you. Check this out."

As Alex walked up, Emily launched a robotic hummingbird that, like a real one, buzzed erratically right, then left, then right again. Three seconds later, their red-tailed robohawk streaked down, grabbed the little bird in its talons, and sped away.

"That was great!" Alex gave Emily a high five. For the past month, the women had been increasingly tuning the robots' fine motor skills. While the robots they used on Ola worked, they wanted to improve their capabilities since some of the repairs the bots might face in space could be incredibly intricate.

"Hello? Is anyone home? Alexandra! Emily!" a female voice came from the path, dousing the two women's excitement like a bucket of Nix ice as they turned to greet their cousin.

"There you are! Isobelle wouldn't tell me where you were. She said she didn't know, but I didn't believe that for a minute. She's so rude. I don't know why you insist on employing a bot," Patricia Olivia Rictor "Pattie" said with disdain as she placed a Marbotab in her mouth.

"I keep saying, 'Give a bot an inch, they'll take a mile,'" Pattie continued, as Emily parroted simultaneously to Alex behind Pattie's back. "I keep telling you, if you insist on keeping her, you should at least have her wear a uniform. Mother told you years ago, and I—"

"Pattie, are those new Ferragasts?" Alex interrupted their cousin's diatribe, knowing if she didn't, two things would happen: one, Emily would get pissed at Pattie's attitude, like that was new, and two, Pattie wouldn't stop. Once, when Emily was away, Alex tested her theory. Pattie spewed for thirty minutes before Alex couldn't stand it anymore and interrupted her.

"Yes, aren't they beautiful?" Pattie stepped gingerly on the flagstones, turning her ankle to show the grape-colored shoes better, as if the women cared.

Emily pulled out the hose and started watering, knowing Pattie wouldn't stay as long, worried she might get her precious shoes wet, much less dirty.

"We heard you were back." Pattie stepped back as she eyed Emily and the hose. "How was your trip?"

"Hawaii is always beautiful. You should visit." Alex knew Pattie never would. The women hadn't told any of the Rictors that Uncle Wally had been murdered.

"I don't know why you don't vacation someplace other than roughing it at your uncle's house." Pattie edged farther away as Emily and the hose moved closer.

"We don't have the extra money to travel like you do. We like it there anyway," Emily said as she started watering her new dill seedlings.

"If you'd stop putting those foster girls up, you'd have a lot more money. I bet you buy them school supplies and clothes, too. If you're so determined to house them, why don't you ask your uncle to just sell one of his inventions—"

"He doesn't want to, Pattie, so there is no sense in asking again," Alex interrupted, wanting to stop that subject.

"Anyway, I told Emily yesterday but wanted to come by today. Mother and Father are having an intimate gathering this Saturday night. 7 p.m." Pattie eyed Emily warily as Emily looked back innocently, hose still in her hand. "Did you tell Alex?" she asked Emily. Not giving her a chance to respond, she added, "Dinner attire. I'll tell them you'll be there?" as she popped another Marbotab into her mouth.

"I hadn't had a chance to tell Alex yet, but I checked her calendar. We'd love to attend. Thank you for the invitation."

Alex knew Emily was being uber polite just to annoy Pattie.

"Well, okay then," Pattie answered, obviously unsure of where to go with Emily's pleasantness. "I should be off," she added before turning to leave.

Alex and Emily followed Pattie inside the house, partially to make sure she was leaving and not prying. Almost to the front door, Pattie spied the draft menu for the hotel's Swan Song Oscar party that Alex had left on the entryway table.

"What's this? Why do you have this? You're not working at the hotel. Are you?" Pattie eyed her cousin. "You know we can always find a place for you to do something at Rictor."

"I just started. The woman handling the opening had to step away." Alex would prefer any hotel over working at Rictor.

"How does it look? No one has been able to get inside yet. Although I hear it looks tacky."

"Interesting, because the hotel looks the best it has in decades," Alex said a bit defensively.

"Well, they must have hired someone with taste because Triton knows they don't have any."

"Who's they?" Emily asked.

"Erik Wolfe and Linc Cussler. Watch out for Erik because he's trash, a snake. And Linc isn't much better. Besides, their company competes against ours." Pattie reached into her purse for another tab.

Alex stepped back when the Marbotab smell hit her. For some reason, that odor always made her feel funny. With Pattie on her third one, the aroma was becoming overwhelming.

"They both went to Brentwood. They were a year ahead of me. Erik was there on a scholarship, while Linc, Hollywood trash." Pattie snapped closed her purple Hermoth purse. "His parents were such a train wreck, and so was he. He had some outrageous parties, though."

Alex had heard rumors about his parties, with the kids raiding his parents' hundred-proof bar and designer-drug medicine chest, getting totally smashed.

"At least until he became friends with that monster, Erik. That was another thing he ruined. Don't see me out. And watch out for that bastard. Actually, both of them. They could charm diamonds from a tight-fisted whore."

Pattie turned to leave, not noticing Alex and Emily's shock at her vehemence. "See you Saturday. I'll send you a contact again for bot uniforms. What Isobelle's wearing is beyond the pale."

As Pattie reached the bottom step, a delivery bot flew up with a package. Pattie took the box from the bot, looking to see who it was for and who had sent it.

Isobelle came up behind Pattie and smoothly took the box out of her hands. "Richard is waiting out front. He has honked twice."

Pattie looked at Isobelle, examined her blouse, sniffed, turned, and left.

Alex joined Emily in the kitchen, turning on the lights since it was getting dark, the copper pots hanging above the autove gleaming.

"You'll never guess who's working next door," Alex said to Emily as she poured a glass of water before sitting at the kitchen table.

"Besides the Space Twins?" Emily plopped into a chair next to Alex.

"Gary Headbone."

"Gary, the ass? Not really. Really?" Emily asked, sitting up straight.

"Unfortunately. He didn't see me. I thought I was hallucinating at first when I heard his laugh. But when I peeked out my office door, sure enough, someone who sure as heck looks like Gary was down the hall. He's added a few pounds. I asked Meg about him later. She told me his name is Gary."

"That blows. Did you find where he works, or if he even works there?"

"He works for the hotel, for the tech department, which would fit."

"Are you going to say anything?" Emily looked at her cousin.

"What's to say? He was an asshole and a bit scary back in college? That was a long time ago. I'll only be there a couple of weeks. I don't want to bring anything up if it's a non-issue. Hopefully he's changed." Alex turned to look at Emily, a hint of wariness edging into her eyes.

"You're a lot smarter now and have backup," Emily said, fists clenched. "Remember that, not to mention a few new devices just in case. I get why you don't want to say anything at the moment, but if he so much as says one word that's out of line or tries anything, the gloves are coming off."

"What gloves?" Isobelle asked as she entered the kitchen holding a box. "Count me in regardless, but tell me who."

"Gary, the asshole of assholes," Emily said, before both women saw what Isobelle had crossstitched on the front pocket of her blouse.

Since March was National Macadamia Nut Month, Alex expected Isobelle shirts to say something about nuts. This one said, "I like big nuts, and I cannot lie." The blouse fit the theme, but Alex could see why her uppity cousin thought it was in bad taste.

"Oh my," Alex said, fanning herself.

"I don't mean to give Pattie any points, but Isobelle, I think Auntie Lani would have disapproved," Emily said, wiping her eyes.

"Unfortunately, Emily's right. Auntie Lani would have disapproved," Alex confirmed.

While bots had basic etiquette programmed in, it took years for them to absorb the subtleties. To help, the women included Isobelle when they taught any of their boarders the etiquette they'd learned growing up. Their Auntie Lani, Uncle Wally's wife, had been a stickler for manners, threatening the girls with her koa cane when they slipped.

"You remember when we told you it's not considered polite to talk about people's intimate body parts unless it's just with Emily or me?"

"And that sometimes other words are used for those parts?" Emily added.

"Yes. You said dick was one, but some people are called Dick—"

"Right, add nuts to the list." Alex held her hand up when Isobelle started to ask. "Nuts when it refers to a male's body parts—"

"And balls," Emily added.

"That word, too," Alex replied, trying to keep a straight face. "Now, who's the package for? Is it my bones?" Alex looked at the box Isobelle had put on the table. Even with the extra work at the hotel, Alex had some downtime and was hoping to start work on v5 of Ola's exoskeleton.

"Yes, it is for you." Isobelle pushed the package towards Alex.

"What are the bones for?" Emily asked as the two headed to the lab.

"A scientist at JPL discovered baked animal bones resist heat really well. Now that we're headed outside the solar system, who knows how hot it could be? I'm thinking if I add the bones to Ola's skin, it might help it survive higher temperatures," Alex said as Emily peered over her shoulder into the box once Alex cut it open.

"The General just sent some materials from Mars, and, don't fricking tell anyone, but I'm so excited, some new samples from Venus, too. I want to see how the bones work with the samples."

Alex started pulling out the bones as Chutney and Betty jumped onto the table.

"Are you going to start tonight?" Emily shooed the cats away before they could start clawing the box.

"Probably, but not until after dinner."

"I don't want to go to the party," Emily blurted out as they headed back to the kitchen.

"You don't have to go. But I expect we'll know most everyone there. And you've been to the house before. It would be good practice. But it's up to you." Alex didn't want to pressure her cousin.

"It's possible the one or ones who paid the killers will be

there." Emily started to bit her nails before she stopped herself, realizing what she was doing. She picked up Chutney, rubbing her chin on his head. The cat immediately started to rumble with the attention. "I know I should go for the practice. I just wanted to whine. It feels surreal to think that Steven and Marie could have ordered Wally killed or that attack on you. I can't believe they'd be that horrible."

"Deborah was horrible when she discovered she couldn't access my trust fund or sell this house after Dad died." Alex would never forget the vile words her stepmother had spewed at her in the attorney's office. "There's no reason to think Marie, Deborah's sister, would be any less horrible. And remember Richard trying to steal Uncle Wally's antique coins that time?"

"Miss Bird saw my shirt and said it was the funniest thing she'd seen in years," Isobelle announced, turning as the women entered the kitchen. Isobelle had changed into a yellow linen blouse with tiny blue flowers embroidered around the cuffs and collar.

"While Miss Bird's brilliant when it comes to ornithology, you can't count on her to know, much less care, about etiquette," said Alex, fondly thinking of the woman whose only nod to fashion was changing the color of the hairband that kept her long, now-white hair out of her face.

"We need to have Miss Bird over for lunch soon. Will you arrange it, Iso?" Alex asked as they heard the front door open and the distant chatter of Bev, Anita, and Jared.

A second later, a loud beeping sounded in the kitchen, followed by the ringing of Jared's comm. Alex grabbed the small tablet they kept in a kitchen drawer, an alert flashing on the screen.

"Someone's trying to access our system," Alex told Emily, fingers racing over the tablet. "Let's go to the lab," she added as she welcomed the girls home and told them to start dinner without them.

"Emily, Alex, can I speak to you a minute?" Jared asked.

"Come with us to the lab," Emily invited.

Alex, tablet in hand, sat down with Emily and Jared at the huge, antique oak-plank table the women used for meetings. Fred had followed them and was now snoring on one of the beds they'd kept in the lab for the animals. Located at the back of the house, the upper lab floor had screened, floor-to-ceiling windows that extended the length of the room. During the day, they opened to a wide lawn and oak trees that stretched towards the hill in back. Dark oak beams ran across the room's ceiling, framing the stucco-white walls.

"It's a remote hack." Alex entered more commands on the comm at the table. "That should trace whoever's trying to break through our firewalls. You wanted to talk with us?" Alex asked as she let the program search for the hacker.

"Honolulu PD called. They found the boat the thugs used to escape." Jared pulled up a holo to show the women. "It was anchored at Hale'iwa. They're continuing their search."

"The boat doesn't look familiar, but there are so many at the islands." Alex looked at the holo of the harbor and abandoned trawler. "Lee?"

"I don't recognize it," Emily said, shaking her head. "By the way, Iso told me the tracer worked on the grey tov that was parked outside last night. It ended up in a parking lot in Venice. It's been sitting there since. I just sent you the coordinates," she told Jared, who took out his comm to check the details. "They were able to bypass the security cameras when they left so that rules out any paparazzi."

"How are you set for tomorrow's test?" Jared asked. "Do you need any help?"

"We're fine," Emily said. "I tested the equipment, including the new antenna."

Emily and Alex also had designed a new antenna that would capture incoming data and then forward it to the competing teams. Alex created the new hardware, and Emily the software. If it worked, Space Force would ship it with Ola v6, the name they'd dubbed the last iteration, which was launching in November.

They were testing v3 tomorrow from their house on Earth to see how well it delivered commands from the Moon to the devices. The next version, v4, of the antenna would arrive on Mars before that test, with v5 headed to Farout.

Alex had created an alloy using Marsirium and Farsid, an element recently discovered in the deep Vavilov crater on the Earth's moon. By combining the two elements, Alex discovered an entirely new channel that Emily then used to compress and transmit data. At least that's how it worked on Earth. If it fuctioned the same in space, the discovery would provide an extremely cheap, reliable way to transfer huge quantities of data. Alex knew many people didn't make a lot of money working in space. If she and Emily could give them an inexpensive way to communicate with family and friends, and even see the latest vid—they knew it could be a life changer.

Since Ola and its antenna would radically alter space communications and the economics associated with it—some companies made a lot of money selling comm time—Alex and Emily weren't surprised that someone would try to sabotage or steal the new tech. If Ola worked, the corporations that could adapt and manage those data loads would be the future's big winners. The companies that didn't would likely become relics.

With those stakes, the women felt lucky no one had discovered their fake identities yet. That didn't mean, however, that they hadn't tried to go after Alex because of her relationship to their uncle. Hopefully, Alex thought, now that she was home, she would be safe.

Alex pushed Fred's ball back to the dog, who'd woken up and decided he wanted to play. She kept another eye on her comm. "Got it!" she exclaimed as a visual of a little puff of an explosion showed on the monitor. "I like the new visual, Em," she grinned at her cousin, who had recently added it.

"Someone just tried to break into Seed's systems," Alex told Jared, who then whipped out his comm to alert his boss.

"We have it under control," Emily added, checking some data on the comm. "So far, they've only found one of the presents we left them. If they're not careful—and hopefully they're not—the other one will completely destroy their system if they try to open it. Now let's go get dinner before the girls eat everything. Tomorrow's going to be a great day."

"Tomorrow's going to be a horrible day!" Pattie said, storming around the family room after pouring herself a healthy couple fingers of Grey Goose XvX and a large splash of Sonix. "We still have nothing! Nothing! While our cousins' uncle and his company ride to glory, we take a back seat!"

"Patricia," Richard said soothingly, not wanting his sister to get agitated. She needed to cut back on the Sonix, he thought. He'd noticed that she was becoming increasingly anxious, one of the nastier side effects doctors had recently linked to the Triton water. And those Marbotabs. He was hearing rumors about some strange side effects surfacing after using them long-term with depressants. "Our data rates are as good as SpaceZ, Verne, and Tiger's, and better than Lockheed's. We'll do fine in tomorrow's test."

"But we don't know how Xtra's are. And we still have to figure out how to boost ours for the final two tests. You know that," she hissed. "God knows Father's drilled that into our heads enough. Has he called?"

"I'm working on our rates." Richard checked his comm for a message from his friends about tonight's party. He then looked around, thinking, not for the first time, how absurd it was that his mother called this sterile, cold room the Family Room. "And yes, Father called and I spoke with him. I told him we're proceeding as planned. You were at Alex and Emily's?"

"Alex got the strangest package today. I didn't recognize the sender. It said it contained some kind of animal bones. What could she be wanting with something like that?"

"Maybe she's making soup," Richard said absently, looking back at his comm.

"My head is killing me." Patti drank some more vodka and Sonix after sinking into the large tan leather chair next to the fireplace. She glanced at Richard, who lounged in the opposite chair typing on his comm.

"They were happy a hawk killed a hummingbird today. Did I tell you?" she asked him, rubbing her head. "When I walked up— they were in the garden — this red-tailed hawk streaked down and grabbed a beautiful little hummingbird. I couldn't believe it! And then they started laughing. They didn't even try to stop it! That poor hummingbird. They're evil. I've always said that. You know that."

"Yes, Patricia," Richard said, not looking up.

"I don't think it's smart that we're trying to explore outside the Solar System. Wasn't Marbola enough?" Pattie popped a Marbotab. "People can't keep exploring further and further out. All the birds almost died. They said they had all the controls in place so we couldn't get any diseases. Instead, they brought back that horrible disease!"

"Yes, and then they created Marbo for the animals, and we have the tabs. We're all okay, although you might want to think about cutting back some." Richard tried to calm his sister before she really revved up.

"And then Isobelle. I told them they have to get that bot a uniform. I did finally get some Marbotabs in Alex's purse," she added, smiling triumphantly.

Richard shook his head. His sister had become obsessed with

Marbotabs ever since they'd been developed. While on vacation on Lunaship, his sister had fallen ill with Marbo. The only thing in the onboard pharmacy that had helped had been the tabs. Now she insisted everyone carry a pack.

"Did you know Alex is working for Erik Wolfe?" she asked Richard, who paused typing on his comm and looked at Patricia when he heard Wolfe's name.

"What's she doing?" he asked, his friends forgotten for the moment.

"She said she was taking over for a woman who was handling the hotel opening. The woman apparently got sick or something. I can't believe she's working at the hotel and for Erik Wolfe! That bastard, and his friend, Linc. Father and Mother will be appalled."

"Are they coming Saturday night?" Richard asked, brushing a piece of lint off his navy slacks.

"They said they were." Patricia finished her drink.

"Well, that will be interesting. Don't forget Wolfe and Linc are attending."

"I'd forgotten until Alexandra told me." Pattie rose, leaving her empty glass on the table. "Did Father say if he'd heard anything from Walter?"

"He still hasn't returned Father's call, which has made him madder." Richard messaged his friends that he'd be ready in an hour.

"I don't know why he won't at least sell us some of Seed's information. Just because we're not close, we are family," Patricia said, checking her nails for chips.

"Obviously not enough of a family. Ever since Mother commented on his wife's hospitality and how they were raising Alex and Emily as heathens."

"It didn't help that Walter caught you stealing his coins," Pattie shot back.

"By the way, I noticed one of your bird feeders looked like it wasn't working." Richard was tired of Pattie harping on the same old subject. "It can probably wait until tomorrow, but just in case." He knew his sister would leap up immediately to go check.

"Thanks, Richard. I have to go check it," Patricia said, leaving the room, still rubbing her forehead.

Confirming where he'd meet his friends, Richard stood, slipping his comm into his back pocket.

# Wednesday, February 18, 2172

A horribly early 5:00 a.m. Pacific Earth Time found Alex and Emily in their lab—Alex with an extra-large latte, Emily with a giant mug of hot green tea, and displays glowing. The women tried to relax as the minutes ticked down before the start of the Farside Moon Base Test. Alex, already dressed for the hotel, wore a sleek, dove-grey Victi pencil skirt and rose-pink lace blouse. She eyed Emily longingly, who lounged in a pair of blue sweats, an old Zuma-Jays t-shirt, and beat-up navy Vans.

She really wanted to pull out some Zopat from her top desk drawer and begin modeling another tiny spaceship. That always soothed her nerves, but she didn't dare risk dropping some on her blouse. It was a pain getting it out of lace. Instead, she looked around their lab, at the pale green walls and golden-oak plank floor—calming colors she and Emily had purposely chosen. A couple of years later, Isobelle had added her orchids, perching them on the countertops that ringed the room after hearing the plants also helped with stress.

"Power's at full. Ready in five," Emily said into her mike, her voice as usual disguised to sound like her male version of Lee.

"Hey Char, how's it going? You handling today's test?" Alex asked the Space Force captain after hearing her confirmation.

Isobelle entered, and Alex almost spit out her coffee when she looked up. Today was Ash Wednesday, and, from the mark on Isobelle's forehead, it was obvious she'd already been to church. Isobelle was exploring different religions. More unusual was the combination of her bright yellow blouse with "Cashew on the flip side" embroidered on the pocket; the amazingly lifelike, tiny orange carrots dangling from her ears; along with the fluorescent lime green slacks. It was a lot to take in this early, Alex thought, before turning back to the displays.

"Switching over in three, two, one, go," said Charlene White at Space Force's command center in Cape Canaveral.

"Roger," responded Alex, the displays lighting up as Ola began capturing the data generated at the Farside Base, then forwarding it for processing.

Eva, who was aboard the network ship, rapidly began switching all of Farside's comms over to the new Seed unit, which Space Force had her position to orbit above the base on the moon's back side. Farside, a key jump-off hub for space travel, had grown a lot over the years due to its lack of interference from Earth.

Scientific instruments, scattered across the landscape like salt from a spilled shaker, surrounded almost forty three-story living and work pods that clustered together into what was now called Farside City. With all the data it generated, everyone desperately needed a new way to manage it all.

"Lee, do you see that wobble in port 23?" Alex asked Emily, seeing an inconsistency in one of the displays.

"I'm working on smoothing it out," Emily said, fingers flying over her keys. "What the heck! I'm losing power. Can you stabilize?"

Alex pulled up her board to check what was happening with their power. "Damn, the power's dropping for some reason. I'm pulling from the hotel. They shouldn't notice since they aren't open yet. I thought the DWP had fixed the lines. Iso, can you check that today? And if they tell you they fixed it, ask Jared to ask the General to help us with that. I'm done with their excuses."

Once Alex had their power stabilized, the port evened out. The second phase of the day's test would start when the competing teams began receiving and processing the real-time data that would pour in from the Ola units at Gateway Station and Farside. Eva had done all she could, her ship already racing to Mars.

"Fuck," Erik roared, fingers flying over his keyboard in the hotel's conference room. The team had dubbed the room BAM for Bel-Air Mission Control. Since they liked BAM best, they'd all agreed to ignore the "C." "What's with the power? What's Playa saying?" he asked Linc.

"They're fine. It's only West L.A."

"I knew we should have gone to Playa this morning," Erik groaned. He wanted to break something; he was so frustrated.

"I'm getting it on the big screen, just a second," Linc said, slightly calmer.

"Meg, have you seen anything from DWP?" Erik yelled out. "Finally," He sat back when the wall display started showing how well their eXo system was handling the heavy streams of data streaming in from the new Seed unit called Ola. "Where'd you pull it from?" he asked Linc, who was still hitting the keys heavy.

"Well, let's just say the only power that's on at the hotel is in this room right now," replied Linc, taking a swig of his coffee while keeping his eyes on the wall display.

"What the heck? Did you guys reroute all the power?" Meg called from the other room. "At least give me some," she added, appearing in the doorway. "I checked the DWP. It's showing there's an issue in West L.A. and they're working on it. How's the test going?"

"We're doing great. What the hell?" Erik swore again as the lights flickered and the screen faded before brightening again. "Didn't we put in that new solar grid?" He turned back to his keyboard.

"We haven't tested it yet. That's scheduled for next week," Linc replied as he continued to work.

"Well, there's no time like the present. We need more power. Even if Playa's up, we still need ops here."

Half a minute later, the lights stopped flickering.

"The guys did a good job." Erik ran his hands over the keyboard, bringing up other parts of the hotel on the new solar grid. "Good thing it's a sunny day."

Linc just grunted, eyes fixed on the main display, which now showed their eXo system rapidly capturing the incoming data streams. "Seed's Ola unit is perfection," he said, turning to Erik. "Al and Lee are geniuses. And so are we," he grinned as he took another swig of coffee.

"Well, maybe I am." Erik ducked when Linc threw a Ferball at him. "But it looks like eXo likes all this data just fine. I can't wait to see General Watson's face."

"Before I forget, the police came by earlier, about Susan's accident," Meg said, still leaning in the doorway. "They wanted to talk to Susan's replacement, so I took the officers to see her. Alex told them that she'd found some discrepancies in Susan's work."

"Did she say what kind?" Erik asked, not happy that Alex hadn't discussed it with him. "I wonder why she didn't say anything to me?"

"She said she'd worked with Susan in the past, and it wasn't like her to make mistakes. She said she'd hoped to have talked with Susan by now. Unfortunately, they still have her sedated. I told Alex she needed to tell you. She said she's planning on it today."

"I meant to tell you," Linc interrupted. "I heard from George about Susan's tov. He found the guy who did it, and it's a dead end. There's no trace."

"Hotel Bel-Air, Events and Occasions," Sally said, answering the department comm at her desk.

"What've you found out?" the sharp voice demanded.

"The hotel was broken into the other day."

"What else?" the voice said.

"Susan Monroe, the event planner handling the hotel opening, was in a tov accident on PCH."

"That's old news."

"The police came today. They're investigating the accident. An insurance adjuster called, too. And Monroe has been replaced by an Alexandra Addington. They should have asked me to take her place," Sally complained. "Addington's had a few problems, though. It seems Monroe wasn't that good at her job."

"Did you say Alexandra Addington?"

"Yes. I don't like her."

"Are Wolfe and Cussler there?" the voice asked impatiently.

"Yes, but they've been locked in the conference room since I arrived. And something's the matter with the power. The lights went out. Everything's back on now."

"Too bad. Have you found anything on their contract bid?"

"Not yet; I've been looking."

"Look harder. There's not much more time, and you already know, if I fail, you fail." And the comm went dead.

Alex saw that Sally was just ending a call when she walked up to Sally's desk. She noticed her thin face was looking pinched again, as if she'd just tasted another sour pickle. Alex wondered if it was her or if Sally always threw off such a dour vibe. Her assistant informed her—somewhat snidely Alex thought—that

Erik was busy this morning. Ready to escape the woman, Alex quickly confirmed the day's schedule, telling her she'd reworked the calendar yesterday. Alex then entered her office, pulled off her tennis shoes, put them in the bottom drawer, and then stepped into her black stilettos.

Today, she'd check the internal orders. She'd been able to order plenty of lettuce from her family friends in Oxnard. Since that was an order she arranged, she needed to let the kitchen know, she noted on her pad. Larry the lizard had followed her to her office, slipping inside without Sally's notice. The little robot had since scaled Alex's desk and was now performing little lizard push-ups to boost his energy.

After observing Larry's gymnastics, Alex started reviewing the internal POs only to find they also had errors. Susan or Sally had made the orders, but as far as the changes, she couldn't find a trace of anyone making them, which was definitely odd. She was going to have to tell Erik.

Thinking of Erik, she was curious how Xtra had performed in today's Farside Moon test. She'd heard a few whispers that Xtra had made some major breakthrough but figured it could just be marketing hype. A noise made her look to the doorway, where she saw an unfortunately familiar face entering.

"Well, well, well. If it isn't Miss Woo-woo," the deep but disgustingly familiar voice drawled.

Alex rose, forcing herself to stand straight, knees locked. "Gary, I'd say it's a pleasure, but that would be a lie." Alex was so very grateful she'd spied him the day before and had had a chance to practice what she was going to say if she saw him.

Not that anyone would say her words were works of genius, but at least they were words instead of her jaw gaping open in shock. In the recent online pictures she'd found, he had added some pounds, and, if she was right, whatever substance he was downing was taking its toll.

Regardless, she felt like her heart was pounding out of her chest. Then she steeled herself. Her experience with the jerk back in college had at first left her feeling damaged. Then, however, after some serious reflection, she'd determined she wasn't going to let Gary dictate her worth. "Why are you here?" She noticed how his eyes and jaw had hardened with her earlier comment. Gary had never liked strong women.

"I'd been told an A. Addington had joined the staff, and I needed to ensure that A. Addington's tech is up and running," the tall, too-tan, slightly paunchy man said, striding closer, preparing to round her desk to look at her deskcomm.

"Mr. Cussler was here yesterday. I'm already up and running. I don't need your services," Alex said firmly, holding her ground.

"Well, aren't you still an ice queen?" Gary sneered. "You obviously have changed, for the worse. Are you still hanging with that creepy cousin of yours?"

Out of the corner of her eye, Alex suddenly saw Erik standing at the door.

"Alex?" His deep voice rumbled through her.

Great, now two unpredictable males were lurking—at least, unlike Gary, Erik pulled on her in the right way.

"Yes, Mr. Wolfe. How can I help you?" Alex turned towards Erik, aware of the growing tension and wanting to bolt out the French doors.

"Were you having a technical problem, Alex? I thought Linc already set you up?" Erik eyed Gary standing close to Alex's desk. Alex, looking flushed, stood stick straight. He wondered briefly if the flush was because she was attracted to Gary.

"The support ticket must not have been updated," Gary said. "My apologies." Gary headed to the door. As he turned to leave, he gave Alex a direct look as if to say he'd see her again.

*Over my dead body,* she thought, relieved that the ice had been broken. Way back in college she'd been such a cliché — the sheltered, brainy, klutzy girl believing the popular boy really liked her. *A harsh lesson, but what makes you stronger, yada yada*. Erik eyed her thoughtfully, as if he was trying to solve a puzzle. She had to pull it together.

"Do you know Gary?" Erik casually asked Alex, senses alert that he'd interrupted something. He'd been grabbing a brief break from today's test when he'd thought about dinner and wanted to confirm with her. As he almost reached her door, he saw Gary, one of the hotel techs, enter her office.

While he couldn't tell if Alex was happy to see Gary, it sure seemed they had history. He'd wanted to storm in and punch Gary, especially when he'd seen how close he'd been to her desk. He found himself almost holding his breath until she answered, noticing the edges of a few greenish-yellow bruises on her neck that she'd missed covering this morning.

"I knew him a long time ago, in college. I haven't seen him since," Alex added at his questioning glance, no emotion showing on her face. When she was a freshman at UCLA, she'd briefly dated Gary, if she could call it that. Once he got in her pants, he dropped her, told her she was a lousy lay, and immediately started seeing Carla, the popular girl bitch back then. He'd then started calling Alex "Ms. Woo-Woo" whenever he saw her because he'd found her crying once over a big old oak that the city hadn't been able to save.

"But that's all," she added. "I didn't think I'd see you until later. Did you need something?"

"I was just stretching my legs and wanted to confirm dinner tonight. 5:00?" Erik wondered what the real story was because certainly there was some kind of history. Now wasn't the time to get answers, though, he thought, needing to get back to the debrief.

"Yes, I'll be there."

"See you at Puck's." Erik turned to leave, then hesitated and turned back. "If you feel uncomfortable around Gary, I would expect you to let me know."

"Of course," Alex said, feeling unusually warm. She wasn't used to people looking out for her.

Erik's comm chimed, so he gave her a nod before answering his comm. "Yes?"

"Get your ass back here. Something's come up," Linc demanded. "We're fine, but you need to see this."

"On my way," Erik said, hurrying back to the conference room.

Once Erik left, and Alex's blood pressure started returning to normal, she quickly messaged Emily to check on Farside's test results.

How's it going?

We're still stable. Not so great for Verne. They're out.

Out?

Yep. Will fill you in later. We rocked it tho. You?

Saw Gary. Hasn't changed a bit. Will fill you in later 2. Having dinner here with E at 5. xo

Alex closed her comm. She wanted caffeine. She trusted Emily to let her know if she needed anything. Ola was humming like a dream. Hopefully, with Ola's new hull she'd just developed, its capture rate would increase tenfold. She wondered what had happened with Verne, but pushed that thought aside. Space Force's ship, along with Eva, was now racing to Mars and then to Farout. They'd also heard the news that Farout's systems were still stable, and that no one else had died.

The hotel was opening in eleven days. Maybe she'd make it a double espresso.

"What's happening?" Erik asked as he entered the conference room.

"First off, eXo managed as much as we'd expected," Linc said, turning to Erik. "Second, we had some noise on line 78, but I cleaned that up. We've passed all the benchmarks, by more than thirty percent, and that's without bringing on any more grinders.

"The other news is Verne. They've dropped out. They also

had a power failure but, unlike us, didn't have back-up. They couldn't make the benchmarks by the time power returned."

"That's a bit suspicious." Erik sat at his display, looking for any information he could find about the outage that had hit Verne. He discovered a vault down the street from Verne in Arlington, Va., had just had a massive failure, with the cause reported as unknown. As Erik delved further, hacking into Arlington Power's comm traffic, he found that the utility had recently serviced the vault. "Where's the team?" he asked, looking up.

"I told them to get some well-deserved R and R and to be ready to go again tomorrow morning." Linc moved to grab a chair across from Erik. "I thought they earned it. Besides, I wanted to talk to you. I dug deeper into Alex Addington's background. Do you know who else she's related to? Do you remember the astronauts Charlie Cash and Sam Zara?" he added when Erik looked at him questioningly.

"Weren't they the ones who were on a routine mission to Eris when their ship malfunctioned and left the solar system?" Erik asked, thinking back. "What's that have to do with Alexandra?"

"Do you remember they were married? When they disappeared, the press was all over it and their wives, coining it something like 'Love Lost in Space Times Two' because the men had married cousins in a double wedding."

"No, don't tell me," Erik said, hoping what he was thinking was wrong.

"Yes, their wives were Alexandra and her cousin, Emily."

"What the hell? No wonder there isn't much about the two after that nightmare. I'm having dinner with Alex tonight. It's not like that," Erik added, seeing his friend's look of surprise. "Here, in the restaurant. I want her opinion on the food and service."

"I wonder why she didn't go to Brentwood with Pattie and Richard?" Linc said, thinking back on their high school days.

"Another good question." Erik stood. "It's almost five now.

I'll let you know what I find out after, unless you want to join us?"

"No thanks." Linc turned back to his comm. "I want to check line 78 again."

*Dang, dang, dang,* Alex muttered to herself. She'd become sidetracked checking an order and then hurried. Then, she was all ready to go to Puck's; it was 4:55, and she caught her jacket pocket on the office door handle as she rushed out, ripping a giant hole in her jacket.

She panted shallowly, the pain in her ribs now worse, thanks to the fricking door handle. She figured her options were to run home, change and be late or remove the jacket. Carefully, she slipped it off to avoid hurting her ribs more. It wasn't risqué, she thought, looking at her reflection in the mirror over the credenza. Her blouse's shoulders and sleeves were sheer lace, while the rest of the blouse had a solid fabric underneath the lace to cover the important parts.

Dropping her jacket on the chair next to the door, she examined her reflection. A flushed face, bright eyes, and rosy cheeks looked back—the blush a result of the pain, not the thought of dining with an incredibly attractive man. She also saw some green and yellow bruises showing through the sheer parts of her blouse. Grabbing her makeup—she'd fortunately stashed a small bottle of base and a sponge—she quickly covered them, wincing as she gingerly touched up her skin.

She hated being late. Absolutely hated it. The rare times it happened, the later she ran, the more her heart rate increased. It was five on the dot as she took one last look in the mirror and tucked her blouse more evenly into her grey skirt. She didn't have time to fix her hair as she strode as quickly as her short little legs and stilettos would allow over the uneven flagstone path that wound through the hotel and led to Puck's.

She hurried up the three steps to the door, glad she'd focused on her cardio lately, and grabbed the door handle as it simultaneously opened. Alex gasped, teetering on the top step before she felt a pair of strong hands catch her and draw her into a warm wall of man.

Dazed, she looked behind her and up, colliding with a set of green eyes before she collected herself and, unwillingly, but intelligently, stepped forward. He felt so good. The man who'd opened the door apologized for almost sending her down the stairs as he eyed Erik nervously. Unfortunately, as she backed up to give the man room, she put herself in the same predicament again, beginning to teeter once more before Erik, glaring over her head at the man at the door, steadied her.

"I'm glad you could make it and appreciate your sense of promptness." Erik reluctantly removed his hands from his pixie as they entered the room. "However, please don't rush in the future on my behalf."

"Of course." Alex attempted to calm her racing heart while checking out the restaurant.

"I'm serious, Alexandra," Erik said, clasping her arm to get her attention. As she focused on his hand, he used his finger—man, she was in trouble; she'd never noticed someone's fingers before—to tilt her chin up so she'd have no choice but to look at him, his green eyes drilling into hers. "Promise me you won't risk yourself because you're running late." He needed her to agree to this. People who hurried could get hurt. He knew.

"I promise," she whispered, gaze locked with his until the sound of the waitstaff's steps on the wood floor broke their connection.

They followed the still-apologetic man, who Erik introduced as Henri, Puck's lead maître d. As they headed to a table near the fireplace, Erik asked him about the new tablets they just started using.

Alex took the moment to look around while wondering at Erik's intense insistence that she not rush. Something must have happened to someone he cared about for him to be that adamant. She leaned back against the pale-pink cushion that matched the restaurant's walls as she took in the beautiful room. Dark wood chairs and tabletops gleamed in the light cast by the chandeliers, gold-trimmed sconces, and fat white candles lit at each table. She was glad to see he'd kept the fireplace, remembering the time she and her cousin had been caught trying to roast marshmallows in the fake flames.

Do you have any allergies?" Erik asked after they sat across from each other, breaking into her thoughts as Henri waited for her answer.

"Only mushrooms," she replied, smiling at Henri, trying to put him at ease.

"Please tell Chef to prepare the tasting menu I mentioned earlier," Erik told Henri and then dismissed him. He focused on Alex, noting the rose pink of her top matched the blush on her cheeks. He hoped he was the reason she was flustered. He then shook himself. He needed to focus. "I already ordered for us. I want your opinion of the menu. Some dishes have received mixed reviews."

"I talked to Chef today. I asked him to make me small portions," Alex said. "Also, his breakfast sandwich rocks. Why don't you have that on the menu?" Alex knew that she was talking too fast, but she was feeling a bit like a rabbit being stalked by a hungry mountain lion.

"I like food, but can't eat a lot of it, and don't like wasting it," she added, feeling her face flush as she mentally kicked herself to just shut up. Her father and stepmother had prized thinness, and Alex's curves, which leaned more towards lush than slender, had always been an issue growing up.

"I'm surprised you've already talked with Chef," Erik said, sidestepping any potential landmines in the food department.

Meg and his sister had always told him to keep his trap shut on that subject. "He's not exactly the most sociable individual."

"Alexandra, buonasera signora," Chef Leon interrupted, launching into a slew of Italian, expressing how glad he was to have her in his restaurant and how he hoped she would love his food. He motioned the servers to place the first course of delicacies in front of them. He then poured what looked like a crisp Pinot Grigio, explaining in English the wine he'd paired with the first dish.

Erik wanted to tell Chef to go away, or toss him off the property. He shoved down his predatory reaction to the man smiling so broadly at Alex. Fortunately, with his limited Italian, he knew the chef wasn't asking anything inappropriate. Alex, though, he noted, was smiling back at the asshole with a warmth he'd only seen directed at him once so far. When she answered Leon in fluent Italian, his admiration only grew. She then switched to English, promising to tell Chef if she had any suggestions for the menu.

After taking a quick glance at Erik and paling at his glacial stare, Leon straightened, excused himself, and quickly strode back to the kitchen, servers trailing him like ducklings.

"Ohmygod, this is good," Alex said, the taste of fresh tarragon exploding in her mouth. "I could date this dish. Yes, this gets a definite yes. Keep this on the menu," she told Erik enthusiastically. She wouldn't normally give this kind of feedback on food when on a date, but this wasn't a date—though part of her almost wished it was. He was also making her nervous; he seemed so attuned to her that she couldn't help but keep blabbing.

She could see that he was amused at her reaction. "What? You asked for feedback. You don't like the asparagus asiago?" she asked, noticing that while he'd sampled the dish and paid attention to the plate's appearance, he didn't seem to like it.

"Not really. I don't care that much for asparagus, but so far, the overall vote's in favor of keeping the dish," Erik said, amused at Alex's enthusiasm. He was even somewhat enthralled at her honest responses, unused to people freely giving him their real opinions, much less the women he dated showing any excitment about food.

"Besides not risking yourself if you're running late, I also don't want you risking yourself around the swans," he added. "Last month Stan, one of the grounds staff, almost lost an eye from one of those birds. And he's a foot taller and has at least 100 pounds on you," he said when she started to object. "I heard you have a degree in swan studies, and Miss Bird told Meg you know your stuff, but at least promise me until I have a chance to talk with Miss Bird myself that you will not get close to the beasts."

"Meg said you could be a tyrant," Alex muttered. While not wanting to argue with him, she wasn't used to anyone questioning her abilities, much less thinking her reckless. "I can't make any promises. Sometimes things happen quickly. If the swans are in danger, I won't be waiting around for you to talk to Miss Bird."

"This is non-negotiable, Ms. Addington."

"You're right. It is non-negotiable, Mr. Wolfe. These birds, your birds, are special. I wouldn't think you'd want anything to happen to them if I could prevent it."

"They may be valuable, but not more than someone's life or safety, especially yours," Erik retorted, amazed at her stubbornness. It had been a long time since a woman had stood up to him.

He had taken Stan to Emergency and was the one who'd been there when the doctors had told him that it would take six weeks to regrow his eye.

"I will promise that I will only get involved if a swan is in danger," she said. "It sounds like Stan was an idiot," she muttered under her breath.

"He was," Erik said, amused at her comment, but making a mental note to contact Ms. Bird tomorrow morning. "Before I forget, I just heard Susan's still being sedated."

"I'd hoped to hear better news by now." Alex looked around to see if anyone was nearby. "I've been wanting to talk with you about Susan and her plans for the opening. They were a mess.

"That's not like Susan," she added when he waited for her to continue. "I've been hoping to talk with her, but at this point, I wanted to tell you. I've fixed almost everything. I'm waiting to see if the florist can move around another order, but I have a contingency plan in case they can't. Regardless, I've worked with Susan before, have known her for years, in fact. It's not like her to screw up like this," Alex said, frustration lacing her voice.

"I'm bringing you just one of my salads this evening — for you, signora, a tiny portion as you requested. Chef Leon eyed Erik warily as he placed a small plate in front of Alex and a much larger one in front of Erik.

"Grazie," Alex responded warmly before picking up her fork to taste the salad. She noticed that Erik had glared at Leon before he dug into the dish.

"Oh my gosh, this is delicious, too. It reminds me of the original HBA salad, but Leon has added something extra. He's a real find."

"Yes, I agree. Chef's amazing when he minds his manners," Erik said, feeling unaccountably jealous of the man. It didn't help that Leon was tall, fit, and handsome. "Thank you for telling me and for fixing the issues." Erik wanted to change the subject from Leon the magnificent. "Please let me know if you need any additional assistance as you get ready for the opening."

He paused to think for a minute and, deciding there wasn't a risk if he told Alex, he continued. "We have reason to believe someone tampered with Susan's tov. That it wasn't an accident," he added, noticing Alex's eyes widen with the news. "We also think it's possible that someone is trying to sabotage our bid on a contract we're trying to win."

Seeing her pale in front of him, he waved off Leon and continued, preferring to rip off the bandage in one move rather than dance around the topic. "You of all people may understand this, I think, considering who your uncles are," he added, gauging her reaction when he mentioned them. "Yes, I know one is Walter Dees and the other's Steven Rictor. I'm guessing you know about the contract and that a best-and-final's taking place right now."

"Yes, in fact, I hear congratulations are in order," she responded simply, maintaining a serene expression. She wasn't surprised he'd dug up her family details, even though she and Emily had hidden them as much as possible.

"You've heard something?" Erik asked, surprised.

"I heard just before coming over." Emily had told her about it earlier, but Space Force had issued a release right before she left to meet Erik.

"Linc and Meg are also aware of your family connections, but we haven't told anyone else. Don't be surprised if Linc hits you up to meet Al and Lee, though," he added, smiling. "He's tried before through your uncle. Do you know them?"

"Yes, they're very nice, although they take their privacy very seriously." Alex was grateful she'd had so much practice acting innocent when others asked her about the mysterious Al and Lee.

"I completely understand and wouldn't ever want to intrude."

Alex relaxed a bit. Usually people prodded, trying to find out anything they could about the two.

Talk of the food and Puck's filled the rest of the meal, with Erik noting her quick intellect as she pointed out a few flaws that no one else had seen and some startlingly insightful ideas for the restaurant. Her blazingly quick mind intrigued him, as did her slight blush when he complimented her.

The hotel's gardens, she told him, should take advantage of Bel-Air's microclimate, giving the hotel another unique edge. He asked that she write her ideas down, especially the ones related to the gardens since he couldn't tell the difference between spinach and dinosaur kale—whatever the heck that was.

"Janice was right when she said I'd be more than pleased with your abilities," Erik told her as they finished their last course.

"Right now, I think my ability to eat too much is forefront.

The chocolate meringue swan masterpiece that Chef created was worth the extra cardio I'll have to endure later."

Peter was clearing their dessert plates too slowly for Erik's preference. He could tell that Peter also had fallen under Alex's spell. He decided to switch to an all-female staff if this continued.

"Thank you for dinner," Alex added, trying to keep things light while fighting the draw of his gaze.

"Janice didn't tell me how beautiful you are," Erik said, deciding to speak plainly, frustrated with his self-imposed employer/employee restrictions.

"I heard you don't get involved with your staff," Alex countered, looking at him directly. While rusty at dating, she found speaking plainly worked best. She was also curious how he'd respond to her comment. She'd been around enough powerful men who had flouted their positions to try and get a woman in bed. She wouldn't tolerate a man like that.

"Technically, you're not an employee, and I never said anything about getting involved. I do not have relationships," Erik said flatly. While he knew he was being abrupt, he didn't want Alex having any delusions.

"Regardless, you're right. I don't seduce women I work with. But you have to admit we have some wild chemistry." Erik noted Alex's answering blush. "And that doesn't mean we should completely ignore the possibility of something after the opening.

"But, enough of that," he added, realizing that while she stood her ground, she also had a bit of innocence to her, unlike the typical Westside maneater, and backed off. He didn't want to run her off. "You mentioned doing cardio. Have you seen the hotel gym? We have the new Peloton XV."

"The new solacycle?" Alex decided to ignore what Erik said about after the opening. She'd unpack that later, at home. For the first time since Charlie, she felt a stir of interest. But she also wasn't into anything long-term. Could she have a one-nighter without her feelings getting involved? He'd hinted at an option to extend her contract after the last party, but she wouldn't be taking it. That was a hard stop. The network contract would be ramping up two weeks after that.

She had to take a break, not to mention help plan her uncle's funeral, before diving into the network launch. And with her identity out in the open, she wouldn't need to hide as an event planner anymore—not that the job hadn't been fun at times.

"It just arrived," Erik said as they pushed back from the table, following Alex closely through the restaurant toward the exit. "Feel free to try it out."

"I will," she responded, thinking it was possible she'd like to try him out, too. "Thank you again for dinner."

"I'll walk you to your gate."

Sensing it wasn't worth an argument she'd probably lose, Alex agreed. She found him outside her office door waiting when she came out, four inches shorter, carrying her heels and wearing her tennis shoes and ripped jacket.

"Don't ask," she responded when seeing his lifted eyebrow at her jacket. She'd sent a comm to Isobelle when she grabbed her things that Erik would be walking her to the house gate. As they walked across the hotel grounds, the dark enveloped them. He'd brought several small lightballs that kept pace with them. The hovering balls lit the area directly around them, making it feel like they were the only two people around.

"So, where'd you grow up?" she asked, belatedly realizing that was a lame question to ask an employer. But she wanted to fill the quiet that felt all too intimate. She didn't want to give him a chance to talk about the contract either or anything regarding space, afraid she'd reveal something.

"Here, in Los Angeles," he said. "Did you grow up here?" He didn't feel like talking about himself and his shitty childhood. He also was interested in her. Typically, with women who interested him, he would have a quickie, then he was gone, never a double-dip. He made sure he left them happy, but he wasn't there for the conversation. However, for some reason, he liked talking with her.

"Yes, born and raised," she said casually.

"Where'd you go to school?" he asked.

"I went to Harvard-Westlake. What about you?" She was curious about Erik and eager to switch the conversation away from herself.

"Brentwood, on scholarship," he added, knowing she could look that up if she wanted to, and interested in her response.

"So, you're either smart or athletic or both." She glanced up at him before walking through the hotel gate he held open for her.

"Both," he said, noting her smile at his arrogance. "I'm surprised we haven't met before this." He was sure he would have noticed her, picturing a pixie face with big, expressive blue eyes, a pert mouth, and long, black pigtails, torturing all the boys.

"I was pretty shy," Alex admitted, remembering how glad she'd been to be done with the social pressures of a private school. She'd always envied Emily for attending public school. She was glad to reach her gate, as their conversation had turned intimate, a feeling she wasn't sure she wanted to encourage.

"Our loss," Erik said softly, brushing a strand of jet-black hair away from Alex's mouth. Suddenly a small white dog of indeterminate breed burst through the slightly open gate and started circling them both, yipping, tongue lolling, and tail wagging so fast the animal was practically vibrating.

"Barney! Stop! Barney, quiet!" Alex said sharply, the last command making the dog sit, black button eyes fixed on Alex in adoration, with occasional glances at Erik to see if he would start petting him. Erik then spied a huge German Shepherd that had quietly followed the other dog through the gate, sitting close to Alex, eyes intent on Erik.

"Are they friendly?" Erik didn't want to lose a finger or arm. *Man, that Shepherd's big.*

"Yes, mostly." Alex made a gesture the dogs seemed to understand as the Shepherd leaned against Alex and the little one sniffed his hand. "That one is Barney. Barney, Erik." Alex put her hand on Erik's forearm to signal to the two dogs not to attack. "The big one is Fred. Fred, Erik. They're both rescues, and we've been told to always introduce them fully to people we don't want them to attack. We did have a problem once, so I wouldn't come onto the property without our knowledge.

Barney actually was the one that almost killed the burglar, but since no one knew Barney was a robot, everyone thought Fred was the more dangerous one. Not that he couldn't cause some significant damage himself. As the medtechs had evaluated the burglar on the gurney, he had insisted that it was the tiny white dog that inflicted so much damage, but the police simply shrugged and charged him with trespassing.

"Alex, is that you?" a soft voice called from inside the gate, which was opening further.

On the other side of the gate, Erik saw an elegant woman. Or was it their bot? He thought he spied a tattoo below her ear, partially hidden by a sweep of grey hair.

"There you are! Oh, I am sorry. Am I interrupting?"

"Iso, this is Erik Wolfe, my boss and owner of the Hotel Bel-Air. Erik, this is Isobelle Sapling, our house manager, who I'm guessing was out for a walk?" Alex said, introducing the two.

"I did not mean to interrupt." Isobelle reached out a firm hand to shake Erik's. "The dogs took off toward the gate, and I wanted to make sure everything was alright," she added, a slight smile on her face. "Nice to meet you, Mr. Wolfe," she nodded to Erik before turning and disappearing back through the gate.

"Thank you again for dinner," Alex said to Erik, a knowing gleam in his eye showing her that he knew she was running. "Will you be in tomorrow?"

"Nice to meet you, Isobelle," Erik called out. "I'll be there. Thank you for joining me tonight." He stepped back so he could close the gate. As he headed back to the hotel, he remembered Meg saying earlier that Alex had asked for her advance. He wondered why she needed it.

Erik stuck his head in Linc's office when he returned to the hotel, hoping to find his two friends.

"Yellowtail," Meg said, arms crossed, sitting back in a pale pink guest chair.

"Come on," Linc protested. "We had yellowtail the last three times. How about gangung?" he asked hopefully, comm in his hand.

"It's not my fault I won the bet. You started it anyway. Want anything before Linc places our order?" Meg asked Erik, unsuccessfully trying not to gloat.

"I'll pass, but thanks. I just had dinner." Erik sank into the matching guest chair as Linc, sighing, entered their dinner order.

"Did Space Force acknowledge receipt of our prelim results?" Erik asked.

"Yes. Did you see the announcement though?" Linc set down his comm. "Space Force confirmed Verne's out."

"When did they issue the release?"

"4:49—I was looking for it," Meg added, when Linc and Erik both looked at her, surprised she knew the exact time. "Why'd you ask?"

"Alex knew when we had dinner tonight at 5:00. She was a few minutes late. She said she'd seen the announcement. I was just checking. I told her that we all know about her family ties," Erik said, thinking her story held up, but something was nagging him, and he wasn't sure what it was.

"She's blindingly smart," he added. "She finally told me that Susan had left a mess, or that Susan's plans had been altered. She said she'd worked with Susan several times and that Susan had always been on top of things. She said it was really weird there were so many errors with the schedule and plans."

"Why didn't she tell you sooner?" Meg asked.

"She said she wanted to talk with Susan first, but since Susan's still sedated, she felt she couldn't wait longer. At least that's what she said. Is there a way to see if she's telling the truth?" Erik asked Meg.

"I suppose. Let me do some digging. Do you think she's trustworthy?"

"I'd like to think so." Erik drummed his fingers on the chair arm, frustrated. "But who knows?"

"Fortunately, we're already locked and loaded, so we don't have to worry a lot about her, at least more than anyone else," Linc said as a chime sounded.

"What's up?" Erik asked as Linc checked his comm.

"Speak of one of the devils we know. Syndi's been busy. She did an interview with the Star. It just went up." Linc scrolled through his feeds to find the interview, then passed Erik the comm so he could read it himself.

"Damn it." Erik tossed the comm on the side table with a clatter.

"Hey, don't take it out on my comm," exclaimed Linc. "It's not my fault your last girlfriend turned out to be such a gold digger."

"Finally," Emily said, turning away from her monitor as Alex entered their lab at the house.

"Whew." Alex dropped her ripped jacket and purse on her desk before plopping herself in her chair. "This was a long day."

"But a good one." Emily sat back in her chair and eyed her friend. "So spill. How was dinner with your wolfy?"

"He's not my wolfy. However, dinner was amazing. Chef Leon's a wizard. You need to come over and try the food."

"Let me know when. How was the company, really?"

"Honestly? I had a really nice time. Ok," she admitted, looking at Emily. "I had a really, underlined and in bold, nice time. He's interesting. I didn't get bored. In fact, he makes me feel interested, if you know what I mean. He told me he's interested himself." She nodded, seeing Emily's raised brows.

"There's a thirty-eight percent probability that he is the killer," Isobelle said, making the women turn and stare at her as she walked in. "What? Bev's taking statistics, and I was helping her. I thought I would make a chart of the probabilities of every executive at the companies competing for the contract."

"Why does Erik have a thirty-eight percent probability?" Alex asked.

Isobelle held up a finger. "One, his company has a lot riding on this project, but actually I took that off the list because all of the companies have a lot riding on winning the contract.

"Two, unlike every other company except SpaceZ, Xtra's core business is space. The other companies diversified, so they do not have as much to lose if they do not win.

"Three," she held up a third finger, "the hacker the other day. I traced them to the hotel before I lost them. Four, Syndi Monroe, Erik's last girlfriend, has been saying he made her get a full body lift and is hinting that he is violent. I am still digging so that thirty-eight percent could change."

"Who stands out most?" Emily asked.

"Rictor and the Lockheed-BRE team have tied for first place at forty-one percent. While both are diversified, Rictor and BRE need money; at least that is the rumor I am hearing. Rictor blew that solar job on the Moon."

"That's right," Alex mused, "and BRE lost their ocean cables and that new sub when that underwater volcano on Europa blew in January."

"Yes," replied Isobelle, "the analysts are sniping at both companies, so winning would make a big difference to either's numbers. But I am still waiting on some information, so everyone, unfortunately, is still suspect. I would not have mentioned it if you were not talking about your wolfy," Isobelle added.

"He's not my wolfy," Alex argued before Isobelle headed back to the kitchen, a smile on her lips while the dogs trailed behind, hopeful for a late evening treat.

The two women sat for a minute, lost in their thoughts.

"With that cheery news in mind, fortunately I have some time to think about whether I really want to have that one-night fling or not. Although I was thinking that if I were to take him up on his offer, that it would be the night after the big party. The next morning—"

"Space Force will be announcing the contract winner, and we'll be revealing ourselves," Emily finished for her. "What if you want more than a night?"

"He already made it quite clear he doesn't do relationships, and frankly I'm not sure I want one either. We have so much to do: the funeral, the launch, not to mention talking to the press after our big reveal." Alex looked at her friend. "I haven't been able to figure out any other way to take control of Seed. Have you?"

"No. And if we don't take control, then we'll continue to hit roadblocks. I'm still planning on it." Emily held up her hand to stop Alex from saying anything. "It's time, Al. I know we can't continue to hide. It doesn't protect us anymore. I think we'll do a better job of protecting ourselves if everyone knows the truth."

"Nothing's ever certain." Alex thought about their uncle.

"I know, but at this point it's more of a burden than a protection. I'm sure Uncle Wally and Auntie Lani would have agreed. We needed the protection before, but we're smart and strong now. It's time. We only have to last another two weeks and we can come out of hiding.

"You know we'll be exchanging one fishbowl for another?" Alex pressed her cousin, wanting to make sure she knew what they'd be getting into once people knew their identities.

"Yes, but someone's trying to crack the bowl we're in," Emily said. "Sometimes I wonder if we'd done it sooner, if Uncle Wally would still be alive."

"Uncle Wally agreed that it was safer to wait until Space Force awarded the contract. The person at fault for his death is the killer, no one else," Alex said firmly. "And that person will pay. Did you tell the General?"

"I wanted to wait until we talked, so it's agreed?" Emily asked one last time, holding out her hand.

"Agreed." Alex reached forward and linked her fingers with her cousin's.

"You are going to do it?" Isobelle asked as she came back into the women's lab.

"Yep, same day the contract winner's announced," Emily said.

"I meant to tell you that someone planted a comm outside the side door tonight," Isobelle said as she misted her plants and refilled the water jug that Emily and Alex had used during the morning's test. "I had squirrel check it out, then bury it and pretend to pee on it. From looking at tonight's vid, it appeared that someone on a mocyke tossed it on the property as they rode past. I told Jared, who said he would tell the General."

"Now the General's not going to want us to go anywhere," said Emily.

"He didn't want us to go anywhere after my attack in Hawaii," Alex reminded her.

Alex had arrived in Hawaii last Friday to close up her uncle's house after his murder. She and her cousin hadn't wanted to run the Space Force tests there after his death, so she'd gone after the police had cleared it and the General had given his okay.

"You know the General blames himself for saying the house was safe," Emily said. "Thank heavens Hilda returned for that book, and the police came in after her."

The attack had come Saturday morning, when she'd wandered out from her bedroom in search of a cup of coffee before starting the day. Wearing just an old t-shirt and underwear and barely awake after having slept fitfully, she didn't realize she was in trouble until the two thugs grabbed her and tied her to her uncle's rattan chair. Somehow, they'd bypassed the security in back.

"Have you heard any updates from HPD?" Emily asked.

"They confirmed it was two men, but that's all," Alex said. The men had demanded she tell where her uncle kept his notes and what she knew about Ola, the device Space Force was using for the new network. She kept saying she didn't know anything, but they became increasingly brutal, alternating questions with blows. She knew, even if she had started talking, they wouldn't believe her. After all, hardly anyone knew she and her cousin were the brains behind Ola.

She realized she might actually die when her vision started to grey after a particularly hard blow sent her and the chair crashing to the floor. Lying on the ground, one of the men savagely kicked her in the ribs as he told her she'd better talk before they really started having fun.

When Hilda, her uncle's housekeeper, had opened the door, looked in and started screaming—she felt a relief she'd never felt before—especially when, a second later, the police pushed in past Hilda, stunners in hand.

Alex banished that thought—she couldn't let that experience define her any more than Gary's actions. She, Emily, and Isobelle finished tidying the room, turned off the office lights, and headed to bed.

Once in her room, Alex washed her face and slathered more Erisalve over her ribs and bruises. She thought about the day's events, including seeing Gary. When she told Emily she'd spotted him, her cousin immediately wanted to act, even offered a few creative ideas. Alex told her she wanted to wait and see if he behaved. If not, she was confident her new jewelry would protect her. She also felt a little safer after Erik told her to let him know if Gary made her feel uncomfortable.

She wanted to trust Erik, but after her uncle's murder and her attack, she didn't feel like trusting anyone new. Too much was at stake. Gary's presence could be more than a coincidence. She'd always believed that employees reflect their bosses—you-know-what flows downhill—which would mean Erik could be a Class A jerk, too.

She then thought about dinner and what Erik had said about not having relationships. She hadn't been involved with anyone since Charlie died. She'd had sex several times, but each time had been an unfulfilling flop. One man had even become a bit nasty when he'd wanted to get together again and she'd turned him down.

At least this time, if there was a chance of a "this time," she'd have her eyes wide open, she thought as she grimaced at her reflection in the big mirror. Dark green and yellow bruises stood out after she'd washed off the concealer. They circled her left eye—fortunately it wasn't swollen—traced her neck, ran down her left shoulder, and wrapped around her ribcage. Hopefully they'd fade before the last party, she thought as she pulled on her favorite pajamas. She didn't want to have to explain them to Erik if they did get together.

As she gingerly slid under her covers, she remembered the picture Emily had found of Erik and Linc on that sailboat. Those ripped, bronzed muscles definitely were tempting, she mused as she turned off the light, Barney curled against her feet, and Fred snoring from his bed.

# Thursday, February 19, 2172

"Son of a bitch!" Pattie yelled, hurling her comm across the room. She'd just tried the bug her man had thrown in Alex's yard last night and ... nothing, not a damn thing! It had worked fine until that crazy-ass squirrel buried it and some kind of liquid dripped on it. She hated those flea-ridden rodents. Apparently, she hadn't thrown her comm hard enough because it started ringing.

"I'm working on it!" she said defensively when she saw the familiar number. "At least Verne's out."

"That's only one team," the voice snapped. "Alex and Emily are supposed to go to *Pierre's* tonight. I suggest you go. See what you can find out about Walter. Seed managed the test from L.A., but there's no sign of him. Who else could have run it?"

"Certainly not Alex or Emily," she said absently as she checked her nails, admiring her new manicure with the platinum accents on the tips.

"Walter has to be here somewhere. Let me know what you find out," the voice barked and then hung up.

"Let me know what you find out," she mimicked. "I'll tell you what I find out when I'm good and ready. And there's no way I'm going to that club. What a waste of time."

She commed her man, telling him she didn't care what he had to do, but he had to find a F270. She wanted it ready for Friday.

Since Erik had caught up on his messages, at least the critical ones, he decided to do a little more digging on Alex for the sake of Xtra's security. At least that's what he'd tell Meg or Linc if either came into his office and saw his screen.

He'd wondered about Alex's bruises more than once as he sipped his coffee. The security check hadn't included any reports of an accident or mugging.

He had a few other avenues to explore. He knew she'd been in Hawaii recently, so after finding nothing in California, he checked the islands, where he hit paydirt—kind of. He found a vague record of an alarm report from Walter Dees' house—or compound, more like it. He still couldn't believe Alex was Dees' niece. Spearing his fingers through his hair as he searched through the police files, it seemed strange that he couldn't find any follow-up report about the alarm. He sent a quick comm to his old surf buddy, Dusty, who owned a security company on Oahu.

While he waited for a response, he took a deeper dive—or as Meg would say, a darker dive—by checking the dark web, including a strand that accessed cams and their backups in the area. It wasn't quite legal, but when it came to protecting Xtra and the hotel, he didn't care.

After a few minutes, he found a short recording from a cam above Dee's house. It showed what looked like military vehicles both in the front of the compound and hovering over the water in the back. Unfortunately, the recording suddenly became blurry and then cut out. He couldn't make out any other details.

He could tell something definitely happened. He had his system hunt further back in case anything else turned up. The only other recording he could find had been logged several weeks before that. It too was short and turned blurry almost immediately.

He could tell that two big someones had carried a large, long object from the house to a small boat in the bay. He couldn't see much about the object, as the vid became really choppy just when the two shapes exited the house. They looked military but weren't wearing military uniforms. Instead, they were dressed entirely in black, with black hoods obscuring their heads and faces.

A bit later, a ping indicated that Dusty had responded. When Erik opened the message, the weirdness only continued. Dusty was telling him to back off immediately. He added that he'd keep an eye out for rogue waves, an old code they had established to let Erik know that he would keep an ear out.

Walter Dees had always been known for his eccentricities, particularly his obsession for privacy. In fact, it wasn't unheard of for Walter to disappear for months. Yet, something seemed even more off this time.

Regardless, he hadn't found anything that indicated whether Alex was trustworthy or a spy—just more mystery. While he wasn't known for always dating the smartest women, he thought ruefully, recalling some of the not-quite-so-intelligent but beautiful women he'd taken out, he did draw the line at thieves or spies. A second later Ron and Linc entered his office, interrupting his thoughts.

"I swear, it's someone on Stone Canyon or very close," Ron insisted.

"It can't be," Linc argued as he walked to the Raleigh to dial a double espresso.

"Walk right in, guys. No, I wasn't busy." Erik closed his screen and turned to the two.

"I'm telling Linc and wanted to tell you, too." Ron sat down across from Erik. "First, DWP said they didn't have a power surge yesterday morning. They said that someone in the neighborhood must have been doing some construction work, which caused the surge.

"Two," Ron continued, glancing at Linc as he sat down in the guest chair next to him. "I think the drain came from the house next door."

Linc shook his head. "The only way that would have happened is if Dees was running the test from next door, which is ridiculous. He's not here in L.A. We'd know that, right? My bet's on Rictor. Did you know he lives up the street on Dolcedo?"

"Fuck. Does everyone live in this canyon?" Erik pulled a bill out of his drawer and tossed it in the bowl. He was getting frustrated with the continued mysteries. "Are we sure Dees isn't here?"

"The infrared showed a major energy flare next door," Ron insisted, looking hopefully at the two and their coffees.

"It hasn't been calibrated," Linc responded. "Right now, it can be off by a mile."

Erik rose to program a coffee for Ron. "It sounds like you want Dees to be next door. Black, right?"

Ron jumped up and headed to the Raleigh to grab his cup, nodding his thanks to Erik. ""Don't you? That would mean that Al and Lee are probably staying next door, too. Then you two could meet your heroes, and we could all move on with our lives."

"You wish," Erik said. "It was probably some too-wealthy prince powering all his fancy tovs at the same time. But my bet's on the Rictors. Keep on looking though," he directed Ron. "The solar should cover us either way."

"We hope," Linc said. "I moved up the solar test to tomorrow, just to be sure."

"I also told the DWP that we have a major test next Monday, so we'd be grateful if they would double-check their systems," Ron added. "If you don't need me for anything else?" The security chief rose to leave, coffee in hand.

"You'll be ready at 8:00?" Erik asked Linc after Ron left.

"Why did we say we'd do this?" Linc groaned, rubbing his face.

"Tonight's for a good cause."

"I can't believe the movie is that popular," Linc replied. "When we said we'd do this, I thought it would be a lark, not this circus. I'm going to kill Jorgé."

Erik and Linc, along with some of their other friends, had cameoed in *Swan Song*'s beach scene as a favor to their movie director friend Jorgé diAngelo. Because of a problem with the original film location, Jorgé had relocated the scene to the back of his property, which sat next door to Linc's Malibu home. The night of the shoot, Erik and Linc's friends were gathered at Linc's for their monthly game when Jorgé commed, pleading that they come over and fill in since the extras had been held up by a mudslide on PCH.

At that time, Jorgé had said the film was a low-budget love story, but then it had become a sensation. Since its release, everything had become swans and feathers: Halloween costumes, decorations for Christmas trees, New Year's parties, ice sculptures, artwork, towels, sheets. When the vid first released and, after a few too many toasts, the friends had promised Jorgé they would help him with publicity.

"You know it's for a good charity. Save the Flocks helps a lot of animals," Erik reminded his friend. "Just because you have to sign a few autographs, dance a few dances, and pose for a few pictures, think of all the critters you'll be saving."

"Yeah, yeah, I'll be ready," Linc grumbled. Linc and Erik both liked to pursue women on their own terms, away from the spotlight. However, tonight would be the opposite. The cameras would be on them as a lot of cosmetically altered, wealthy women vied for their attention, women who would think they could buy whatever they wanted, including the two of them.

Alex pushed back from her desk; she'd accomplished a lot for the day. Next, she had a meeting with Erik, then home to change before heading to Pierre's. The pain in her ribs, still extreme, was taking a toll on her health. She was relieved she'd planned on staying home tomorrow night to prepare for the upcoming Mars test.

After checking the mirror to ensure the cover-up still concealed her bruises, she grabbed her comm and skimpad and headed to Erik's office. Knocking on his door at precisely 5:00, she felt the now-familiar spark of awareness when he looked up and locked eyes with her. As Erik stood, Alex noticed his biceps straining against his shirt sleeves as he placed his hands on his desk. Alex's heart rate rose as she smelled the hint of his woodsy scent. She wished the air conditioning would kick on. Better yet, she wished another skunk was nearby. She could use the distraction.

"May I," she asked, motioning to his Raleigh.

"You seem to know your way around it," he said, taking in the sight of her crossing his office to the shiny copper machine. He also enjoyed seeing how her lithe fingers moved deftly across the buttons. He wondered if her fingers would move as deftly over him.

"We haven't had a chance to talk about tonight's party at Pierre's." She turned and leaned against the counter as she waited for her latte. "I talked with Mr. DiAngelo's rep. She seems to have everything under control."

"I want you there tonight," Erik informed her. "I'd meant to mention it before, but with everything else, it slipped my mind. Problem?"

"Actually, I've already planned on being there. I'll be busy for about thirty minutes at some point in the evening due to a prior business commitment, but I'll be available the rest."

"I'll pick you up at 8:10." Erik said, feeling pleased he'd finally capture the woman's attention for some conversation during the drive.

"Thanks, but my cousins are coming with me." Alex set her latte on the high table, then carefully climbed into the high chair. "I'll meet you there." With their chemistry, she didn't want to be in a tov with him all the way to Pierre's, much less with Emily and Jared, too. "I sent you a new version of the *Swan Song* party release. I fixed some errors. If you wouldn't mind looking at it now?" Alex asked. After passing her skimpad to Erik, she absently picked up the unsolved nine-level holo puzzle sitting on the table.

She tried not to stare at Erik's broad muscles filling out his dress shirt. Instead, she spun the morphing cube, returning it to its single-color sides before it could change. The crystal bowl on his credenza had considerably more chips in it today. She then remembered yesterday's test and how Seed had monopolized the local power.

"What were the mistakes?" he asked, looking up.

"The time was wrong in the head. In the copy, the date was wrong. Your name was spelled wrong in the boilerplate." Alex listed off the errors as she put the finished cube down.

"Did you look to see who touched it last?" he asked, frustrated with the continuing errors as well as the fact she'd declined the ride. He wasn't used to anyone, especially women, turning down his offers. Usually, they tried all kinds of maneuvers to be with him.

"Susan was the last one to see it, but she was always meticulous about releases."

Erik took a small box from his desk drawer and, opening it, pulled out what looked like a small, black dot. "While you're working for me, I want you to keep this tracker on you," Erik said, pushing it towards her. "Attach it to your comm."

Alex started to protest, but he cut her off. "We're now sure that Susan's crash was deliberate. I'm not taking any chances. And if you don't like it, you'll find yourself talking with my lawyers, as our contract includes a security clause that says you'll accede to any protections I deem necessary. And I think the tracker's necessary," he added, even more frustrated that she balked at him protecting her.

Alex had dealt with enough strong protective males, including her Uncle Wally and the General, to know when to argue. But she also didn't want someone else keeping tabs on her. The General had already invaded their space with Jared. After being blindsided in Hawaii, she was hyper alert now.

One more person monitoring her and snooping in her business, all while she and Emily were hiding their Al and Lee personas and conducting the network tests, would drive her crazy.

"Thank you for your concern," Alex said soothingly to Erik, who raised an eyebrow at her quick acquiescence. "I greatly appreciate it," she added quickly when she saw Erik's jaw clench. "and will use it when away from the hotel and providing you services," her mind automatically going into the dirt and visualizing other services she could provide him.

"I expect you to have the comm with you regardless of what you're doing while you're under contract. That's not negotiable."

"What!" Alex protested, hearing her skimpad creak as she gripped it. Taking a breath, she reminded herself she owed Susan and that the assignment would only last another week. The General would probably be happy when she told him tonight. "Fine." She smiled sweetly at the man as she loosened her hold on her skimpad, already deciding to reprogram the tracker so it only monitored her when she wanted. "Thank you very much."

"Fine?" he asked, surprised and suspicious.

"Yes, thank you very much for your concern."

"Since it's so small, I suggest you put it on your comm now so you don't accidentally lose it." He didn't trust her for a second.

"Of course. I wouldn't want to lose it." Alex turned over her comm, peeled off the backing on the dot, and stuck it on. She couldn't wait to hack it.

Erik didn't trust his pixie any more than he could talk to the swans, but until he could prove anything, he decided to move on, glad that she'd agreed. While it looked like a regular tracker, which was the point, he'd designed this one himself. Even Linc hadn't been able to crack it yet.

"This looks good." Erik signed off on the new version. "May I ask who you're meeting at the fundraiser?" While he realized he sounded like a prying, pompous ass, he rationalized that to safeguard Xtra, he had every right to pry.

"I mentored Mark Bagdasarian, Pierre's new GM, during the remodel. I promised to come tonight in case he needed any support. Also, my uncle provided the animatronics for the club, including some swans for tonight's charity as a donation. I told my uncle we'd make sure they're in place and working," Alex replied, glad she had her cover story.

Space Force had discovered discrepancies between the data it had captured and the data on the drive she and Emily had taken to the General after the Space Station test. Tonight, they were giving the General the Farside test data to compare. He hoped it would hold some clues about the people trying to sabotage the new network as well as ensure they had clean numbers.

"Jared, my cousin, just came into town. Emily and I promised him we'd take him out tonight." Alex thought that the way Emily and Jared constantly bickered made them seem like they were related. "Is Meg going?"

Right then Meg entered Erik's office.

"Am I going where?" she asked.

"Are you coming with us tonight to Pierre's?" Erik knew he was goading his friend. She'd already said wild horses couldn't drag her to watch women drool over the two men.

"No, thank you. Besides, you guys are the draw or, should I say, the chum in the water."

Meg sounded a bit too happy at Erik's expense. Alex smiled, obviously liking Meg's humor.

"For that comment, I think we should make Meg join us, don't you, Erik?" Linc said as he entered Erik's office. "If we have to be chum, we need protection, or someone to suffer right along with us."

"I've got the wrong parts. Besides I'm sure Alex will protect you both." Meg smiled at Alex.

"She's certainly nicer to us than you are, so it will be an improvement," Linc countered. "Will you dance with me, Ms. Addington? Meg never dances," he complained, smiling at Alex as he sat down across from her.

Linc, while extremely good-looking, did nothing for Alex, and for that, she felt grateful. If anything, he reminded her of a classmate who'd been like a big—emphasis on the big—brother during college. He'd been her first real male friend. When he died two years ago in an airship accident, part of her heart had shattered. Linc reminded her of Jim. "Only if you don't smash my toes."

"You'll never have better," Linc said as Meg groaned.

"Excuse me?" Erik said, giving Linc a stink eye he hadn't leveled at him since college. "Bragging much? You'll have to excuse his exaggerated sense of self. He takes one Astro Dancing class, and he thinks he's Ric Speath.

"I'm not touching that," Alex said, smiling. "I need to go. Meg, if you change your mind, let me know."

"I hope she's for real." Meg said as she rose to leave. "I think I like her."

"Say who finished the cube?" Linc picked up the puzzle he'd been working on for weeks.

"Our new event coordinator." Erik realized Alex must have finished it while he was reading the release because it wasn't solved before she'd entered his office.

"No way! Did you see her do it?" Linc turned the cube to check that all the sides were complete.

"No, I was reading the hotel draft she'd brought."

"How close were you to finishing?" Meg eyed the colored, nine-rowed cube.

"Not close at all."

"Damn, the Bel-Air princess is smart and nice. Too good to be true?" Meg looked at Erik.

"I don't know." Erik still felt something wasn't adding up with Alex. "I'm just not sure."

Alex was ready to leave the hotel and head home when Richard commed her to ask if she was around. Sighing, she messaged him back that she would be heading home from the hotel in two minutes. He responded that he'd meet her out in front. Alex sighed again. She really wasn't in the mood to talk with her cousin. She had a long day ahead of her, and he always seemed to ask about Walter and Seed's work.

"Allie," Richard said as Alex spotted him out front near the hotel's footbridge. She could tell he'd been out running, considering his hot face and sweaty tank. Richard had been running since elementary school. She'd always figured it was his way to escape his parents.

"Hi Richard." She liked her cousin, even though he was shallow. He couldn't help it. Her aunt and uncle had raised their kids on money. The complete opposite of her Uncle Walter and Auntie Leilani, his parents had a coldness that sometimes surfaced in Richard and Pattie.

*Could any of them have caused her uncle's death*, she wondered. If she was honest, she wouldn't be surprised if either her aunt or uncle were responsible. As for her cousins, she hoped not. Feeling guilty for thinking so poorly of her "family," Alex tried to compensate by grabbing Richard's hand and giving it a warm squeeze. She prayed it was someone else.

"Are you okay, Allie?" Richard glanced at his cousin as they walked to the gate.

"It's just nice to see you. How've you been? How's the testing going for Rictor?"

"Great on both counts." Richard motioned Alex up the street, avoiding the large green bug on the camellia bush. "Although Father would really appreciate it if your uncle would share some of Ola's code."

"Richard, we've been through this before." It felt like a knife when Richard said Walter's name. Alex especially didn't want to discuss giving Rictor Seed's tech again, something Walter had adamantly opposed.

"I know, I know. I'm sorry. It's habit, father and all that," Richard apologized. "Say, have you also hung bird feeders? I swear there are more birds here than at our place." He tried to wave off an unusually pesky hummingbird darting around them. "That's not why I stopped by. I wanted to offer you and Emily a ride tonight. You're going to Pierre's, right?"

"I already told Emily I'd go with her and her friend." Alex opened the side gate to her property. She knew Richard wouldn't buy the "Jared is a cousin" story. Marie had investigated all of the "other" family from both sides of the tree, hoping, but not expecting, to find some successful entrepreneur she hadn't heard about who she could mine. "Do you want to come in? You still haven't met our newest boarder?"

"You're still handing out free room and board?" Richard closed the gate, carefully avoiding a spiderweb. "Honestly, Alex. Your roof looks like it's going to fall in, and the fence needs repair." Richard looked around at the less than pristine yard, distaste showing on his face.

"The fence's still sturdy, and we just hired a roofer." Alex was used to Richard's disparaging remarks about the old mansion, just like his father.

"How about I pick you up for Saturday's party then?" Richard asked as they reached the door.

"Let me check with Emily. Besides, won't Stephen and Marie kill you if you're not at the house greeting guests?"

"They won't mind if I step out to pick up my favorite cousins."

"I'll let you know. I've got to run. I'll see you at Pierre's?" For a second, Alex thought she'd seen Richard's expression harden when she hadn't accepted either ride offer.

"Yes, cousin. I wouldn't miss it," he replied breezily before turning to continue his run back home.

Alex wondered why he wanted her and Emily to ride with him as he headed toward the street. He couldn't still think there was a chance he'd be able to talk her uncle out of any of his inventions. On the other hand, if Richard thought her uncle was still alive, that would mean Richard wasn't the murderer, she mused —unless he was trying to distract them from thinking he'd been involved.

Besides, she wasn't sure the thugs realized they'd killed her uncle. When they'd been discovered and fled, her uncle hadn't died yet. It wasn't until he arrived at the hospital that he passed. Shaking her head in frustration while trying to tamp down the deep sorrow she felt welling up within her when she thought of how much she missed her uncle, she glanced at her comm. She needed to hurry if she wanted to shower before getting dressed for the evening.

"Did you check out that tov?" Linc asked. "The one that just passed with the "Allee Cats" license plate?"

"The blue one?" Erik asked as they pulled out of the hotel parking lot. "I think that's Alex and Emily's."

"That's a hot tov."

"You're only saying that because you've heard their uncle made some modifications."

"They're going to *Pierre's*, right? Maybe we can catch up." Linc switched to manual. "Have you heard the rumor about the shield Seed built that repels dirt, water, everything? I think they're calling it Blastglas."

"I hear it can withstand anything," Erik said, amused at his friend's excitement.

A half hour later, they pulled into *Pierre's* lot, spotting the blue tov for the first time since they'd left the hotel, already parked in the back of the lot.

"Damn," Linc said. "I'd like to take a closer look at that."

"Me, too, but judging by the crowd, we have other duties at the moment. Besides, its owners are inside." Erik winced as the valet opened his door to the screaming women waiting to see the arriving celebrities.

"Who would have thought Jorgé's movie would be so popular?" Linc grouched to Erik as they strolled into the club amid comm flashes and women yelling their names.

"I feel like fresh meat," Erik replied as the door closed on the madhouse outside.

"You owe us, asshole," Linc told their friend Jorgé, who was walking up, smiling broadly.

"Come and raise some money for the animals." Jorgé grasped their hands in a warm handshake. "Seriously, thanks for coming," the producer added, clapping both men on the back. "Although what women see in you motley, techno stiffs is beyond me."

Leading them deeper into the club to join the rest of their friends, he explained how the fundraiser would work.

"We created an auction where people could bid to dance with you in five-minute increments, which is the length of each dance. If, after their time, they want to give you their number," Jorgé continued, arching a heavy brow at the group, "they've been told they'll be able to leave their info in the front room. At the end of the evening, you'll get any messages left for you," the director concluded, adding that they'd get a five-minute break every hour and that all the timeslots had been filled.

"This is going to be a long evening," Erik sighed, wishing he could be doing just about anything else instead of this.

"Yes, but you're all strong, virile dudes. Too bad you aren't great dancers. You should have joined me in that dance class last year," Jorgé said, laughing at their incredulous looks as he turned to lead them into the main dance room. "Come on, you guys. You can deal."

When they entered the room, Erik noticed Alex standing next to who he assumed was her cousin Emily and that familiar hulk he was getting tired of seeing lurking around Alex. As if sensing Erik's perusal, the hulk began scanning the room, stopping when he spied Erik and Linc. After a second, he nodded, his jaw hardening, before turning his attention back to the women who were talking with a young, trim, well-dressed man who was gesturing while looking a little panicked.

Interested, and not at all hesitant in barging in on conversations, Erik motioned to his friends and strode across the room to intercept his pixie and company.

"...and now it won't work," the young man finished as the men walked up.

"We'll be happy to come look at it," Alex said, relief evident in the man's whole demeanor at her words. "Good evening." She turned to Erik, who looked appreciatively at her silver feathered outfit, causing a slight shiver to run down her limbs as their eyes connected.

"I bet you didn't know that you had certified swan specialists in your midst," Erik told Jorgé after introductions had finished and the women had congratulated Jorgé on the movie's success.

"You both have degrees from Stanford?" Linc asked, looking at Emily.

"It was that or we wouldn't be allowed to go to the hotel," Emily said. "Besides, Miss Bird was our real teacher."

"I bet she was a dragon." Erik told Jorgé about the ancient wiry woman, no bigger than the swans.

"She was if we weren't top in the program." Alex confided, her heart beating a little quicker once she'd seen Erik walk in. The music ramped up as the DJ tested the system. Noticing Mark nervously hopping back and forth, she gave Emily a sideways glance. "It was a pleasure meeting you all, but if you'll excuse us, we have to help Mark with a little issue."

Emily looked a bit dazed and a lot nervous around Linc, who seemed intrigued by her based on the unwavering smile he continued to direct her way. Alex grabbed Emily's arm, seeing both her and Mark's relief that they were going.

"I'll be available in about a half hour," Alex told Erik. He looked hot tonight. She could tell he'd freshly shaved and put on cologne that smelled like it had been made for her, its scent weaving its way into some kind of crazy olfactory sensor she hadn't known she had.

Entering the front room, the women needed to see why the roboswan wasn't working. Odette—they'd dubbed the big white robot Odette II after the real one at the hotel—had been moving when she and Emily had left last week. Only half as big as the real swan, the bird still spanned a wingtip more than three feet across.

As Alex looked up at the bird and clicked the remote, Odette was supposed to open its wings, fly, and then land in the 'water' that flowed like a wide stream around the sides of the nightclub's rooms. Instead, it hung frozen mid-flight, wings outstretched. Everything else moved—the fake water, the multicolored fish, the seaweed and grasses.

That meant, Alex sighed, she had to climb the ladder, clip on to the cable, and then let Emily lower her so she could reach Odette's robotic brain to hopefully fix the bird. Emily was actually better at robocoding, but she didn't like hanging from cables, not that it was Alex's favorite activity either.

The robot was so cool when it worked, Alex thought as she carefully slipped off her dress in the small bathroom off the club's control room. Fortunately, she'd worn a silver bodysuit under her dress. Juliette knew she wouldn't wear the dress without something covering the peek-a-boo gaps that appeared as the feathers moved. She prayed the only one who would see her in the bodysuit would be her cousin. She felt naked in it as the stretchy material clung to her body. While in shape, she was no supermodel.

"What do you think happened?" Emily asked, hanging up her bronze-colored dress since she also had to climb up the tube. A year ago, Emily never would have scaled the ladder, much less worked from the high platform.

"Maybe I set Odette's sensor too low?"

After climbing up inside the almost forty-foot-tall metal tube and cautiously climbing onto the small, square, semi-screened platform, the two women peered over the side. Only Pierre knew how special the club's robo-animals and fish were and, from their perch, they could see them all.

Alex and Emily had created all the water scenes. The effort had given them an opportunity to push their robotics designs while also helping raise funds for the ocean they loved. Pierre was committing a percentage of his L.A. profits to the local nonprofit Heal the Bay. The more successful the club, the more Pierre could donate.

Over the past couple of centuries, humanity had really trashed the oceans. Only about fifty years ago, people had begun a serious effort to reverse that damage. Now the Pacific was about seventy percent clean. For the oceans to fully recover, however, the waters required more work, which meant more money.

After Alex clipped her harness to the boom above the platform, she carefully climbed over the safety rail. Emily peered over the platform's side, ready at the controls to start lowering Alex.

As Alex and Emily left with Mark, Erik noticed that Linc seemed a bit taken by Emily. Hell, he was definitely attracted to Alex. The two women looked especially vibrant tonight, Alex wearing silver and Emily bronze. In California, he'd found women either grew up plastic or sun-kissed. Those two definitely were natural. They exuded a confidence that made a man realize if he wanted their attention, he'd have to work for it. For a someone as wealthy as Erik, that was an unusual experience.

After watching Alex and Emily walk away, Jorgé couldn't stop talking about the two.

"Do you think they'd be willing to consult on the next movie?" the producer asked. "I'd like to be a swan, if you know what I mean. Are they single?" he continued, unaware of Erik and Linc's glowers as he led the group back into the main room. "Is this place amazing or what? Pierre was able to add some swans for tonight, although there's a bit of a problem with the big one."

"It should be working any minute." Mark replied, pointing up as he overheard Jorgé's comment. As the group looked up, Erik suddenly saw Alex hanging above the large swan.

"What the hell?" He couldn't believe what he was seeing: his pixie hanging from a thin cable at least forty feet in the air.

"Alex and Emily are trying to fix the big swan." Mark paled when he noticed Erik's thunderous expression.

"And you let her up there without a safety net?" Erik gritted his teeth, his eyes glued to Alex, who was barefoot and barely covered by some kind of silver bodysuit, dangling high above the floor. He then spied Emily further up, peering over a short wall, probably controlling the cable holding Alex.

"Their uncle designed and donated the robotics. I was told to contact them when the swan stopped working." Mark's voice became fainter at Erik's incredulous look.

"I'll be damned, do you see the two of them?" Linc asked, astonishment and awe in his voice.

Suddenly the bird came to life, which was the only way Erik could describe it, as it drew up its wings and then dove down. It barely missed clipping Alex with a wing. The men below, along with several servers distracted by the aerial show, gasped when the swan grazed Alex. They all let out a breath when she stopped swinging erratically, the cable slowly raising her up. A minute later she carefully climbed over the rail and onto the platform.

He was going to wring her pretty little neck once she made it back down safely. Erik hated the helpless feeling that washed over him when it looked like Alex was going to fall. What the hell was she doing up there? They were going to have a long talk about why she wasn't to take risks like that, especially when she was working for him. Not that he liked the thought of her taking risks at any time, but that was something he'd think about later, watching Emily help Alex unhook the harness before the two disappeared from sight.

"I can see the swan is now working," Pierre declared before Erik could say a "hell no!" to his friend.

As the men looked back at the swan, it launched into the air again, rising up to the top of the club and what looked like a starry sky.

"You said their uncle designed that?" Linc asked Mark, a gleam of interest in his eyes.

"Yes, he's brilliant!" Mark began to gush. "You should see—"

"Mark, Bianca asked if you could come to the front," Pierre smoothly interrupted. "Gentlemen, the ladies are waiting to enter."

"It's showtime!" Jorgé announced as the first group of bidders streamed into the dance room, half of them oohing and ahhing at the décor, the other half happy to see the handsome men.

Erik and Linc stood where Pierre's assistant had told them to wait, sandwiched between their other stoic friends. Two obviously enhanced women rushed over to them, ready for their dance. Like the other women in the room, these two women had embraced the theme and were covered, although not covered enough, Erik thought, with feathers.

Tina, his first partner for the night, had chosen to adorn

herself in red feathers, which unfortunately clashed with her ruddy skin tone. As they danced—Jorgé had picked slow songs from the film—feathers began to fall off, and there wasn't much dress underneath. Erik wondered if the slow reveal as the feathers fell was on purpose. Tina kept fluttering her eyelashes, which had tiny red feathers attached, making the woman look like a crazy, molting bird. As the evening progressed, feathers from the women's outfits continued to drop.

After his break, Erik returned to the dance floor to find feathers everywhere, sticking to shoulders, shoes, and people's hair. Across the room, Erik saw one friend trying to blow a feather out of his mouth as another plucked a feather out of his ear.

After a while, Erik found he was enjoying the evening, smiling at his next dance partner—Sheena?—especially since the night was for a good cause. As the second hour passed, none of the women clung to the men when their dances ended, even though it was obvious that many would have liked to do just that.

Earlier he'd seen both Alex and Emily at the edge of the room checking on what looked like all of the robots. By then, Erik had let go of his fury and fear and had calmed, recognizing Alex was safe and would still be working for him tomorrow. They'd talk, that was for sure, he thought as he twirled his dance partner, but the discussion could wait until tomorrow.

"You really have to be more careful," Pierre lectured the two women as he led them down the hall to meet the General. "Both of you." He was still shaken from watching Alex almost fall. "If Mark ever, ever asks you to do something that dangerous again when spotters aren't available, I'll have his hide. In fact, he may not be working for me any longer!"

"Don't take it out on Mark. He's a great manager, and you know it. Besides, Emily tracked the cable carefully, and it just jerked a bit." Alex rolled her eyes at Emily as they walked down the hall, trying to placate Pierre, who had a neon blue feather stuck to the back of his suit. She knew he wasn't happy with all the feathers floating around the club and would recoil at the thought of one attached to his clothes.

"Don't think I don't know you're making faces!" Pierre said to Alex as he opened the door. "And you're no better!" he added to Emily as the two entered the room. "You both need someone keeping an eye on you to keep you out of trouble."

"What happened?" The General stood to greet Emily and Alex, amused as Pierre vainly tried to grab several hot pink feathers that had followed them into the room. The two women hugged the General. The man, dressed in black, with steel-grey hair cut short and piercing green eyes, could be easily mistaken for an actor, he was so attractive and fit. Alex and Emily had seen several high-profile women fall at his feet over the years, only to be disappointed to discover he was happily married.

"A near mishap, a very near mishap. Alex could have fallen and killed herself! She was hanging from the ceiling!" Pierre caught the two pink feathers and stuffed them in his pocket.

"We had it under control." Alex looked to Emily to confirm. "I had the harness on, so I was perfectly safe. The cable only stuck for a second."

"Where was Jared during this?" the General blustered. "Jared!"

"Yes, sir?" Jared entered the room, unfortunately for Pierre, with a yellow feather attached to his lower right pant leg before it dropped to the floor. "My apologies, sir. I thought Alex and Emily were checking on some robotics. I didn't realize they were talking about the giant swan stuck near the ceiling."

"It's not Jared's fault." Emily motioned to Pierre to turn around so she could pluck the blue feather off the back of his suit. "Besides, you know we're always careful, General, and certainly know our way around a simple cable. We appreciate all of your worries, but we do know what we're doing and how to do it safely." She handed the feather to Pierre, who looked like he was going to torch it in the fireplace.

"Just promise to tell Jared in the future if you're doing anything remotely dangerous so he can double-check your equipment. It's always possible whoever attacked you in Hawaii could sabotage something," the General said, seeing Alex and Emily's expressions pale with that comment. He knew that they were brilliant, that they held degrees in more than just the sciences. But the diminutive women weren't trained soldiers.

"Now on to yesterday's test," he continued, gleefully rubbing his hands. "That went superbly."

"Too bad Verne's out," Alex said. "I'd hoped Mike's team would have done better."

"Was there anything suspicious about them dropping out?" Emily asked as she warmed her hands at the fireplace. Pierre had spared no expense with the club, so the fire felt and even smelled as if real wood was burning. "I heard something about their power failing?"

"We're checking to see if the outage was accidental or if someone cut their power. We should hear soon. But Mike's solution wasn't working well anyway," the General said. "In the meantime, I'm not sure it's a good idea to continue working at the hotel."

"We've extended our security over there, which gives us a great opportunity to test it out." Alex was reluctant to give up the assignment, for reasons she preferred not to explore. She didn't want to mention that she needed the money for the roof because the General would offer to help her. "Jared's keeping an eye out, too, and if I'm not mistaken, Erik and Linc have their security dialed up tight after the last break-in."

"After Hawaii—" the General started to say.

"This is not Hawaii. The house and grounds are a fortress," Alex stressed.

"I still don't like it. Are you still planning to reveal yourselves after the contract award?"

"Yes, that's the plan." Emily started to lift her fingers to her mouth before she realized it.

Alex recognized that Emily was feeling anxious if she was even thinking about biting her nails. But she also understood Emily was determined to follow their plan.

"How're the other competitors doing?" Alex asked, hoping to change the subject. She was also curious about Erik's team. She knew the General probably wouldn't tell her, but she had to ask.

"You know I can't tell you that, but I can say one company in particular stands out over the competition, at least right now." The General held his hand out for the tiny drive that Emily was pulling out of her concealed pocket.

"Which one?" Emily handed him the Mimant drive. "Can you give us a hint?"

"I'll give you one," the General said as he smoothly slipped the drive inside his coat.

"Yes?" the women asked simultaneously. They'd both talked about the different teams, and they definitely didn't want their uncle's company, Rictor, to win, or the Lockheed-BRE or Tiger teams for that matter. Lockheed's lead, Hector, was a sexist jerk, and Tiger's AE on the project, Dahlia Germaine, was a full-on sabotaging witch. They didn't want to have to work with any of them.

"I can tell you that it's an Americas-based team." The General smiled as the women's faces fell, realizing that this was no real hint since all of the companies headquartered there.

"I thought you were going to at least give us a clue, but one team's standing out already?" Alex was surprised, knowing that to really stand out required some groundbreaking tech.

"If this company continues to manage the data Ola's sending so well, this project will drive a huge breakthrough for space comms." The General beamed at the thought. "In the meantime, let me know if you have any more power changes at your house or the hotel. If someone hacked both grids that Verne and Xtra use, that would take some real sophistication."

After a terrorist attack had crippled the Americas' power grid forty years ago, the government had finally hardened its infrastructure. That meant the only answer for yesterday's power loss would be an inside job at both plants, which would take money and planning.

"I need to get to a meeting at Farside," the General continued, checking his comm. "I'll see you both Monday night after the Mars test. Will you have enough time to get everything on a drive for me?" he asked as he picked up his coat and plucked a green feather out of Emily's hair and handed it to her.

"Easy peasy," Emily said. "We'll see you Monday night. Tell Mary you're missing a button on your coat."

"Stay dry, General. It's started sprinkling," Alex added, looking around for any sign of the general's missing brass button.

The smell of damp salty air rushed in when the General stepped out the side exit, replacing the faint aroma of wet feathers and sweat that had seeped in from the club's front rooms. Waiting as Emily adjusted her shoe, Alex looked through the wooden shutters as lightning shot across the sky.

Suddenly, she saw her cousin Richard striding past the window, headed toward the front. With a start, Alex quickly closed the shutter, hoping he hadn't seen her. He looked really angry, she thought, as she turned to find Emily talking with Pierre.

"I just saw Richard coming inside. He looks like he's in a foul mood."

Erik was starting to feel annoyed. He hadn't pursued a woman since, well, he couldn't remember when, as he looked around for

Alex. He'd expected her to hover nearby. Instead, he'd last spotted her with her cousin almost an hour ago. In the meantime, he was on dance number three with Mrs. Plastica, his name for the poorly aging matron who should have stopped trying to pass for middle age decades ago.

He'd thought more than one dance per woman was illegal—if it was possible to have something illegal at a fundraiser. Nevertheless, the woman, more enhanced than the latest Bulgetti, was actually nice, albeit a bit scatterbrained, probably the result of all her skim treatments. During each dance, she'd tried talking him into coming to her daughter's thirty-fifth birthday celebration. He'd had to endure hearing about the daughter's accomplishments every time. This third recital was draining every bit of generosity out of him. When he glanced over at Linc, he saw that the lucky bastard seemed to be enjoying his dance partner.

Finally, the song ended. He gratefully extricated himself from the matron, telling her he would check his calendar and let her know if he was free for her daughter's party—no way in hell—for the third time. He also wondered, again, where the hell Alex was.

He thought he'd seen her and Emily enter the same door that Alex had gone through the other night. While Linc was on his five-minute break earlier, Erik had motioned to his friend to see if he could figure out what the draw was down the hall. Now that he was free, he left the floor and found Linc standing across from the mystery door.

"I couldn't get past the door," Linc mouthed softly to his friend. "But, look what I found on the floor right outside the door." He palmed Erik a silver feather just like the ones on Alex's dress. "And, check this out." Linc slipped Erik what looked like a brass button for a jacket. Erik noticed it had a military motif and the initials GW stamped on it.

As Linc dropped that bit of info, the door opened, and Pierre, Alex, Emily, and Jared emerged. Erik noticed that Jorgé had positioned himself near the door, holding court with the press, and wondered if his friend had also seen the women enter. When

Jorgé spied Alex and Emily, he excused himself and joined them as Pierre and Jared stepped away, deep in conversation. A minute later, Erik saw Richard Rictor walk in and head toward the bar. When Richard spotted Alex and Emily, he abruptly changed his course toward the group, a mask of sincerity settling over his features.

"Still, think about it, ladies. I'd make it worth your while," Jorgé said.

"Seriously, cousins, you should consider it," Richard broke into the conversation, joining Jorgé's plea to get the women to work on his next movie. "Richard Rictor, these ladies' cousin, and a fan of your work," he said, holding out a hand. "My sister, Patricia, is an avian expert. If these two don't have time to help, please feel free to call upon her.

"I don't mean to interrupt; however, I saw you two and wanted to offer you a ride Saturday night." Richard said to Alex and Emily, then added, "Mr. DiAngelo, our family is having a small gathering Saturday night, and if you're in town, we'd be pleased if you could come."

"That's so kind of you," Jorgé started, only to be interrupted again, this time by Erik, who had walked up with Linc. At this point, Erik's annoyance had only grown after being propositioned and pawed all night, while Alex, the one he'd actually like to paw, hadn't so much as looked his way. She'd only stopped by once to inform him of some press queries when he was on a break. Another time, he saw her standing on the sidelines, chatting with Emily. Another time he saw her with a man who looked very interested in getting to know her better.

Right now, he wanted to grab her and claim her as his. He resisted, knowing that action would look strange to everyone, even him, now that he thought about it. He'd just met her four days ago. He had to get a grip. He eyed Richard, the pompous jerk he'd known from way back.

They'd all gone to the same private high school. While he'd been there on scholarship, Linc, Richard, and Richard's sister,

Pattie, were full-fare students. If the rumors had been correct, Richard and Pattie's parents had paid more than full fare after they'd been caught doing something that even Erik hadn't been able to discover.

"We can give the ladies a ride," Erik said as he and Linc joined the circle. "It will be on our way, and it will save you from driving down. 7:30, yes? It's been too long, Richard. Thank you for the invitation." Erik stuck out his hand to grip Richard's.

"And if you all don't mind, Alex promised me a dance this evening," he told the group as he reached out to take Alex's hand to pull her towards the dance floor. "Since the charity dances have ended, now's the perfect time."

Stunned that he'd take such liberties and annoyed that she'd been manipulated so effortlessly, Alex found herself on the dance floor in Erik's arms before her mind could catch up. Taking a deep breath, she prepared to chastise him for his audacity, but his warmth, strength, and heavenly aroma sent her brain to the Kuiper Belt. Pull it together, woman, she told herself.

She suspected that if she dared risk a taste, he'd be as addictive as chocolate—her biggest weakness. He wasn't for her. But oh my, could he move.

He maneuvered her effortlessly around the dance floor, holding her just close enough to be a whisper of a tease but not so close as to make her uncomfortable. If she looked up the word "suave," his picture would surely be front and center. She knew she'd be a wreck if she gave him even an inch. He'd leave her on the sidewalk gasping, not knowing what had hit her. It was best to leave his kind to the women who were used to the game.

"What have you been up to besides talking with the press while I've been trodding the floors for charity?" Erik finally relaxed now that he had her in his arms.

"I was reviewing some last-minute marketing details with Mark and Pierre." It was good that she worked for Pierre as a cover, already distracted by Erik's warm hand on her back. She sighed, deciding to simply enjoy being encircled in his strong arms and dancing to beautiful music with this captivating man. Since Hawaii, she'd been hyper-focused, on the lookout for danger every second she wasn't home, and even a little bit when she was. She probably wouldn't get another chance to feel this safe for a while.

Minutes later, as the song ended, an insistent tap on her shoulder jarred Alex back to reality. Turning, she saw one of the women who'd been eyeing Erik earlier. The woman, whom she and Emily had nicknamed Ms. Mars, had legs that reached as high as Alex's chest, her torso barely covered by an indecently short, gold-feathered dress.

"Erik, you promised me a dance." The woman dismissed Alex like she was cheap Grundic on the bottom of her shoe.

"You go ahead. I need to go." Alex stepped out of Erik's arms, thinking Ms. Mars was more his type. "See you tomorrow." After saying goodbye to Pierre and Mark, Alex asked Emily if she had the bag for the captain as they pulled on their coats and headed to the door.

Emily pulled out the container Isobelle had packed from under her coat, which she then buttoned up to her chin. "The captain, then the tov," Emily said, relieved they'd done their duty and could go home.

Alex and Emily had met Captain Albert, who was living on the street, his piece of claimed concrete in front of the club when Pierre bought the establishment. For a while, Pierre, Alex, Emily, and the rest of the staff had all tried to convince him to settle in a home or shelter, anything that would offer more protection. But the trauma of the interplanetary war had set its talons in too deep; the captain preferred where he lived. With that clear, Alex and Emily helped Pierre design a tiny house that sat in the back of the parking lot. With a command, the building would turn translucent or open completely whenever the captain felt confined.

After delivering the container, Alex and Emily climbed in their tov, Jared entering after. Before he shut the door, Alex noticed Cata and Lina across the ocean silhouetted by the full moon. The two islands, once connected, had split apart in the big quake of 2111. Everyone had been so busy getting their lives together, they'd started calling the two new landmasses Cata and Lina. It had stuck.

"So, are they coming?" Marie Rictor asked Richard, her speech only slightly slurred as she poured herself another drink from the bottle sitting on the Family Room's long bar.

Hewn from the Frankin Mines on Charon, the bar had been created at great expense, his parents would readily tell anyone who would listen. Multicolored gems from other planets the Rictors had visited spread across the shelves lining the walls. Across from the bar, large white upholstered chairs circled the huge fireplace, framed by a giant piece of red Charon Smite. The room had a feeling of solidity and permanence that usually was a space that calmed Richard, unlike the rest of the house.

Richard figured it must have been an okay night if his mom wasn't a lot more wobbly by now. Wobbly, he thought to himself with disgust, a term she'd used with him and his sister since childhood when they arrived home from school to find her "wobbly."

"Yes, they're coming." Richard wondered why she was at the house. He wanted to retreat to his rooms, tired after a long day at Rictor, working on the network contract and then attending the charity event at *Pierre's*. He should have never stopped in the Family Room to grab a Ceoat. Usually, it was a room he could escape to without feeling trapped.

"Good, did you offer to bring them? Although why that interloper has to come, I don't know. All she does is sit in a corner. Remember that time she drank Silfa out of the bottle?" Marie took a generous sip—she would never gulp her drink—of the Chabat she always kept close. Richard and his sister often wondered how she was still alive after all the alcohol she'd poured down her throat over the years.

"Yes, I did, mother, but they already have a ride," Richard interjected before her mother could continue her complaints about Emily. She'd hated Emily since that family Christmas, when Walter and Leilani introduced her as their adopted niece. He still remembered the half-starved waif standing between them. Walter and Leilani had discovered her homeless, sleeping on Olokele Avenue in Waikiki.

There was no way Richard would mention that Alex and Emily were coming with Erik and Linc. Marie tolerated Linc only because his father was a famous celebrity and Linc was rich. But Erik? She'd despised him since he'd made a speech on a fundraising night that had wowed the whole high school and brought in record-breaking donations. She loved to rant about how she'd been in charge of the silent auction that night and how Erik had ruined it all.

"I worked my fingers to the bone for months," she slurred more times than Richard could count. "Instead of me getting credit for that night, all anyone could talk about was that free-loader." When she found out later that Erik was at Brentwood on scholarship, Marie had gone ballistic, drinking herself into one of her more memorable binges.

"What about Walter?" Steven Rictor asked, entering the room, a glass of Lemon Shasha in his hand. "Did they mention him? We have to get more from the system. Fuck Walter for not sharing any of Ola's strings with us. Well? Where the hell is he?"

"They didn't say anything," Richard said, resenting both his parents and wondering where Pattie was. "We raised three million tonight," he added, feeling quite ambivalent about the fact but wanting to change the subject.

"I can't believe they're giving all that money to animal research instead of focusing on birds," Pattie huffed as she entered the room, still wearing the suit she'd worked in all day. "The movie features swans, not bears or dogs, for alum's sake."

"We were talking about Walter. I don't care about any damn birds," Steven said to his daughter, his voice flat. "Did they say anything about him?"

"They only said that he was working hard and is unavailable," Richard told his father, hating what a rude bastard he was to his sister, who'd clammed up after their father's cutting remark. "I'm heading to bed. Tomorrow will be another long day." He gave his mother the expected air kiss on her cheek before heading to his rooms.

"We were just leaving." Steven put his half-finished drink on the bar before turning to Pattie. "But first," he said, fixing his gaze on his daughter with a dangerous glint in his eyes, "you've been spending altogether too much time on those birds. You need to focus on Rictor and getting a husband. If I hear you've been in that bird room during the workday again, I'll exterminate all your feathered friends and make the conservatory a tritball court," he threatened before stalking out, Marie behind him.

Pattie stood in the empty room. For her, the room didn't offer the same solitude it gave her brother. Instead, the deep quiet threatened. Heading behind the bar, she poured herself another Grey Goose and Sonix, her hands shaking in anger. Kill her birds? She'd kill him first.

# Friday, February 20, 2172

The downpour started just as Alex stepped out the kitchen door to head to the hotel. She hoped the rain wouldn't wash away the concealer covering her bruises. At least the purple marks were starting to fade to a paler green and black, though the pain hadn't lessened much yet. Whoever developed Erisalve deserved a lifetime supply of chocolate. She angled her umbrella into the rain and tightened her collar.

Finally at the hotel, she reached down to pull off her rainboots, balancing over the mat someone had thoughtfully placed just inside the side door. She slipped off her raincoat, letting it drip on the mat as she waited for the mbot to arrive. She smoothed her deep-purple pencil skirt and pale gray blouse before stepping into the heels she'd stashed in her bag. She wondered how people in wet climates managed to look so put together all the time. When the bot arrived, Alex stashed her rain gear in its hold when she heard a noise further down the dark hall. Turning, she thought she saw Meg.

"Crazy storm, right?" Meg asked as she switched on the hall light. "The mbot will leave your things in the closet outside your office once they're dry."

"Thanks, and good morning," Alex said cheerfully, hoping

the rain hadn't washed away any of her makeup. She felt like a moist, if not drowned, rat, while Meg looked ready for a fashion shoot in her trim black suit edged in bright pink piping and matching heels.

Entering her office, she stared in dismay when she glanced at her reflection in the mirror. A few fat drops of rain had slid down her face and neck. She quickly repaired the damage, grateful she'd become adept at it. Returning to the short hallway between her and Erik's office, she noticed Meg standing next to the Raleigh, looking frustrated.

"The machine's really quite simple if you understand the thinking behind it." Alex soothed as she walked up beside Meg and showed her how to make a decaf latte.

"This is nectar from the gods." Meg practically purred as she took another sip of her drink. "You have my gratitude forever. Have you heard anything new about Susan?"

Alex noticed Meg looking at the places on her face and neck where she'd touched up her makeup. She appreciated her not asking questions. "I talked to her sister this morning. She said the doctors still have her sedated, but they're planning to take her out of the recovery pod soon."

"Please keep me updated. I liked her. Erik said she's a friend of yours?" Meg asked as they headed towards the door.

"We're not real close, but more because of life circumstances with her usually being in one place and me in another. We've worked together a couple of times over the years. That's why I told Erik I was surprised by the errors she supposedly made."

As Alex reached her office door, she still thought the errors were strange. A few hours later, the storm intensified, much to her dismay. When a hard gust pushed open the French doors, she leapt up to shut them before the rain drenched the carpet. Earlier, she'd cracked open the doors, hoping the fragrance from the flowering orange and lemon trees would replace the faint aroma of new paint and construction that still lingered in her office. She hoped that the dredging they'd done on the stream and the new gates they'd installed didn't create any problems for the hotel's lake.

The heavy cell moved on, and the rain lightened. The quiet sound of the heater clicking on and off, along with the occasional baritone murmur from Erik's office, made Alex feel like she was wrapped in a cozy blanket. Erik's voice had provided a welcome distraction from the storm, helping her settle and focus on the upcoming events. She hadn't seen him all morning, except for a brief hello.

Lost in thought, she picked up Larry, which sat on some sample menus piled on her desk. The lizard-shaped robot had successfully slithered, crawled, and walked between the house and hotel four times now. It wasn't until the last trip in the rain that the material underneath had thinned, and the color began to leach from the bottom of its feet and belly.

An hour later, Emily knocked, then entered Alex's office, placing a box on Alex's desk. "Have you seen the Space Men in the pool?" she whispered. "Come quick. Look." Emily motioned Alex to the small side window.

"Oh my." Alex started fanning herself when she spied Erik and Linc, who had just climbed out of the pool and were standing under an overhang to dry off. This was the second time in a week she'd been treated to an almost naked Erik, and she was going to savor every second. Linc, also in a speedo, wasn't bad looking either.

"It looks like their bananas are from the species giaganticus," Emily whispered, the two women breaking into giggles. "If I were braver, I'd try to peel Linc's," Emily added.

"Quick! They're turning this way. Move!" Alex dragged Emily away from the window over to her desk and leaned back against it. She willed her face to cool and her heart to slow. Spying Larry, she remembered she wanted to talk to discuss the robot lizard with Emily, which would also serve to cool her off.

"Check this out." Alex showed Emily Larry's underside. "The material isn't holding up. Hopefully it won't be an issue for Ola, but I want to try mixing the bones that came yesterday and see if that makes a difference."

"Have you looked at Larry under the scope yet?" Emily asked, peering closely at the lizard's feet.

"I will tonight. For the moment, Larry's a desk ornament." Alex turned the lizard over and placed him on the menus. "So, let me guess, you want to go to lunch, and you've brought Isobelle's bread to give to Chef as a cover to come over?"

Alex peeked into the box Emily had placed on her desk. Emily knew storms made her nervous, and Alex was grateful to see her.

"Iso wanted Chef to try it while it's fresh. So, how about lunch? I need to go into Westwood. I think the rain's letting up, so we could have lunch there."

A huge flash of lightning lit the room, followed closely by a boom of thunder. A big gust of rain rattled the French doors.

"Did I hear something about lunch?" a deep voice from the doorway asked. "Hi Emily." Erik prowled into Alex's office. Having seen him around the pool, Erik reminded Alex of a great white shark at its peak, with his white dress shirt's sleeves rolled to reveal tan arms, silver-grey slacks that hugged his large, muscular thighs.

"I wasn't eavesdropping, but I heard you talking about lunch and the rain stopping," Erik admitted as another flash of lightening illuminated the room followed by a loud boom of thunder. He noticed Alex jerk at the sound. "Seeing that's not likely, I have a favor to ask, and it would be much drier." He walked further into the room. "We're having a tasting lunch today before finalizing the menu. All of the crew are invited. I'd be grateful if you two joined us and gave us your votes."

At that moment, the skies opened and yet another downpour began.

"Well, I guess that's your answer. Thank you," Alex said. "I'd love to join you. Emily?"

"Thanks for the invite." Emily eyed Alex before looking at Erik. "Can I meet you there? I'd like to drop off the bread first.

Our house manager, Isobelle, is friends with your chef," she explained to Erik. "She sent him some bread to try." Emily held up the box as she edged around Erik and hurried out the door.

"Emily's pretty shy," Alex confided when Erik looked at her, one eyebrow raised in question. "She's actually become a lot better. Before, she wouldn't have come to lunch, much less talk to you."

Alex thought back to when they were young and Emily hardly left the house. Alex also felt a strong urge to retreat to the safety behind her desk as Erik moved closer. Suddenly, he stood right in front of her, reached around and plucked Larry off her desk.

"What's this?" He looked intently at the reptile, unable to identify what it was made of. The material seemed to suck the moisture out of his skin, which was still damp from his swim. The lizard also felt light, lighter than it should be for its twelve long inches.

"My paperweight. I've had it for years." Alex hoped he couldn't tell Larry could move and start asking questions.

"Where'd you get it?"

Alex wanted to snatch the robot out of Erik's hands before he could study it further. A second later, a huge crack of lightning and almost simultaneous explosion of thunder shook the room, causing Alex to gasp and grab hold of Erik's arm. Erik immediately put the lizard down and grasped her hand when he saw her trembling.

Embarrassed, Alex started pulling out of his grip when a brighter flash and louder boom shook the hotel. She turned her face against his shoulder.

"It's okay. It's just a storm." Erik gently stroked his hand down her back, as if calming a skittish Eurfish. Like his sister, she obviously didn't like storms, he thought as Alex slowly calmed.

After taking a deep breath, she looked up, embarrassed and ready to apologize for grabbing him.

When her eyes met his, Erik's protective instincts changed gears. Her body inches from his, her lips moist and slightly parted. He needed to taste that mouth—

"Hey guys—oops, sorry to barge in." Meg, who'd stepped into Alex's office, quickly backpedaled as Alex and Erik jumped apart.

"What do you want, Meg?" Erik ran a hand through his hair, trying to gain some composure. Damn. He hadn't slipped up like this since he was a teen.

"I wanted to see if you were coming to lunch, but you can let me know later." Meg turned quickly and left, her soft snicker echoing in the hallway behind her.

"I'm sorry. I should never have done that. It won't happen again. At least unless you want it to once your contract's up," Erik said, a gleam in his eye, relieved to see the color flooding Alex's face.

Erik's almost-kiss, combined with almost being caught by Meg, sent a rush of heat through Alex as she tried to compose herself. While she felt mortified, she was grateful for the distraction from the storm.

Eyeing Erik, she confessed, "No apologies necessary. I'm starving. How about you?" She slid around Erik and headed for the door.

"Oh yes, I'm hungry," he murmured as he trailed her. Hungry for the pixie fleeing in front of him.

"I hope you're hungry," Linc said to Emily as he pushed in her chair. He'd spotted her while leaving the lobby. She'd been running into the restaurant, a bag in hand, trying to avoid the rain. Before Henri could lead her to another table, he suggested she join his and Meg's table, assuring her that they would save space for Alex and Erik.

"Chef Leon and the crew have been working their butts off creating samples of everything that's in the running for the menus."

"Dessert, too. Don't forget to save room for that," advised Chef, who set down tiny ramekins of something that looked like huevos rancheros.

"Isobelle asked me to bring you this bread." Emily handed Chef the bag. "It's a new recipe."

"Please tell Isobelle thanks. I'll call her later tonight."

"I didn't know you knew Isobelle, too," Erik said to Leon as he and Alex joined the group. "How'd you meet?"

"We met at a Le Baptiste," Leon reminisced. "Isobelle could have worked for anyone. I know one restaurant owner who said he would redesign his whole kitchen if she'd said yes. She refused —claiming she wasn't keen on the environment in the city at the time." He regarded the women thoughtfully. Alex remembered Isobelle mentioning her decision to leave Paris when huge anti-bot demonstrations erupted.

"What's in the ramekins?" Alex nudged Emily, wanting help in changing the subject.

For the next two hours, the serving staff brought out tastes of every menu candidate. The conversation flowed as everyone debated which dishes should be kept or eliminated.

Later, after lunch, Alex joined Erik in his office to review plans for the opening and parties.

"I think I'm going to die I'm so full," Alex groaned. She wished she could loosen the top button in her skirt.

"You have to admit it was worth it." Erik rose to stretch his legs and make a cup of espresso.

"How can you consume anything more?" Alex asked incredulously, admiring how Erik's shirt stretched tightly over his muscular back as he reached for the cup. "I still vote to include the passion fruit crème brûlée for dessert and passion fruit and orange waffles for breakfast. Those were too good and unique."

"Now that we know there's a lot of it growing in back. I thought Leon was going to kiss you when you told him that." He would have fired him for sure if he had. "Damn, that's lousy," he grimaced, putting his full cup down on his desk.

Alex grabbed it, took a sip, and immediately spat it back. "I think you selected the clean program instead. Let me print out some instructions. In the meantime, come, I'll show you again."

Erik followed her back to the Raleigh. Any excuse to keep her in his office.

He really enjoyed brainstorming with her, her lightning-fast mind keeping pace with his. She had a refreshing way of approaching challenges, not to mention her quick wit, which he truly appreciated. He'd been debating asking her to join his team, although that would preclude any relationship, leaving him unsure of his next move. He was having a hard enough time keeping his hands off her as he walked up behind her.

Dragging his focus back to the Raleigh while Alex explained its workings, Erik noticed she'd draped her braid around to her front, unknowingly exposing the bruises on the back of her neck. Tentatively he lifted a hand and touched the edge of a yellow-green bruise, causing Alex to gasp and almost knock the espresso cup off the holder.

"I'm sorry." Erik quickly stepped back. "What—"

"Ron has some news about Susan," Jenny announced through the speaker on Erik's desk. "Are you free to meet?"

"Tell him to come over," Erik sighed.

Silently Alex placed the cup of espresso in Erik's hand. She knew that at some point he would flat out ask her about her injuries. "I think we covered everything, so I'll head back to my office." Alex rapidly skirted around Erik, trying to figure out why they kept getting into these situations and why he flustered her so much.

"Stay," Erik said before taking a too-big gulp of his espresso.

"Fuck, that's hot. Good, so thanks, but hot." He grabbed a bill out of his desk and threw it in the bowl. "Please, sit down. It sounds like Ron's discovered something regarding Susan. You should probably hear it. I won't pry about those bruises, at least not at the moment. I don't know what comes over me when you're close."

"Okay," Alex sank into a chair, relieved and surprised that he wasn't peppering her with questions.

"If you're in trouble, though, all you have to do is—"

"Hey boss. Hi Alex." Ron nodded to the both of them as he entered Erik's office.

"Have a seat. I asked Alex to be here since she replaced Susan. What do you have?"

"After I heard that a lot of Susan's orders for the parties had errors, I started looking into the system. Someone definitely accessed her files and comm." Ron sat down next to Alex. "What was really interesting is the way they did it. Even if Susan had still been here, she would've never noticed the changes unless one of the vendors asked her about them."

"Do you have any leads?" Erik asked, thinking he had to get a grip if he was going to get irritated any time another man sat close to Alex.

"No, whoever did it was good, really good," Ron said, frustration evident in his voice. "I haven't been able to trace it to anything or anyone. I haven't even been able to discover what days they made the changes. The emails are a bit easier, but since those were done on days when everyone was in, it doesn't tell me much. Sorry, boss. I wanted to let you know the little I've discovered."

Alex would love to examine their back system, but she didn't want to reveal how good she was. They might become suspicious, maybe even think that she was the one trying to sabotage them. Why she'd want to do that would be anyone's guess, except maybe they'd speculate that she was spying for Rictor. She'd just keep her mouth shut and her eyes open.

"Is there a way to know if any changes have been made since I came onboard?" she asked the two men.

"I haven't found any yet. Linc finally gave me some of those authentication chips you two've been working on," Ron said to Erik. "Those should automatically alert me to any changes. I'm adding them to all the comms. I'll start on yours, boss, if it's a good time."

"If it's okay with you, I'm going to head out." Alex stood, thinking it was a good time to go home since the storm had quieted.

"You should take a tov home," Erik told Alex.

"Thank you, but it's not that muddy."

"At least let me walk you home," Erik offered, reaching for his raincoat.

"Boss, I'm going to need you for the next fifteen minutes."

"I'm fine. Seriously." She quickly escaped back to her office, grabbed her things and left before Erik could join her. It wasn't that she didn't like him. It was the opposite. That's what scared her.

She wasn't in the market for a man. Perhaps that would change after they—fingers crossed—saved the colony, Space Force awarded the contract and she and Emily revealed themselves. Right now, though, she had too many secrets. Later, well, she'd think about it. For all she knew, Erik might be turned off if he knew how smart she really was.

"We had another attempted burglary," Ron said quietly as he closed Erik's comm. "On the south side of the property this time.

"Damn!"

Meg entered the office as Erik tossed another chip in the rapidly filling bowl. "Well, we'll be making a nice donation this month. What?" she asked after noticing Erik's glare.

"Another attempted break-in," Ron explained. "Fortunately, the new alarms worked. Unfortunately, whoever it was got away before we could get there. The person wore a mask; we didn't get any kind of ID. The only clue was an empty container of Marbola tabs, which Mario found. He swears it wasn't there this morning."

"What about a tov?" Erik asked, pacing.

"That's the interesting part. We didn't see any on the vid before or after the attempt, nor any broken brush or other evidence of a tov in the area."

"Could someone living nearby have walked in, like the hunk next door?" Meg asked before heading to the Raleigh to make herself a latte. "It looks like they headed west but could have circled back."

"Ron, have you found anything out about him yet?" Erik watched the vid Ron had pulled up of the burglar starting to cut the fence before sensing someone coming and sprinting away through the trees.

"One of my guys thinks he's special forces. That he's seen him before on an op, but he can't place him, and certainly not by the name Jared. I'm still digging."

"Make it a priority," Erik ordered, frustration lacing his voice.

"Someone tried breaking into the hotel again," Alex shared as she sat at the kitchen table with the others for dinner. She'd overheard Ron telling Erik about it as she left. "The alarm sounded before the burglar could do any damage."

"That's great," Bev said, reaching for a roll. "It is, like, isn't it, that the alarm scared them away?" she added, looking around the table.

Everyone was home tonight, including Jared, who at first seemed uncomfortable joining the women. It was clear he wasn't used to family-style meals with a bunch of women. He was settling in though, Alex noticed, observing the generous portion of stew he piled onto his plate as he joked with the girls. When he first arrived, Alex overheard the two girls discussing how they thought he was equal parts scary and hot, which had amused both Alex and Emily when she told her. Earlier today, though, she heard Bev admitting that Jared had slid further into the hotness zone.

Suddenly a loud alarm sounded. Jared jumped up, looking around as Isobelle headed to the counter for her tablet.

"There is an intruder on the north side," she said, tapping her screen as Alex and Emily joined her.

Peering over her shoulder, Alex saw a big, silver, heavily weaponized, two-legged droid moving steadily towards the house.

"Shit, that's an F270!" Jared stood stunned, looking at the screen. He then pulled out his Gunter and switched it off stun as he confirmed he'd correctly identified the ten-foot-tall, heavily armored android.

"Yes, it is." Isobelle calmly continued to tap the screen as the droid moved closer. "Fortunately, we have a few welcoming surprises."

"See if you can keep from damaging it," Alex told Isobelle.

"Damage it! Are you serious?" Jared asked, shocked. "I think my Gunter will injure it enough to stop it, but you should go to your safe room just in case. Hey, what happened?"

"As Iso said, we have a few surprises around the property, including a trap, which the F270 just fell into," Emily said. "And you said that little afternoon project was a waste of time."

"I didn't say it was a waste of time. I said that we were on deadline that day and had some other things to finish," Alex said, sticking her tongue out at her cousin.

"Tomato, tomahto. You owe me twenty lines of siycode, cousin."

"Fine," Alex sighed. Emily loved to knit with siy yarn, but hated coding it herself. "Iso, will you secure it in the lab?"

"Done. Let us finish dinner." Isobelle set her tablet down before turning back to the table.

Anita and Bev, used to unusual activities at the house, had

already finished their first bowls of soup and were ladling out seconds as the rest sat back down.

"Don't worry, Jared," Bev said to the speechless man, patting his arm. "This isn't the first time a robber has, like, tried coming on the property. We're safe here."

Jared gaped at the women, all of whom had resumed eating their soup and chatting about the latest vid heartthrob. F270s were no ordinary intruders. They were state-of-the-art killing machines. He'd already tried comming the General. Though from the looks on Alex and Emily's faces, he realized they wanted him to finish his dinner. Taking a breath, he grabbed his spoon. He had a lot to tell the General.

"Yes, sir, yes, sir. I tried to call you, but for some reason my comm didn't work." Jared paced the length of Alex and Emily's lab, talking to the General while watching the women dismantle the F270 on a back table. "It's an F270. Right now? Right now, they're taking it apart in their lab."

"Tell the General he can have a look after we're done, right, Al?"

"Yep, finder's keepers, but we don't mind sharing." Alex was intently unraveling the computronics in one of the android's hands. "Will you look at that, Lee? I would have thought they'd upgraded it by now, but they're still using our old tech. Idiots."

"Tell the General that his intel was wrong, please. They're still using the materials they stole from Seed in '69; though they've improved their scanning circuitry." Emily glanced back at Jared. "Someone can pick it up tomorrow. Have them ask for Isobelle."

Jared stared at the women deep in conversation as they dismantled the droid, which was twice their size and armed with an arsenal of weaponry. "Yes, sir, I will let you know if anything else happens, sir. Good night, sir."

"The General requested that you not silence my comm in the future and reminds you that I'm here to help," he said, clearly frustrated and struggling to grasp how resourceful and sneaky these petite, seemingly innocent and fragile women were.

"We didn't silence just your comm, Jared," Alex said as she stripped down the droid's right foot. "Iso shuts down the whole complex per our protocol whenever there's an intruder."

"How often do you get intruders?" Jared asked, trying to stay calm.

"It depends on what you consider an intruder."

"Yeah, human or not, armed or not, family or not?" Emily asked. Alex snickered as Jared choked on his water. "What exactly are you asking?"

"Does the General know about all your intruders—the kinds you mentioned?"

"Most of them." Alex had finished with the foot and was now deep into one of the F270's legs. "There was an E270 a while ago that we kind of forgot to mention, and the R230. Remember that one, Lee?"

"The General was on his first vacation in forever, and we didn't want to bother him with that one," Emily said. "And there were those little E3s a couple of months ago. That was ridiculous that anyone would send those here."

"Really. And each time we dealt with them without anyone suspecting anything," Alex said as a loud thud sounded. "The storm's really picking up. I've looked at everything, including its improved but still lousy circuitry. Ready to call it a night, Lee? I'm done here. Isobelle will pack this guy up and have him ready in the morning," Alex told Jared.

Alex craved a long hot bath and some smooth jazz to soothe her nerves. The storm was triggering old memories, making her feel wound tight since it started. Isobelle would be on watch, and while the roof needed repair, it and the walls could withstand hurricane-force winds. She'd made sure of that.

As she left the lab, Alex bid good night to Emily and a still-processing Jared. Emily said she'd check in with Isobelle. Bev and Anita had gone to their rooms to study after dinner, leaving only Barney and Fred to keep her company as she walked down the hall and entered her room. She always kept the dogs near during a storm, their presence a comfort.

An hour later, Alex climbed into her bed, pulled up her blue comforter, and patted the mattress for Barney to jump up. After a long, hot bath and generous application of Erisalve, she'd received a frantic call from the lieutenant at Mars Base. The woman sounded panicked, claiming Ola wasn't working. Alex walked her through the set-up process once more, step by step.

At least that had taken her mind off the still-raging storm. She turned off the lamp by her bedside, with Barney snuggled against her. Fred was already snoring. To distract herself from the storm lashing against the windows, Alex envisioned her happy place: was diving off the coast of Oahu. Picturing a large green turtle swimming next to her and a tiny school of seahorses keeping pace, she slowly drifted off to sleep.

"Al, Al, wake up!" Emily was calling her, which Alex couldn't understand since her voice was coming from a naked Erik lapping the hotel's pool. "Al!"

"What? What time is it?" Alex asked, reluctantly surfacing from the hot visuals as she pushed her hair out of her face. She must have been thrashing around for her braid to fall apart. She could hear the storm still raging outside as the semi-dark room lit up with another flash.

"It's 1:30 in the morning."

"In the morning? What's wrong?"

"Erik and Linc are here. The gates for the stream failed. The swans are missing." Emily tossed Alex some clothes to put on.

"The gates failed?" Alex repeated as she hurriedly dressed. "They just replaced the motors, didn't they? Where's Jared?"

"Yes, about the gates, at least I think so. Jared went to see the General. He's not back yet. I'll get the lightballs and meet you in the kitchen. Don't forget your coat and boots." Emily turned and hurried out the door.

What the heck, thought Alex, as she quickly rebraided her hair. Grabbing her rain gear, she rushed after Emily. Upon entering the kitchen, with Barney and Fred on her heels, she blinked against the bright lights and focused on the two men pacing.

"Why do you think the swans are here?" Alex asked after greeting the men and sitting down to pull on her boots. "Did you look around the lake?"

"First, thanks for getting up to help," Erik said, looking, Alex thought, for the first time, disheveled, his shirt misbuttoned, a pant leg caught on his boot. However, that disarray didn't detract from his appeal. He took in her rumpled state, his piercing gaze stripping away her weak defenses as she tried to fully wake-up. "The stream alarm woke us," he added. "When we checked the vids, we saw the gates open and the tail end of one of the swans heading toward your place."

"It's not the first time they've come here," Emily said as she entered the kitchen. Four big lightballs trailed behind her, stopping and hovering over the table while she sat and tugged on her boots. "We have a greenhouse with all kinds of lettuce, among other things. They probably remembered it from the last time they escaped. They almost got sick they gorged so much."

"We have people searching the hotel property, but they haven't found any sign of them, so we're pretty sure they're here." Linc pet Fred and Barney, who were shamelessly sucking up to the men for attention. "We really appreciate your help. Even if we found the birds, we wouldn't know how to get them back to the lake."

"Lee, why don't you take Fred and Linc and look around the pool area? I'll take Barney and Erik and check around the greenhouse," Alex proposed, her face paling as a clap of lightning struck, followed a second later by a booming crash of thunder.

"We'll comm every ten minutes." Emily stood and grabbed two lightballs. She knew why Alex had suggested Emily look by the pool. It was hard enough for Alex to go out in the storm, much less by the pool. She didn't need any help with her nightmares.

The men pulled on their raincoats, which had been dripping by the door.

"Don't worry about the water," Alex said when Erik looked around for a towel to dry the floor. "Iso will take care of it. We need to find the birds before a tree or even a branch hits them. They're not used to being out in the elements, much less in a storm like this."

Another flash of lightning hit as everyone left the kitchen, thunder following two seconds later.

"Man, that was close!" Erik said as he and Alex headed to the left as Emily and Linc headed right. Suddenly they heard a big crack and thud. Something had fallen nearby. Another flash lit the sky. Erik noticed Alex looked unnaturally pale, remembering her reaction to the storm earlier that day.

"Are you ok? You don't have to come."

"I'm fine." Alex crouched down to talk to Barney. "Barney, find the swans," she ordered the dog. "Search!"

Erik couldn't believe she'd trust the animal, but damn, the dog turned, sniffed the air, and headed north. As they followed Barney, debris flew through the air while trees and bushes whipped madly around them. Erik ducked to avoid a blast of leaves, beginning to think that maybe they should give up. He'd somehow become attached to the big turkeys, but he also didn't want anything to happen to Alex, who'd grown even paler as they fought through what felt like a hurricane.

Fifteen minutes later and still no swans. Suddenly Alex tripped and fell. Right then, lightning struck the top of the big oak next to them. A branch cracked and fell, hitting Barney, who stood exactly where Alex would have been if she hadn't fallen.

"Are you okay? Did you hurt anything?"

"Just my ego." Alex scrambled up, wondering which god she'd pissed off. She shoved down the panic that threatened to overwhelm her. "Damn, Barney." She saw the dog lying partially beneath the fallen branch. She tried lifting the branch, but it was too heavy. Suddenly, it rose as Erik lifted the branch and shoved it aside.

"Is he okay?" Erik bent down next to Alex, who was inspecting Barney. Instead of the dog whimpering, Barney appeared normal, even though a tree limb had punched a huge hole in his back leg. Expecting to see blood oozing out, he was surprised to see what looked like some sort of metallic substance. "What the heck?"

"Barney will be just fine," Alex said with a sigh, realizing that Erik was too smart to be convinced that Barney was a real dog. "He's a robot. I'll explain after we find the swans," she said, wanting some time to figure out how much she was going to tell him.

"Would you mind carrying him?" She asked Erik since Barney couldn't walk. "Which way, Barney?" she asked once Erik had picked him up. The dog looked to the left. "That way then, toward the greenhouse."

If they weren't in the middle of a giant storm searching for giant birds, Erik knew he would be peppering Alex with questions. He'd heard rumors of her uncle's special robotic inventions, but nothing concrete. While robotics was a well-established field, he would have never guessed Barney was a machine. Hell, he'd even petted the thing, and it felt like a real dog. He couldn't wait to tell Linc.

Another streak of lightning lit the sky and, a second later, thunder ricocheted through the canyon. Questions could come later, he assured himself. A minute later, Barney barked.

"Where are they, Barney?" Alex asked.

Barney looked straight ahead at a cluster of bird of paradise growing next to what looked to Erik to be a huge, old, dilapidated building. Before he could say anything, Alex stepped carefully between the plants, calling out the swans' names. He followed, ready to assist if she needed help, scanning the area for anything white.

"I need your help," she suddenly said. "A branch has fallen and trapped them. I can't lift it."

Erik put Barney down against the building, hoping the structure would protect it from further damage. He turned and went back into the bushes, where he found Alex struggling to lift a giant sycamore branch. The swans, clearly spooked, looked wild-eyed and drenched. "Step back," he commanded.

"They might peck you. I should stay here," she replied.

"I don't want them biting you. Step aside. I'm going to grab the branch fast," Erik said, sizing up the best place to grab the big tree limb, aiming to keep his hands as far away from the birds' beaks as possible. When Alex moved, he stepped in and quickly lifted and shoved the branch away before retreating as fast as he could.

"Chloe, Athena, Hercules, Odette! Come here!" Alex directed the birds once they were free, motioning for Erik to back up and stay silent. First, one wet and bedraggled head and body appeared, then a second, followed by a third and fourth waddling out.

"Come. I'll give you some lettuce, and maybe if you're lucky, some snails," she told the gang of four, gesturing to Erik to back up more. Turning, she coaxed the swans to follow. Eyeing Erik and the dog, the birds slowly waddled after Alex as she headed to the building. Erik held back, giving the soaked birds ample space before following the bizarre procession.

"We found them," he told Linc over his comm. "Alex's leading them to a building. They look okay, just wet," he added after Linc asked. "Will you tell the hotel and Iso? We'll comm when we head back."

Erik watched as Alex pulled open the big door to the rickety old building. She disappeared into the gloom inside, followed by the gaggle—was it gaggle, Erik wondered—waddling behind her. He waited a few seconds before following, not wanting to scare what had to be a traumatized group. He wasn't sure if the swans knew the dog wasn't a dog, but in case they were as gullible as he'd been, he decided to hang back.

Once inside, Erik couldn't believe his eyes. Row after row of ceiling lights switched on as he pulled the door shut. What had looked like a giant run-down shack now looked sturdy enough to be a bomb shelter. Once he'd shut the door, the raging storm outside quieted to a mere whisper. Thick walls encased just as impressive floor-to-ceiling windows and an enormous skylight. Everywhere he looked, rows of plants on raised beds spread across the room.

"Come to your nests and I'll give you your treats," Alex called to the group, luring the swans toward the back of the building. Erik sensed something at the end but couldn't see it clearly. Suddenly, Alex disappeared, then the swans seemed to vanish until a soft light illuminated the area. As Erik approached, still holding the robot dog, he realized there was a big space at the end.

"Would you mind helping me?" Alex asked, grabbing two baskets from a small table. "You can put Barney on the bench," she added, pointing to a bench along the wall. "I promised them treats, and could use some help gathering them."

Erik carefully set the dog down—he still had a hard time thinking of it as a robot—took the basket she'd offered, and followed her down the aisle. About halfway down, she started picking something green and leafy.

"Can you pick some spinach for me?"

Erik looked around. He thought he knew what spinach

looked like, but in the array of greenery, he wasn't sure. Seeing his confusion, she pointed to the rows of plants on her left.

"If you see any snails, grab those too," she added, breaking off more leaves.

He was happy to see that Alex's face had brightened as she focused on filling her basket with what appeared to be another type of lettuce. The storm sounded distant as they worked.

Alex noted that Erik obviously hadn't done much gardening, glancing at him as he very precisely picked one leaf at a time.

Suddenly, a flash of lightning raked across the sky. A second later, something large hit the side of the building, the loud thud making Alex gasp and drop her basket.

"When I was thirteen, a major storm hit the area. They called it the Storm of the Century," Alex said quietly as she resumed searching for snails and picking greens. "I'd gone outside to look for my cat, Boo, who always spooked in a storm. I found her hiding under an old picnic table we had. I'd crawled under the table to get her when lightning hit the sycamore tree next to it.

Erik barely breathed and kept picking. He suspected his pixie rarely opened up, so he didn't say a word, hoping she'd continue.

"A big limb fell on the table, crushing it, and trapping me and Boo beneath it. A piece of the table broke off and speared through my leg. They didn't find us until the next morning. I almost died. My father was so mad; he wanted to kill Boo. Fortunately, she hid until I could rescue her. I haven't liked storms since."

Alex wasn't sure why she was sharing this story with Erik. Maybe she didn't want him to think she was a nervous nebula—at least not one without cause. She continued picking.

"I remember that storm. I was fifteen," he said, as another thud hit the building. "My dad got laid off that day and came home smashed on Spark. I worked at the market down the street after school. When I got home, I found my mom and brother out cold on the floor—my dad had just started on my sister.

"I knew if I didn't stop him, we'd all end up dead. We started fighting._ He had his back to the front window. One of my punches landed better than the others. He fell back through the window and hit his head on the bricks outside. Died immediately. My mom passed away five minutes after getting to the hospital."

Erik didn't know why he had told Alex that story. Besides the police, only Linc and Meg knew about it. He'd never been prosecuted. The police hadn't even taken him to the station. Instead, they put him in their tov and took him to the hospital.

"That's awful," Alex said softly. "I'm sorry."

In that moment, Erik felt a deep connection with this woman, her gaze filled with compassion. Pull it together, bro. "Thanks. It was a long time ago, but storms aren't really my thing either," he said gruffly.

"I found one," Erik reported a minute later, carefully holding a snail between his thumb and finger, clearly not comfortable handling the slimy creature.

"Great. I found two. We need one more."

"Why do we need four?" Erik asked, ready to hurl.

"If we only have three, one of the swans will start to sulk. Believe me, you don't want a sulking swan. Got ya!" Alex announced, pulling a snail out of a patch of lettuce. "Iso will hit the roof when she hears we found four so easily. Let's go feed the gang and shut them in for the night."

Alex headed toward the back of the building. Erik kept pace with her, not wanting to miss whatever was going to happen next. He realized he hadn't been this interested in someone in a long time as he watched Alex's lithe figure in front of him. She had a really nice ass, he noticed for perhaps the millionth time. His intrigue peaked when he spied a hole in her sweats, revealing a glimpse of a pink bottom. She was so different from most of the women he knew. Most would discard an outfit after a couple wears. From the look of Alex's sweats, she'd worn them for years.

Alex felt Erik's stare as she walked ahead of him. Dressed in some of her old sweats and a thin t-shirt, she had removed her jacket when they'd entered the greenhouse. Not very glamorous. The clothes Emily had thrown her were threadbare, something she'd wear when gardening and no one was around. Suddenly, she remembered the hole she'd been meaning to mend after catching them on a thorn and torn them. She felt a wave of embarrassment wash over her.

Stepping into what appeared to be the end of the greenhouse, Alex raised the light just enough for Erik to see the four swans sitting serenely on what looked like four old nests.

"Here you go, you escapees." Alex divvied up the greens for the birds. While they ate, she grabbed a large round porcelain bowl on the floor by the wall and filled it with water from a nearby spigot. She then gave the birds the rest of the greens, placing a snail on top of each pile.

"What is this place?" Erik asked, glancing around the back room, which, with its black, rounded, stone-like walls, resembled a cave more than the back of a greenhouse, not that he'd been in a greenhouse before.

"It was a wine room. My father's third wife wanted one, so he built this. Then he divorced her, and Emily and I started using it for other things. About ten years ago, your gang escaped and found the greenhouse and the lettuce. The door wasn't quite so sturdy back then. Since it was night and they were already inside, we built some nests for them. After that, we didn't need the room for anything else, so we left the nests in case they ever escaped again."

At the back of the room, behind the nests, Emily and Alex had installed a concealed staircase that led down to their lab, providing an escape route if needed. They'd stacked some gardening materials around to hide the entrance. For a moment, Alex thought someone had rearranged some of the equipment. She figured Emily had moved the stacks when she'd been looking for something for her seedlings.

"They're settling," Alex said as the swans began to quiet down after finishing their snack.

The swans did look sleepy, Erik thought. He also noticed that Alex was trying to keep her front facing him. She'd probably remembered the hole in her pants. Really, it didn't reveal much, at least not as much as he'd like. Not to say that her front view wasn't spectacular. He bet she hadn't realized when she'd filled up the bowl of water for the swans that some had splashed onto her shirt, making the thin material and lace bra underneath almost translucent. The view made his pulse pound.

"Would you mind helping me pull this across to keep them in until tomorrow?" she asked, side-stepping around him to keep her front facing him before unlatching a tall piece of folded wood lattice. Together they pulled the lattice across the room and secured it at each side to a metal loop in the wall.

"That should hold them for the night. We'll be back in the morning," Alex told the birds.

She lowered the light until it was almost pitch black and then turned to lead Erik out. She couldn't get her coat on quick enough.

"You go on ahead. I forgot to grab the baskets." Alex stepped to the side.

"I'll get them and meet you at the door," Erik offered, then headed back to grab the baskets.

By the time he returned to the front, she'd unfortunately slipped on her jacket. As he picked up the dog, he was amazed to see that big hole in the dog's leg closed by a third. He hoped she wouldn't mind if he told Linc.

"I know it would be too much to ask you not to tell Linc about Barney," Alex said. "I will ask that you not tell anyone else and will tell Linc the same. If word got out about how rapidly his skin repairs, someone would try to steal him. And, I know it will sound weird, but besides him being unique, we're attached to him, and so is Fred. No," she added before he could ask, "Fred's a real dog. We're not sure if Fred knows Barney isn't, though."

"I know you don't know me enough to trust me, but I promise I won't tell," Erik said. "And I appreciate you letting me tell Linc. He won't tell anyone. He's very good at keeping secrets."

Alex nodded before turning to open the door. "I hope so," he heard her murmur before the greenhouse door flew from her hand and banged against the side. Outside the storm screamed. Amazing, he thought, how quiet the greenhouse had been.

It took them what felt like an hour, although Alex knew it had to be less than ten minutes, to fight their way back to the house. At one moment, the wind blew so strong she was plastered against Erik's huge body, grateful for his strength and heat as he helped her fight through the storm, one arm around her, practically holding her up, the other holding Barney. With his support, they crab-walked the last ten feet to the house.

By the time they entered the kitchen, she was ready to rip her jacket off she'd become so heated being flush against his body as they fought to the house. After removing her jacket, she slipped on a long shirt hanging on the hook before entering the kitchen.

Emily and Linc sat at the table. Isobelle was pulling out of the autove what looked like her oatmeal cookies. The three looked up as she and Erik entered. Alex took a double take when she got closer, realizing that Linc had put on a pair of her uncle's old sweats and t-shirt. Her uncle hadn't been a tall man. In fact, he only cleared her by a few inches. He had loved food though and had made up in girth what he lacked in height.

"Can you take Barney for me?" Alex asked Emily.

"What happened?" Emily jumped up to cover a side table with a towel, then motioned Erik to put Barney down on it.

"A limb fell on him and punched a hole in his leg. The gang, though, is settled in the greenhouse." Alex used a towel to blot her dripping hair after handing one to Erik. "I'm going to change into some dry clothes and find something for Erik. In the meantime, tell Linc about Barney, but have him swear upon penalty of death that he won't tell anyone, including Meg. Not that I don't like her," she added hastily when the two men looked at her.

"I put some of Walter's clothes in the spare room for Erik," Isobelle said as she plated cookies.

"Thanks. We'll be back in a minute." Alex motioned for Erik to follow.

"You're sure your uncle won't mind?" Erik asked when they met back in the hall after changing. He struggled to tighten the waistband of her uncle's way-too-large sweatpants to keep them from slipping down his lean hips. If she didn't miss her uncle so much, she would have laughed at the sight. Erik looked like an overly handsome hulk who'd just shifted, his pants riding high above his ankles, a too-big waistband, and a t-shirt stretching so tightly across his pecs and around his biceps that the fabric seemed seconds away from ripping.

"No," she said wistfully, realizing she could smell her uncle's familiar scent coming from the clothes. "Here's a bag for your wet things."

Erik looked around as they headed down the hall back to the kitchen. Framed pictures lined the walls. One captured the women when they were young, sandy and sun-kissed on what looked like a Hawaiian beach. Another showed Alex with what must have been her husband on their wedding, and another, probably taken just a year or so ago, of Walter, Emily, and Alex together.

He would have loved to stop and study them, but he knew it was late and not the time. The guest room he'd changed in had been nice but had lacked personal trinkets, containing only some huge old conch shells and wooden carvings of tropical birds. They passed a big high-ceilinged living room before entering the large kitchen and breakfast area.

"I promise I won't breathe a word," Linc was telling Emily as they leaned over Barney. When Erik walked up and looked down, he could see the hole in Barney's leg had almost closed. As he and Linc stared at it, the hole completely disappeared. "Man, would I love to talk to your uncle about that."

"I'm sorry, but that won't be possible," Emily said. "It's okay, boy," she added, patting Fred, who was whining. "Barney will be fine."

"Would you like a cookie?" Alex asked Erik.

"We should offer them at the hotel if Isobelle would share her recipe," Linc suggested to Erik before he could respond.

"I'd be happy to send it over to Leon," Isobelle said as she brought over another plate, having seen that Linc had already demolished the first.

Erik noticed the teardrop tattoo below Isobelle's right ear. He'd thought he'd seen it the other day. Interesting that the women didn't introduce her as a bot.

As Alex sat, she motioned to Erik to pull out the chair next to hers.

"I don't suppose Al and Lee are around?" Erik asked, taking a bite out of a cookie and groaning in delight.

Emily nearly choked on her drink, having just sipped her chocolate.

"Why do you ask?" Alex asked.

"Linc should be president of their fan club," Erik cracked, getting an evil eye from his friend. "Not that I don't admire them. I do. I'd like to talk with them about some of their innovations. But I'm not obsessed like he is."

"I'm not obsessed," Linc protested. "Have you met them?" he asked Emily. "What am I thinking?" he said sheepishly. "Of course you have, haven't you?"

"Um, yes," Emily responded, obviously uncomfortable, glancing at Alex for help.

"I mean the way they solved the nanobot issue ten years ago. No one else could figure that out. It was such an elegant solution. And then their gummagad invention, and what a great name for a space glue. And—"

"Dude! Chill!" Erik cut in, not wanting to turn off the women. "You'll have to forgive him. He's usually better behaved. He's been working too much."

"Aren't you also celebrities?" Alex asked, thinking of some of the papers the two had published.

"We like to think we have minds, unlike that *Galactic Style* article implied," Erik said stiffly, thinking she was referring to the magazine article that had nicknamed them the Space Men and the unending ribbing they'd received from their friends.

"I wasn't talking about that, but now that you mentioned it," Alex said, eyeing Emily, as both tried not to laugh at the offended expressions on the two men's faces. "I heard you both wrote some groundbreaking papers on astrobiodefense. My uncle, in fact, talked about one. I think it was about the risks from Arrokoth's Pewsodoter? He said you two were up-and-coming— what was it he said, Emily?"

"He said you were a force to watch, and he expected Xtra would become a major player in the space industry," Emily finished for Alex, remembering his comments. "That was about two years ago."

"Really?" Linc blurted. "Wow, that just made my day, or night as it is."

"Yeah," Erik added. "Hopefully we can meet him one day."

"The storm seems to be dying down." Isobelle placed a bag of cookies on the table. "Those are for you two," she told the men.

Grateful to her for changing the subject, Alex smiled her thanks at Isobelle before turning back to Erik. "Call us in the morning. We'll help you get the swans back to the hotel."

"Should we call Miss Bird?" Erik asked.

"No, Emily and I can manage getting the birds back. The important thing is to get the gates fixed."

"Those gates were fine yesterday. We just tested them." Linc said, looking at Erik.

"You've had a few break-ins, haven't you?" Emily asked, stirring her drink.

"Since you're our neighbor, and you've told us your secret, it doesn't hurt to return the trust." Erik reached for another cookie. "Besides Susan's tov accident, we've had two break-ins, the first one causing a lot of damage and theft. Both of them were at the top of the property."

"Do you have vids up there? Did you see anything?" Alex

knew they had vids. Heck, she and Emily had vids up there too, but their sensors hadn't tripped.

"Yes, but we didn't get much. The burglars wore masks, and their tov didn't have a license plate," said Linc. "We're asking for access to the neighborhood comms to see if they picked up anything. The police said a gang's hitting places in the hills."

Seeing Alex cover a yawn, Erik grabbed the cookie bag before Linc could open it for round three and moved toward the door. "We'll let you get some sleep and get some ourselves. Thanks for your help, and the cookies, Isobelle."

"I have brought the tov around to take you back to the hotel," Isobelle said, ready to lead the men to the front door.

"That's not necessary. We can hoof it back," Erik said as a flash of lightning hit, followed closely by a rumble of thunder.

"The storm has not completely finished, and the tov is right outside."

"Yes, ma'am," Linc said, grabbing the cookies from Erik before following Isobelle.

"Hey!"

"Thanks for everything," Linc said, smiling at Emily and Alex, who had also stood.

"I'll call you in the morning," Erik added.

"We'll walk you to the door," Alex said, both she and Emily enjoying the sight of the two men walking in front of them, dutifully following Isobelle, their clothes tight against their extremely ripped bodies. After the men left, Alex and Emily straightened the kitchen, then headed down the hall to their bedrooms.

"Do you think they'll keep the secret about Barney?" Emily asked.

"I think so. I hope so. The last thing we need right now is a bunch of people asking if Seed's created a new material," Alex replied wearily.

"They didn't ask where Jared was either."

"Yeah, he should be back by morning. What'd you tell your wolfy about the cave?"

"Only that Dad built the wine room and then abandoned it." Alex ignored Emily's wolfy comment.

"Do you think he saw the door behind the nests?"

"No, it was too dark. Besides, he was looking at the hole in my butt. I can't believe you threw me those sweats!" Alex admonished her cousin.

"I thought you'd fixed them," Emily said as she stopped at her door. "I like them," she admitted. "I hope they keep their promise."

"Iso liked that they cleaned up after themselves," Alex said, remembering that they had given their mugs and plates to the autowash. "I like them, too."

It had been a long time since she'd felt someone truly had her back. Even Charlie had been a bit oblivious, not that she hadn't loved him. Charlie had always had his head in the clouds—more specifically in space—always ready for the next adventure.

He'd loved her, she knew that. But he wasn't the type to provide physical support. He'd been fit, but not as fit as Erik, nor as big and built. And it wasn't like she was looking for someone to protect her. She'd always done that herself. But it was amazing how it felt—novel really. To have someone cover her back, literally, so she didn't have to be on her own or in charge for just those few minutes, felt heady. As she fell asleep, she reminded herself to ask Emily if she'd moved anything in the old wine cellar.

"Well, that was interesting," Linc said, opening the bag of cookies and reaching for yet another as the two men entered the hotel lobby. "Those women are hot, and I think they're smart, too."

"I agree. Hey, leave some for me!" Erik grabbed the bag of cookies from his friend. "I think they know more than they show.

Barney, for instance. If I hadn't seen that hole repair itself, I would have never believed it."

"Do you think they work with their uncle?"

"I don't know. You'd think we would have heard about them if they did. There's something we're missing though, something more than just that robot dog."

"Maybe, or maybe they just like their privacy after their husbands were lost in space and all the publicity before and after," Linc said, reaching for the bag.

"We need to save the last two for Meg," Erik said, holding the bag away from Linc.

"She'll never know." Linc tried to grab the bag again.

"You know she'll find out. Go get some sleep. We should be up by eight to collect the swans."

"Damn, you're right. At least it will give us another chance to see the women and maybe get some more cookies. By the way, where was that big guy? Did you see him?"

"No, I wonder where he was? He sure doesn't look like a cousin. We should have asked about him to see what they would've said," Erik added as he opened the door to his suite.

Dumping his wet shoes and socks in the tub and fighting to pull off the damp sweats and t-shirt, Erik stepped into the hot shower to warm up and rinse off the assorted debris he'd collected while struggling through the storm. He found the water didn't need to be too hot when he thought of Alex in his arms as they practically crawled the last stretch back to her house. She was a tiny thing, but not stick-thin. He didn't like skinny women, he thought as he soaped himself.

Besides that, he appreciated how kind she seemed, both to animals and people. When they'd been eating lunch at Puck's earlier, a busboy had accidentally dropped a fork off a plate. It had landed right in her lap. He'd seen women tear into what they'd called "the help" for a lot less. Heck, he'd wanted to yell at the guy for his clumsiness. Instead, Alex had almost comforted the distraught kid.

Still, it wasn't his first rodeo, and he'd experienced enough betrayals to know that kind gestures and smarts could be a cover. Then there were those bruises. He remembered her gasping when he'd wrapped his arm around her middle to steady her in the storm. He wondered if she had a broken rib.

She was definitely hiding something, and whether it was a big something, a bad something, or a no-big-deal something, he was sure it was something. She hadn't said anything about her bruises, and if there was ever an opportunity to share, discussing his father certainly provided one. Regardless, too much was happening right now. Someone was targeting him, the hotel, or the company, and he wasn't going to be distracted by a compassionate pixie with a beautiful face.

# Saturday, February 21, 2172

"He's good as new," Emily said, looking at the little robotic dog now prancing around the kitchen. She and Alex nursed their tea and coffee, trying to fight off the fatigue caused by last night's rescue.

"Pattie is coming up to the front door," Isobelle warned from the autove.

"You-hoo! Alexandra, Emily!" Pattie called from the porch. With a nod from Alex, Isobelle opened the front door.

"Darn, it's too early for this," Emily muttered.

"We're in here, Pattie."

Alex knew their cousin would enter, whether they welcomed her in or not. She and Emily had been discussing last night's events while Isobelle experimented with some new dish featuring macadamia nuts, successfully by the smell of it.

"You two look like you've been up all night. Did the storm keep you up? Jacques is coming to do my make-up and hair before the party. I can call to see if he has time to help you two." Pattie scrutinized the women. "Isobelle," she sniffed, looking with disdain at the bot's sky-blue blouse that read "No nuts, No glory" on her blouse pocket. Alex and Emily had made it clear years ago that if Pattie didn't acknowledge Isobelle, they wouldn't talk to her until she did.

"Good morning," Isobelle said, before turning back to the autove, a small, tight smile on her face.

"Well, at least it's not X-rated today." Pattie sank onto the seat next to Emily, who scooted away, seemingly to make room. Pattie was decked out in what looked like another new Ralime jogging outfit.

Pattie also had trainers—usually muscular, European men—whom she hired to prod her to keep thin. "Prod" being the operative word, Emily had observed one day after she and Alex had seen another one of Pattie's trainers. They always had one thing in common beyond their athletic abilities: big packages that bulged noticeably—packages, which the women assumed, Pattie frequently unwrapped.

"You two really should have Jacques come. You have so much sun damage," Pattie said, popping a Marbotab in her mouth.

"We're fine, but thanks. So is your mom ready for the party tonight?" Alex asked, wanting to change the subject.

"Mother's always ready for a party," Pattie said, smoothing her hair to ensure every strand was in place. "The caterers and decorators were setting up when I left."

Isobelle plunked down a plate of macadamia nut bread, glistening with butter, on the table along with plates and napkins for each. She then set down a carafe of coffee and heavy cream, adding another mug for Pattie, who recoiled at the display as if a Rimpa had landed.

"You know I don't eat carbs, Isobelle," Pattie said, "much less have cream, of all things. Do you have any oat milk?"

"No, they were out at the market." Isobelle turned back to the autove to shut it off. "I am going to the garden if you need anything."

"I still don't know why you don't fire her and hire humans," Pattie hissed under her breath to Alex. "I know there's oat milk at the market. Sandra just picked some up yesterday!"

"Well, maybe there wasn't any when Iso was there," Alex said before Emily erupted. "Now why are you visiting us today?"

While Emily told Alex to give up, she couldn't help but continue being nice. She could tell how unhappy Pattie was and how her mother still had her under her critical thumb.

"I was just passing by on my jog and thought I'd stop in to make sure you didn't want Richard to pick you up."

Alex was sure either Pattie's mother or father had sent her for that specific reason.

"Erik and Linc already offered to bring us since they'll be next door. We didn't want to put Richard out," Emily said, obviously enjoying shutting Pattie down.

"But Richard doesn't mind."

"Neither do Erik and Linc, and we already accepted. It would be rude to renege now," Emily said, as she poured a healthy amount of cream in her coffee and then took a big bite of bread.

"Those two are trouble. You should stay away from them. I can't believe you're working there, Alex!"

"At least we trapped him," Erik told Linc as they headed over to Alex and Emily's.

"Or her."

"Or her," Erik agreed. "Whoever it is, they're good at jacking around stock prices. For sure this isn't their first space ride. At least we haven't lost them. Damn, it's wet." Erik pulled a boot out of the mud with a big sucking sound.

They'd almost made it to the stream. Manny and his crew had arrived earlier, trying to figure out what had happened with the new gates.

"Hey, boss." Manny stood up, wiping his muddy hands on a

rag. "The gates are working now. It looks like they malfunctioned. We found a big branch that was holding them open."

"But?" Erik asked, noticing Manny's hesitation.

"Something feels off. The debris fence should have caught the branch before it reached the gates. Also, the branch would have had to hit the gates perfectly to have landed between them and wedged them open," Manny said, scratching his head.

"Tree limbs certainly had been flying around along with a lot of other stuff," Linc pointed out.

"Yeah, maybe. We had an alarm go off about thirty minutes before the gates stuck. We didn't see anything, or I would have told you. I sent Gary out to take a look around, and he didn't see anyone, so we figured it was an animal or the storm. Nothing showed on the vid. At that point the gates were still closed."

"Let us know if you find anything else," Erik said. "We're headed to get the swans. How much longer do you think you'll be?"

"We're just wrapping up. We should be out of here in the next ten minutes. I'm guessing you don't want us spooking the swans when you bring them back?"

"Right. Alex and Emily will be helping us get them back," Erik said.

"I'll finish up then and let you know if I see anything else." Manny turned back to the stream and bent to pick up something.

"What's that?" Linc asked.

"Another one of those Marbotab holders," he said, putting it in his pocket. "Some people love those things."

"Let us know if you find anything else," Erik said before he and Linc headed towards Alex's property.

"Do you think the cat's a robot too?" Erik asked as they saw one of the women's cats lounging on a rock as they walked through the garden.

"I have no idea. I'd have bet big money that dog was real." Linc knocked on the kitchen door.

"Good morning. Come on in. The girls are waiting for you,"

Isobelle said as she opened the door. She turned back into the kitchen. "Girls, the boys are here."

Erik glanced at Linc, both amused at her calling them boys.

"Those two are nothing but trouble. You should stay away from them. I can't believe you're working there, Alex!"

"Pattie, that's not your concern," Alex said seeing Erik and Linc walk in the kitchen.

"But Alex—" Pattie stopped as she saw the two men enter.

"Hello, Pattie," Erik said.

"Yes, hello, Pattie," Linc echoed.

"What are you two doing here?" Pattie asked. "Never mind. I have to finish my run. I'll see you tonight," she added, turning and heading out of the room. "I'll see myself out."

"Well, that was interesting." Alex glanced at Emily before shifting her gaze to the two men. She'd really like to know the story behind whatever was going on there. She'd have to ask Pattie later, though she didn't expect to get the full truth. "Good morning," she said to the men, noticing how handsome Erik looked. He was dressed casually again, at least casually for him, with his pressed designer jeans and ironed blue Quent shirt. His thick, black hair, however, was a little messy. "We'd offer you some coffee, but we should probably go get the gang. I'm sure they're anxious to get home," she said as she and Emily rose and grabbed their jackets.

"Hey, that's the cat from outside," Linc said, spotting the big tabby now lounging in the window.

"Chutney?" Emily asked, stopping to stroke the huge cat, its tail flicking.

"Is he a robot?" Erik stepped closer to inspect the giant cat.

"Chutney? No, he's just a big boy," Emily said, scratching under his chin.

"Do we need anything to get the swans to follow us to the hotel?" Linc asked.

"We'll get some romaine at the greenhouse." Emily said, grabbing some hemp bags before following the other three out the door.

Thirty minutes later, with some cajoling and freshly picked romaine, the half-animal, half-human group had almost reached the hotel gate when Linc asked about the women's gate to their property.

"Did your uncle carve the gate or was it one of you two?"

"That was Emily. She's the wood carver. She did it the first summer she came to visit. My stepmother had a fit when she saw it."

"That was my last visit here," Emily added.

"It worked out though. I got to go to Hawaii the summers after that. Deborah was Dad's wife number four. Marie Rictor was her sister," Alex added when Erik looked at her. "Deborah felt the gate's aesthetics had been ruined. She'd demanded my dad beat Emily."

"She was a fine person. May she rest in peace," Emily said.

*Amen*, Alex thought to herself. Deborah had been the worst of her stepmothers. Alex had had mixed feelings when her father died in the tov crash. Who wouldn't? He'd been so cold and uncaring, but she'd felt no loss with Deborah's death. The woman had criticized her daily about her weight, her grace—or lack of it. When she'd demanded her father beat Emily for the gate, she'd almost lost it. Worried he'd do it, she'd grabbed Emily and hidden her at Natalie's.

"Come on, you guys. Time to go home," she said, dismissing the lousy memories as she held out a bunch of romaine to lure the swans through the gate.

"Do they seem kind of, you know, a bit unusual?" Linc whispered to Erik as the two men followed.

"A bit?"

"Yeah, okay, a lot unusual?"

"They certainly don't fit any mold, that's for sure," Erik said as he sidestepped a puddle.

"Is it that they're not coming on to us? Is that the attraction? I didn't think I was that shallow."

"Man, you've always been shallow when it comes to women, but no, I don't think that's it. They do seem skittish the minute we get physically close, and they're very matter of fact. They certainly don't flirt."

"I wonder if it's our reputation? Meg said it would bite us in the ass one day."

"You'll get another chance. Remember, we're picking them up for tonight's party."

The two men hurried to catch up, rounding the last bend in the stream in time to see the women feeding the swans the last of the romaine. Suddenly Hercules tried to shove Odette out of the way to steal her treat. Erik and Linc tensed, worried that the big male would bite Alex or Emily.

"Hercules! You already had your treat," Alex scolded the big bird. "And stop pouting. You'd better check your lake to make sure no new birds have taken your spot."

With that, Hercules looked around, and, spotting two ducks paddling at the other end, hurried off, wings slapping the water as he honked at the intruders.

"I can see Miss Bird knew what she was talking about," Erik said as they walked up. "I'm glad we didn't have to disturb her."

"Can we take you to dinner as a thank you?" Linc asked.

"Thanks aren't necessary," Emily said. "We care about these birds. Besides, we're working on a project, and our nights are pretty much taken right now."

"What kind of project?" Linc asked.

"Oh my gosh, did you see the time?" Alex interrupted. "We have to get going if we're going to get everything done before tonight's party. If you don't have time to pick us up, we can get there ourselves."

"It's not a problem," Erik said. "Does 8:00 work?"

"That's perfect. See you then," Alex said. She and Emily turned to head back to their property.

"Did you notice how they didn't want to talk about the project they're working on?" Linc asked as the men headed inside the hotel.

"I also noticed that they didn't want to have dinner with us. That's a first. It would almost be refreshing if it weren't so irritating," Erik replied. "I'm going to the gym."

"Need to work off some frustration? I'll join you. I want to try out that new holobike. I hear the new Mars challenge is out of this world."

"I bet those two noticed you changing the subject," Emily said to Alex as they entered the kitchen. "They'll probably ask about it on the way to the party."

"Yeah," Alex said as she poured a glass of water. "So, what kind of project are we working on? How about something with the swans. I know, how about a fundraiser to help swan research?"

"Then we'll have to come up with a fundraiser that's taking place soon. What if they want to go, or worse, tell Jorgé about it? He may be there tonight," Emily said, absently raising her hand to her mouth before realizing it and dropping it.

"I know, how about the upcoming Foster Family Fundraiser? Cheryl can cover for us."

"Perfect, the fundraiser isn't for another month. Besides, we asked Pierre to donate a year's VIP pass to his club for the auction. You don't mind calling her?"

"I've got it," Alex said as they headed down the hall. "Before I forget, you're wearing your hair up, right?"

"I thought I would. Why?"

"I have a surprise. Iso, I'm going to show Emily the sticks. Can you help?" Alex called out.

Emily followed Alex, who grabbed a slender green-colored stick off her dresser, then headed to the backyard. Isobelle was propping up two sycamore branches that still had leaves on them. Once Isobelle stepped away, Alex pointed the stick at a sycamore leaf. A second later, what looked like a pale-yellow beam shot out and enveloped the leaf.

"Oh my gosh! You did it!" Emily exclaimed. "When did you finish?"

"The other day," Alex said proudly. "I'm calling it the Numser."

Alex had been tinkering with the contraption for months. She'd discovered if she blended Haumic, a sand-like material from the dwarf planet Haumea, with some of Earth's silica, the resulting alloy worked like glass in a laser. But instead of cutting or destroying whatever the yellow beam hit, it would put the object in stasis.

"Here, this one will match your dress tonight." Alex handed Emily the long stick.

"How do you activate it?"

"First, I added our biometrics so no one else can use them. Turn the thicker end counterclockwise one turn, then push the button that appears on the tip. Aim at one of the leaves, then push the button again."

Emily, following Alex's instructions, hit another sycamore leaf with the Numser.

"It's really only for extreme emergencies because it will freeze someone for an hour if my calculations are correct," Alex added. "I'm working on a mini one we can conceal easier."

"Hopefully we'll never need them, but this is awesome,"

Emily said, twisting her hair into a bun. After making sure she deactivated the stick, she tucked it into her hair.

As Erik and Linc strolled up to the women's front porch, they could hear Isobelle calling out, "The boys are here." They'd barely reached the front door when it opened and the two women walked out, coats in hand.

"Fuck" was all Erik could think. He'd been around his share of beautiful women, but something about Alex made her stand out. She'd put her hair up again, and he itched to pull out the thin sapphire-colored stick that held it, just to see her hair cascade down like a silken river.

Shaking himself, he smiled and offered to help her with her coat. Holding it open, he practically had a seizure when she turned and he saw that her dress was open to the very bottom of her back. Created from some kind of fluid-like material he'd never seen before—the color like a hot summer sky right before the night turns dark—the gown slid down Alex like a Mimas hanging orchid, sapphire petals dripping to the ground.

It was a good thing she had put on the coat, as otherwise, he would have wanted to see if her creamy-looking skin was as soft as it looked. She turned, the porch light illuminating her dress's bodice, revealing a lacy inset that revealed her deep cleavage. A feeling of pleasure swelled inside him at the thought of having such an interesting and lovely woman in his care, even if it was just for a mile up the canyon. Alex smiled at him, secretly questioning his sudden silence.

He motioned for her to go first, noticing his friend was just as bemused by Emily. Tonight Emily she exuded an earthen magic; her short, tight, pale green, off-the-shoulder dress skimmed her figure, her white blonde hair styled up as well.

"I don't know about you ladies, but I'm starving," Linc admitted once they'd all climbed into the tov.

"You're always hungry."

"I forgot," Emily said, holding out a bag. "Iso gave me these cookies for you two."

The men immediately reached for them, Erik snatching the bag before his friend could. He took out two cookies, handing one to Linc. "We're almost there."

"Don't you ever eat, or are you always hungry?" Alex said, a little amused at the way they became so excited over some homemade cookies. "Did no one ever make you cookies?" The thought made her a little sad for the men, if true, remembering how her Auntie Lani's coconut-mango shortbread treats had always filled the cookie jar.

"Marie always has a spread," Emily said. "She has a greenhouse out back and loves to talk about how almost everything she serves is sourced from there, as if she's ever gotten a finger dirty." Emily immediately covered her mouth.

"I take it you're not a fan?" Linc asked as he popped the last bit of cookie in his mouth.

"Let's just say Marie usually likes to stretch the truth a bit," Alex said. Emily suddenly looked like she was searching for something on the floor.

"So, what's the project that's captured all your free time?" Erik asked.

"We're helping with a foster fundraiser," Emily said. Alex could tell she was happy to change the subject, especially since she had a ready response. "We promised we would work on the silent auction. In fact—"

"Look, we're here," Alex interrupted. Emily always started babbling when she fibbed. One time, long ago, Alex, her aunt, and uncle listened for a half hour while Emily insisted she wasn't hungry, only for her to finally confess that she hadn't eaten for two days.

"Erik, Linc, so nice to see you. Alex, Emily," Pattie gave the two women air kisses as they entered the foyer. "Mother's in back, giving a tour of the greenhouse."

The women removed their coats and handed them to one of the young, handsome men working the party. Typically, the men were first-year UCLA student athletes, dressed in black fitted slacks and shirts, a signature style of Marie's parties.

"Interesting dresses," Pattie added.

Alex knew Marie wouldn't like the colors, so Pattie wouldn't either. Her aunt only allowed her decorator to use bold red accents–Alex thought they looked like bloody slashes–throughout the house, muted with gold, silver, and white. Marie expected everyone in the family, including Alex and Emily, to conform to her theme.

"They're Juliettes." Alex knew Pattie or her mother wouldn't snub them with that pedigree.

"Father's in his office. His cigans just arrived," Pattie said, a hint of tenseness to her tone, which Alex attributed to her dislike of Erik and Linc. "More guests are coming. You know the way. Go socialize."

As the four entered the living room, Alex recognized the usual wealthy society sharks attending the Rictor's events, including Claudette Michaels, a snotty friend of Pattie's whom Alex and Emily despised. Claudette, pushing sixty, was eyeing one of the young servers. Poor guy, she thought. He looked like a scared guppy in front of a barracuda.

While examining the boy, Claudette talked to Mildred and Brad Wine, owners of the powerhouse Oro Properties, as Marie walked in from the back. Alex recognized her friend, Sonja Roberts, a man, and three other women with Marie. One of the women, Christine something, she thought was the city's new mayor.

"I can't believe people actually think that bots should have rights," Marie said as they entered. "That BAPB, BAPT, BART group, whatever they're calling themselves, is delusional. I mean, they're just machines. The fact that they want to be paid is ridiculous. Christine, surely you don't support that."

"I believe the group is BAPT, for Bots Are People Too," Christine said as they walked up.

Alex, a BAPT supporter, waited to hear the mayor's response.

"Silly name," Marie sniffed before Christine could respond. She then introduced the group, inspecting Alex and Emily's dresses. Alex hugged Sonja, whispering to her friend that her ex-father-in-law, Peter Anwai, and his latest wife had just arrived. Sonja had divorced Peter's son after catching him in bed with a client. None of the Anwais understood why Sonja demanded a divorce. Alex bet that Marie and Pattie had purposely invited Sonja and the Anwais, hoping for some drama that everyone could gossip about later.

"Alex is it?" Christine's partner asked during the lull in conversation. "Your dress is gorgeous; yours too," she said to Emily. "Are they Juliettes?"

"Yes, thank you," Alex said smiling. When Marie had walked up, Alex could tell that she disapproved.

"Gentlemen, so good to see you. Ladies, you look lovely," Richard added as he strolled up, slipping his comm into his pocket. "Father and some of the men have gathered in his office. A box of Lunas just arrived. Erik, Linc, if you'd like to join me, I'm headed that way."

"Tell Steven I'll be there in a minute," Peter told Richard as he and Belle walked up. "Alex, a minute please." He reached for her arm, guiding her a few steps away.

Alex had never liked Peter, especially after he told Sonja she was acting immature when she had demanded a divorce from his son.

"What can I do for you, Peter?" Alex asked, already eager to end the conversation.

"I don't know if Steven has told you yet, but I've just invested in Rictor and wanted to ask you for an introduction to your uncle. Is he in town, or working the contract from Hawaii? If he's at the islands, I can take my yacht over to meet him next week."

"Why?" she asked, disliking him even more, if that was possible, for mentioning her uncle. Hearing his name triggered a deep misery within her.

"Don't you worry about that, Alexandra. I wouldn't expect you to understand. I'd just like to talk to him about some opportunities that a joint Rictor-Seed operation could offer."

*Oh my god, did he really say that?* She decided to play the airhead since he believed all women were stupid.

"Gee, Peter, I have no idea where he is right now." She fluttered her eyelashes, hoping she wasn't pouring it on too thick. "When I see him next, I'll be happy to give him your message though."

"When do you think that might be?" He asked, clearly frustrated with her.

"Oh, I don't know. Emily and I have some parties to go to. Did you know Pierre's just opened? It's so much fun. Pierre let us help decorate the place. Isn't that sweet of him? But Uncle doesn't really like to go to parties, which I really don't understand, so we see him when we see him," Alex rambled, enjoying the disgusted look on Peter's face.

"Please convey my message. Steven and I would both like to meet with him as soon as possible," Peter said dismissively before turning and stalking off to Steven's office, ignoring his wife as he passed.

"These Lunas just came off the ship from Europa," Steven said, offering the fat long cigans arranged in an intricate silver box to the men already in his office. "It's a great excuse to stay in here," he added, waving a hand around the large office. "Marie hates cigans so the women won't come in. Erik, Linc, good to see you boys. I hear that Xtra's showing some real possibilities in the tests.

"Rictor's a shoo-in, but there might be a few projects we can send Xtra's way after we win," the man added, holding the box out to Erik, Linc, and Jorgé. "Have a seat and relax a bit. All that business about that stranded colony has been a bit tiring.

"You must be the Jorgé who directed that fun film, *Swan Soup*?" Steven continued, turning to Erik and Linc's director friend. "I told Marie we really must see it. I don't suppose you'd share the access key to the director's cut?"

"I don't have it at the moment," Jorgé said.

Erik could tell he was offended by Steven's arrogance.

"That's okay, my boy. I'm sure I can find one. Now gentlemen sit and relax." Steven sat at his desk, and began puffing away. "How do you like my pet?" he asked, stroking the life-size replica of a Rhodesian Ridgeback, its snarling face and lifted ridge of hair arrowing down its back. "Caligula looked just like this. He was a wonderful dog."

As Steven droned on, Erik took in his competitor's office. A huge crimson and gold USC banner hung across the wall, surrounded by photos, including one of a much younger Steven in football gear and a more recent image of him standing alongside the latest SC wonder player and coach.

His desk was glass, the walls were glass, even the coffee table, which was surrounded by a white leather couch and several white leather chairs. It looked like his desk rarely saw any work, Erik thought, in contrast to his own, which was full of skimpads, several keyboards, and a large monitor, besides the huge monitors on his wall. The only item that wasn't glass, apart from the seating, was a large silver credenza featuring a floating, turning 3D model of a spaceship. Erik recognized the ship as one of Rictor's. The latest USC game played on the wall behind it.

"You can probably tell that I'm an SC alum. Too bad you boys didn't go there," Steven nodded to Erik and Linc. "SC's colors don't quite go with Marie's decorating, but as I told her,

'Go Trojans and fuck the décor.'" Stephen laughed, tapping his cigan in the large crystal bowl on his desk. "And check this out. I just had it installed," he boasted as he pushed a button, which turned the walls opaque. "Marie doesn't need to know everything I do in here."

"Daniel, come in, come in," Steven said, motioning to a well-groomed man standing at the door. "Shut the door behind you. For those of you who don't know him, this is Daniel DuBois. USC just named him 2172's Engineering Leader of the Year.

Erik had heard nothing good about Daniel. The evening was looking worse by the minute. Had he not known that Alex was coming tonight, he would have ditched the party. He knew without looking that Linc was ready to flee, with Jorgé on his heels. He originally accepted the invitation to mingle with the other executives he'd heard would be attending. When he discovered Alex was coming, he hoped to spend some time with her that wasn't work-related.

"Dinner's ready, dear," Marie's cultivated voice sounded in Steven's office. "Please join us on the patio."

*Thank God*, Erik thought, as did his friends, from the looks they shot him. Even that Raul guy looked relieved.

Steven pushed another button on his desk, and the glass wall facing the back disappeared.

"That cost five mil," Steven said, waving at the lifting wall before rising from his desk. "Boys, leave your Lunas. There's plenty for later. Now let's go mingle and make the ladies happy."

"Have you talked to Alexandra?" Erik overheard Stephen quietly ask Daniel as he headed for the patio. Before he could slow and eavesdrop further, Jorgé grabbed his arm.

"I could use this guy in my next movie," he whispered.

"What's the title?" Linc asked, overhearing. "Entitled Douchebags?"

The men grinned as they left the room.

Alex already regretted coming this evening; the pain in her ribs was a dull ache even with the Erisalve. Daniel had just arrived, a jerk she tried to avoid at all costs. Fortunately, he'd gone into Steven's office. Meanwhile, Marie and her group of friends were droning on about clothes, how someone stole someone's maid, and how hot the Zaras' new chauffeur looked. Since tovs didn't need drivers, using a chauffeur was merely a status symbol.

"Wasn't that Daniel?" Emily whispered to Alex, the two having moved away slightly from the other women to catch up with Sonya. "I don't know if you've met him," she added to Sonja. "He's a douchebag, an old friend of Richard's."

"He offered to give me a ride home after the Children's Bureau Ball three years ago. When he tried to paw me on Bellagio and I told him to back off, he kicked me out of his tov. Told me to walk home, which was fine with me," Alex said, remembering the exchange she'd had with the jerk. "I should have known better. I'd heard rumors."

"He works for Rictor now," Emily replied.

"More like steals for Rictor," Alex added, determined to keep an eye out for Daniel so she could keep her distance. "How he was named Engineering Leader of the Year is beyond me."

"Good to know," Sonja said, looking around. "Have you noticed Marie's servers keep getting younger? These guys look like boys. At least Peter Jr. isn't here tonight," she added, suddenly wide-eyed. "Alex, look out!"

It was too late. Alex felt something cold splash against and then run down her back.

"Oh my god. I'm so sorry," the boy-man who was delivering drinks exclaimed as he frantically tried to blot her back with cocktail napkins.

"You imbecile," Marie said angrily, pointing at the server,

having immediately come when she saw what happened. "What are you doing?" She grabbed his arm and yanked it away from Alex's back. "Lisette!" she snapped, searching for the head of the catering company, who was scurrying up. "This idiot just spilled a drink down my guest's back. Her dress is probably ruined. Get that cleaned up off the floor and fire that imbecile immediately.

"Alex, come this instant," Marie ordered, clutching Alex's arm, practically dragging her out of the living room. "We don't need your help," she hissed, dismissing Emily, who had started to follow them. Alex nodded to Emily that she was fine.

"Thank heavens you wore dark blue, even though you know I'd prefer you wear black or silver at my parties," Marie continued once they'd entered the powder room. She watched her maid as she blotted Alex's back and dress.

As the maid swiped at the liquid running down her back, Alex tried not to wince. The woman, she knew, was trying to be gentle once she'd seen her bruises.

"What are these horrible bruises?" she exclaimed as the maid's efforts removed the concealer on Alex's back. "You must take your hair down. You can't walk around with those showing. Besides, that stick in your hair looks ridiculous."

Marie plucked the numser from Alex's hair and tossed it in the trash after dismissing its value. Alex wanted to dive into the trash and grab it but didn't want to call attention to it in case Marie decided to look closer. She could always return and get it later, she figured. For now, her hair covered her back, and her dress was drier.

Alex decided she would no longer attend any more of her so-called family's events after the upcoming reveal. She'd tried to be nice, but she'd tapped out of nice. Besides, when the Rictors found out they'd been deceived all these years, they'd likely be furious. Eyeing the silver clock on the wall, she groaned to herself. Only an hour had passed. They had to stay at least through dinner.

The stress was getting to her. The doctor who had seen her

after the attack in Hawaii had lectured her that her numbers were off, emphasizing that she needed to take it easy. She was worried about the colony on Farout, keeping her uncle's murder a secret, whether Ola would work, anxious about Susan's recovery and all the hotel party errors. The stress of keeping her and Emily's identities confidential, not to mention Gary's sudden unwelcome appearance and ensuring her injuries remained unknown—the pile kept growing.

If she could, she'd escape to Europa, and that new ocean resort, Atlantica. She'd heard it had a whole non-sensory section —no noise, only natural light generated by the moon's fluorescent creatures.

An artist friend had just returned—she'd gone to regenerate— and told her that the translucent rooms where guests could rest and watch the animals swimming in the Europan ocean had refreshed her enough to continue her art.

Only nine more days to go. Then she'd leave for Atlantica.

"Fungi Frappe?" the young blonde Adonis asked, holding out his tray as Alex rejoined her friends.

"Alex, you must try these," Sonja said as she and Emily sipped their drinks.

"No thanks. I'm allergic to mushrooms."

"Oh no you're not, dear," countered Marie, miffed that Alex had refused the special drink. "I've told you time and again that's not possible. The same goes for your silly allergy to wasps. I was talking with Dr. Roberts the other day. He said it's just in your head," she said, addressing the other guests nearby. "Nobody has allergies anymore."

"Mushrooms are quite good for you," Pattie interjected. "You should really give them a try, Alex. Mother grows these in her greenhouse. Raul, you grow mushrooms. Have you ever heard of anyone allergic to them?" Pattie asked as he approached.

"I think Alex knows what's best for her, don't you?" Raul said as he leaned in to kiss Alex's cheek in greeting.

"Raul, I didn't know you were here," Alex said, happy to see her handsome friend. She had grown up with Raul; his family owned a huge farm up north in Oxnard. The farm was one of the suppliers of greens for the hotel's upcoming parties. When she was little, her family frequently visited his, as the Sepulvedas and Addingtons shared a multi-generational friendship. As kids, she and Raul had been thick as thieves, which Raul's dad often said. But to both their fathers' dismay, they'd never had any chemistry, particularly on Alex's side.

Over the years, she'd thought Raul was going to propose a couple of times, once before she married Charlie and another, a couple of years back. Fortunately, she'd evaded both proposals. She didn't love him but didn't want to hurt his feelings either.

Meanwhile, Erik felt he would bust a gasket as he watched Alex talking to that Raul guy. They looked like they had history—lots of it. He wanted to shove that guy away, possibly to another country, if not planet.

"Who is that guy?" Linc asked, also noticing Raul getting cozy with Alex, his hand on her arm moving to her back. "Shit. Did you see that?" he exclaimed.

When Raul moved his hand, Alex's hair moved, revealing a huge green and yellow bruise on her lower back before her hair fell back to cover it.

"That must hurt like hell." Erik felt a surge of anger and protectiveness wash over him. He wanted to grab Alex, shake her, demand she tell him what happened, and ensure it never happened again. Then he'd rip apart the bastard or bastards who'd dared lay a hand on her. "I'll kill him," Erik swore, starting to move towards Raul.

"Raul didn't do that," Emily said softly, having overheard him as she was walking by and seeing the concern etched on the men's faces.

"Who did?"

"That's not my place to say."

Fortunately, before they could press her for more information, Claudette walked up, eyeing Linc and Erik like they were fresh meat. Emily wished she and Alex had come up with a story about her bruises. Earlier, when she'd applied the waterproof concealer on Alex's back, they'd never expected that the Rictors would serve Champardd tonight, much less that anyone would choose to drink the vile stuff. Made from an element found on the Pluto moon Charon, the drink, not only had an extremely bitter taste but also broke down chemicals, including, it seemed, the ones used to make the concealer waterproof.

Emily silently thanked the universe that the top of Alex's bodice circled her neck, hiding the bruises there. Judging by Erik's expression, he looked about to explode. Good thing Raul hadn't seen Alex's bruises either. He would be just as upset.

"How about a dance?" Raul asked Alex, the two unaware of the drama behind them.

"I believe it's my dance," Stephen said as he stepped up. He took Alex's hand and led her to the white, floating dance floor as the human four-piece combo started a slow jazz tune from the silver platform in the corner of the large patio.

Alex stiffened as her uncle's stinky cigan breath wafted towards her, his firm grip on her back hurting. Darn, this night is just getting worse. She would have declined the dance, but after the attack and the issues at the house, she needed to see what he would talk about. Unfortunately, the Erisalve was starting to wear off sooner than she'd expected.

"I've been trying to reach your uncle, but he's not returning my calls," Stephen said, frowning. "Is he in Hawaii or here?"

"I believe he's in Hawaii, but I'm not sure." Alex realized that technically this was true before quickly slamming the door in her mind on the fact that her uncle was dead. "Why?"

"You may or may not know, Alexandra, but a big contract's up for grabs right now. There's also a colony on Farout that needs saving, or everyone will die, but that's not public. Your uncle's company developed something that everyone's using to save the colony and for the competition. It's important we have that tech. I want Walter's help."

"Peter also said he wanted to talk to Uncle. Is that why? He mentioned that he'd bought into Rictor."

"Damn him. He shouldn't be talking about that yet. Just ignore that he said anything. Comm your uncle. Tell him it's urgent. We're family after all. We'd do the same if the situation were reversed."

Alex didn't believe that for a second but kept quiet.

"I have an offer I think he'd be interested in. It's imperative I talk to him as soon as possible. I need your help, Alexandra," Stephen demanded quietly, tightening his hold on her back and hand.

Alex stiffened as his grip tightened, fearing she might pass out from the pain. Unable to speak, she nodded tightly. The only good part of this conversation, she thought, was that it was unlikely Stephen had killed Walter, as it sounded like Stephen needed him.

She'd give anything to have just one more minute with her uncle. Having Stephen talk so casually about him hurt, a lot. She was doing all she could to keep it together until the competition was over. Wouldn't Stephen be surprised then when he found out it was her and Emily who had designed Ola and its data compression formulas. It had taken them years to get the compression rates where they needed to be. For some reason, Stephen thought he was owed all that for free.

When Erik saw Alex stiffen in Steven's arms, he felt like storming up onto the dance floor. Stephen's hand was resting right where he'd seen Alex's bruise, and even though Erik had known Alex less than a week, he sensed Stephen was hurting her. It also looked like whatever Stephen was telling her wasn't anything she wanted to hear. What was it with her that she was putting up with the jerk, he wondered. Was she spying for him? After all, he's family. It wouldn't be the first time a woman had betrayed him, he thought ruefully.

Regardless, he still wanted to rip Steven's hands off Alex. Linc and Jorgé, the jerks, had left him with Claudette, excusing themselves to ask Emily and her friend to dance. Erik could tell Linc was upset about being ignored, though he didn't think Emily doing it on purpose. She seemed completely oblivious to Linc's interest.

"I can see it already: Rictor and Seed headed to space together," Stephen continued as he danced with Alex. "Daniel is leading the team, Alexandra. Which brings me to the second reason I wanted to talk to you. Don't you think it's time to marry again? Charles has been gone a long time. If you don't want to marry Raul, Daniel would be a good choice. You're not getting any younger, in fact—"

"I believe this is my dance," Raul interrupted, smoothly cutting in as a new song began, ignoring Stephen's frown.

Turning back, Erik spied that Raul guy already on the dance floor, cutting in. His green-eyed monster roared as he saw Alex smile warmly at Raul and relax into his arms. He grabbed Claudette without ceremony and pulled her onto the floor, positioning them close to Alex and Raul in an attempt to overhear their conversation. He didn't care if he was acting irrationally, although he saw Linc give him a look. Try as Erik might, he couldn't hear a word Alex and Raul were saying. But she sure was smiling.

Dancing with Raul was so easy, Alex thought. He kept their conversation light, sensing Stephen had upset her. It was a shame they didn't have any chemistry, because they jelled so well. Not enough to get married, though. One and done was it. When Charlie's ship went missing and the judge had declared him and Sam legally dead, she'd shut the door on her heart. Emotions equaled pain—she'd learned that first from her father, who after her mother died and he married one woman after another, had no time, much less love, for her. Then she'd risked her heart for Charlie. It had taken these last five years to dig herself out of that depression. Now she was content with working, volunteering, and hanging with friends.

As for Daniel, who was trying to catch her eye, the creep, that would never happen. Besides, she knew that when he found out she and Emily were the brains behind Ola, he would feel threatened and become an even bigger ass. As the song wound down, she saw him head her way. *Darn,* she thought, suffering through Stephen was bad enough. She had to get out of here. Looking around for a plausible way to escape, she locked eyes with Erik, who stood behind Raul.

"May I cut in?" he asked, his deep voice sending a hot caress fluttering across her skin. After subtly questioning Alex and seeing a brief nod, Raul stepped back to let Erik take his place as a new song started.

Alex stiffened, bracing for another stab of pain in her back, but before she knew it, Erik had shifted his hand higher as if he had seen her bruise and was trying to keep from hurting her. She looked up into his eyes, questions brimming in her gaze.

"I won't ask tonight about that huge bruise on your back. It looks like you've already had a rough night, at least when you were dancing with Stephen. I also won't ask you what he was saying that upset you so much," he added, seeing Alex's eyes widen in shock that he'd read her so accurately.

"But I expect some answers Monday. No one in my employ gets harassed or abused, especially not anyone I have a relationship with, and make no mistake, Alexandra, we will have a relationship. We have too much chemistry not to. You can't deny it."

Thankfully Erik didn't say another word. Nor did Alex; his comments capped off an already exhausting evening in a spread of exhausting days. Instead, she decided to just enjoy being gently wrapped in his arms again, feeling the sense of security similar to the other night at Pierre's, along with that same shiver of desire.

As the song ended, she noticed Daniel eying her like a hungry Botabit sighting a tasty Cresta. She did not want to deal with him, much less dance, and from the way Erik was reading her, she could see the two coming to blows. Daniel had an explosive temper. She didn't think Erik would care. Thank heavens the floor had stopped near Emily, who was looking her way.

"Alex, I'm sorry to bother you. Iso called. Anita had an accident," Emily said, a worried look on her face as she clutched her pendant. "She's one of the UCLA students living with us. She doesn't have any family," she explained to Erik as Linc walked up.

"We should go," Alex said stepping back and turning to head towards the front door. They had left Anita at home studying for a test, so Alex figured she was safe, but still. Emily had been playing with her pendant, a code that something was up.

"Can we take you two home, unless Emily wants to stay?" Erik asked, concerned.

"Iso sent the tov. It should be here any moment, but thank you. And I'll be going with Alex," Emily added, relieved she was escaping, too. Linc had walked up right as she'd told Alex the Anita news. He made her nervous, not in a bad way, but being around this many people already made her nervous.

"We should say goodbye," murmured Alex. "Oh good, there's Marie."

"We'll wait with you until your tov arrives." Erik and Linc followed the women across the living room.

"Marie, thank you for a lovely time. Unfortunately, we have to leave now. One of our student boarders has had an accident."

"Alexandra, really? How old is she, 20?" Marie asked, a frown flashing across her face before she smoothed her features when she noticed Erik and Linc standing behind the women.

"Nineteen, and she has no family," Alex responded tightly.

"Honestly, Alexandra, she can wait an hour or two at the least. Why do you even have those girls living there? Besides, Daniel wanted to spend some time with you."

"I'm sorry, Marie, but this is urgent," Alex said, turning away, eager to escape. She'd been right. Daniel had been trying to get to her.

"You two aren't leaving, too, are you?" Marie asked, ignoring Emily, as Linc and Erik followed the women toward the front.

"We'll be back in a minute. We want to make sure their tov comes." Erik inwardly seethed at the callous woman. He'd have given anything for someone to look out for him and his siblings when they were young. He was still amazed that his sister Marion had turned out to be such a good mother. "Let me know if you need anything," he told Alex as they walked out the door.

The tov was already in the driveway with—wouldn't it figure—Erik grimacing at the sight of the women's "Cousin Jared" holding the door open. The more he saw the guy, the more he seemed like a bodyguard, at least going by the steely stare the man gave him and Linc as they followed the women outside.

Spying Jared and their tov, Alex and Emily turned and thanked the men for the ride over. Alex couldn't wait to get inside and learn what was really happening.

"What's going on?" she asked after the door closed and the tov flew down the street.

"We've had another attempted break-in," Jared said. "Everyone's okay. No one entered the house, but the General thought it best that you two return home until we have the area searched. I'm sorry you had to leave the party."

"We aren't," Emily quipped.

"What happened?" Alex asked as they pulled into the garage where Isobelle was standing, waiting.

"Two men, at least based on their size, came onto the property," Isobelle said as everyone headed inside. "The sensors went off, and our defenses kicked in. For some reason, though, the grapnets did not take them down, and our visuals did not work. By the time Jared arrived outside, they had already taken off down the street."

Jared scrolled through data on his comm. "They took off in a black tov, but it was too dark to see what kind. Hopefully the Bel-Air Association's visuals got something."

"They had time to leave a tracer in the front oak tree," Isobelle said. "We have not touched it yet."

"Good. Let's go hack it and set up a loop until we decide if we want to lay some bait." Alex slipped off her shoes and, carrying them, headed barefoot to their lab.

As Daniel finished his business in the Rictor guest bathroom, he spied a familiar dark blue stick peeking out of the trashcan. Interesting, he thought, realizing it was the stick that had been in Alexandra's hair earlier. It didn't look like a normal hair thing, he thought as he peered closer, seeing a tiny hole in the top. He reached in with a tissue and picked it up. He'd wanted to talk to the bitch tonight but hadn't gotten a chance.

He was sure she knew where her uncle was, if he'd even survived the attack. *The idiots*, he thought as he fixed his tie. They were just supposed to rough him up until Walter gave them the code to his safe. Since then, no one was talking, and no one had seen Walter.

It already looked like Rictor would win the contract, but he wanted every advantage possible, which meant getting Ola's source code. With that, Rictor's value would quadruple. Rictor needed that money for the mining project on Palma. As he slipped Alex's hair stick into his inside coat pocket, he decided he'd comm Alex tomorrow and invite her to dinner at Versailles. No one turned down an invitation there. He had to get this charade going. He'd wasted too much time already.

"You two must join the Cosmic Club," Claudette droned in her nasally voice, her arm on Linc's. Bobby, Claudette's husband, had just left in search of a drink. More likely to find a reprieve from his wife, Erik thought. The minute Bobby escaped, Claudette had almost literally sunk her nails into Linc, confident in the allure of her skinny, overly bleached, and overly sculpted body.

Lauren, Richard's plus one, had set her sights on Erik. At this point, he felt like one of Charon's threatened Trebits. Jorgé had bailed already, the traitor. It had been no more than ten excruciatingly mind-numbing minutes since Alex had left. He and Linc had talked with two execs they'd wanted to meet this evening. They'd just walked up to the third on their list, unfortunately trailed by Claudette and Lauren, when Erik's comm started vibrating. Excusing himself, he saw a message from Ron that someone had broken into both his and Linc's offices.

"You'll have to excuse us," Erik said, interrupting Lauren's latest diatribe. "Unfortunately, we have to leave due to some unexpected business."

"Not you, too! The evening's young," Marie said when she overheard his comment, trailing the men to the door. Erik could tell she'd had a bit too much wine and suspected she really didn't care they were leaving, except that their presence added mass to her party. Once Xtra had become successful, Marie had decided they were acceptable additions to her gatherings, at least as long as they had money.

# Sunday, February 22, 2172

"They had some kind of new tech. Almost took the team down," Pattie said after feeding her birds and entering her home office to comm her contact.

"That's unfortunate. Could they tell what it was?" the man asked.

"No, that guard—they think they're so smart calling him their cousin—came out. They had to abort."

"They didn't get a chance to drop anything?"

"They dropped a tracer," she said as she checked her manicure. Earlier, she'd dialed in purple passion, the latest shade, which matched her plum suit perfectly. She was really getting quite tired of talking to the man, arrogant asshole that he was. She had a brunch date at the Polo. It wasn't her fault they hadn't found Walter.

Her attempts to sabotage the contract competition hadn't delivered any real results either. At least SpaceZ and Verne were out, but the competition was still moving ahead, along with the damned rescue mission. She had to stop Space Force from exploring into the Oort Cloud. Her birds could die if she didn't. At that thought she tightened her fists until her nails dug painfully into her palms. The pain centered her. She clenched her fists even tighter.

After Marbola had killed almost all the birds on the planet, she had expected humans would stop exploring. Sure, if they wanted to mess around in the solar system, that seemed safe enough. But beyond it? Who knew what diseases lurked? The thought of her precious birds at risk made her dig her nails in deeper.

"What about the hotel?"

"They overrode the vid system. They got into Wolfe and Cussler's offices," Pattie replied impatiently. She really wanted to get off the comm. "They didn't find anything."

"That's too bad."

When he said things like that, Pattie's skin crawled. She'd heard whispers about his cruelty. She wished she could figure out who he was. She also wished he didn't know who she was. That had been a mistake.

"We have some surprises planned for the Mars test," she said. "We should see some results then."

Pattie heard nothing after that. He didn't bother with niceties. He just disconnected. She didn't think he'd come after her, but he was even more unpredictable than her father. *Damn him.*

"You can't discount the fact that the women left the party and ten minutes later someone broke into your offices," said Debbie Cockerill, Xtra's VP of Security, her holo pacing in front of the men gathered in Erik's office.

It looked like she'd been up all night, Erik thought. Considering she was on Ceres conducting a spot security check of Xtra's operations, that was likely. The dwarf planet's day totaled just nine hours, making sleep schedules erratic.

"Two people broke in, one at each office," added Ron, who had joined Erik and Linc that morning.

"Their technology had to be pretty sophisticated to override the vid system," Debbie continued.

"We can keep Alex and Emily on the list of possibilities, but I just don't see them breaking in," Erik said. "Besides, they had to go home because one of their boarders had an accident."

"So they claimed," Ron pointed out. "If anyone could do it, Walter could develop tech that can break through our systems."

"Yes, but why would they want to break in?" Erik got up to program another Americano. It was only 8 a.m., and they'd been up late last night checking to see if anything had been stolen.

"Maybe they want to help Rictor?" Linc suggested, leaning back in his chair.

"You mentioned seeing a big bruise on Alex's back. Any idea how she got it?" Debbie countered, nails tapping on her comm.

"No," Erik grumbled, annoyed after seeing a picture of Alex dancing with Raul in the news earlier. "It doesn't look like they broke into the safes," he said, straightening the skimpads on his desk. The men had looked carefully through their offices again this morning but couldn't find anything missing.

"I can't believe we lost the hacker, too," Linc added.

"For a minute we thought it was someone in the hotel, but we couldn't pin it down." Debbie looked like she wanted to throw something. "The trail jumped off planet after that. We haven't given up," she added before signing off.

"What do you have?" Daniel asked impatiently, his fatigue evident from the late night. The Rictor party had been a complete bore, but he'd stayed late for appearances. All he wanted to do now was relax. Erika was waiting in his bedroom, ready to help him. He always used real women. People who used bots were either disgusting or didn't have enough to afford the real thing.

"We couldn't get in," one man said, shifting nervously in front of the vid, while his partner tried to edge out of view. "An alarm went off, so we had to cut it short."

"What exactly am I paying you for?" Daniel asked softly, the sound of breaking glass making the men more nervous. "And you set off the alarm?" The men couldn't see him. As always, he had blurred his image so they wouldn't be able to identify him, but they could hear him clearly. "I told you to not set off any alarms. You said you were alarm experts."

"We did find safes in the wall behind Wolfe and Cussler's desks," the shorter man said, glancing at his companion.

"I already knew about the safes. I'm the one who told you they were there. Did you manage to get into either of them?" Agitated, Daniel picked up his cat and started petting the Siamese. He'd found Caligula lurking outside his home a year ago. Later, he'd learned that his elderly neighbor, Mrs. Wishbone, owned the cat. He didn't care. Caligula suited him. Finders keepers, and all that.

"We didn't have time to get in," the first man answered, a trickle of sweat running down the side of his face.

"You said at all costs to not get caught," the short man added.

"So you didn't get anything, and you set the alarm off. Now they'll be even more vigilant. Certainly, you don't expect to get paid?"

"It wasn't our fault they had some kinda new alarm tech," the short man whined, nervously twisting the edge of his shirt. He'd heard rumors about this client, how if you blew a job, then you were the one to pay. When they'd taken the job, they believed it would be a breeze, in and out, quick. But the place had some kind of strange new tech he'd never seen before. Just his luck; he hoped it hadn't completely run out.

"It seems my sources weren't as well informed as I thought when they told me about you two. I'll tell them about my dissatisfaction. You can deal with them for payment."

Daniel cut the comm. Pattie had told him the men hadn't found anything, not that they hadn't been able to break into the safes, which was different. He wondered why she'd lied. She'd been acting stranger than usual lately.

# Monday, February 23, 2172

"Five, four, three, two, one, Mars systems in multi-phase lock loop," the Space Force captain announced, signaling the start of the Mars test. "Data coming in. Teams, on mark, ready for downlink. Three, two, one, all systems go."

"Pushing data down. One hundred percent uplink," Alex said into her mike, her voice digitized into Al's male tone. It was 5 a.m., and both Alex and Emily sat in their lab, feeling sleepy yet excited for the Mars test. The only drag about living on the West Coast, since Space Force ran this project out of Goddard, the tests started at 8 a.m. Eastus Earth Time. Alex cradled her warm latte while monitoring the displays. She'd taken lead this morning, letting Emily hang in the background until Alex left for the hotel.

Alex scanned the readouts, including the links' connectivity rates and data uploads and downloads. Ola was performing perfectly as it hovered above the red planet's Jezero Base gathering, compressing, and forwarding all the data Jezero could transmit. On the wall across from them, an image displayed live shots of Goddard's mission control room, as well as each team's project leads with their backgrounds blurred to protect competitive information.

Their view showed a thin man with a dark beard and short,

spiky hair, aka Al. To stay anonymous, she and Emily had created avatars of Al and Lee early on that mirrored their movements. Initially, they had fun altering their appearances, making them fat, then skinny, changing their hairstyles from short to a manbun, adding long bushy beards. Once Alex even added buck teeth. At that point, their uncle warned them that their continuous morphing of Al and Lee's images would generate more interest. Since then, the women kept their avatars' looks consistent, only aging them a little over time.

On the middle left, next to the screen of Goddard, Alex spotted Dahlia, Tiger's project lead. The horrible woman had worked for Seed twenty years ago on a Voyager contract until Walter had discovered her stealing company secrets. Alex and Emily had often wished Walter have been able to prove it, but Dahlia had been too slick. Nor had they been surprised when Tiger Express announced a platform remarkably similar to Seed's after Dahlia joined the company.

"Seeing Dahlia made me think of Marie. I called her about my numser," Alex told Emily as she checked the readouts.

"And?"

"She said Shari had already cleaned up. She was still mad we left early."

"Good thing you tied the stick to me so no one can activate it."

"I should put a tracker on them," Alex said as she continued to scan the displays. To Dahlia's right, Claudia Little filled SpaceZ's spot. She hadn't heard much about Claudia besides that she was smart and capable. "Right after I hung up with Marie—by the way, she didn't like the colors of our dresses, even though they were Juliettes—"

"You're kidding me."

"Daniel commed."

"The dick?"

"He invited me to Versailles for dinner next week."

"Did you barf, or just disconnect and then barf?"

"You would have been proud of how diplomatic I was. I told him to get shanked." Emily, who'd just sipped her tea, started coughing. "Actually, I thanked him. Said I was busy. Then I cut the comm."

"Look at him sitting there." Emily leaned on her desk and glared at the display. "That suit looks like it cost a bundle. I bet it's a Forducci. Want a muffin?" Emily got up and walked over to the counter where Isobelle had left a plate of macadamia nut muffins.

"Sure, thanks. I bet that tie is the exact blue Space Force uses in its logo," Alex added after taking a bite. "Wow, these are really good. He's such a kiss-ass."

"Interesting that Xtra has two leads."

"I like Carlos and Denise. I guess Erik and Linc wanted both a software and hardware engineer for leads."

She and Emily had previously worked with the two engineers and liked and respected both, which spoke volumes for Erik and Linc. She suspected Erik and Linc stood ready to step in if their system needed tweaking. So far, all the teams were performing well. No one was sweating, but the ramp-up had yet to start.

"Increasing download speed on my mark—five, four, three, two, one, active." Alex keyed in the controls to double the download speed. This was the moment when Ola would take off and the team that had the best network solution would be revealed.

"Did you see that?" Emily asked suddenly. "There, there it goes again." Emily started entering commands on her keyboard to even out the numbers.

"Ola team, are you seeing that wobble?" Alex switched from her broad comm to speak directly with their support tech team on Oahu. Even though the women hadn't wanted to run the test from Hawaii after Walter's murder, the rest of the team had remained on-island.

"I'm seeing a high-temp read," Ruthie responded. "It looks like there's a breach in the skin at 3500."

"Activating repair now," Alex said, keying in a series of commands.

Alex and Emily held their breath as a third screen lit, showing Ola, glowing like a golden orb, hovering over the Martian base.

"Can you zoom any more, Ruthie?"

"Trying, Al. Have asked Space Force to either give us cam control or increase zoom."

Suddenly Ola's image expanded, giving the team and Space Force a close-up view of the orb, a hatch sliding open, and a tiny mechanical arm coming out and beginning to seal the orb's skin. Everyone held their breath. After a minute, the arm slowly retracted and the hatch closed.

"Temp falling," Ruthie reported.

"The anomalies have stopped." Alex sat back and took a calming breath. With new materials, there was always the possibility they wouldn't hold up in space. She turned to Emily after muting her comm. "Did you see a flash come from Jezero Base before the wobble started?"

"No, but I was focused on the readouts."

"Hmmm." Alex couldn't be sure she'd seen anything. Fortunately, she'd had the foresight to install the autorep arm and her special space glue in case of a rupture.

"That wear could be the same as what's happening to Larry," Alex told Emily, referring to the robot lizard and the problem she'd noticed with its undercarriage. "I'm pretty sure the new glue will fix it. I'm testing Larry 1.8 tomorrow."

"Didn't you give Space Force some Gummagad for the Farout test, too?"

"I finished it just in time for them to include. Captain, please increase download from the base to Ola. Do not, repeat, do not increase the download from Ola to the teams."

Ola's capabilities far outstripped any data management abilities any of the teams had yet exhibited. At the moment, Alex felt comfortable testing Ola but didn't want to risk any of the teams' equipment, which was all working well enough.

"Space Force, respectfully request download increase to eXo," Erik said over the comm. "We take full responsibility."

"He's crazy!" Alex declared, muting her mic. "Ola's funneling 100 tbp now. However, it's their funeral. Look how smoothly Ola's running though. Good baby Ola." Alex felt like a proud parent as she watched their orb manage the mega loads of data streaming from the Mars base.

"She's humming, but check out eXo."

Alex glanced at eXo and did a double take. eXo was pacing Ola.

"Maybe the rumors are true," Alex said. "Looks like Lockheed's shutting down," she added, seeing their screen go dark, signaling the company was pulling out of the competition. "Are you okay with babysitting the end of the test?" she asked, finishing the rest of her forgotten muffin before pushing away from her desk. Their work with Ola was complete for the Mars portion.

"Farout colony's hanging on," she heard the Space Force captain report as she stood and stretched. "Everyone there wanted to relay their congratulations and is glad to hear Ola's heading their way."

Alex prayed that Ola would reach the base in time.

"I'm good. I'm going to try a few tweaks to see if I can amp up the bandwidth more." Emily said, already focused on her desk display as she delved into Ola's system.

"I'm heading to the hotel. Yell if anything comes up."

"I'm paying you big for results," Daniel warned when Gary accepted the comm. "I'm not seeing them. That attempt to have your contact at Jezero take down Ola failed. Instead, it just gave Al and Lee the opportunity to test some new glue they developed. They should be paying you!" he barked.

When Gary heard the comm go dead a second later, he threw

his litpen across his office so hard it stuck into the wall. Furious, he yanked it out of the wall, broke it in half, and chucked the pieces into the trashcan next to his desk. He wasn't sure who he was angrier at, himself or the asshole on the comm. At least he was pretty sure it was a man, having never actually seen him. The guy had contacted him six months ago, right after Xtra hired Gary. He'd promised to pay an exorbitant amount—half upfront—if Gary would do some undercover work for him. Even though Gary had seen the initial payment arrive in his account, he hadn't heard from the man until last week, right before the tests began.

At least Erik and Linc had gone to Playa. With them and their support staff out of the way, and Ron and his team distracted with a security test they'd scheduled earlier, he could start the loop on the vids covering Erik's office, slip in, and snoop some.

A minute later, he pulled the Camelia painting away from the wall safe hidden behind Erik's desk. Even though the safe had an intricate lock, Gary smiled as he got to work. Locks were one of his specialties.

"What do we have here?" he murmured a minute later, spying a tiny matte-black metallic tube inside. Not wanting to risk setting off any alarms by trying to open it, he pulled out his dampner case, a tool of his that had come in handy many times in the past, and put the tube in the case. If Erik had planted any kind of tracker on the tube, the case would keep it from working.

"I bet this fetches some credits," he said quietly as he stuffed the box back into his pocket. "Unless the asshole's interested." He figured he'd offer it to him first. Then he quickly closed the safe and left the office before anyone discovered him.

Alex padded barefoot toward Erik's office, more than ready to head home once she left her report on Erik's desk. She was relieved he hadn't been at the hotel today. He distracted her too much. She knew he thought she was hiding something, which she was, but not anything that would affect him. She also knew that at some point, he would pry about her bruises. Combine that with her growing attraction to him, which was more than just physical, she felt flustered, for lack of a better word. The more time she spent with him, the more he seemed genuine, not the callous playboy she'd heard about from a few acquaintances. That realization felt even more dangerous.

Noticing the door ajar, she entered his office, shoes in one hand, and looked around to see if anyone was there. She placed the menu samples for opening party on his pristine desk. If he saw her desk in the lab, he'd probably be shocked. Not that it was dirty. It was just a tad messy. Spying the painting behind his desk hanging at an angle, she walked over to straighten it before leaving.

"I'm headed home," Alex told the most sullen assistant she'd ever had. However, at that moment, Sally looked weirdly happy. She'd even smiled. Over the last couple of days, Alex had tried to be friendly, but the woman had a chip on her shoulder the size of Ceres.

"It's a little early, isn't it?" Sally asked, looking pointedly at the pink wall clock, which read 4:55.

"Yes, and we'll both be putting in extra hours soon enough. I can't believe guests will be arriving in three days. You should go home, too." Alex tried to make the woman feel part of the team.

"I still have things to do," Sally said stiffly, turning away to face her keyboard and screen.

*Okkayy,* Alex thought as she commed Jared to let him know she was heading home via the street. Ron had told her he was running some kind of security in the back and advised her to avoid the area. After stepping outside the building, she crossed the footbridge to the parking lot. Jared acknowledged her comm. Just in case, she touched her ring to an earring to activate it. She determined she would never be a victim again as she stepped onto Stone Canyon, looking both ways for anything suspicious.

She waited as the star-tov slowly glided past, the autobot droning on about the hotel, celebrities who had stayed there, and past and present neighbors, both famous and infamous. She smiled and waved at the tourists, cams in hand, who were trying to determine if she fit any category. When summer came, three times as many star-tovs cruised the street, with visitors gaping at the historic pink hotel and neighboring mansions, hoping to spot someone famous.

After it passed, she thought about Erik as she headed home. The more she was around him, the more his appeal grew. Since Charlie, a couple of men had briefly caught her interest, though none like this.

Should she risk a one-nighter with him? She'd only known him a week. She figured he'd be an amazing lover, considering all the women who'd notched their names on his bedpost. Most of those women still adored him and would gladly hook up again, at least according to what she'd read. He'd probably spoil her for anyone else afterward. But would that really be so bad?

He was also super smart. Alex had always found intelligent men attractive. She'd tried to hack that stupid tracking chip he had her put on her comm the other day. She was sure he'd designed it. Granted, she'd only spent a few minutes on it, but she hadn't been able to break into it, which was unusual for her.

Lost in thought, when a tov pulled alongside, she looked up, thinking it was someone asking for directions. Instead, a huge man in a mask jumped out and reached for her arm while holding a white cloth in his other hand.

Trying to jump away, she teetered when her shoe hit a small rock, the man grabbed her arm—the one with her ring. As he raised the cloth to her face, he moved his hand higher on her arm, just a little bit higher. He pushed the cloth over her face. She began to lose consciousness. Some kind of chemical must be on the cloth. Frantic, she reached to touch her ring to his chest. As she finally made contact, the world turned grey. She felt herself falling and heard someone yell her name.

"I'd sure like to get a chance to meet with Al and Lee, or make that Al or Lee," Erik told Linc as they came up Stone Canyon, their tov headed for the hotel. "The way that orb ramped up blew my mind."

"Speaking of getting a moment with someone, what's happening with you and your event planner?" Linc asked. "She seems to be getting under your skin. And, hold on—let me finish—while I think she and that cousin of hers are both hot, something's suspicious, or, heck, I don't know. I just feel we're missing something with those two," he added, drumming his fingers on the tov.

"I know. I get it, but we have some mad chemistry. Regardless, she doesn't want to admit it, at least not yet. I'm trying to take it slow, at least until after the parties."

"Good plan, in fact—"

"Wait, is that her?" Erik grabbed Linc's arm. "What the heck?" One second, Alex was walking up Stone Canyon; the next, a tov rounded the bend, and a big man with a mask and hood covering his face leapt out and ran towards Alex.

The moment Erik saw the masked man heading for Alex, he slammed open the tov's door and jumped out as Linc took the tov's controls and started reversing out of the hotel's lot. As the man grabbed Alex and began dragging her towards the open-doored tov, Erik heart thundered. He worried he wouldn't make it in time. Suddenly, the man shoved a cloth over Alex's face, preventing her from running. Erik summonded every bit of energy he had, fearing he wouldn't get to them before it was too late.

Almost there, he thought frantically, seeing Alex begin to sag. Suddenly, the man made the strangest move, as if he'd been electrocuted, and fell. Not giving a shit about the man or the tov, which was racing away, Erik sprinted toward Alex as she crumbled. Unable to save her completely from hitting the ground, he at least slipped his hand under her head so it didn't split like a melon on the rock in the road.

"Freeze," a deadly voice spoke, and Erik, knees in the mud, slowly turned, still cradling Alex's head. Alex and Emily's supposed cousin was aiming what looked like a special-issue stunner at both him and the masked man, who, still on the ground dazed, was groaning.

"This scum was trying to kidnap Alex." Erik nodded towards the groaning man. "He knocked her out with something. We need to get her to the hospital!"

Just then Linc rode up as Emily ran out of the house.

"She needs to get to the hospital," Erik repeated, standing with an unconscious Alex in his arms. "That asshole knocked her out with something."

"We'll take her to the hospital," Emily told Jared. "Can you deal with that?" she asked, pointing to the masked man who was struggling to get up.

"Yes, I'll call the cops." Jared jabbed his stunner into the man's side. "Once they come, I'll follow to emergency."

Erik leapt into the tov, placing Alex on his lap, while Emily scrambled in behind him. Linc sped down the street, the door closing.

Alex was hearing strange beeping noises. Why was Emily making those sounds in her bedroom when she was trying to sleep? Also, why the heck did her arm hurt, and why did her ribs feel like they were on fire?

Cracking an eye open, she realized she wasn't home. Instead, it looked like a slip in UCLA emergency. What the heck was she doing there? Slowly the haze started to clear. She vaguely remembered a big masked man trying to grab her and putting something over her face. After that, nothing. Suddenly, Emily's worried face came into view.

"Hey cousin. How are you feeling?"

"Like I was hit with a truck," Alex whispered, keeping her voice soft to avoid worsening her pain.

"Do you remember what happened?"

"I—"

"That's enough. No talking, only resting. Her blood pressure is spiking, and we need her calm."

Alex slowly turned her head to see a doctor beside her bed, checking her monitors.

"The lab work will be back soon, and we'll know what he knocked her out with," Alex heard him say as the darkness came again. "She has a nasty bruise on her arm, I expect from her struggling with the kidnapper. She also has other bruises and what appears to be a couple of broken ribs, but those injuries look older." The doctor directed a pointed look at Emily.

"She tripped over a branch about a week ago," Emily said.

"She's a shitty liar," Linc mouthed to Erik as they left the room to head towards the waiting room down the hall. Halfway there, they saw Jared approaching with another big man.

"Thanks for helping today." Jared stopped to look at the two men. "This is my brother, Joe. And that's Marty, my other brother." He nodded towards another well-built giant who was walking up. "We'll take it from here. Do you need a ride back to the hotel?"

"No, we have a tov here. Did the police know anything about that man?"

"They've taken him into custody. They'll let us know what they find out."

"Please keep us informed. If that was a random kidnapping or if someone's targeting Alex."

"Of course," Jared said, dismissing them.

"Brothers, my ass," Erik said to Linc as they headed to the exit. "They don't look anything like either of the women, much less each other. Those guys are military, or I'm a Kuiper doughnut," Erik added as he banged open the exit door in frustration.

As they headed home, Linc wailed on the keyboard. "There's no record of the police coming out."

"Could it be too early to appear?" Erik asked. "Though nothing ever makes sense with that woman."

"It's possible it's too soon for the police report to show. I tied an alert to it in case anything comes up. Speaking of alerts, someone's at it again with Xtra's stock."

"Damn, at least the Mars test went well, but damn. Still no clue who's buying it up?"

"Not yet, but Meg's hot on it, and you know how she can get. By the way, Jorgé asked us to meet him at Pierre's for dinner tonight. I could use a bit of distraction and some celebration after this morning. Want to go?" Linc asked, tucking his comm away as they pulled into the hotel lot.

"Sounds perfect. I'll be ready in fifteen. I want to stop by my office for a second before changing."

Erik and Linc walked down the hall, continuing to discuss their hacker. So far they were down a million, but they knew they'd be able to recover the money.

"I could have sworn I locked the door last night," Erik said, noticing his office door ajar.

"You did. I saw you do it." Linc followed Erik inside.

"Everything looks the same. Let me check the safe." Erik moved the picture and scanned the lock. "Well, lookie here. Someone's taken the bait." Eric stepped aside so Linc could peer in.

"I want a list of anyone who was in or near my office today," Erik commed Ron, filling him in on the theft.

"Give me a minute to check the vids," Ron responded.

"Interesting they just took the tube." Linc continued to rifle through the safe. "They didn't take anything else."

"Ron, when you have the list, copy Debbie when you send it to us. Ask her if anyone stands out." Erik closed his comm with the security chief and turned to Linc. "I could really use a drink now."

"Me too," Linc said. "See you in five?"

"Four."

A half hour later, Erik and Linc pulled into Pierre's lot.

"What are they doing here?" Erik exclaimed, spotting the familiar "Allee Cats" license plate as they entered Pierre's lot. "Is she really that much of a partyer? I don't get it. It's almost as if she's two different people."

Just when Erik felt he understood Alex, she did something that seemed, at least to him, out of character. He couldn't keep up, he thought. He was tired of the social scene, and if Pierre's restaurant didn't serve such amazing food, he wouldn't have bothered coming. The fact she was there, after almost being kidnapped and a trip to ER, made him wonder who she really was.

"Looks like the rest of the relatives are here, too," Linc said, noticing Jared, Joe, and Marty at the bar trying to blend in. Erik was busy watching Alex, who was standing with Emily near that same door she'd disappeared into before.

"Is Jared coming?" Alex asked, checking her dress after she floated into the tov and sat next to Emily. They were going to Pierre's. She knew she probably should have stayed home, but she was done hiding. She had a new numser, and had charged her earrings and ring. She was ready to take down any asshole who tried even looking at her wrong. They also had reinforcements the General had assigned after this morning's kidnapping attempt. Alex almost laughed out loud at the thought of the three special forces men saying they were brothers, their only similarity being their massive builds.

The med the doctor had injected her with had cleared her system of the drug she'd inhaled. It had also numbed her pain. In fact, she felt great. She was ready to hand the disc to Pierre and dance.

"Right on our tail with his 'family,'" Emily said, making quote marks around the last word.

"I don't think Erik and Linc bought that story," Alex said as the tov pulled into *Pierre's* lot, Jared and company close behind.

"We only have seven days left, and actually that seventh doesn't count since that's when the interview runs. We only have to hide for six more days," Emily said as they entered the club.

"Ladies, thank you for coming. Even though we're being very careful packing the roboswans for their move to the hotel, I'm glad you came to check everything." Pierre motioned Alex and Emily to the door; Jared and the other two men rose to stand an unobtrusive guard.

Once the women and Pierre reached the back room, Alex handed Pierre the disc. Later that night he would deliver it to General who hadn't been able to come tonight. Then Alex and Emily checked to make sure the swans had been packed correctly for their move to the hotel for the *Swan Song* parties. Finished, they reentered the main part of Pierre's. The floors were filling, and several women and a few men had started flirting with their 'cousins.'

"Check out upstairs," Emily subtly nodded to the restaurant on the third floor.

Alex looked up to see the beautiful waitress she'd met a month ago while preparing the club for its reopening. She was serving Erik and his friends, all of whom were smiling broadly as she took their orders. Alex had heard another employee call her 'sex on a stick.' While she found the waitress stunning, she had found her nice, as well as smart, hearing later she was working her way towards a joint Ph.D. and M.D. in Marcology.

"Well, they certainly look like they're enjoying themselves," Alex muttered, not liking the sharp stab of jealousy spearing through her. She had a roaring impulse to grab the waitress, hit her with volts, and then chuck her over the balcony. Catching herself, she told herself to chill, relieved no one could read her mind. She also made a mental note never to accept the med the doctor had given her again, especially if she had something important to do.

"Come on." Alex nudged her friend toward the dance floor. "There's Raul. Let's go dance with him."

Three songs later, Alex felt the med begin to wear off. Soon she'd want to head home, smear some Erisalve on, crawl into her soft bed, and nurse her aches until they numbed again or she fell asleep, whichever came first. She figured she'd last a couple more dances, and unless Emily wanted to leave sooner, they'd leave. Pleading thirst and, seeing her friend Tracy, Alex left the floor to talk to her. As she walked up, she motioned to Tracy to follow her below the balcony so she couldn't see Erik glowering down from the restaurant.

"Hey Alex, how's it going?" Tracy smiled at her friend. "I noticed your new boss upstairs. He didn't look too happy to see you down here enjoying yourself. Come to think of it, Cussler didn't look happy either, but he was looking at Emily. What gives?" she continued, keeping her voice low. "I hear the doctors still have Susan sedated. And I'm hearing it might not have been an accident?"

Alex and Emily had met Tracy one summer day while walking on Waikiki Beach. Tracy's mother was in the habit of dumping Tracy at the beach everyday so she could go off and spend time with husband number six. As a result, Tracy spent the entire summer with the girls, Alex and Emily's Auntie taking her under the family wing. They'd been tight ever since.

Now a reporter at the *Global Times*, Tracy was the only person who knew Al and Lee's true identities besides the General, his wife, and Pierre. Tracy'd discovered it accidentally one summer when she'd gone to visit. She'd then told them her secret, which cemented the friendship. Back then, Alex and Emily had nicknamed her the shark because she was so freakishly intuitive and ballsy when it came to sniffing out a story.

"I'm hearing it wasn't an accident either, but not a word," Alex said under her breath before downing a glass of sparkling Taka water.

"Damn," Tracy said. "Are you still planning on coming out, so to speak, once the contract's announced?"

"Yes, we're ready. Still want the exclusive?"

"Does a hot space man play around?" Tracy rubbed her hands together with glee. "I told my editor that I'll have something really big that day. No, I didn't give him a hint even though he tried to bribe me with a box of Chocmate."

"That's playing dirty. Did you grab the box before telling him you couldn't say anything?"

"How'd you know?" Tracy asked, taking a sip of her martini. "By the way, what do you think of your new boss, besides the fact that he's extremely attractive? His admin commed me today. She said they want to give me and Raygan, that reporter from *Space*, semi-exclusives on an Xtra development."

"I wonder what it is? So far, he's been professional," Alex answered, ignoring Tracy's attractive comment.

"Interesting that you're ignoring my comment about his looks, not to mention that you've turned pink. What gives?"

"Alex, come dance some more." Raul grabbed Alex's hand and pulled her back to the dance floor.

"Come on." Alex, glad for Raul's rescue, motioned to her friend to join them.

Several songs later, Alex motioned to Emily that she was done dancing and to Tracy that they were leaving. She felt they'd been there long enough to make it look like they'd come to party, barely long enough, but it was the best she could do. She noticed Tracy, who waved back and blew them a kiss, looked like she was having fun with Raul. *Interesting*, she thought. Since Raul was trustworthy and Tracy was no idiot, she didn't worry about leaving her with him.

"Let's get out of here," Alex said as a wave of weariness nearly leveled her.

"You're on. Darn, Erik and Linc are both looking this way, and neither looks happy. Quick," Emily said as they grabbed their coats and headed outside. "Crap, alert, alert, Daniel the Dick's approaching," Emily whispered as they stepped outside.

"Alexandra, I should have known I'd find you at LA's hottest club," Daniel said. "Oh, that's right, didn't you help with the decorations or something? Emily." He didn't count Emily as someone worthy of attention. He never had. He also knew Emily didn't like him after that little scene when he'd dumped Alex on Bellagio. "You aren't leaving. It's so early," he said, placing his arm around both women, smiling for the paparazzi out front.

"I have a terrible headache." Alex smiled for the vids, realizing she wasn't even lying to the odious man as their tov pulled up.

"Yes, she has a bad headache," Emily said, grabbing Alex's hand. "We're going home. Our tov's here."

Jared and his brothers suddenly appeared and stepped in front of them, making an open path for them to get to the vehicle.

"Later," Emily called as she practically shoved Alex in the tov. "We just dodged that bullet. To top it off, I think I saw Linc and Erik coming through the door." Emily noticed her cousin's pale face. "Jared and company are behind us. We can relax. And you're safe; that's what's important. Did you see that bimbo practically sitting in Linc's lap?" Emily asked with a huff.

Alex would be more interested in her cousin's reaction if she felt better. As she pulled the numser out of her hair, letting it cascade down, she thought she'd have to mull it over later when she felt halfway coherent. She then leaned back in the seat with a sigh.

"Alex, Emily, you have a silver tail, and, damn, another tov just blocked us," Jared said over the comm. "Can you pull that trick you showed me the other day?"

"Not until we're off Sunset. But give us a sec. Engage manual." Alex rattled off a command that generated three duplicate holos of their tov, complete with Alex and Emily as passengers. The replicas appeared behind their tov, causing their tail to swerve with their sudden emergence. Alex told the comp to create two more holos in front of them. "That will give us a bit of a breather."

"A bit," Emily said. "Let's exit at Wilshire." She keyed some commands into the board she'd pulled out.

"Jared, we're pulling off the 405. One of the holos will run up Wilshire towards Westwood. The rest will stay on Sepulveda with us," Alex reported, looking behind her, spotting an unfamiliar silver vehicle jetting in and out of traffic, trying to keep up.

"Hold on. We're going to exit fast," she said as she dropped the craft two levels, barely squeaking between a cruiser and lumbering autobus, and sped across three crowded lanes to exit the airway onto Wilshire right on the tail of another autobus. Using the bus as a shield, Alex pulled a quick U-turn, with loud horns, yells, and unfortunately their tail following them as they flew up Sepulveda.

"Damn, we didn't lose them, but we're almost to Montana." Emily looked back. "Fortunately, we can go invisible when we turn into Westwood. There shouldn't be too many out on a weeknight."

"Stealth," Alex commanded as she turned. Two of the remaining holos sped up Sepulveda. "We just have to cross Sunset, and we should be home free. Jared's tov's behind our tail."

"We're trying to stop it, but it keeps outpacing us," Jared said over the comm.

"Since they can't see us, we should be fine." Alex quickly

glanced back, keeping the tov so low it almost touched the ground.

"Watch out!"

"I see it! Dang cat," Alex answered, as they both sighed in relief that the cat, sensing something was headed for it, had fled back to the grass.

As they crossed Sunset, heading further into the hills and towards home, the two remaining holos slowed just enough so the silver tail following them could see as one holo turned left and the other right.

"They fell for it, and we got a trace, too," Jared said. "Be careful; we're about thirty seconds behind. Let me know if you see anything suspicious. We'll be coming in hot behind you."

"Will do," said Alex with a sigh.

This day had been horrible, except for the Mars test. Eva had blazed through all the necessary operations to get the Ola unit working above Jezero Base. Later, Alex planned to make the system completely autonomous. She had to wait for the test to finish first.

Eva had saved some valuable time on the schedule, which would likely be crucial once her ship reached Farout. So far the planet's backup systems were holding, but they would need every available second to set up the Ola unit and reload the systems before the colony's systems completely failed. As it was, she'd heard they'd already cut their environmentals to fifty percent.

# Tuesday, February 24, 2172

"This looks good." Erik closed the final report Alex had brought him. The two were meeting in his office, sitting in the guest chairs facing his desk, as they reviewed the last details for the hotel opening and upcoming parties. "Did you put Chloe in the Grace Kelly Suite? She called me yesterday. I meant to confirm that with you. I told Susan about it several weeks ago."

Alex could chew nails. Unfortunately, Susan, or someone, had assigned Chloe the Swan Lake Suite instead. Not only did she feel that ugly snake of jealousy upon hearing Chloe had called Erik directly, but she also felt intimidated by the beautiful, talented actress, a feeling she rarely experienced, especially as she hadn't even met the woman.

She also felt frustrated, as she'd just finished reviewing the room assignments with Martha, housekeeping's manager, to ensure each VIP had the right suite as well as the items they'd requested. She couldn't believe Samantha's agent had commed, telling them the actress expected toilet paper in her suite—perfumed and pink. Who used toilet paper anymore, much less heard of any colored and scented? Fortunately, Martha had been able to locate some.

"That's not a problem, is it?" Erik asked. "Oh, that's wrong, too?" comprehension hitting when he saw Alex's expression.

"It seems that way. I had her in the Swan Lake Suite. I'll fix it."

"Jorgé was supposed to be in the Swan Lake Suite."

"I have him in the Bel Suite," Alex answered, making notes on her comm.

"He hates heights," Erik said simply, raising an eyebrow at her questioning look.

"Okayyy," Alex said, looking at her options. "Do you think Mr. Fieldstone would be good for the Bel Suite?"

"Put him in the Camellia Suite."

The two went over the rest of the VIPs, and thankfully the rest were fine. Closing her comm, Alex rose to return to her office and meet with Martha to review the changes.

"One other thing." Erik watched as Alex sank back into her seat. She's always so ready to leave, he thought grumpily. He could have any other woman he wanted, usually with just a nod, but this one was practically immune, "practically" being the key word he had to keep in mind. He'd noticed the perplexed look on her face when he caught her gazing at him the other day, and that day at the pool, he knew he'd seen interest in her eyes.

Now, after yesterday's attempted kidnapping—about which Ron still hadn't been able to uncover any leads—and the latest news regarding the wasps that Manny had just told him about, her reluctance to be with him chafed.

"Manny told me this morning he'd found little piles of raw beef all along the hotel's fence that runs parallel to your property and on the grounds between the fence and your place. Wasps were buzzing around each of the piles," he added, seeing her confusion turn into alarm. "How allergic are you?"

"Deathly," Alex whispered, turning pale, as she tried to grasp the implications. Even though medical science could eliminate 99.9% of allergic reactions, Alex's body for some reason reacted differently, and the doctors still hadn't been able to figure out why. She'd discovered that after a near-fatal wasp sting when she almost didn't make it to their medpac in time. Fortunately, they'd had a Level Five pack.

"What's going on, Alexandra?" Erik demanded, leaning forward in his seat, frustration mixing with alarm at her pallor. "You have bruises that look like you've been beaten, someone tried to kidnap you yesterday, and now this!" Seeing her withdraw, he wanted to shake her until she spilled the truth.

With Erik's concern, she felt herself crumble. A tear slipped down her face as she stood looking at him through watery eyes. She couldn't answer, couldn't tell him the truth. Someone was after her—someone who killed her uncle and might try to target Emily. She had to stay quiet for just six more days.

"Damn you, I can't stand that you don't trust me," he gritted out, pulling her into his arms and sitting back down, cradling her in his lap. Since his sister was little, this was how he soothed her, gently rubbing her back until she calmed.

He'd seen lots of tears before, mostly as attempts at manipulation, but that single tear undid him. He stroked her back, up and down, as gently as possible so as not to cause her any more pain. God, he didn't want to cause any more pain as she sat rigidly until, finally, she leaned into his chest, silent tears wetting his shirt.

Finally, exhausted, she sat up, creating space between them, which he hated. When she finally looked up at him, her beautiful blue eyes glistened like bright crystals. He couldn't help but raise a hand to gently caress her cheek, giving her time to pull away if she chose. He leaned in closer until his lips met hers. After a second, she tilted her head for better access, clutched his shirt, and pulled him close.

She knew she shouldn't be kissing him—nor he her—but these last weeks had been horrible. Her defenses had shattered. The attraction she felt for him—well—she'd never felt this heat or pull, even with Charlie. And right now, she craved his warmth and caring because she felt so very cold inside. As he deepened the kiss, she felt herself melt.

"Alexandra, Miss Bird is here to see you," Sally announced, standing at the door to Erik's office.

Caught off guard, Alex and Erik jerked apart. Incredibly embarrassed, Alex jumped off Erik's lap and turned toward the woman, catching a flash of what looked like hatred in her eyes.

"Well, that was an interesting seat you had, my dear," Miss Bird said to Alex as she entered the office. Alex almost tripped in her haste to separate herself from Erik. Regaining her balance, Alex walked over to Miss Bird and gave her a big hug, drinking up the love the woman had always shared with her.

"Thank you, Sally." Alex turned to the woman who was still standing in the doorway, her gaze fixed intently on the scene. "Miss Bird and I will be having lunch at Puck's if you need anything."

"That woman shouldn't be trusted," Miss Bird said once Sally left, closing the door behind her. "She's about as friendly as a rabid rattler, and possibly as dangerous. I thought I'd told you that already, young man." She turned to Erik accusingly after linking arms with Alex.

"We're not keeping her on after the opening." Erik felt like a boy being lectured, a feeling he only had around Miss Bird. "You're going to lunch?" he added, hoping for an invitation, curious to see Alex and the old lady together.

"Yes, and you may join us if that's alright with Alexandra," Miss Bird said. "Well, Alex, speak up."

"Yes, Miss Bird, that would be fine." Alex noticed a gleam of satisfaction on Erik's face.

"Before we go, I'm must tell you both that I was shocked to see that display in the office. First, you shouldn't be carrying on where others can see you." The tiny, white-haired lady wagged her finger at them. "Unless you're both exhibitionists, making out should not be a spectator sport.

"Second, young man, to quote an old saying, 'If you like it, you should put a ring on it.' Alex is a special woman not to be trifled with, or you'll be hearing from me, and I'll stop taking care of your birds. Lecture is now over. Let's go eat."

With her arm still linked with Alex's, Miss Bird marched out the door, leaving Erik wondering what had just happened.

As Erik headed back to his office, he wished he had another piece of Isobelle's pie. Unfortunately, there hadn't been any left. When the bot had entered the dining room earlier with Chef Leon, each carrying a macadamia nut pie, Erik wasn't sure what was up.

Leo, as Erik secretly called the demanding chef, was dressed in his usual spotless whites, keeping pace with Isobelle, wearing grey linen slacks and blouse. When she turned to ask one of his hovering servers to bring some forks, he saw intricately embroidered on her back the words, "I would challenge you to a battle of wits, but I see you're unarmed." He wondered if she knew how funny she was. Alex had mentioned something about Isobelle studying humor. Leo placed the pies on a side table and, after greeting Miss Bird, proceeded to cut slices that Isobelle then put in front of everyone, the two expectantly waiting for a reaction.

"This should be on the menu," Chef Leon said adamantly, ready to do battle for the pies. "Miz Isobelle just brought them over and es willing to share her recipe," he added, sincere admiration for the housekeeper evident in his expression as he looked at her.

"It is macadamia-nut month," Isobelle said simply, "and I heard you were here, Miss Bird."

After the pies had been demolished, everyone unanimously agreed they were a hit. In fact, Erik was ready for another piece. He'd left Alex and Miss Bird in Puck's, where the two were huddled together, finishing their coffee and tea before heading to the back storage room. Alex wanted to show Miss Bird the robotic swans that had just arrived from Pierre's and would hang from the ballroom ceiling for the *Swan Song* parties this weekend.

Lost in thought, Erik stopped mid-stride as he glanced into Alex's office. On one side of her display, pictures scrolled of Alex and Emily from the previous night at Pierre's, dancing and talking with their too-close friend Raul, the pompous Daniel, and several other men he didn't know. On the other side, it looked like some kind of code was scrolling, but the screen went dark before he could examine it closer.

Damn, he thought, he must have been seeing things. Alex was an enigma, and it was making him crazy. One minute he thought she needed protection; the next, he wondered if she was a thief. He decided to step into her office for a quick look around to see if anything else seemed unusual.

Aside from a packet of Marbola tabs on the floor next to the trash can—did everyone really use those vile things?—and that weird lizard, the only other thing he saw was a basket of mushrooms sitting in the middle of her desk. Suddenly, he remembered her saying at the Rictor's party that she was allergic to mushrooms, too. Picking up the basket, he took another look around before walking out to find Sally at her desk.

"Sally, where did this basket come from?"

"It was delivered while you were at Puck's."

"I'm taking it to my office. If Alex asks about it, please tell her I have it," he said.

Once inside his office, he placed the basket on a side table and, spying a card, opened it.

*"Mushrooms are brown,*
*Violets are blue,*
*Please accept this gift because*
*I love you."*

"What a lousy poem," Meg said, looking over his shoulder. "Sorry, I thought you heard us come in," she added when Erik jerked around.

"What poem, and what's the basket of fungi for?" Linc asked, dialing an Americano before sitting down.

"It was delivered a little while ago for Alex."

"Didn't she say that she's allergic to them when we were at the Rictors?" Linc asked, sipping his coffee.

"Yes, that and wasps. This morning, Manny found little piles of meat along the fence and in the area between the hotel and her house. They were covered with wasps."

"That's weird. It's as if someone's trying to hurt Alex," Meg mused out loud.

"Everything is weird when it comes to Alex," Erik muttered, increasingly weary of the mystery.

"Well, it will all be over in five days, unless you want to keep Alex on the payroll longer," Linc said.

"She's really good at what she does, but she's not the only event planner," Erik replied. "No, I don't think I want to keep her on." He didn't want her to keep working for him so he could explore the hot chemistry that was driving him increasingly nuts.

"You certainly want to do something with her. You've never been this wound up by a woman." Meg said, innocently stirring her mocha, topped with a mound of whipped cream and some chocolate sauce.

A half hour later, after Linc left and Erik cleared his comm of the latest messages, he decided to check if Alex was back in her office. He wanted to tell her about the mushrooms, show her the card, and see if she knew anything about the sender.

As Alex walked into her office after her lunch with Miss Bird, she almost ran into Sally. "Can I help you?"

"I was just putting the latest orders that came in for the party on your desk," Sally said briskly as she turned to leave, almost pushing Alex out of the way.

What a lovely person. Sighing, Alex logged into the hotel comm, but nothing happened. After a few more tries, she asked Sally to call tech support.

"Well, well, well, what did you do now?" Gary asked nastily as he strolled into her office a few minutes later. "Can't you manage a simple comm?"

If Alex had a knife, she would have stuck him. As it was, she really wanted to shock him—the big shock, not the little one.

"If you don't fix this now and get out of here, I'm going to HR," Alex hissed, carefully keeping her voice low so Sally couldn't hear them. "You were an ass before, and you still are."

"Look who grew some balls—itty, bitty ones. However, you're still a frigid bitch," Gary snarled back, stepping forward and invading her space. "You think you're so smart. If there weren't so many people around, I'd—"

"Alex, is everything okay?" Erik asked, as he entered her office, noticing Gary standing altogether too close to her.

"Her comm stopped working," Gary told Erik, then turned back to Alex and glared. "I think someone must have spilled some ice water on it, but it's fixed now. Call the help desk if you have any other problems."

"Do you have some kind of history?" Erik asked, feeling a familiar stab of jealousy. Gary was a smart guy and ok looking, although something seemed off about him.

"We have the wrong kind of history, but I don't want to go into it. Suffice to say, I don't like working with him."

"I'll see to it that you don't have to deal with him anymore." Erik suddenly felt a sense of relief with her honesty and the fact that she didn't like Gary. "I came to tell you a basket of mushrooms came for you today, along with a card." He handed the card to Alex. "And yes, I took the liberty of reading it. Aren't you deathly allergic to mushrooms? I remember you saying that at the party last Saturday."

"First the wasps, now the mushrooms," Alex said, reading the poem. "I have no idea who could have sent them, much less this terrible poem. I know I said I'm allergic. I'm not. I just hate them, and I say that so I don't have to eat them at Marie and Stephen's. They always have a lot of mushroom dishes."

"Someone thinks you're allergic," Erik says, walking around her desk, spying the lizard again, and picking it up. Strange, he thought absently as he turned the lizard over, trying but failing to identify the material it was made of before setting it down. "I didn't know you were going to be at *Pierre's* last night. Don't you think you should have rested some? And how well do you know Daniel DuBois and that Raul Sepulveda?" Erik thought of the pictures he'd seen on her display.

"Daniel DuBois is an all-around ass," Alex said, not caring about her present lack of filter. "And Raul's an old family friend."

"How close a family friend?" Erik growled, misinterpreting her smile when she talked about Raul. "I hope he's not going to be a distraction."

"Are you kidding me?" Alex exclaimed, angry by Erik's implications.

"Why were you at Pierre's last night? You didn't say anything about going earlier," he added as she started clearing her desk for the day.

"I didn't know I needed to tell you what I do in my free time," Alex replied, feeling cranky after a full day ensuring everything was ready for the opening, the parties, and all the incoming VIPs and their stupid demands. Not to mention his continuing pull, which was beginning to completely fray her nerves. "If the offer's still there, I planned to use the Pelo2000 in the gym. I left today's report on your desk. Also, don't forget I'm taking a personal day tomorrow," she added as she turned to grab her coat, comm, tennis shoes, and flee.

"You promised 24x7 availability," Erik said stiffly, stepping in front of her to block her path, standing so close that if she moved an inch forward, her body would brush against his.

*Do not back up; do not back up. Don't let him see how he affects me*, she told herself.

"You already approved that. Good night," Alex snapped, starting to brush past him.

"What you do to me, little pixie," Erik said, hauling Alex up against him. "I know Miss Bird said no PDA, but you make me crazy," he muttered as he slammed his mouth on hers.

Alex, overwhelmed by the heat she felt from Erik's lips on hers, gasped, giving Erik the opportunity to dive in and deepen the kiss.

Hearing Sally slam a drawer jolted Alex back to reality, just enough to wrench away. Grabbing her gym bag, she rushed out and down the hall, crossing the brick path to the gym without even bothering to change her shoes. She had to pull it together. Too much was happening. *And who the heck sent her those mushrooms?* she wondered as she changed into her old black yoga pants and favorite blue top. The top had a few holes, but she had a workout bra underneath, so they didn't expose anything important. Besides, she wasn't there to look like a model, not that she ever did. She was there to sweat and release all this anxiety.

A few minutes later, she felt as though she'd gone to heaven. The new Pelo adjusted perfectly to her height—short—and legs—short—and arms—also short. She and Emily had an ancient Pelo1000 at the house, courtesy of her father's second wife, and, while that was better than nothing, this felt like full-on fricking luxury. The seat was soft but supportive, and she barely noticed the goggles. The display was amazing as she scrolled through all the ride choices, stopping with utter glee when she discovered the new Enceladus ride she'd heard about.

Dialing in the Saturn moon, she jetted down through the icy, bright-white atmosphere to the surface, speeding around craters and giant jets of water vapor shooting ice up to feed Saturn's E-ring, the ice then falling back down like snow. As if that wasn't enough, once she reached Enceladus' southern region, the ride cut through a wide crack in the moon's surface. She screamed down twenty miles below the surface to a hidden ocean, where she could see all the bizarre but beautiful sea creatures explorers had discovered as she pedaled through the water, fighting against the heavy current she'd dialed into the program.

Erik walked in thirty minutes later, needing to let off some steam. He hoped Alex would still be there. He felt he should apologize. He didn't know what came over him when she was around, but she was like a drug, distorting his thoughts, his actions, everything. There she was. She was beautiful, with a smile on her face as she rode like a bat out of hell through some imaginary world. He wondered which one she'd picked. It didn't surprise him that she wasn't wearing the latest workout gear. She hadn't styled her hair in some fancy way like some women did for their 'workouts.' Instead, she was sweating profusely, bits of hair plastered to her flushed face, sweat soaking through her top.

He was sunk, he thought, as he stepped on the tread. He'd planned to try a run on Ganymede, another new Pelo adventure, but instead feasted on the sight of the woman next to him reflected in the mirror as he started to pound away.

When she finished the ride, she felt so much better, drenched, hot, and her muscles loose. As she stepped off the bike and started to stretch, she glanced around the beautiful gym, shocked to see Erik sweating on the Pelo tread to her left. She hadn't heard him enter, or notice him start running next to her, she'd been so into her ride. Now she drank him in, captivated by his powerful thigh muscles bunching and releasing as he powered through an interval. Sweat dripped from his face, dampening his tank in a sexy path that trailed past his waistband. The man could have been a model. In fact, she bet he'd been approached when younger. Suddenly, as her gaze rose back up to his face, she saw him looking at her. *Great, you dummy,* she thought, embarrassed to be caught staring at him like he was an ice cream cone she'd like to lick. She had to get out of there.

"Thanks for letting me ride. See you Thursday," she blurted before fleeing.

"You can ride any time you want," Erik called after her, especially him, he thought. He'd seen her checking him out, and by the guilty look on her face, she approved of what she'd seen. If he caught her in the gym again, he thought unashamedly, he'd skip the tank.

"Unfortunately, when we found the tov that was tailing you last night, no one was there, and it had been cleaned," the General said, his holo pacing in front of Alex and Emily as they sat in their lab. "We did get some information from the guy who tried to kidnap you, though not much. Turns out he was a bot."

"I didn't see a tattoo," Emily said. "I'd have remembered that."

"That wasn't the only interesting thing. Someone deactivated him remotely, but before that happened, we were able to get a few bits. He was working for Solars."

"Solars is real then," Alex said, getting up and almost tripping over Fred's paw hanging off his dog bed.

The anti-expansionist group they'd heard their uncle mention was more of a threat than they'd expected, she thought.

"Do you think the group had anything to do with Uncle Walter's death or my attack?" Alex asked.

"We're looking into it. We've activated a task force. Even if they didn't, the fact that they sent a bot means you have to be even more careful."

# Wednesday, February 25, 2172

As Alex stirred her coffee, she looked out the kitchen window to see the jumble of reporters, cameras, and tovs milling around in front of the house.

"They showed up early," Rosie commented, glancing out, before putting a plate away in the cupboard.

"Did you hear what they're calling it?" Alex asked.

"Let me guess. Something stupid?" Emily muttered as she stirred some honey into her mug of tea.

Five years ago, when the Space Force officer arrived at the house to tell Alex that Charlie and Sam's ship hadn't landed at Farout's Base Station or responded to any messages, Emily had just come from Hawaii. Once the media discovered their disappearance, the news rose to a froth, reporters detailing every aspect of the two handsome explorers and the cousins' double wedding. In the wake of the astronauts' disappearance, humanity both on- and off-planet waited anxiously—hour-by-hour, then day-by-day—for any news. Yet, no news ever came—no peep, no blip, nothing. The media, milking the tragedy, labeled the incident a heartbreaking love story, dubbing it "Love Lost in Space Times Two."

Now, on the five-year anniversary of their disappearance, to Alex and Emily's dismay, the press resurrected the headline, adding "Five Years Later: Where Are They Now?" In the last couple of days, they'd been inundated with requests for interviews. Now, reporters had set up camp in front of the house. Earlier, one reporter had even captured a hazy vid from the street, mistakenly believing he had seen Alex with the dogs. It was really Isobelle.

"I'm so grateful you're here." Alex slung her arm around Emily and rested her head against her cousin's shoulder before they both donned their jackets, called the dogs, and headed up the hill.

"At least it isn't raining," Alex said when Emily grumbled about the "lousy, foggy, cold weather" as they crested the top.

"There's that," Emily agreed, unzipping her jacket, now warm from the climb. "Why did we decide to put the memorial up here?" she asked as she slipped off her jacket and set it on the ground to sit on.

"We thought it was a good idea at the time." Alex nudged her cousin aside, making room for herself to sit on Emily's jacket as well.

"Hey, that's my jacket!"

"It's already muddy. Why should I get mine dirty?"

"Next year, it's your jacket. I can't believe it's been five years." Emily peered through the fog that hung over the canyon to the hills misty in the morning light. "How are you feeling?"

"Honestly, kind of numb." Alex rested her chin on her knees and looked out. "I'm more upset about Wally. Is that terrible? And I'm surprised at the publicity. I thought the press would have stopped the annual rehash by now."

'Me, too. I feel the same about Uncle Wally, too. I still can't believe he's gone. We need to plan his memorial after the tests finish." Emily took a slow, deep breath, one of her ways to settle her anxiety.

"Let's get the new lantern in place," she added a minute later.

Once on her feet, she started pulling out the weeds that had grown into their makeshift memorial.

After the judge officially declared the men dead a month after their disappearance, Space Force held a big formal funeral. Following that, Alex and Emily privately climbed the hill behind the house and left a lantern at the top to shine out into the night. They knew the lantern wouldn't change anything but, for them, the symbol of hope comforted them as the chance of finding the men's spaceship faded. Since then, every year, they climbed the hill, checked the lanterns, and added a new one. This year they added a fifth, which Emily pulled from her pack.

Alex silently cleaned the four other lanterns with the water and rags she'd brought. As she righted one that some animal had knocked over, she thought of Charlie, her wonderful, fun-loving, life-loving husband.

She realized she was finally ready to say goodbye and let go. Not let go of the memory or the warmth she felt when she thought of him, but possibly the chains she'd wrapped around her heart. Walter had always told her and Emily that they shouldn't stop living. That Charlie and Sam wouldn't have wanted them to hide away. However, until now, she hadn't been ready to step out of Charlie's orbit.

After Alex righted the lamp so it stood at attention alongside the four others, each one upright like a sentinel, she sat next to Emily and linked arms with her. As Fred laid his head across her feet, they listened to the robins and jays chattering as the fog burned off and the butterflies and bees meandered from poppy to poppy.

"Five more days," Alex said as the women and dogs trekked down the hill.

"I'm ready," Emily said after noticing her cousin's concern. "Let's plan Walter's memorial after that. Decide on a time when everyone can come, Walter's friends, the General, and Mary."

"I'm not going to invite Charlie's family. I forgot to tell you. Charlie's mother, Bernadette, called. She wanted to thank me, actually she wanted me to thank Uncle Wally for trying one last time to reach Charlie's ship."

Alex didn't even know how to feel about Bernadette's comm. She hadn't talked to the woman in five years. Bernadette's choice, not hers. Part of Alex understood, but it had really hurt when Charlie was lost, and Bernadette, along with the rest of Charlie's family, had closed ranks and not included her. Bernadette had always made it clear that she believed Alex wasn't good enough for Charlie. He came from old Boston money. Once Alex had overheard his mother call her an L.A. hussy. Alex figured Bernadette somehow blamed her for his loss. That if she'd been a better wife, Charlie would have stayed on Earth instead of traipsing all over the Solar System. Alex knew that wasn't true. Charlie was a traveler—it was in his bones. And while she hoped Ola that would help find his and Sam's ship, she knew it was impossible they'd still be alive.

"She still hasn't given up hope?"

"Doesn't sound like it," Alex said as they navigated the old path down the hill. "I also don't want to invite any of the Rictors. Is that bad?" She almost tripped on a fallen branch.

"We're only inviting the people we want—the people who were important to Wally." Emily grabbed hold of Fred's collar to steady herself on a steep part of the hill, the German Shepherd being more surefooted than her.

"Barney, stop it!" Alex admonished the little white robot dog that was circling her, nearly causing her to trip. "That new download makes Barney act like a puppy. I think I liked him better as an old dog."

"Iso said he was running around so much yesterday she locked him in the pantry. Then he chewed a hole in a bag of rice. There was rice everywhere. I'll change his code back," Emily said as the two entered the house.

"Hey Iso, what's up?" Alex asked, seeing Isobelle waiting for them.

"Sergeant Kahue from Honolulu PD commed. Someone broke into Walter's house. Fortunately, they set off the alarm, and HPD was close by. However, they did not find anyone there when they arrived. He asked Hilda to go through the house. She told him it did not look like anything was missing. The Sergeant said he notified the General."

"Damn it, why can't they leave us alone?' Emily asked.

"They must still be looking for Uncle Wally's files," Alex said. "That's the only thing that makes sense."

"What the hell's your problem? I've paid you a shit ton for Seeds' files, and again you come up with nothing. And you set off the alarm! What the hell? You were supposed to be good. Did you get anything?" Daniel spewed, pacing furiously in front of the giant desk that had just been delivered. He knew he shouldn't have spent so much on the custom piece, but once Rictor won the contract, he'd be flush again.

"No, they must not be there," the man whined. "They must be hid someplace else. I found the safe; it was empty. I can't find things if they're not there. And that alarm system was unlike any I've seen before.

"I want my money back," Daniel said. "You've been nothing but a waste of time."

"I can't find anything if it's not there," the man repeated. "And no refunds. I made that clear up front. I've broken in twice now. There's nothing there except a lot of old Hawaiian junk."

Daniel cut the connection as he sat at his desk. "What?" he said, punching his comm to answer when he saw it was from Gary.

"I just sent you something interesting," Gary said.

"Don't waste my time. What is it?" Daniel said as he opened the box that had just arrived.

"It's a little something I found in Erik Wolfe's safe the other day."

"What is it?" Daniel asked as he peered at the black tube sitting in a clear container.

"I'm not sure. I didn't want to set off any alarms by opening it. The dampner's containing it right now."

"I'll have my lab look at it," he said, placing it in his top drawer. "What about the mushrooms? From what I heard, Alex didn't even get them. Wolfe grabbed them."

"Who told you that? If that bitch —"

"You worry about your own ass."

After disconnecting from Gary, Daniel pulled out the container and examined the tube inside. He needed to find a secure location to analyze it further. Whatever it is, it might help Rictor with its bid. Gary was proving to be somewhat worthwhile, despite seeming a bit unstable. Getting good help was becoming harder. He was glad he'd disguised himself while recruiting everyone. If the police caught anyone, they couldn't squeal on him.

"Manny said the front lawn is still a bit damp from the flood but thinks it will be fine tomorrow when the guests start arriving," Erik told Linc as they sat at Erik's conference table reviewing the plans for the opening one last time.

"Listen to you talking about lawns. Soon you'll be a regular horticulturalist."

Erik chucked the empty Marbotab case across his desk, aiming it at his friend. "Yeah, right."

"What's with all the bottom feeders outside?" Linc tossed the case in the trash can. "You'd think it's opening day. Where's Alex?"

"She said she needed a personal day today when she took the job, so dammed if I know either answer."

"I know why she took the day off and the reason for the paps," Meg said as she walked into the room and turned on the display before heading to the Raleigh. "Check that out."

"... the fifth anniversary of Charlie Cash and Sam Zara's disappearance," the reporter said to her co-anchor. "Where are their families now, Jim? What happened to their wives, Alexandra and Emily?"

"We don't know much," Courtney, the co-anchor, said. "They're living in Alex's family home in Bel-Air and have been spotted at the city's newest nightclub, Pierre's L.A. Rumor has it that Alex is also helping Erik Wolfe and Linc Cussler prepare for the Hotel Bel-Air's opening and *Swan Song* Oscar party.

"We did reach out to the women's uncle, the famous inventor and scientist Walter Dees, but couldn't get a hold of him either. We only received a statement asking people to respect the women's privacy."

As the reporter continued, sounding more like she was gossiping, a series of images flashed on the screen: the hotel, Alex and Emily marrying Charlie and Sam, their uncle, and even Erik and Linc, finishing with a hazy picture of a woman with a big German Shepherd.

"That's such a tragic story," Meg sighed as she stood watching the images flash by.

"That's not one of the women," Erik said, stepping closer to take a look at the last image. "That's Isobelle. Those idiots."

"Why so cranky?" Meg took a seat at the conference table. "Do you think your woman's still in love with her husband?"

"She's not my woman, so no, I'm not upset," Erik responded gruffly, pulling up docs at the table's comm for everyone to see. "What?" he asked, seeing his two friends exchange a look. "Let's finish this before midnight."

An hour later, Ron entered Erik's office and turned on the wall display as the three were finishing.

"Sorry to bother you, but I thought you'd want to see this. I asked the system to scan each day's data for anything suspicious, given what's happened lately. It flagged this."

On the screen, they saw Emily and Alex walking through their gate onto the property located between the hotel and their home, trailed by their two dogs. A second later, the women vanished, but the dogs remained visible. The image changed to another vid showing the dogs walking up the hill by themselves. Just before the top of the hill, the dogs disappeared into the fog.

"Don't we have any eyes up there?" Erik asked, frustrated that he couldn't see the dogs anymore, much less the women.

"We did. Something happened to them. I have Gary checking it now. But look at this." Ron switched to another vid of the hillside. Suddenly, the dogs reappeared out of the fog, this time heading down the hill; the women still nowhere in sight. The dogs walked down the hill, occasionally glancing at something behind them, but there was nothing there. Once down the hill, the gate leading to the women's property opened, and the dogs walked through, with the gate closing behind them.

"Wait. Zoom on the gate right as it's closing," Erik said. "Focus on the top of the gate. Look, is that a hand on the top pulling it closed?"

"It sure looks like one," Meg said, peering at the display. "And look at the ring. Doesn't Alex wear one just like that? Do they have some kind of invisibility capability? Does anything like that exist?"

"I've heard rumors, but that's all we thought they were." Erik thought about the whispers he'd heard lately.

"If anyone could pull it off, I bet Al or Lee would be the one to do it," said Linc. "Among other things, doesn't one of them specialize in molecgen? Maybe they're testing it out for them."

"Yeah, I heard that too," Erik agreed.

"I wonder if the women would tell us about it."

"Yeah, just flex your pecs and they'll cave for sure." Meg rolled her eyes. "They don't seem the type to be swayed by beefcake."

Later that evening, as Erik stripped down to shower, he found himself thinking about Alex and Emily. Al and Lee's names kept popping up when talking about the women. The names were also similar. They couldn't possibly be one and the same. For them to keep that kind of secret for this long seemed impossible. Suddenly his comm rang. It was his buddy in Hawaii.

"Bro, someone broke into that guy's house again. The HPD comm was going off. First the police showed up, then military types swarmed the place. They're still there."

"Thanks for keeping an ear out," Erik said, rubbing his head in confusion. "Let me know if you hear anything more."

"Will do. Are you coming out soon? The waves are peaking."

"As soon as this competition's over, I'm planning on it. Save a break for me," he added, before disconnecting the comm.

Erik wondered what it all meant, worried he was missing something important. People trying to kidnap Alex; her uncle's house broken into. She had bruises around her neck, arms, and back. She and her cousin vanishing into thin air, not to mention the wasps and mushrooms. Then there were the burglaries at the hotel; the theft from his safe, Susan's accident, her plans hacked, much less the stock runs.

Maybe he should add more security, he thought as he stepped in the shower. But if he added any more, there would be more guards than guests. He needed to get a handle on what was happening. He wondered if multiple people were behind the chaos.

# Thursday, February 26, 2172

Finally, the sun was out, Alex thought as she grabbed her jewelry from the charging box and headed to the hotel. The bright day matched her mood. Happy to hear the update about the Farout colony, that their backup systems were still operational, she opened the hotel's gate from the side yard. She didn't see Erik waiting for her. Suddenly, she felt a hand grip her upper arm. Having armed her ring before leaving the house and instantly reacted, grabbing the person's arm before turning.

"What the hell!" Erik exclaimed, rubbing his hand on his pant leg. "What was that?"

"I'm sorry," Alex said, pasting on an innocent look. "That must have been static electricity. It's so dry today with the Santa Anas blowing."

"Static electricity?" Erik said somewhat dubiously, looking around at the trees before the two entered the hotel. "I don't see any wind."

"Do you have time to go over the final plans?" she asked, wanting to distract him but also wanting to go over the schedule since people would begin arriving that afternoon.

"Come in once you've put your things down and changed

your shoes." He looked at her muddy orange tennis shoes, wondering what was wrong with him that he was starting to think them cute. "How are you feeling?" he asked when she entered his office, noticing the dark circles under her eyes.

"Okay," she said, wondering why he was asking as she went to get a double espresso. She hadn't slept much the night before, had risen early, and desperately needed more caffeine.

"Yesterday must have been difficult," Erik said, feeling a bit awkward bringing it up.

"Oh, that." Alexandra busied herself with making her drink. "I'm just glad the day is over, to be honest."

"You must miss him," Erik said, thinking of her lost husband, and mentally kicking himself for even mentioning him.

"I do, but now I think I miss the idea of him more than him. Does that even make sense?" she asked the handsome man sitting quietly at his desk, concern etched on his face. It hadn't even been two weeks since she'd met Erik. However, today she almost started vibrating when she approached him. It was something about the way their energies mixed, like opposite polarities rubbing together, created a tension that felt ready to explode.

"Actually," she added, as she played with her ring, deciding to go for broke, not wanting him to think she was still heartsick over Charlie. "A friend died recently. He was someone I really cared about, and that's what made yesterday really hard."

"A friend like a friend-friend, or a lover?" Erik asked, finding himself needing to know. He wasn't going to pursue anything with her if she was mourning another guy. That simply wasn't his style. Competing with a dead hero-husband was already humbling enough. But if she'd just lost a lover, well, he wanted her to desire him for who he was, not as a mere substitute.

"Not a lover," Alex said. She was beginning to feel overwhelmed with all of the secrets she had to keep. "But that's what made yesterday hard. As far as Charlie, I think I've finally put him to rest."

"I lost my brother a long time ago. I hate that my memory of him has become so dull and faint," he admitted, feeling an unusual lightening in his chest as he spoke. He hadn't talked about his brother in years, he realized. Most people didn't even know he had had one.

"What happened?" Alex asked, feeling a sense of intimacy build between the two in the quiet morning.

"He—Ulrich was his name—died in a skaboarding accident. I was 20; he was 17. He'd been running with a fast crowd. My little sister, Marion, was home when the officer came to the house. I was at the office, trying to get Xtra going. He'd been racing down Topanga Canyon, heading towards Malibu. A tov came up on him on a blind curve. He apparently swerved, fell, and hit his head on a rock. He died before the ambulance arrived.

"I don't know why I'm telling you this," he added, looking at her, feeling uncomfortably vulnerable. "It keeps happening. First, I tell you about my father, now my brother. Next, I'll be telling you I'm sensitive," he said, trying to lighten the mood.

"Maybe you're trying to make me feel better?" she said, looking at the man—sexy and powerful—with his shirt tight across his chest as he leaned back in his chair. If she didn't have all her secrets or work for Erik, she would be tempted to go sit in his lap again and spend some serious time exploring his lips and a few other body parts.

"Anyway, about today, everything should be ready for your guests," Alex said lamely, getting up to head to her office. This was too intense, especially after yesterday, she thought.

A couple hours later, Alex sat at her desk, checking off details for the *Swan Song* Oscar party. The fabricators who made the giant white metal birdcage, which would sit at the entrance of the ballroom, confirmed they would deliver it Saturday morning. The cage would open on both sides, allowing guests to walk through.

Tomorrow, the giant perches would be installed, and the robotic swans hung. The footbridge over the stream that connected the parking lot to the hotel would be transformed with feathers and wood into a tree limb and giant nests once the fog burned off. Still wanting to check the VIP suites and swag, she decided now would be a good time as she grabbed her comm and stood.

"I'm going to check the swag bags," Alex told Sally as she left her office and headed down the hall. Alex swore she'd seen some kind of code on Sally's display before Sally changed her screen to the schedule that Alex had sent her.

"Fine," Sally answered, not even looking up.

Alex turned right, toward the Bel Suite. She felt pretty confident that Martha had kept a close eye on the swag bags, making sure the right one went in the right suite, but after all the mistakes, she wanted to double-check.

Celebrities treasured swag. In fact, many people would sell their souls for swag, especially items given as part of a blockbuster movie. From a promoter's standpoint, celebrities flaunted the bag's expensive trinkets to friends, adversaries, the media. Because of that, it paid to have unique, high-end items.

Susan had done a great job selecting pieces for the hotel's *Swan Song* bags. The only errors had been with the quantities, but Alex had been able to fix those mistakes in time. So far, so good, she thought as she exited the Grace Kelly Suite. Only the Camellia Suite was left.

As she entered the semi-dark suite, the hotel's new signature scent almost overwhelmed her. The bags, which they'd put together on Monday, included custom, swan-shaped crystal bottles that held a special scent crafted by leading perfumer Hadid Monchant. As her eyes adjusted to the dark, she saw the silhouette of a man standing in the suite's dining room, a bag's contents spilling across the table.

"Gary. Is that you?"

"What do you think?" Gary sneered, an ugly expression on his face when he recognized her. "Oh, that's right, you always need the obvious spelled out for you." He grabbed the bottle, which perched open on the table, and, with a pipette, dripped a gold-colored liquid into the bottle.

"What are you doing? What is that?" Alex asked, suspicious that something was drastically off.

Gary didn't quite look like himself. His slacks and shirt, which were always clean and pressed, looked like he'd slept in them. A few strands of long, brown hair, usually neatly back, had escaped its tie.

"Just checking that everything's ready for the guests," Gary said, setting the pipette down and taking a step towards Alex.

She raised her comm to call security, but before anyone answered, Gary rushed her, grabbed her comm, and twisted her arm behind her back.

"You just have to be a meddling little bitch, don't you?" he hissed at her.

"What the hell, Gary? Are you crazy? Are you the one behind all of the problems here? Isn't the hotel paying you enough?"

"No, it isn't. And I've been told that I won't be kept on after the opening, probably thanks to you. So another opportunity landed in my lap. One you aren't going to ruin. This was my last assignment, and I'm finishing it. Then you can come along with me for a little fun."

"What makes you think I'd go someplace with you?" Alex said, struggling to free her arm so she could tap her ring to her earring. This situation felt too similar to what happened in Hawaii when the men grabbed her. However, she couldn't use her ring on him, so she kicked him as hard as she could in the shin. His crotch wasn't close enough, otherwise she would have aimed there.

With a curse of surprise, Gary loosened his grip on her arm. Turning to run, she touched her ring to her earring, but before she could tap it a second time, she felt a wrenching pull on her hair. Gary had grabbed her braid, stopping her in her tracks.

"Oh no, you don't," he laughed maniacally, quickly pulling his tie from around his neck. "Finally, these stupid things come in handy," he added as he grabbed her arm. "Fuck!" he howled, dropping her arm as the shock hit him.

Alex turned again to escape, quickly tapping her ring to her pendant again, knowing she had to make the last shock count because then it would be out of juice. She reached the door—she was almost clear—when she felt something catch her blouse, followed by a ripping sound. Gary had grabbed her blouse. If she could just reach the hall, and if she screamed loud enough, maybe someone would hear.

She wasn't quick enough, fear flooding through her. She told herself she couldn't shut down. Gary had definitely lost it, and if he caught her, she realized, she may not survive. But he was too strong. Slapping his hand over her mouth before she could yell, he dragged her back inside the suite and threw her on the floor, swearing when she shocked him again.

"We're going to have some fun, you bitch," Gary snarled. "You'll pay for sticking your nose where it doesn't belong."

Alex gasped, trying to suck air into her paralyzed lungs after hitting the floor. Little lights sparkled in her vision; her ribs spasmed in pain. Gary leaned down, furious, a bit of spittle on his lip. She saw the tie in his hand and realized he meant to tie her up. Suddenly, somehow, he flew up and away from her, a shocked look on his face.

Erik wondered where Alex had gone. He checked the hall cams, then commed Martha. She said Alex had gone to check the VIP suites. Erik could tell Martha was miffed, thinking Alex hadn't trusted her. He explained that because of the mistakes Alex had discovered after Susan's accident, she was even double-checking him.

He then checked the tracker that he'd asked Alex to attach to her comm. She'd entered the Camellia Suite. He left his office and headed across and up the brick path edged by giant birds of paradise and pink-flowered camellia bushes. Erik wanted to tell her that he would like her with him in the lobby when guests arrived tomorrow. At least that was his excuse.

The hotel looked great, he thought as he looked around. Fresh white paint covered the original wood doors and window trims, the walls once again their signature pink. They'd printed new red Spanish tile to replace the old ones on the roofs. They'd used red clay from Mars after discovering the red dirt, when formed into tiles, repelled fire and insulated better than Earth clay. A century of celebrities and elite visitors had graced the hotel, and Erik felt a deep sense of pride in updating and protecting the icon without comprimising its glamour.

As he approached the Camellia Suite, Erik heard a strange, muffled noise. Looking towards the end of the path, Erik was momentarily stunned to see what appeared to be Alex struggling in the suite's doorway with a man who looked like Gary. When the man yanked her through the door, Erik began to run.

Later, his actions would replay in his mind, but at that moment, he turned cold and felt deadly. Reaching the door, he looked in to see Gary throw Alex to the ground. He burst in, grabbed Gary, yanked him up, threw him against the wall, and started beating him. Seeing a man hurting a woman, much less Alex, triggered him instantly, fury riding him like a shark tasting blood as he slugged Gary in the kidneys.

Even as Gary doubled over, Erik continued to pummel him. First, an uppercut that snapped Gary's head back; then, before Gary could raise his arms, a punch to his face that produced a satisfying crunch. Erik hoped he had broken Gary's nose. He drew back to hit him again when a hand landed on his arm.

Snarling, thinking it was another attacker, he almost hit out but pulled back when he saw Alex's face.

"I'm okay. I'm okay. You can't kill him," Alex said, gripping his arm, her soft voice dousing the cold rage coursing through him. "Erik, I'm okay," she repeated, breathless as she clutched her side.

Gary lay moaning on the floor, blood running from his nose. Erik, still enraged, wanted to kick the ass. Sucking in a deep breath, Erik slowly began to regain some sanity.

"Ron, get the police," he snapped into his comm, breathing heavily while keeping an eye on Gary. "We're in Camellia."

"I think he was doing something to the perfume," Alex whispered, her gaze fixed on the crystal swan, a cold beginning to freeze her body and mind. "I think we should pull all of them until we find out," she said, pushing her hair out of her face.

"Fuck the perfume," Erik swore, seeing her flinch at the anger in his voice. "I'm sorry. Are you okay?" he asked, taking in her torn blouse and wild hair loose from her usual neat braid. "Of course you're not okay," he said, fury surging through him once more. "I'm going to kill him for laying a hand on you," Erik growled, ready to give the man cowering on the floor another violent kick or ten.

"Even though I think that's a great idea, I don't want you going to jail if he dies," Alex said, rubbing her arms, desperately trying to warm up. "He didn't hurt me, at least not much. You saved me," she added gratefully as she heard footsteps in the hall.

Ron raced into the suite, skidding to a stop upon seeing a bloody Gary lying on the floor, Erik looking wild eyed and panting, and Alex, her face pale, and clothes torn and disheveled, her hair a mess.

"Say boss," Ron said quietly, trying to diffuse Erik who looked ready to go ballistic, not that it looked like he hadn't already.

"Did you comm the cops?" Erik demanded, trying to regain some semblance of control.

"Yes, they're on the way."

"He attacked Alex." Erik gestured angrily at Gary, starting to wind up again.

"I was checking the swag bags," Alex explained, still rubbing her arms. "I found him in here doing something with the Monchant bottle. He told me it was his last assignment. That someone was paying him to cause problems, and that once he was done in here, he was going to take me someplace to have some fun," she said, her voice falling to a whisper as she felt herself starting to lose it.

Erik quickly walked over and gently wrapped his arms around her. "Ron, have the police take this scum out of here. Alex is pressing charges, and so am I. Get Martha to pull all of the Monchant bottles from the suites and get someone to check their contents. "What did you do to the perfume, you asshole?" he snarled at the man on the floor.

"You're not getting anything from me," Gary said defiantly, wiping the snot and blood from his nose as he slowly stood. "You broke my nose! I'm going to press charges against you, you asshole."

"Well, if that's the case, then here," Erik growled, released Alex, and punched the man in the gut again.

"Hey! You can't do that! I'll sue you for everything you have. You saw that, Ron. You can't deny that you saw him attack me," Gary cried, once again on the floor, gasping. "I think my ribs are broken now."

"I didn't see anything except Erik trying to defend himself and Alex," Ron said calmly.

A minute later, the police swarmed in and took Gary and the Monchant bottle away. Erik told them he and Alex would sign complaints later. Ron assured Erik that he would take the remaining officer and collect the rest of the bottles. Martha and some of her staff were already waiting outside the door for the police to finish and leave so they could clean and straighten the room.

"Let's go to my office," Erik said, helping Alex up from the chair she'd been sitting in as they told the police what had happened. "I'm calling the doctor to come take a look at you," he added, concerned at her paleness.

"No, no doctors. I have a good doctor. If I feel I need to see her, I'll give her a call," Alex said as she walked back with Erik to his office. She hurt. Her arms hurt; heck her hair even hurt, and her ribs. It felt like whatever healing her ribs had managed had been erased.

Feeling hysteria rising, she wondered if some entity had placed a target on her body. Trying not to breathe deeply, she didn't want the hotel's doctor—whoever that might be—to see her old bruises and start asking questions she didn't want to answer. It was bad enough that Emily and Iso would freak when she got home, not to mention Jared and the General. Once there, she planned to slather on more Erisalve, take a sleeper, and crawl into bed.

"Let's get the police over with," Alex said as she entered Erik's office. "Gary had to be doing something with the perfume bottles."

Erik was worried she looked so pale. She wasn't walking that steadily. He grabbed his comm and punched it so they could join the conversation already underway between Ron, the police sergeant who'd booked Gary, and Dwayne, Xtra's legal counsel.

"Glad you're here, Erik," Dwayne said. "How's Alex?"

"I'm fine," Alex responded when Erik moved the comm so she was in view.

"She won't see a doctor."

"Miss, you should probably get checked out," the Police Sergeant said.

"I will if I need to when I get home. What do you need from me besides signing a complaint?" Alex asked, barely holding onto her sanity. She'd thought she was going to die. Gary had a crazy look in his eyes, as if he was looking forward to hurting her further. While she hadn't had a great childhood—she'd been verbally abused by her stepmothers and ignored by her father—

she'd never been physically hurt. Now, in less than two weeks, she'd been attacked twice, each time to the point she'd felt she was close to dying.

"I'm sending the complaint now," the Sergeant said, interrupting her thoughts. "Once you sign it, that's all I'll need for now. I'll need your signature, too, Mr. Wolfe."

"Forward them to me after you sign them, Erik," Dwayne said. "I'll review them and then forward to you, Sergeant."

"Fine, thanks Dwayne, Sergeant. Once we're done, I'm taking Alex home."

"I can get home—" Alex started to say until Erik shot her a glare that made her stop. He obviously hadn't calmed down.

"You don't have to be here tomorrow," Erik added as they left his office after forwarding the signed complaints to Dwayne. "The tov's up front."

"I'll be here tomorrow," Alex replied, determined to face her demons; otherwise, the hotel would haunt her forever. "And you don't have to go with me. The tov can take me home."

"I know I don't have to, but I need to," Erik admitted, keeping a careful eye on her as they slowly walked across the bridge. "When I saw Gary throw you down, I thought he'd killed you."

"I will always be grateful you came along when you did, not to mention beat the crap out of Gary," she said.

"I'd have never guessed you'd be so bloodthirsty," Erik said trying for a lighter tone, hoping it would help soften the shock of what had just happened.

"Sometimes," Alex said, thinking about Hawaii and what she'd like to do to the people who killed her uncle and hurt her.

"Thanks for seeing me home," Alex said as he helped her get out of the tov at her house.

"I'm seeing you to the front door. I'm not sure I trust you to tell Isobelle or Emily," Erik said, grabbing her arm as she stumbled over a rock. "Shit, I'm sorry," he added when she gasped. "You have to see a doctor."

"I'll tell them," Alex said, thinking about her plan to slip into her room before Emily or the girls, much less Jared, saw her. She also noticed that Isobelle hadn't opened the front door as she usually did; instead, she chose to let Erik escort her to the porch.

"Now we can make sure, can't we?" Erik said as Isobelle opened the door.

"Alex, what happened?" Isobelle exclaimed, opening the door wider to usher Alex and Erik inside.

"She was attacked at the hotel and should see a doctor," Erik said quickly, cutting Alex off. "She wouldn't let me comm the hotel doctor."

"You have been attracting trouble like a cup of gold to bees. Do not worry, Mr. Wolfe," Isobelle assured Erik. "I will be sure to keep an eye on her and call the doctor if necessary."

"I told you I'm fine. Thank you for escorting me back, and, if you'll excuse me, I'm going to take a hot shower. I'll see you tomorrow morning." Alex walked past Isobelle, heading down the hall before Isobelle could look too closely at her. She just wanted to get to her bedroom, take a long hot shower, spread on a bottle or two of Erisalve, and lie down.

"Thank you for looking after her. God knows she won't listen to me."

"She is a stubborn one. She has been on her own for a long time, always the one to take care of others."

"I've noticed."

"By the way, I have just made a big pot of stew for dinner. I have made more than anyone here can eat. Would you like to join us?"

"Stew sounds great. I haven't had a home-cooked meal in a long time. Thank you, Isobelle."

Alex's heart started thumping when the doorbell rang. She could have zapped Iso for inviting Erik. She'd just woken from a long nap, the sleeper having knocked her right out when she'd climbed in bed earlier, and the Erisalve thankfully muted her pain. She'd desperately wanted a quiet evening. She knew that was why Iso had asked him, so she couldn't hide. Erik made her feel anything but quiet.

When she opened the door, her heart raced even faster. He'd changed out of his suit into light-blue jeans, pressed of course, that caressed his strong thighs, and an open-at-the-collar, light-blue linen shirt under a green slicker wet with rain. Darn, she thought, the sleeper definitely hadn't worn off; even his neck and the hint of his chest looked good enough to nuzzle. She jerked her eyes up to his face.

"Can I come in?" Erik asked, a smile on his lips.

Damn the man. He knows his effect on me.

"Of course. I'm glad you dressed casually." She took his coat to hang on the hook near the door.

"How are you feeling?" Erik glanced down at Alex's body, clad in soft blue pants and a matching blue top that was slipping off her shoulder. His attraction to her climbed as she reached to hang his coat, her shirt lifting to show a small strip of pale skin.

He hadn't seen her dressed this casually before, except during the storm when the swans escaped. This time, her clothes, the same blue as her eyes, caressed her form, her ebony hair in a simple braid that hung down her back. Then he spied the new bruise below her collarbone, which showed when her shirt slipped further down her creamy shoulder. Anger surged within him at the sight, a desire to pummel Gary more erupting again. Noticing where his gaze had landed, Alex quickly yanked up her shirt.

"A little stiff from this afternoon, but nothing a good night's sleep won't help," Alex said, hoping that was true. Without the Erisalve, she probably would have been in bed with ice packs or at ER. Even though she was still tender, the worst of it was numb.

She knew she'd have to be really careful for a while. When the medtech in Kailua said her ribs were broken, he'd also told her that if she didn't take care, she could puncture a lung. They'd injected the latest regeneration glue, he'd said, but her ribs were still extremely fragile. She'd felt something crack again when Gary threw her down, but even though it hurt to take a breath, her lungs felt okay.

As she and Erik walked to the kitchen, she kept slipping him glances, feeling extremely tiny next to him and safe. She could tell he was fuming about something, though.

Erik was working hard to tap down the rage that resurfaced when he thought about Gary and what could have happened if he hadn't gone looking for Alex. The sight of his petite pixie, impossibly strong, yet so fragile, transformed his rage into a powerful sense of protectiveness. Then they entered the kitchen. He hadn't spent much time—actually hardly ever—in anyone's kitchen, much less for a home-cooked meal.

Isobelle was stirring a big pot of stew. The two college girls he'd heard about were carrying a large bowl of salad and a plate of what looked like muffins to the long hammered-oak plank table. Jared, looking entirely too comfortable for Erik's liking, was setting butter and what looked like honey on the table as Emily poured water. The room almost looked like one of those old-timey images, he thought, a fire crackling in the old river-stone fireplace, the fire looking and smelling so real he wanted to reach his hands out to feel its simulated warmth. Rain spotted the big windows at the end of the room, while occasional flashes of distant lightning lit the yard. The women's big cat slept on an old blue rug in front of the fire.

Large, old German steins, carved scrimshaw globes, giant conch shells, and wooden carvings competed for space on the white shelves running between the fireplace and windows. A multicolored cloth ran down the table's middle, covered with bunnies, colored eggs, and four fat pewter candlesticks holding cream-colored candles.

He could see where the Easter decor came from. How could

he help, he thought, with Isobelle wearing a neon orange blouse and lime-green linen pants. Dainty orange filigree carrots dangled from her ears. When she turned to greet him, he didn't quite know where to look, at her blouse, which had "Silence is golden, duct tape is silver" embroidered on the pocket, or her extremely garish make-up. The blackest, biggest eyelashes he'd ever seen competed with her bright orange lipstick. He noticed that except for one of the women, the others wore little if any make-up.

"You haven't met the girls," Alex said, introducing Beverly, a busty blonde fusion engineer, her makeup almost as heavy as Isobelle's, and Anita, a slender brunette with a fresh face and ready smile who had just started UCLA as a Sipta engineering major.

"Alex, tell Erik where to sit, and you sit down, too," Isobelle directed, concerned at Alex's paleness. Isobelle ladled stew into bowls, which the girls carried to the table, placing one at each seat. "Everyone, sit," Isobelle commanded, carrying over the last two bowls and then sitting down herself.

"Iso's a general in the kitchen," Emily said to Erik, passing him the muffins.

"From the smell of everything, that's a good thing." He wanted to grab more than one of the crisp warm muffins, hoping they were cornbread.

"Young man, you might as well ask why I am wearing so much make-up," Isobelle said, noticing Erik glancing her way.

"Okay," Erik said, not sure where the conversation was heading.

"My theatre class teacher, it's a GE, our project is, like, to create a clown face that doesn't actually look like a clown face," Beverly said. "What do you think?"

"Well, it looks like you accomplished what you set out to do, but I don't know a lot about the subject." Erik thought Beverly's make-up wasn't much different from Isobelle's.

"I think she should have made Iso scarier, maybe with a scar running down her cheek," Anita piped up.

Before Beverly could reply, Fred and Barney ran in and immediately came over to Erik, wanting to explore the smells he'd brought with him. Erik noticed that Barney looked completely normal again.

"I hope you recovered after your accident, Anita," Erik said, remembering the women left the Rictor party because something had happened to her.

"Accident?" Anita asked, confused by Erik's comment.

"Anita, stop feeding Fred your Kraksnot," Alex scolded the girl, attempting to change the subject. They hadn't told Anita that they'd used her as an excuse to escape the Rictor party. Fred had moved to sit between Anita and Jared, drooling happily as he obviously scored some treats.

"Jared started it," Anita said, forgetting Erik's question, ratting out Jared, who had also been feeding Fred the superfood.

Isobelle used a lot of Kraksnot because of its nutritional value. She tried to camouflage it, but many people struggled with the viscous, some said snot-like substance that oozed from the inside of the semi-hard kernels when chewed.

"Jared, quit getting suckered by Fred. He already gets plenty with his dinner. He needs to lose weight," Alex lectured.

"Besides, Kraksnot's good for you, and these just arrived from Hyperion," Emily added.

Erik, who was trying to hide his Kraksnot under a few lettuce leaves, kept his mouth shut. Jared caught Erik pushing one beneath a lettuce leaf just as Erik looked up at him. When Jared didn't out him, Erik thought he might be an okay guy.

"This stew is really good, Isobelle," he said, trying to take the attention off of the other man. "Would you mind sharing the recipe with Chef? I think it would make a good addition to the menu, especially during the winter. What do you think, Alex?"

"I think it would be a good addition, although I'd make the Kraksnot an option," Alex said, casting a suspicious eye at Erik and his salad plate after noticing him trading looks with Jared.

"Before I forget, Iso, how did your BAPT meeting go?" Alex

asked. "Did you and Eva talk Congresswoman Reynolds into taking BAPT's manifesto to the senate?" She turned to Erik. "Did you know that Iso's involved with Bots Are People Too?"

Alex wanted to shift the attention away from herself and Emily. Erik wasn't dumb. She and Emily had shown more scientific knowledge than she'd intended. Discussing in detail the challenges and possibilities Marsium offered had been fun. Usually, just she and Emily tossed around ideas, with the girls occasionally chiming in. As they'd rapidly thrown out different scenarios where the Mars element could be used, in her excitement she'd completely forgotten to dumb down. She didn't know what Emily's excuse was.

"No, but Ms. Reynolds did promise us she would take it around to some of her fellow Congresspeople and see who might support it," Isobelle replied. "Eva is a friend of mine—a bot, too." She gauged Erik's reaction to the fact. When she didn't see any horror or distaste on his face, she continued. "It helped that she volunteered for the mission to save the Farout Colony."

"Farout's at the edge of our Solar System, which is, like, where our planet is," Beverly said.

"Mr. Wolfe knows where Farout is, Beverly. His company does a lot of work in space," Alex told the girl.

"Really?" Beverly asked, batting her eyelashes at Erik.

"Eva's quite brave," Alex said. "We'll miss her while she explores the Kuiper Belt. She's like family, isn't she, Iso?"

"I have known Eva for sixty-six years. I will miss her terribly," Isobelle said. "That is why that new network will be important, which I believe you are hoping to work on, Mr. Wolfe? If the network works, Eva and I will at least be able to talk if Space Force allows it."

"Yes, my company's competing for the contract," Erik admitted, just realizing that Isobelle was friends with the now famous bot. That made sense since Walter had created them both.

"That's also why it's important that BAPT's charter's approved," Alex said. "Just because she's a bot, some organizations don't think it's necessary to give Eva the bandwidth to communicate with anyone other than Space Force. They think it's okay to treat bots like slave labor."

"If approved, the charter will give bots full human privileges, right?" Erik asked. "Isn't Destinee Montaro involved with BAPT?"

"She is a friend," Isobelle said, admiration in her voice, her carrot earrings swinging as she nodded. "How do you know her?"

"Linc and I met her years ago at a convention. She attended a presentation we made and hit us up for access to the tech we'd developed to help a bot that was heading out to Styx. She was relentless. Little did she know we were going to offer it anyway, but we waited until she bought us dinner. We were hungry back then and didn't have a lot of money," he said, smiling at the memory.

Alex could picture a young Erik and Linc, both blisteringly smart and likely skinny—what young men weren't with their metabolisms cranking—hungry for food and their new company to succeed.

"Is it true, Mr. Wolfe, that besides the *Swan Song* cast, Mick Jagger will be staying at the hotel?" Anita asked dreamily when the conversation had paused.

Erik could tell Anita, whose t-shirt displayed a picture of the rocker, was a fan. "Yes, he's supposed to arrive tomorrow."

"That is such a crazy story, like how he and his band—the Rolling Stones, isn't it—have been in cryosleep for, like, the last ninety-five years?" Beverly asked. "Has it really been proven that, like, they're the real thing?"

"Yes, I saw Mr. Jagger's ID since he's staying at the hotel."

"Do you want to hear his new tracks, *Second Time Around*?" Anita asked, poised to start the music.

"May I have a raincheck? I need to get going. If there's a chance, however, I'll see if I can get you an autograph from Mr. Jagger," Erik added after seeing Anita's face fall in disappointment. "Thank you everyone for a very enjoyable dinner."

"I'll see you out." Alex pushed back from the table.

Erik followed her over to the sink with his plates and glass. "Can I help clean up first?" he asked, hoping to scrape his plate, especially the hidden Kraksnot, into the recyk before anyone saw.

"I will take it from here," Isobelle said. "Alex, you see Erik to the door, and then take a hot bath."

As Alex walked with Erik, he thought about how much he'd enjoyed the dinner tonight. Not only was the food good, but so was the company.

"Thank you for including me," he said to Alex as she opened the door. The rain had stopped, the clouds were gone, and a full moon shone down, lighting up the drive and Alex's face. *Damn it*, he thought as he turned and looked at her. He couldn't resist her any more than the moon could stop shining. He bent down and kissed her softly on her lips, lingering, teasing, hoping she'd open up. When she did, he slipped inside, taking care to not scare her away. A moment or ten later, he stepped back, tucking a stray bit of hair behind her ear.

"I'll see you tomorrow," he said as he stepped outside. "10:00? We have the final competition for that contract we're bidding on before that. Wish me luck?"

He would have liked to have stayed longer, to take the bath Isobelle mentioned with Alex and enjoyed soaping her back and her front even more. And maybe even ask how she knew so much about Marsium. She'd clearly wanted to change the subject when Anita talked about how smart she and Emily were.

Regardless, he was beginning to feel that Alex was more than just a one-night stand. But what she truly was, he wasn't sure. Anita hadn't acknowledged she'd had an accident either.

"Luck," she said, thinking how ironic it was that if Xtra won the contract, this man might be in her life for many more years than he realized. That meant she really needed to think hard about getting entangled with him, even if it was for just one night.

That kiss had been a wowza, though. Boy, could the man kiss. She could tell he'd leashed himself; he'd been so gentle. What would he be like if he slipped that leash? she wondered, feeling a shiver slide down her spine. Did she want to find out? She wasn't sure, although he was certainly wearing down her resistance. In the past, she would have never considered it. Now she was. She felt crazy, certifiably so. Thankfully, she and Lee had the test tomorrow to focus on. It was going to be a full day.

# Friday, February 27, 2172

Hand clutching her coffee mug, Alex stepped into the lab and carefully took as deep a breath as her ribs would allow. She then paused to center herself as Fred plopped down on his bed under the left wall display. So much depended on this day. Before the accident on Farout, Space Force had planned to use the planet, the furthest one in the Solar System, for its final test of the deep-space network. If it worked, she and Emily would then make one last attempt to search for Sam and Charlie's lost spaceship.

The new network, with Ola as its backbone, would give anyone or anything leaving the Solar System and entering the Oort Cloud a lot more security since they'd be able to communicate, and send and receive data. The existing network just didn't have the juice to go that far. It even had problems within the Kuiper Belt, where the Solar System's most distant planets lived.

Shaped like a giant spherical shell, the Oort Cloud surrounded the System like a big, thick bubble packed full of trillions of icy debris the size of mountains. Everyone itched to explore those big bits of rock.

Now though, everyone was focused on Farout. Someone had leaked to the media, and now everyone, on- and off-planet, was watching, waiting to see if the colony could be saved. The ship with Eva had already arrived, breaking all speed records, and now hovered over the pink, icy planet.

The test started in thirty minutes. Alex set her mug on her desk and started bringing up the monitors, comms lines, and the big displays on the wall. Once the left screen lit, Alex linked to their support team in Kahaluu and brought up the screens that showed such details as connectivity and data upload and download rates.

On the right screen, she could see Goddard's Mission Control Room, where Space Force's engineers moved around, checking their systems. She could almost feel the tension, what with such high stakes. Everyone understood that if Ola didn't work, the entire colony would perish. Although Space Force had dispatched another ship, it wouldn't arrive in time. The other sections of the right display featured Seed's logo and the competing teams' identifiers. Twenty more minutes.

A minute later Emily shuffled in, followed by Chutney, who lazily made a circuit of the room before stopping at Fred's bed, butting the dog in the head so he'd make room.

"I'm nervous. How about you?" Alex asked Emily as she rechecked the uploading comm lines.

"I feel like I could knit a king-size blanket right now," Emily admitted, looking longingly at the full basket of synthyarn on the couch.

Alex tore a chunk of green modeling sopat from the jar she kept in her top drawer. "Goddard's almost ready," she added, nodding to the monitor where Space Force's engineers were settling at their desks.

"Is Capt. Walker there? I don't see her," Emily asked as she sat and brought up her keyboard.

"She just stepped away."

"Do you think she's going to ask you for your private comm after the test?"

"I hope not," Alex said as she shot the mini sopat spacecraft she'd molded across the room. "I've tried to discourage her."

"That hasn't seemed to deter her."

"Too bad she's so nice. I got another message from Charlie's mother last night," Alex confessed as she molded another mini craft. "It was about today's test. She wanted to make sure I had thanked Walter for trying to recover the ship. She also said that she'd be willing to pay for the funeral expenses if his body's recovered."

"How perfectly nice of her," Emily said, a disgusted snort escaping her lips. "What'd you say?"

"Nothing. She can wait," Alex said, her jaw set.

"Hey missy! You haven't picked up the last ones you made," Isobelle admonished Alex as her latest mini ship barely missed the bot as she entered the lab. "I bear gifts and do not deserve such ill treatment."

"Are you reading Susanne's historical romance again?" Alex rose to see what flavor muffins Isobelle had set on the counter.

"Quit changing the subject. There are altogether too many of your little crafts lying around from the last test." Isobelle plucked an orange one out of one of her prized orchids. "My babies don't like sopat. It dries them out," she added as she started misting the plants.

"I'll get them all after the test. I promise."

"You had better," Isobelle said before leaving the lab.

Alex finished molding another craft—this one with tiny boosters—and set it aloft. Seconds later the tiny ship skidded to a stop in front of Fred's nose.

"Five minutes to launch," Capt. Walker said, entering the screen and alerting the teams the countdown had started.

Twenty minutes later, Alex and Emily started to relax. Space Force had successfully completed the download to Farout Base in time, and the base was resetting its systems, much to everyone's relief. Ola's transceiver was sending and receiving data at a space-breaking ten yottabytes per second. At the moment, all of the teams, except SpaceZ, were keeping up.

Suddenly, the left monitor went dark. Alex quickly glanced at the right, which was fully operational, showing everyone's eyes bouncing between different screens, trying to determine what was happening.

"Lokahi team, we have a blackout. What are you seeing?" Alex asked their team in Kahaluu as she and Emily started rapidly entering commands on their keyboards.

"We've lost eyes on Ola. No data's being received," Keanu responded calmly. Keanu never stressed out, which is one of the reasons she and Emily had named him lead engineer.

"Initiating reboot," Emily said, checking her desk monitor for additional details. "Contact made with Ola. Ola coming back online."

"Confirmed. Ola rebooting," reported the Space Force Captain.

Slowly, the screen filled with data, and transmission rates returned to yottabyte speeds. Alex glanced at the right monitor and saw the Space Force team glued to their screens. In Xtra's area, Erik sat behind his team, his shirt sleeves pushed up, intent as he typed rapidly on his keyboard. Linc, sitting beside Erik, looked a bit rattled, his hair sticking up as if he'd run his hands through it a few times. Their capture rates had recovered, as had Rictor's. In fact, Daniel the Dick, Alex noted, looked calm as Rictor's capture rate smoothly climbed. Xtra's rates, she saw, while slightly erratic, began to creep higher than Rictor's.

Alex noticed Tiger's system, though, was silent. In fact, all she saw was Dahlia screaming at her team. Fortunately for everyone, someone had muted Tiger's comm. Suddenly she saw Dahlia sweep everything off her desk, comm equipment flying, and her team ducking the onslaught. Then Tiger's screen went dark.

"Tiger's out."

"Good riddance," Emily mouthed to Alex behind her hand so no one would see. "Dahlia deserved to fail."

"Yeah, but her team didn't. There were some good people working the project," Alex mouthed back, turning away from the camera. Although viewers saw what looked like the male Al and Lee, every motion, including facial expressions, mirrored Alex and Emily's.

"I know, but you have to admit that woman's evil. Maybe we can lure away some of her team when this is over. Everyone except Dahlia."

"Everyone except Dahlia and Dave. He's a sanctimonious ass-kisser."

"Ola's fully up," Emily informed Space Force.

"What do you think happened? I don't see anything that would indicate a crash, much less a shutdown," Alex questioned as she and Emily pored over the data Keanu was sending. "The Lokahi team can't find anything."

"Me either. Captain, do you see any anomalies that might have affected Ola?" Emily asked the Space Force engineer.

"Negative. Nothing to indicate a system failure. However, a two-second power surge hit the ship right before Ola went dark. We'll continue to investigate. Test is continuing with the remaining teams."

"Did you hear?" An unusually flustered Isobelle entered the lab, wringing her hands.

"What, Iso?" Alex asked.

"Eva. Something happened to her ship. I just received a message from her saying goodbye. Instead of heading to Arrokoth, her ship's malfunctioning. It is heading out of the Kuiper Belt toward the Oort Cloud."

"Al, Lee? Direct Time in five minutes," the Space Force Captain reported.

"A minute, Captain," Emily responded, looking at Alex.

Alex looked back at Emily, raising her eyebrows and cocking her head. She silently asked if Emily was thinking the same thing as they watched Isobelle sink down on the bench seat, staring blankly across the lab. Alex and Emily had provided Space Force with an extra Ola orb, which was currently aboard Eva's ship and ready to launch after completing the Farout test. They had planned to use it to search for Charlie and Sam's ship one final time.

"We know they're not alive," Alex said slowly. "It's not possible they survived all this time."

"Agreed."

"Captain, please alert the General; we need to talk to him immediately," Alex said.

"Al, Lee?" the General said over the comm.

"We heard the craft piloted by Eva Pab has malfunctioned and is headed toward the Oort Cloud. We're authorizing that the extra Ola unit stay with the ship."

"We won't be able to search for Cash and Zara's craft. Please verify."

"Verified, sir. We have authorization from Seed and the men's widows," Alex said, looking at Emily, who nodded. She was fudging the Seed authorization a bit, but technically, with their uncle's death, they already owned Seed.

"You would do this for Eva?" Isobelle asked the women, rising from her chair.

"Yes, Iso. Eva's a person, just like you are, just like Lee and me," Alex said after temporarily turning off their cam.

"Initiating change, General," Emily reported as she and Alex entered Ola's new commands. "Ready in five, four, three, two, one—new link's up."

"We'll have to comm Charlie's family before they hear it on the news," Alex said as the two women sat back in their chairs for a breather, their comms muted again. "And the you-know-what's going to hit the fan when they discover we're Al and Lee."

It's not like his family had stayed a part of her life after Charlie had disappeared. Sure, if they'd sent out the extra Ola unit to find Charlie and Sam's ship and actually found it, Space Force could have possibly retrieved the vessel and determined why it had malfunctioned. But that possibility was remote at best and really made no difference regarding the lost men.

Not giving Eva the ability to communicate as her ship flew into the Oort Cloud would have been criminal, she thought. Eva likely would be alone for a long time; that could drive anyone mad. She and Emily couldn't have lived with themselves if they'd had the chance to give Eva the ability to comm others and hadn't allowed it to happen.

So far eXo was chugging like a champ, Erik thought as he looked around the Playa control room. With the amount of data their system was downloading, processing, and uploading—both on Earth and at the various bases and stations—eXo had to be the frontrunner.

Thank Ceres that Farout Base was back online. While he wasn't close with anyone at the base, he'd known and liked a few of the scientists and engineers there. Sitting back, he noticed Carlos and Denise taking a breather, getting coffee—Denise with her lucky cup in hand while Carlos sank a crafball into the hoop on the wall. They deserved bonuses, he decided, preparing to get up for a cup himself. Suddenly he saw a light dim. The left screen had gone dark.

"What the hell is that?" Linc asked Erik as both began poring over the readouts.

"No idea, but it wasn't eXo." Erik rapidly began resetting the key algorithms responsible for the communication links and processors that had just crashed.

"Carlos, anything from Goddard?"

"They're saying two power surges hit the ship."

A quick glance, and Erik saw all the teams as well as Space

Force glued to their seats, rapidly checking readouts and gauges for any information while restarting their systems.

"Initiating reboot," Lee said. "Contact made with Ola. Ola coming back online."

"Confirmed. Ola rebooting," reported the Space Force Captain.

"Space Force will take into account Ola going offline and the teams' systems performance managing the outage," added Frank, the Space Force engineer assigned to monitor the test at Xtra. He was sitting next to Erik and Linc, equipped with his own monitor, keyboard, and mic.

"Damn, it's taking longer than I'd like for eXo to ramp up," Linc said.

"Don't worry. eXo's resilient. We built that and some into the system."

Erik hoped that proved to be true as he scanned the data eXo was transmitting from each of the bases. "Outgoing transmissions are wavering. I'm switching to eXo algorithm 3.9bv in three, two, one, active."

Erik and Linc held their breath as the eXo team and Space Force looked on.

"3.9bv has leveled out the waver. How's incoming?" Erik asked Linc, who was furiously keying in data on his keyboard.

"I have an idea," Linc said. "Game?" he asked his friend.

"Game."

"Going live in three, two, one, live," Linc said.

"Look at that." Erik saw eXo's rates climb another ten yottabytes. "What'd you do?"

"You know that program you said you just finished? Well, it seemed like a good idea to try it."

"Shit. No guts, no glory," Erik said, fist bumping his friend.

"No guts, no glory," Linc replied, bumping back.

"Do you realize your system is now moving a thousand yottabytes a second?" Frank asked, incredulous at eXo's performance.

"Yes, and we may be able to get more from this baby. Heck, look, something's happening at Tiger."

Erik and Link and the rest of the eXo team saw Dahlia screaming and knocking stuff off her desk before the Tiger team's screen went dark.

"Tiger's pulled out," Frank acknowledged a minute later.

"No comment re: Dahlia," Erik said.

He thought good riddance to a nasty woman. She'd come on to him and Linc years ago during a conference. Erik had turned her down, but Linc had fallen hard for her, only for her to dump him when she set her sights on richer prey—Tiger's CEO. And that was her nice side.

The test had forty-five minutes left. During that whole time no one from the remaining teams or Space Force relaxed. No one moved. In fact, no one spoke except to relay readings and other test data.

"Test complete in five, four, three, two, one—all systems off. Thank you, teams. We'll respond to your bids and announce the contract winner on Monday. Over and out," the Space Force Captain relayed as the team monitors and then Space Force's went dark.

I feel like we almost got leveled by a twenty-footer at Mavericks," Erik said as he stood and stretched.

"Yeah, but we stayed up, came through the tube, and rode it all the way in. Now we'll see whether the other teams made it to shore or got crushed," Linc said, smiling and reaching out to shake Frank's hand after Erik. "Hopefully we'll be seeing a lot more of you, Frank."

That should cement the contract, Daniel thought as he stood to shake Tiffany's hand. "When will you know what happened on the ship?" he asked the Space Force engineer assigned to Rictor. He wondered if he tried hitting on her again if it would help secure the win. No, he decided, casting a disdainful look at her hideously ugly brown suit, her drab brown hair pulled tightly into a bun, and the bright red nose she claimed was caused by his cat.

He bet she'd never seen the inside of an enhancer shop. He'd tried cozying up to her during the first test, and she shut him down immediately. Just like Alexandra, he thought, but Alexandra would be his after they had their little conversation. They would get married, or he'd reveal her little secret.

When he examined Alexandra's stick device that he found in the Rictor's guest bath—he'd been able to bypass its security protocols thanks to his little obsession with collecting DNA—and discovered its abilities, he began to add two and two together. While it made sense, he still had a hard time thinking of her and Emily as Al and Lee. He had no idea why either one of them would have hidden that information all these years. Although he was sure they had some altruistic, sappy reason for it.

Stephen would be furious when he found out after he'd spent decades trying to get Walter to share his data. Yeah, Alexandra would marry him in exchange for his keeping quiet—if not for her, for her cousin. Alexandra would get her eggs fertilized with the sperm he already had in storage, and he could start his dynasty. He wouldn't even have to fuck her.

When Ola had gone offline and then back up, Daniel tried to act flustered, at least for a minute, while loading the reboot so it wouldn't seem like he knew the blackout was coming. Rictor had performed like a champ, thanks to the secret program Daniel had built that rapidly restarted the system. In fact, he couldn't fathom any other team's system reacting as smoothly as Rictor's had. If anyone was going to explore the Oort Cloud, it would be Rictor. Rictor, and he deserved it, and by controlling Ola, they could keep their little mining operation secret.

With the win in the bag and his plans set for Alexandra, the next stop was president of Rictor. After Tiffany left, he picked up

Caligula and started stroking the cat. Stephen had basically told Daniel that if he won this contract, the Rictor presidency was his. Daniel knew Stephen had hoped Richard would prove he deserved the position, but he hadn't. He was too interested in partying, and Pattie was delusional if she thought Stephen would even look her way.

At first, Stephen had wanted him to marry Pattie. As if, he chuckled to himself. Pattie had served her purpose, but he could tell she was living on the edge, ready to fall off, with her obsession with her birds and opposition to exploring the Oort Cloud. He deserved someone brilliant, just like Alex, just like himself.

Yes, things were looking solid. As long as that captain he'd paid to set up that power surge was taken care of, no one could pin anything on him. Standing up, he plucked a brown cat hair off his lapel after setting Caligula down. Heading for the door, the cat following, he accidentally knocked over his cup, spilling coffee across his desk and onto his chair. The janitor could clean that up, he thought, as he continued out the door. He was too important to deal with something so mundane. Besides, if the stain didn't come out, he'd have his admin buy a new chair. Rictor's new president couldn't have a stained chair.

"Did you see Al and Lee's reactions when Ola went down?" Linc asked Erik later, while they were sitting in Erik's office having a celebratory coffee after returning from Playa.

"They looked as panicked as everyone else," Erik said, thinking back. "Their images wavered a bit, which was weird, but what wasn't?"

"Alex and Emily's approval to give up the search for their husbands' ship so that bot could keep her comms open sure ranks up there," Linc agreed.

"Eva worked for Walter. He created her. Also, last night they said they support BAPT, so I'm not surprised they gave the okay."

"I bet Alex catches grief from her husband's family, not to mention the companies that exploit bots. The morning talk shows have already started discussing granting rights to bots. I bet this sets some kind of precedent," Linc added as he picked up the puzzle from Erik's desk.

As Linc started spinning the cube, Erik thought about the women's actions. He'd always believed that actions spoke louder than words, and while he still felt Alex was hiding something, he couldn't believe it was anything malicious. No one who saved a bot—which is basically what she did—could be evil.

"I wonder what caused the outage?" Linc mused.

"It'll be interesting if Space Force finds out, and even more if they tell us. Regardless, eXo was screaming."

"Hopefully we've won the contract."

"Did I hear that right?" Dwayne asked as he entered the room. "You won the contract?"

"No, back down, Dwayne. We don't need your lawyering skills for that yet," Erik told the man, whose excitement dimmed.

"But we think the odds are in our favor," Linc added.

"Quit saying that. You're going to jinx us. Now what made you crawl out of your hole?"

"I resemble that remark, but I digress. If you're going to press charges against Gary, it's time to do it, although do you still want to?"

"Yes. You won't be talking me out of it," Erik said, starting to get heated just thinking about Gary.

"With those expansion plans you're looking at implementing when you win the contract—I know, I know, it's not a done deal yet—and Xtra looking for additional capital, investors aren't going to want to see any drama. They're already skittish about the hotel.

"They think it's a distraction, especially with one of your employees being attacked. Yes, yes, I know, technically she's not an employee, but still, and then having the police involved. If you file a report, it will hit the press, if it hasn't already. The police, even if they wanted to, can't keep this covered up."

"The bastard assaulted one of mine. Heck, he could have raped her or killed her. No way am I not pressing charges. In fact, I want you to file every possible charge against him. If that means we lose any investors, we lose them."

"I'm with Erik on this one," Linc added. "I hope that guy rots on Europa."

"Are you sure you want to go to Pierre's tonight? Why don't you stay home and take it easy? I can take the drive. You have a big day tomorrow, and you look like hell." Emily added.

"Wow, thanks. I'm glad I look so good," Alex snapped as she headed to her room to get ready for the club. "I'm sorry," she said, immediately apologizing to Emily. "I'm tired, but we both need to make an appearance. We have to keep up the pretense for these next few days."

"It doesn't look like you slept a wink. Even if you hide those bags, you're still running on fumes."

"I agree with Emily, for what it is worth, missy. You should take a hot bath and go to bed with a good book," Isobelle chimed in as she entered the hall, holding a pot she'd thrown on a wheel she built in the backyard. Isobelle had taken up yet another new hobby. "I have a good book that I can forward. It's about an alien named Jorg," she said, smiling at Emily.

"Jorg, hunh? You can send me that even though we're going out," Alex said to Isobelle, momentarily distracted. "We won't stay long, okay?" she added, absently twisting the end of her braid. "I need to get out. I need to do something. Otherwise I keep feeling Gary's hands on me. It keeps replaying in my head, and a hot bath isn't going to change that. I need to hear music, dance a bit after we give Pierre the drive. Now go get ready."

The Erisalve had worked its magic, Alex thought a few minutes later as she slipped on her special earrings. She really needed a distraction. Even though Farout had been a success and the colonists had been saved—that had added more stress—and then there was Eva. Deciding to abandon the search for Charlie to save Eva—that decision had been a doozy.

Tonight, she needed to dance. She refused to take any stress meds—they just made her sleepy or numb the few times she'd tried them. Dancing, though, that helped. And it didn't hurt that it helped her keep her cover. No one would ever think that Alexandra Addington, an event planner and clubber, was the same brilliant scientist who just that morning was working with Space Force to save a colony and expand humanity's reach into space. She slipped on her favorite aqua dress. It was one of her designer friend's first creations. Alex had been offered a ton for it since, but she'd never part with it.

"I think the new Pierre's a success," Alex observed as she, Emily, and Jared walked up to the club's entrance, the sound of surf crashing on the sand competing with the drum of a song's heavy bass inside. Usually, they could barely hear the waves, but massive ones were hitting the beach at the moment, thanks to a cyclone up north. Rain had been falling earlier but stopped before they pulled up, so it was damp, but the air was clean and smelled a bit salty, just like Alex liked. Fortunately, the patch on the roof was holding. Next Tuesday, the new roof would go on, and she could stop worrying about that.

"Looks like the paps like your outfit," Alex told Jared, eyeing the slacks and shirt Juliette had designed for him. When she first saw Jared, she mentioned she'd been thinking of branching into menswear. She confided to the women that Jared was such a fine-looking specimen that she couldn't help herself. Jared was dropping off the women tonight and leaving them under Pierre's protection. He had to do something for the General and promised to return when they were ready to leave.

"It looks so much better with the swan decorations gone, not that they weren't slammin', but I thought it was a bit busy," Emily said as they entered the club. With the swan décor removed, the club's ocean theme shone brightly, featuring robotic great white sharks, dolphins, and orange Garamundi swimming amidst giant kelp, which created intimate nooks throughout the club.

"There's Pierre. Let's give him the drive," Alex said as she spotted him approaching.

"Ladies, how nice to see you both. Alexandra, I have a few final questions about the renovation that I'd like to discuss. It will only take a minute. Emily, if you'd like to join us, you're always welcome," Pierre said, leading the women down the hall into the room where they'd previously met.

"Have you heard anything about the power surge during this morning's test?" Alex asked as she handed over the Mimant drive.

"All I've heard is that some things aren't adding up and they're investigating further. I also heard your avatars failed for a second during the outage. And I heard about yesterday's attack," Pierre said, his brow wrinkled with worry. "I could have come over to get the drive. In fact, why don't you two let me call your tov so you can go home?"

"Thank you, but no. Emily and I want to stay and let off some steam."

"Besides, if we're not safe here, with you and your staff looking out for us, where will we be safe?" Emily added. "We just want to relax and dance a bit, then we'll head home. Did you hear how well Ola worked, Pierre? It was smoking."

"Smoking?" he asked, confused. "The General said Ola did great."

"Smoking is good, Pierre," Alex said. "We're going to go dance some. We'll let you know when we're leaving."

"Hey ladies, I've been looking for you," Tracy said as the women entered the main room. "I heard you were here," she added when they looked at her puzzled. "Do you have a minute? I have a table upstairs in the back."

As the women headed upstairs, Emily elbowed Alex and nodded up toward the third floor. Erik and Linc, along with Jorgé and she assumed the friends they had been with earlier were having dinner, surrounded by different flavors of women, their dresses cut low on top and short on the bottom.

"Are those Juliettes? I swear, if I had the money, I'd have a closet full of her outfits," Tracy said, admiring their dresses. "I don't know which I like better. You look like a mermaid, Alex, and you, Emily, you look like a sea nymph rising out of the ocean in that seafoam dress."

"Are you on features again?" Alex teased their friend, who usually started throwing around flowery descriptions when her editor assigned her a feature story.

"How'd you guess? Becky's out, and they want me to do a society piece. Gag me," Tracy complained. "But that's not why I wanted to talk. Although, if you do have any inside dirt, I'd appreciate it."

"Sure, but spill. What's up?" Alex asked. Tracy didn't usually drag them to a back table, so she had something to say. She had contacts like nobody else.

"Well, don't freak, but I'm hearing a rumor that Daniel has eyes on you, Alex. Eyes like marriage eyes. I also heard that during this morning's test, the two of you showed up Al and Lee's place when there was some kind of glitch? Is that true?"

"Damn. If you're right about that, which you are, off the record, I hope that doesn't mean you're right about Daniel the Dick," Alex said.

Tracy nearly spit her drink out when she heard that description. "Can I quote you on the Daniel part?"

"Don't you dare; at least don't attribute it to me."

"You can say that an unidentified source called him that," Emily added helpfully.

"Remind me again to not get on your bad side," Tracy said. "Anyway, your avatars really glitched?"

"Yes, but just for a second."

"No way. Way?" Tracy asked, looking first at Emily, then Alex.

"We've put out the word that Al and Lee were having fun and had made avatars of us. If you don't mind spreading that around, that'd be great," Emily added, before taking a healthy gulp of her spicy Mimas.

"Are we still on for our interview tomorrow night?" Alex asked their friend.

"You bet. I'll be there at 7:00. I'm so excited. Though now I have to go talk to Jessica van der Hoosen. Talk about a mood damper. She just returned from the newest spa on Venus. It's called Romans. What a dumb name. She claims to have the first Venus tan. Is that exciting stuff or not? Thank heavens you two keep my mind from atrophying. See you tomorrow night."

"Hey, there's Raul," Emily said after Tracy left. Their handsome friend was talking to another man on the first floor. "Let's see if he wants to dance."

By the time the women wound their way through the crowded tables on the second floor and down the stairs, Raul had disappeared.

"I think he went that way," Alex said, pointing to the left.

"I could have sworn he went to the right."

"Hmm, let's find him. First one who does gets to drive home."

"You're on," Emily said, turning right to search. Alex purposely made it a game to distract Emily from the crowd pressing in around them. She'd found that challenging her cousin helped Emily cope much better.

Looking up for a second, she spied Erik still at dinner up on the third floor. Her breath quickened as he turned and locked eyes with her, ignoring everything else, including the twin brunettes vying for his attention. Alex broke eye contact first and turned away. She didn't want to deal with the man, or her feelings for him, not tonight. As she resumed her search for Raul, she felt a hand on her arm.

"Alexandra. You look lovely tonight. Doesn't she, Daniel?" Richard said, eyeing his cousin.

"Yes, she does. She looks stunning," Daniel said, giving her a calculating once-over. "And just the person I'm looking to dance with," he added, firmly grabbing Alex's arm and tugging her towards the dance floor.

*Darn*, Alex thought. Daniel the Dick—she had to stop calling him that—was the last person she wanted to run into tonight, especially if what Tracy said was true.

"So, where've you been hiding? At the spa? You look amazing," Daniel smiled as he pulled her into his arms and a slow piece started playing.

*Ewww*, she thought, pulling back from him. Daniel was wearing waaaay too much cologne. He always wore Calypso. She'd overheard him call it his 'signature scent' once. It always made her queasy.

"I'd hoped to talk to you at your family's party the other night, but you left before I had a chance," he said, looking down at her accusingly. "To be blunt, I think it's time we married. You've done enough traipsing around the Solar System with that cousin of yours. Marie told me she would be happy to plan the wedding. We could have it at the hotel. She already checked, and there's an opening June 8$^{th}$."

Alex stared at Daniel in shock. Whatever made him think she'd agree to even go on a date with him, much less marry him? He had to have suffered a major blow to the head.

"Come on Alexandra, or should I call you Al?" he said. Alex, struck dumb, could only continue to look at him in disbelief. "Yes, I know your and your cousin's little secret," he whispered into her ear after pulling her closer. "I was already suspicious, but when I found that stick you had in your hair in the Rictor's trash-can, everything fell into place. That stick's an interesting little device, by the way. I bet I can find lots of uses for it.

"If you don't marry me, I'll just have to out you two, and I don't think people would be happy to find you've been deceiving them all this time. I bet Space Force would be equally upset at the fraud. Besides, just think, with our brains, our children would be brilliant.

"Oh, we don't have to have sex, Alexandra," he added when she didn't say a word. "If you don't want to. Although I wouldn't mind, much. Think hard about it. I expect an answer no later than Monday, or I'll reveal your little secret. And before you think of running to Stephen, he's all but said that with the contract win, which is in the bag, and you on my arm, he'll make me president. And that's before he finds out about you. Won't that be a surprise? He didn't offer his precious daughter for marriage; not that I would have wanted to marry her, but you've always been an acceptable choice since you're part of the family. When he finds out you're the famous Al—after our wedding I think would be best—he'll shit. Now let's enjoy this music. I think it would be a good piece for our reception."

Alex was in shock. That was the only reason she was still dancing with the odious man, much less said anything. Everything he'd just said—from knowing who she and Emily were, to believing Rictor had won the contract, to marriage and sex. *Oh my God*, she couldn't think which was worse, though sex with him had to rank at the top. Thank heavens they were revealing themselves Monday. As far as Rictor winning the contract, she hoped that wasn't true.

"May I cut in?" Erik said, not really asking permission, as he smoothly took Alex's hand when a new song started.

"Monday, Alexandra," Daniel said, before turning and strutting off the dance floor.

"What's Monday?" Erik asked, thinking Alex looked a little pale.

"Oh, Daniel wants to have a meeting," Alex said, mind racing.

"About what?" He didn't like the man's possessive gaze. If anyone had any claim to his pixie, it was him, even if it was only a professional claim for now—a matter he intended to change soon.

"I hope you'll talk to me first if you're looking for additional work. I didn't want to bring it up until after the party. And I'd rather explore this crazy chemistry between us," he declared, drawing her closer as he guided her around the dance floor.

Alex felt like she'd fallen down a rabbit hole, first with Daniel, then with Erik, even though Erik's declaration had a lot more appeal than Daniel's. Unfortunately, what she'd hoped would be a low-stress evening had morphed into quite the opposite. She needed to pull herself together.

"While I agree there's chemistry between us, I'm not sure it's a good idea to explore it," she told the altogether too sexy male. She wasn't someone to go off half-cocked, pun intended, just because someone said they had chemistry. She still hadn't decided what she wanted to do with Erik, literally. Besides, she was still working for him. She needed to think a while longer.

"You make me crazy. My brain goes on vacation when I'm around you," Erik said, his soft breath against her ear causing a completely different sensation than when Daniel had drawn her close. "Let me try again. I would like to explore what's between us at whatever pace works for you. I know, or at least I think you're not the type of woman who has quickies in a side room, although if I'm wrong, please let me know."

"You're incorrigible," she said, seeing the hopeful look on his face. She also saw a youthful spark in his expression that she hadn't seen before, as if he was genuinely enjoying himself.

"I know, but I had to put it out there. Anyway, back to being serious, not that I wasn't serious about that, too. I'd like to explore the possibility of an 'us'. I've never said that to anyone before, mind you, so I'm not sure how to go about it, but it's something I'd like to explore, if you feel the same. Don't answer me right now. I'd rather hear a 'yes' later than a 'no' or 'maybe not' now. Am I rambling?"

"Yes, actually I think you are," Alex replied, touched he was being so honest, something she'd never expected from such a playboy.

"Let's just finish the rest of this song, and then you should go home. You look tired."

"Funny, that's not the first time I've heard that tonight. I think I need to go get a new makeup program or go to that new spa on Venus I've been hearing about."

"You're perfect just the way you are. At least don't argue with me about that."

Alex chose to stay silent and just revel in the feeling of dancing with a man who wanted her for her, not that he knew who she really was. When the song ended, he walked with her to find Emily.

"Thank you for the dance and the offer," Alex said. "I'll think about what you said."

Well, he'd obviously bungled that, Erik thought to himself as Alex and Emily headed to get their coats. He hadn't felt this inept since he was a kid. What was it about her that made him lose his mind? Sure, she was pretty—beautiful in fact—and whip smart. He still wasn't sure if he could trust her completely. He and Linc sensed that something was off with her and that cousin of hers.

Deciding he was ready to leave, he went to tell Linc he was heading out. Tomorrow would be an early day. Hopefully it would be drama-free, but when dealing with celebrities, one never knew. He must have been out of his mind to schedule the opening so close to the contract competition. To be fair, Space Force's schedule had slipped by a month.

A few minutes later, the two men stepped outside, with Linc

also opting to leave, only to find Alex and Emily waiting for their tov, along with an elderly man approaching the women. Worried he might cause trouble, they moved to intercept the man.

"Can I help you, gentlemen?" the man asked, the two men suddenly blocking his way. The man looked slightly unsteady on his feet, maybe homeless, although once he got closer, Erik noticed his clothes looked clean but rumpled.

"Hey Alex, hey Emily," the man said, peering around Erik and Linc.

"Capt. Joe, we were looking for you," Emily said as she and Alex came around Erik and Linc, the two women regarding the men as if they'd fallen off their rockets.

"Capt. Joe, meet Erik and Linc," Alex said. "They're okay. I'm doing some work for them."

"Harumph," the Captain uttered, peering suspiciously at the men.

"Iso gave me some cookies to give you. They're in the tov," Emily said. "It's coming now."

"Cookies?" Linc asked hopefully.

"For the Captain," Emily said, giving the large bag to the elderly man. "He watches over us when we're here," she explained to Erik and Linc.

"Not that they need any help, but some nasty sorts do live on the beach round here. Can't be too careful," the old man said as he checked across the parking lot before taking a cookie out of the bag. "If you two boys ever need anything, don't hesitate to call out, and I'll come a-runnin'. That is, anything except one of Isobelle's cookies," he added, chortling to himself before taking a big bite. "Well, I'll be seein' ya'all. Give my thanks to Isobelle." He nodded to the four before shuffling off to a dark corner in the parking lot.

"Is that a house in the corner?" Erik asked, peering into the dark.

"Yes, that's the Captain's place. He came with the club. Walls make him nervous," Emily said. "Pierre built him a tiny house on the back corner of the parking lot."

"The fact that he talked to you two, you should feel flattered," Alex added.

The Captain only spoke to people he liked, snubbing a few over the years, much to the amusement of some. He could id a jerk faster than anyone Alex knew.

Erik felt more than flattered. He was impressed that these two tiny women were so friendly with someone like the captain. He was involved with several charities that helped homeless vets, and that's surely what the Captain was. He knew helping vets suffering from PTSD required a special touch. Especially those who'd fought in the Enceladus Conflict, which he suspected the Captain had.

During that horrible war, many soldiers had become trapped in malfunctioning warships that endlessly circled the Saturn moon. When nations finally agreed to a ceasefire, ships raced to rescue the soldiers, but most had died when their oxygen ran out. Only a precious few had been saved. Their minds had been a different matter. Recently, a mining ship had discovered another one of the old fighters on the surface.

Just then, Erik noticed the women's tov pull up, and Jared, "the cousin," step out and hold the door open for them.

"See you tomorrow," Alex said as she and Emily walked over to the tov and got in, Jared eyeing the men before following inside.

"There's no way that guy's related," Erik said as he and Linc watched the vehicle pull away. "Still no word about an ID?"

"Nothing," Linc said as they waited for their ride.

# Saturday, February 28, 2172

Alex definitely felt wired, and it wasn't because of any lattes, she decided, as she straightened her desk at the hotel. She'd be out of there after the parties tomorrow and didn't want to clean up then. Last night, she and Emily had met with Tracy to record their interview, revealing their identities. Both women were relieved to have finished that. Now Alex was reviewing the hotel's plans for the evening party a final time when Erik stuck his head in her office.

"Ready?" Earlier, he'd asked if she would escort some of the VIPs to their suites, making it clear that if she wasn't comfortable with the assignment after Gary's attack, he'd get Meg to help.

Of course, Erik had to look amazing, she thought, as she rose and slipped on her jacket. His dove grey Amani suit, paired with a Hotel Bel-Air-pink dress shirt open at the collar, covered his body like she'd like to cover him. Ironically, she was dressed in the same colors. Blessings on Juliette, who had created her current outfit and the amazing ones hanging in her closet for the pre- and post-Oscar parties. Alex had protested at first, but Jules insisted it would be great advertising for her and told her to shut up.

Erik was already struggling to keep his hands to himself. He needed to stay focused on the opening and the network contract.

He'd worked too hard to let himself get distracted by a woman, no matter how hot. She did look amazing in her suit, and he quelled the fleeting fantasy of removing it, followed with a quickie on her desk.

"Chloe and Jorgé should be the first to arrive. Are you okay seeing Jorgé to his suite? I promise you, having known him for a long time, he won't pull anything."

"I'm fine," Alex said, fingering her ring as they entered the lobby. "I don't mind taking him to his suite. I like him."

*Jorgé?* Erik wondered if it would be too late to switch and have him take Jorgé while Alex escorted Chloe.

"Dahlings," Jorgé drawled as he entered the lobby a second later. "You two look like you're posing for the cover of *Interiors*," he remarked, bussing Alex's cheeks before clasping Erik's hand. "The hotel looks great, but I'm beat and need a nap. Care to take one with me, pretty lady?"

"Jorgé, really?" Erik said, a red haze starting to emerge when thinking of Alex with his friend. "Maybe I should take you to your suite, or should I change your room to the dungeon we've just renovated?"

"Erik, I'm fine. Besides, Ms. Chambord will be here in a second, and you said you wanted to escort her to her suite."

"Yes, she's fine. Come along. You can show me what Erik's been doing around this place." Jorgé said before spotting Chloe Chambord entering the lobby. "Chloe, you look tired. Who put you through the ringer?"

"Jorgé, I can always count on you being blunt," the actress said as she removed her wool Pradica coat and draped it over the back of the lobby sofa. Admittedly, she did look a bit frazzled, Alex thought, but that didn't detract from her stunning beauty or elegant clothes. Even when tired, the *Swan Song* star knew how to dress. Watching first Jorgé and then Erik greet her, she felt a small —*okay, not so small*—twinge of jealousy as Erik gave her a very warm kiss and a too-lengthy-for-strangers hug. It seemed she was nice, as well, Alex thought irritably. At least she was gracious when introduced to Alex.

"It was the spacraft that did it. It hit a ton of turbulence coming in from Europa. It knocked me off the bed. Spacorp isn't getting any recommendations from me."

"Well, you can sit by the fire here while Mr. Big Hotel Owner figures out which room he put you in. I'm taking Alex and heading to my suite. I'll see you later, maybe much later," Jorgé said, clearly enjoying poking his friend. He'd noticed that every time Alex was around, Erik couldn't keep his eyes off her. Something was brewing there, and it was about time. At least for his friend, who'd always sworn he had a commitment phobia. Jorgé linked his arm through Alex's and winked at Erik as he led her away.

"You know he's all bluster," Chloe said, noticing Erik's glower at the retreating Jorgé, looking like he was about to go after the two. "Besides, who's she, and when did she catch your eye? Don't deny it."

"Honestly? You heard about the accident with my event planner?" With Chloe's nodding, he explained how he'd found Alex. "I've only known her a couple weeks," he continued, "but it feels like I've known her a lot longer. She's smart—"

"Very pretty."

"That, too. Nice. She could be the one."

"Really? The great Erik Wolfe's leaving the bachelor ranks?"

"We'll see," Erik said, uncertain of how Alexandra felt about the idea, though he hadn't admitted that much to her yet. "Let's just say stay tuned. Her contract ends with the parties. So, how do you like the hotel? And do you still want me to keep quiet about your news?"

"Yes, I do. And you're avoiding the subject, which I'll let you do for now," the actress said as Erik walked her to her suite. "Sometimes it seems so strange, doesn't it, Erik? Whoever would have thought that we'd be here today?"

"I never had any doubt."

"No, you didn't, did you? You just put your head down and worked away."

"It's not like you didn't pay your dues. All those shows you did in those off-world dives? I'll never forget seeing you in the Bedford Bergère on Triton," he teased as they entered her suite.

"I'll have you know that was a great show," Chloe protested, swatting Erik's arm. "Ok," she conceded, "it was great training."

"Training you how to duck, for sure."

"Ha ha. Thanks for arranging the juice by the way," she added, picking up the chilled glass of tomato juice that had been resting in a silver bowl of ice. "Oh Erik, the hotel looks amazing. The last time I was here, it looked decrepit. Even the swans seem shiny today," Chloe added, looking at the birds gliding across the lake after Erik opened the suite's French doors.

"The bones were always good. Now—"

"Oh my god," Chloe said as she stumbled, splashing juice on Erik's suit. "I'm so sorry." She quickly tried wiping it off, but it had already soaked in. "Take it off. Let me run cold water on it."

"It's an Armani. I don't think that will help," he said wryly as he slipped off his coat.

"It's on your shirt, too," Chloe said lamely as she dampened his coat with a washcloth before turning to try and absorb the juice staining his shirt front. "At least your shirt was already pink."

"I don't think that's helping," Erik said, grabbing the washcloth out of Chloe's hands before the whole front became wet. "I have other shirts and jackets. Now, before you collapse and take a nap, tell me, is Mick still coming? And are you keeping it a secret until the Oscars tomorrow?"

"Yes and yes. He should be arriving in about an hour. Will you unlock the connecting doors between our rooms? You did get him the connecting suite?"

"Yes. You have Alex to thank for that. She was the one who shuffled everyone's room."

"I owe you and her. Thank you, Erik," Chloe said, reaching up and kissing his cheek.

One down, Alex thought as she headed back to the lobby after dropping Jorgé off. He really was a nice man. She could see why he was so successful. He'd told her he was determined to get her and Emily to consult on his next movie, *Swan Lake.* He mentioned the script had a couple of holes and wanted it to be believable. She said she'd think about it when he had a more concrete idea of the details. She wouldn't mind helping if she had the time, especially since he so cleverly offered to bribe her with the promise of a hefty donation to Venice's swan rescue project. Lost in thought, it took her a second to notice Erik coming out of Chloe's suite, jacket in hand, his shirt disheveled and damp, and was that lipstick on his cheek?

It was a good thing she hadn't made up her mind about him yet. He must have been playing her. Now he was messing around with that actress. He hadn't seen her, so she stepped behind a pillar, circling around it as he passed, probably headed to his office to change. She would shove her hurt and stupid gullibility aside and slam the door on both. She had today and tomorrow to get through, and then she could leave and never see the jerk again.

Entering the lobby, she found Rex Fieldstone, the movie's male lead, had just arrived. As she escorted him to his suite, she noticed his short black hair was sticking up like he'd just gotten out of bed. Maybe he had. With his 6'5" lanky build, chiseled face, and sparkling emerald-green eyes, he probably had no shortage of willing women. Isobelle had mentioned that she'd read the whole package was natural, no enhancements needed anywhere, wink, wink, nod, nod.

Next came Samantha Stevens and Clint Johnson, up for best supporting actor and actress and supposedly in love with each other. She led them to their suite, a two-bedroom, which made her wonder if the rumors were true. After ensuring the couple was settled, she returned to the front lobby to check on Tuesday. Unfortunately, she saw Erik already there, talking to her.

"I can see all's well here," he said in that oh-too-sexy cheating voice as she walked up.

"Everything is fine, Mr. Wolfe."

Alex noticed that Erik had changed into a different pink shirt and grey slacks. She also saw a small bit of lipstick still on his cheek.

"How many of those shirts do you have?" Alex blurted before thinking. Here he'd been trying to get in her pants, inferring he'd like a relationship, or at least explore one, and then he carried on with Ms. Movie Star. Maybe she should reconsider Jorgé's offer. He certainly thought she was interesting. Too bad he didn't push her buttons like Erik did.

"As a matter of fact, I have several since they match the hotel's brand. Why do you ask?" Erik wondered if she'd seen him leaving Chloe's room without his jacket on and with lipstick on his face. Damn the meddling woman. He knew she'd kissed him on purpose.

"Did Jorgé behave?"

"Yes, perfectly. In fact, he offered me and Emily a job on his next movie."

"He did, did he? I don't need to warn you that he's a bit of a player."

"Pot, kettle, you two run in the same circles. Besides, it's not my first time off-planet. Speaking of off-planet, isn't that Mr. Jagger coming across the bridge? Do you want me to take him to his suite, or will you?" Alex asked.

"I'll take him. You should head home for a break. Tonight's party will run late."

As Alex checked her list for the pre-Oscar party and tried not to fume over her philandering boss, she wondered why Erik wanted Mr. Jagger to have that suite. It couldn't have anything to do with Chloe or with what she'd seen, damn him. At least she'd seen him in action before she risked her heart, or her body.

She'd briefly considered confiding in him the other day about her and Emily's big reveal. Thank heavens she'd wised up before spilling the details. She finished clearing out her desk, packing the few personal items she'd brought. She'd already taken Larry the Lizard home. And that was also depressing. The little time she'd spent getting to know Meg, or Linc for that matter, had been nice.

She was trying not to feel nervous about Monday. She suspected their lives would change, but how much she or Emily couldn't guess. The fact that they'd be able to attend meetings and conferences as themselves would be freeing.

Switching thoughts, she was glad she'd seen Erik leaving Chloe's suite. There was no way now that she would accept his offer. She'd been tempted, having considered a night of sweaty sex and a swan song the following morning. If she would have even stayed the night, she thought as she left the hotel and headed home. Now, none of that was happening.

"Ladies, Tracy's on the comm," Isobelle said as she entered the kitchen.

"Can you tell her we'll comm her back in ten?" Alex asked, taking a last spoonful of carrot barley soup before pushing her chair back. "Ready?" she asked Emily, who nodded slowly. "You know we can still cancel," she added, concerned about her friend's pale face.

"No. I'm tired of holding you back, and myself," Emily added before Alex could protest, nervously chewing on a fingernail.

"You've never held me back. I've wanted to avoid the attention just as much as you."

"You never showed it," Emily said, looking at her nail with disgust. "I wish that hot sauce remedy had worked."

"At least it cleared your sinuses," Alex said, remembering when Emily had dipped her fingertips in some extra spicy Ziki sauce to try and keep from chewing her nails. Then, when she'd forgotten, she'd nibbled, gasped, turned a bright red, and raced to the sink to gulp water. "And that's not true. I just show it differently. I haven't been sleeping."

"Is that because you haven't decided what to do about your wolfy or because of our reveal?"

"Probably both." Alex absently started braiding her hair. "As for my wolfy, I didn't get a chance to tell you. I think he's seeing Chloe."

"The actress?"

Alex told Emily what she'd seen, disappointment growing as she told the story.

"The bastard! After coming on to you?"

"I knew he was a player."

"Yeah, but still. I bet Linc's no better. What're you going to do? I know you were thinking about maybe, you know—"

"Maybe what?" Bev asked as she walked into the kitchen with Anita, backpacks on their shoulders. "Spill, please. Like, inquiring minds and all that," Bev prompted, eyebrow raised as she put her soup in the robocook. "Great soup, Iso, and no, no macadamia nuts on top, thanks."

"Where did you get that recipe?" Alex asked, seizing the chance to change the subject. She so did not want the girls to overhear her talking about having sex with Erik.

"You know the macadamia website I found?" Isobelle said.

"How many nut dishes have you planned?" Emily asked, eying Alex, thinking that they may have to do an intervention.

"Only a few," Isobelle said as she opened another can of nuts.

"I'm beginning to feel that I may be developing a bit of an allergy to them," Alex said, as Emily hid a smile. "Ready to comm Tracy?" she asked as she rinsed her bowl and put it in the robowash.

"So, what are you going to do?" Emily asked as the women entered their office, Fred and Barney following. "I'm assuming you're going to the opening party tonight."

"I have to go, and no, I'm not going for it," Alex sighed. "And even if Chloe hadn't happened, I would have waited until after tomorrow's after-party. Then I could've escaped the next morning since my contract would be up."

"All the women say he's very attentive. I haven't seen a single complaint about the wolf man," Emily added, sorry her friend was hurt.

"Regardless, it's moot what with him hanging with, or should I say, banging Chloe?"

"Bastard."

"Who's banging Chloe?" Tracy asked as her holo appeared. "Good afternoon, ladies. Are we still on for tomorrow? Any cold feet?" Working at home, the reporter had on her favorite worn shorts and an equally faded blue t-shirt. A litpen tucked behind her ear, she sat at her desk cluttered with skimpads and tablets, while her old tabby snoozed on the back of her high-back chair.

"We are on, aren't we, Alex," Emily said determinedly.

"Yes, we're doing this. What time's it airing?"

"8 a.m. EET. Same time the contract will be announced, from what I hear. It's going to be a busy news day. When are you planning on being available for other interviews? You know others will be baying for time."

"Towards the end of the week. Okay, Emily? Iso can field calls until, say, Wednesday?"

"Do we even need to talk to anyone else? I mean, we've said everything in your interview, Ms. Nosy," Emily said, eyeing their friend on the screen.

"If Tracy's piece runs, we'll still have to talk to others at some point."

"Alex's right. Those harpies will want to talk to you, and the sooner you talk to them, the better," Tracy said, leaning back in her chair. "Play it like you're eager to talk to them. I know, I know you're not, but if they think you are, and you give them some time, then they'll lose interest that much faster. It's pure psychology."

"We'll become old news, and they'll get distracted by something else," Alex agreed, unraveling the braid she'd just braided.

"Do you want to watch the vid again before I tell Elenor it's a go?" Tracy asked.

"I don't. It looked fine. Lee, what about you?"

"It will only make me more nervous if I watch it again, so no. Thank you."

"We'll be going dark around 11:00 Monday for a couple of days, just so you know," Alex told Tracy. "But you can always reach us on our private comms."

"You aren't trying to distract me from the comment you made about Chloe, are you? A little bird tweeted that Wolfe's interested in you, in more than a professional way. Was my little bird right?"

"Off the record, I thought he was interested, in an uncommitted way, but now I think he's more interested in Chambord."

"He and that friend of his are such players. I'm sorry, Alex. Yours unfortunately wouldn't be the first heart he's broken. By the way, did you hear the good news? Susan's awake. They're not letting her talk to anyone yet, but it's progress. Gotta go. Catch you later."

# Sunday, February 29, 2172

"Everything looks great. This all wouldn't have happened without your help, so thank you for all your hard work, especially for stepping in in the middle of everything," Erik told Alex as they waited in the hotel's bar for the VIPs to arrive.

"I'm not so sure about that, but thank you," Alex said as she looked around, checking for flaws. Yesterday's opening and *Swan Song* Oscar party had been a huge success. Everyone only had compliments. Media requests for follow-up interviews and access had poured in, while the public had flooded the reservation desk.

This evening's Oscar after-party would start soon. Everyone associated with the film, their dates, and a few select guests were coming. Alex felt on edge. Chloe had shocked the world when she appeared at the Oscars arm-in-arm with Mick Jagger. The actress had not been linked to anyone for years. With the two revealing their relationship, the streams had anointed Chloe and Mick the new it-couple.

That news had only increased the buzz surrounding *Swan Song*, much to Jorgé's delight. Alex herself was reeling with the realization that Erik wasn't involved in a torrid affair with Chloe. Yesterday, she had resolved to not have anything to do with him.

Now, she didn't know what to think. For the past two weeks, she'd felt like a ball in one of those new vid games pinging frantically back and forth.

Despite everything, the chemistry between them was still off the charts, and he *was* single. She covertly eyed his physique in yet another beautiful suit, this time without a tie and open at the collar. A whiff of his cologne enveloped her, sending her senses soaring. Maybe she could indulge for one night—if he was still interested. However, he'd been all business yesterday and, so far, tonight.

*Swan Song* had swept the Oscars. While the cast had dinner at the Governors Ball, she knew they wouldn't eat much before making the rounds at the Vanity, Derby, Beverly Wilshire, and Elijah after-parties. Knowing the group would be hungry when they arrived at the hotel, Chef Leon had been madly preparing another gourmet feast, Peking Pulled Jackfruit and Amgukyu Filet just two of the delicacies.

Alex had tasted the Amgukyu beef the other day and had to admit it was amazing. A conglomerate of Japanese and American ranchers had bred and raised what they called Amgukyu cattle on Uranus' moon, Miranda. The first shipment had just arrived on Earth. How Erik had scored some, she had no idea.

Chef had also prepared Shallot Agrodolce with Raka nuts from Neptune's Triton, along with repeats of everything served at yesterday's party, including the famous *Swan Song* butter-lettuce salad. He didn't skimp on dessert either, serving chocolate and vanilla versions of the hotel's famous meringue swan-shaped Floating Island—another dish that had everyone going gaga over last night.

From the bar, besides the traditional offerings, Erik had somehow located both red and white wines from the new winery on Jupiter's moon, Ganymede, another amazing accomplishment.

"Jorgé just commed that he's on his way and is hungry," Linc reported as he walked up. "As a matter of fact, so am I," he added, grabbing some Raka nuts from a bowl on the bar.

"You're always starving," Erik said to his friend. "Quit eating all the nuts before everyone arrives."

"Relax. I saw the big can of Rakas behind the counter. Besides, Chef prepared a ton of food. I don't think anyone will go hungry. Too bad your cousin couldn't come tonight, Alex. What's she doing that would beat Chef's food and my company?"

"She had another engagement," Alex said, thinking of Emily's engagement with a hot bath. Linc made Emily nervous in a way that Alex hasn't seen before. Besides, her cousin had enough to manage with tomorrow's reveal. She wasn't up to braving Linc tonight, either.

"Well, I'm heading to the kitchen to see what I can sneak from Chef." Linc left, still munching nuts.

"You thought I was interested in Chloe," Erik murmured as they watched Linc walk away.

"I saw you come out of Chloe's suite. You looked tousled. You had lipstick on your cheek."

"Tousled? Is that even a word?" Erik asked, tugging on an inky, silky lock that had escaped from Alex's intricate braid. While beautiful, he itched to unravel it and run his fingers through it before putting his hands on her. She'd looked stunning last night, dressed in a sleek, sleeveless black dress made from what looked like black swan feathers that hugged her body. A slit in the dress had run high up her thigh that, combined with her lethal black stilettos, made him feel like a hungry Raptin tracking a favorite snack all night long.

Tonight, she looked just as hot in a pale pink number, this one short. She wore matching pink stilettos that, together with the dress, made Erik want to scoop her up, throw her over his shoulder, and escape to any room with a door.

"Yes, tousled," Alex prompted.

"Linc and I have known Chloe a long time," Erik said, trying to get himself under control. "She's like a cousin, a bratty one. Besides, I already told you I'm interested in you, Alexandra. And while I don't believe in long-term, I'm never intimate with more than one woman at a time."

Well, that was kind of good, Alex thought, in a no-strings, purely physical kind of way. She looked at him. He took her breath away. She decided she wanted this, wanted him, even if it was just for one night. "So, what are you doing after the party?"

"Hopefully spending it with you."

"I think that would be nice."

"Maybe we shouldn't wait until the party's over," Erik suggested, feeling a tightness ease in his chest now that she'd finally acquiesced. Ever since he'd met her professionally—even before, when he'd first discovered his mystery pixie sleeping under the oak tree—he'd been entranced. "These movie people can stay up all night, and if I'm going to be awake, I think I'd rather be doing something other than talking to them."

While he still suspected there was more to her than she revealed, and he answered all of his own questions, it wasn't as if he'd spilled all his secrets either. He couldn't see how she could be the spy or thief they were searching for, or the one trying to sabotage the company, even though she was connected to the Rictor family. After his experience with Syndi, he'd learned to pay attention to any subtle signs of deceit. He hoped his gut would alert him if someone wasn't genuine. At least he hoped so.

"Erik. My favorite swan lady. Did you hear?" Jorgé asked as he walked up waving his Oscars around. "We swept them, the whole damn thing. It's time to celebrate. Everyone's on their way. Do you have a table where I can park these?"

"We originally had a small table set up, but when we saw how many awards the movie won, we had to pull out one of the conference rooms," Erik said, a smile on his face as he saw Jorgé's giddiness. He was happy for his friend and gave him a congratulatory slap on the back. Jorgé had earned this success after working so tirelessly and paying more than his fair share of dues.

"You'd better not let this go to your head, or we'll have to pound some humility back into you, boy-o," Linc chimed in, walking over while munching on an appetizer he'd swiped from the kitchen. He clasped Jorgé's hand and pulled him into a celebratory hug. "You also better not rope us into any more movies. We won't be so gullible next time."

"You loved the attention. Besides, it gave you publicity for this relic. We'll talk later about the next one. Alex, you can tell me later that you and your cousin will be helping us, too. Tonight's for celebrating. I'm ready for some of that famous Ganywhit I heard you scored."

Soon, the rest of the group arrived by twos, fours, and more, settling in for some serious eating, drinking, and celebrating. Mick arrived with a radient Chloe, who showered Erik and Linc with huge hugs and kisses. Samantha arrived, arm-in-arm with Clint, while Rex came in with a woman who looked familiar, though Alex couldn't place her, followed by the remaining cast and crew.

"Everyone looks settled," Erik whispered to Alex a couple hours later after they'd circulated and congratulated everyone. A little earlier Mick had borrowed one of the musicians' guitars and serenaded the group with a song he was releasing next week, a treat Alex wouldn't soon forget. The group then insisted Chef come out and take a bow, much to his embarrassment.

"Interested in disappearing?" he asked, hoping desperately that she still was. "Rumor has it there's a beautiful suite called the Crow's Nest that needs attention."

"The Crow's Nest, hmm," Alex said, linking her arm in Erik's and taking a breath. "I guess we'd better make sure everything looks good in there."

As the evening had progressed, Alex felt as if she'd been downing espresso; at this point her body was vibrating. Now that she'd decided to spend the night with Erik, she felt hyper alert, the occasional brush of Erik's sleeve or hand on her back as they conversed with the others further heightening her anticipation of finally having the freedom to slide her fingers and explore his sleek, taut body.

As Erik snagged two glasses and a bottle of Ganeyred, Alex

tried to stifle her sudden jitters. She hadn't had sex in so long. At least her bruises had finally disappeared. Otherwise, that would have certainly been a mood dampener.

"Are you okay?" Erik asked as they entered the suite, noticing Alex seemed nervous.

"I'm a bit out of practice with this kind of thing," she admitted. "You're, well, you're you and I, well, the last time I saw a naked man was quite a long time ago."

"I don't think I want you remembering other naked men right now," he said as he set the glasses down on the credenza. He began unraveling her intricate braid, running his fingers through the long, glorious mass as it fell to her waist. "I've wanted to do this since I met you."

"Thanks," she said, feeling herself unwind as his fingers gently threaded through her hair. "I'm not sure I know what to do," she said, trying to keep her nerves in check while he turned to pour them some wine.

"They say it's like riding a cycle." He handed her a glass. "You never forget."

"I don't know how to ride anything but a stationary cycle," Alex said, feeling a bit breathless.

"That's okay. I know how to ride," Erik murmured as he drew her close, leaned down, and plundered her lips.

# Monday,
# March 1, 2172

Erik woke to the sound of his comm vibrating. It stopped for a moment, then started again. Swearing softly under his breath, he carefully lifted Alex's arm, which had been splayed across his chest, and slipped out of the bed to avoid waking her. This had better be important, he thought, as he walked over to grab his comm from the table near the door. It felt like they'd just fallen asleep again. He could tell it was early; the early morning light barely illuminated the room. The hotel, tucked in the canyon, didn't see the sun until at least 8:30. Whatever it was, it wasn't good because he'd left explicit instructions not to be disturbed unless it was an emergency.

"I need to see you as soon as possible. It's urgent," a message from Ron said on his comm.

Erik messaged Ron that he would meet him in his office in five, then began searching for his clothes. He thought he should have something casual delivered for Alex to wear, glancing at her dress pooled on the floor where he'd removed it. With a smile on his face, he slipped out the door thinking whatever was happening, it wouldn't diminish the night he'd shared with Alex.

He'd never experienced a connection like the one he had with her. Between the explosive sex, they'd quietly talked about their lives. He still felt she wasn't telling him something since each time he asked about her future plans, she evaded his questions. Somehow, though, he felt certain she would open up to him in time. As he entered his office, he couldn't believe he was actually considering he might want more from her than just a single night.

"Boss, I am so sorry to disturb you, but I know you'd want to see this as soon as I discovered who'd broken into your safe," Ron said, not looking happy.

"Who was it?" Erik barked, thinking this wasn't enough of an emergency to pull him away from Alex.

"This had better be good," Linc interrupted grumpily as he entered Erik's office, still buttoning his shirt.

"You both probably want to sit down." Ron moved to start the vid on the wall.

Silently the men watched as the vid began, showing Erik's office and the picture of the Camelia behind his desk that hid the safe. Alex appeared on the screen, placing a folder on Erik's desk before looking across at the painting. She circled his desk and reached out toward it. Then there was a glitch; the screen blacked for a second before revealing the painting swinging open. A familiar female hand wearing a familiar gold ring placed a device on the safe door, pressed a few buttons, and the safe opened. The hand then reached in, took out the decoy papers that Erik and Linc had stored in the safe, closed it, and swung the painting back into place. Another jerk in the vid caused the screen to blur for a second. Finally, they saw Alex straighten the picture, turn, and walk out of view.

"I'm sorry, boss. I just finished cleaning up the vid enough to see Ms. Addington, and ...well, what do you want me to do?" Ron asked, clearly not happy to be this messenger.

Erik felt numb. Linc and Ron looked at him uncomfortably. It wasn't a secret he'd been interested in Alex from the start, and it probably wasn't a secret he'd just spent the night with her.

"I want her escorted off the property immediately," Erik said, a coldness seeping into his body. He'd trusted her. He'd trusted her, and now she was trying to steal from him, from his company.

"Do you want to press charges?"

"I'm not sure we can since technically she stole a decoy; therefore, no damages," Linc said quietly, sorry for his friend and equally angry that Alex was the thief.

"I want her gone immediately. And Ron, tell her why and that Xtra's legal counsel will be contacting her," Erik added, anger burning like the ice on Europa that he'd accidentally touched when he'd been careless so many years ago. He'd almost lost his hand that time. This time, it felt like he was losing his soul. Never again, he thought. He would never again trust a woman.

Alex was dreaming she was napping on a beautiful beach when a lifeguard walked over and shook her. When she realized that someone really was trying to wake her, she dreamily opened her eyes, expecting to see Erik, hopefully with a coffee and one of chef's passion fruit croissants. As the face looming above her came into focus, she quickly realized it wasn't Erik. Instead, it was Ron, and he didn't look happy. She pulled up the sheet to cover herself fully as he dropped her dress on the bed.

"Mr. Wolfe has instructed me to tell you that you are to leave the property immediately. I will give you five minutes to get dressed before escorting you out, starting now," Ron said stony-faced, glancing at the comm on his wrist.

"What? Where is he?"

"Four minutes, fifty seconds. Mr. Wolfe does not want to talk to you, Ms. Addington. He did say to tell you that he knows now that you were the thief who stole the papers from the safe in his office. He also said to tell you that Xtra's legal counsel will be contacting you shortly. Four minutes, twenty seconds," Ron added before turning his back.

It was clear Ron wasn't going to leave the room, Alex thought dazedly as she sat up and started pulling her dress over her head. Untangling herself from the sheets, she stood, yanked her dress down, and looked around for her underwear, bra, and shoes. After zipping up her dress, she stepped around Ron and changed her stilettos to flats before slipping them on.

"Three minutes."

Frantically Alex looked for her bra and underwear. They were her favorites, and she'd be damned if she left them behind, she thought as the reality of her situation started to set in. Why they thought she had stolen any documents was a mystery, but being accused without given a chance to defend herself felt like a kick to the gut.

"Two minutes."

She finally spied her bra on the credenza and grabbed it. She stuffed it in her clutch along with her comm, figuring she didn't have enough time to put it on before Ron made her leave. Seeing her image in the mirror, she groaned.

She looked exactly like she'd imagined, like she'd spent the night in bed but not sleeping, the bastard. She wasn't going to cry, holding tight to her anger. She didn't give her body frivolously, and last night had been the best ever, even better than with Charlie. Dousing that thought, she smoothed her hair as best she could, turned, and walked out the suite, not bothering to see if Ron was following. Staring straight ahead, she headed towards the back gate that led to the side yard and her house.

"You have to leave through the front," Ron said, grabbing her arm to steer her in the opposite direction. "The code on the back gate has been changed. I probably shouldn't do this, but there are a lot of paparazzi out there. Here," he paused briefly before abruptly handing her a giant, grey sweatshirt with a hood.

Grabbing the sweatshirt and slipping it on over her dress, Alex strode towards the entrance, pulling the hood up. Eyes straight ahead, she didn't look into anyone's office as she passed. Tuesday, looking puzzled, called out to her as she entered the lobby, but Alex kept on walking, out the door, across the bridge, and out across the parking lot. Turning left, she ignored the still sleepy paparazzi and headed for home, starting to shake as what had happened began to crystallize.

Grateful the paps thought she was just an employee and not worth their time, she hoped she wouldn't run into any of her neighbors. Nothing worse than taking the walk of shame on Stone Canyon. At least she'd washed off her makeup last night, so she didn't look like a raccoon. And, of course, there was Mr. White across the street, walking his toy collie. He tentatively waved to her as he peered over his glasses. In a half hour, the news would be all over the neighborhood.

When she entered the kitchen, Isobelle turned, surprised to see Alex so early. Her expression shifted to concern when she saw Alex's face.

"What happened to you, dearie?"

"Erik. Erik's what happened to me," Alex said, walking into the woman's arms. "He threw me out. He thinks I stole some stupid papers of his. He didn't even give me a chance to defend myself," she added, tears starting to streak down her face.

"Is that my slutty cousin?" Emily joked, coming into the kitchen. "What happened?" she asked, seeing Alex crying in Isobelle's arms.

"He kicked me out of the hotel. Gave me five minutes to leave. Said I stole some stupid papers," Alex said, hiccupping as she tried to get control. "He sent the security guy to tell me to leave. He didn't even have the decency to face me and accuse me himself. I was still in bed."

"The bastard!"

"And I left my favorite underwear there," Alex added, mopping her eyes with the napkin Emily handed her.

"Not the pink Pragrain ones? The double bastard," Emily

declared when her friend nodded in response. She wrapped her and Isobelle in a big hug, resting her head on her cousin's shoulder. "I'm sorry, so sorry."

"So am I. I thought he was a nice guy. Obviously not," Alex said, taking a deep breath. "I need to take a shower," she added, wanting to get the smell of him off her.

A half hour later, clean but weary, Alex entered the lab, hearing a reporter on the vid talking about her and Emily's interview with Tracy. As the reporter wrapped up, Alex looked at herself on the screen and sighed. She'd looked a lot better just a few days ago, suddenly feeling tired of life. Looking across the lab, she noticed the hidden door to the steps that went up to the greenhouse standing open.

Next to it, Pattie stood, pointing a blaster at Alex. She looked terrible, her hair all messy, faint smudges of what looked like dirt on her blouse and skirt, and a streak of something on her cheek. What was the matter with Pattie? Why hadn't Iso told her Pattie was here in the lab? And why was Pattie pointing a blaster at her?

"How could you? I trusted you. You've been lying all these years!"

"What are you talking about, Pattie? Did Iso let you in?" Alex asked in as quiet and soothing a voice as possible. She noticed with alarm the slight tremble in Pattie's hand.

"No, that bot didn't let me in. I got in through the secret stairs. Oh yes, I found them years ago. What I never discovered was that you're the famous Al! You lied to me," Pattie shrieked. "Everyone always lies to me. First Father, then Mother. He said I could be president. Ha! That was a lie! 'You can always have another baby,' Mother said." Pattie weirdly mimicked her mother's voice. "That never happened. Then Richard and Curtis—both liars, the cheaters. Now you, Miss Famous Al! And where's that Famous Lee hiding? Oh Lee! Lee!"

"Alex, did you call me?" Emily asked as she stepped into the lab. "We already have a ton of comms requesting interviews. I asked Iso—"

"I bet you've gotten a ton of comms," Pattie hissed at Emily, who turned in surprise.

"Hi Pattie, what are you doing here? And why do you have a blaster? You should be careful with that thing. They're not toys," Emily said automatically before realizing something was wrong based on the look on Alex's face and Pattie's disheveled appearance.

"They're not toys! They're not toys! Of course I know they're not toys. And they call you brilliant," Pattie said, mimicking Emily, before launching into a fit of laughter.

"I'm sorry I lied to you, Pattie," Alex said, desperately trying to think of anything that would appease her. "I didn't want to, but do you remember that boy who was kidnapped and killed back when we were thirteen?

"After he died, Uncle Wally and Father wanted us to pretend we were average kids. They worried that someone would try and take Emily or me. And then Charlie and Sam came, and they agreed it was better to stay undercover. But now we don't have to have any secrets. I don't have to have any secrets with you." As Alex talked, she slowly edged towards Pattie, worried that she was now aiming the blaster at Emily.

"Stop moving! Stop confusing me! It's all over now. The contract's going ahead. Those bastards won it. I suppose you spilled all Seed's secrets to Erik when you spread your legs for him. And now it's too late. Don't you see that?

"Wasn't Marbola enough? We can't keep exploring further and further out. The birds almost died because of that freaking disease. God knows what someone will bring back when they travel further out.

"But if the Famous Al and Lee aren't around to make Ola work, then Space Force won't be able to explore further. I would have thought you'd have agreed with me after losing Charlie and Sam. Then you picked that bot, Eva—a bot over your husbands! She's not real. How could you? Now you two can join them," Pattie said, waving around the blaster.

"Pattie, do you really believe bots shouldn't have any say over their existence?" Alex asked, hoping to somehow reach her cousin.

"Of course I don't! They don't deserve any rights. They're dangerous! Just because Mother doesn't mind screwing them—oops, wasn't supposed to say that. Mother will be mad," Pattie said, waving the blaster around more. "Anyway, who cares about bots? You won't have to in a minute," Pattie added, beginning to laugh again. "The important thing is to keep Ola from working. Gary and I had a plan, you know. But now he's been arrested. That's your fault, too. But if I get rid of you, you can't press charges either!"

"Pattie, if you feel you need to kill us, I get it." Alex slowly edged closer to the woman. She touched her ring twice to her earring. If she could just get a hand on Pattie, she could shock her and then grab the blaster. "I understand. The world did suffer terribly when Marbola arrived. Before you kill us, though, can I hug you? I would like to think that at least a little part of you loved me like I've loved you all these years."

"Sure, because I'm going to kill Emily first," Pattie said, her eyes darting back and forth between Alex and Emily. "I don't need a hug from her. She should go first anyway. If your uncle hadn't found Emily, then you and I could have been sisters—sisters who don't keep secrets from each other."

"I would love for you to be my sister." One more step and she could reach Pattie. "I always wanted that, just like I could really use a hug."

"Sure, in the meantime, say goodbye, Lee," Pattie said, her finger tightening on the trigger.

Alex leapt towards Pattie, who jerked the blaster towards Alex in surprise. As Alex landed on Pattie, shoving her down and shocking her with her ring, she felt a searing pain in her side.

"Noooooo! Emily has to die first!" Pattie shrieked before passing out from the jolt.

"Alex, Alex, are you okay?" Emily ran around the desk as she yelled for Isobelle. "Oh my God, are you alright? You're bleeding!" she cried as she helped Alex off Pattie.

"Get the blaster," Alex whispered, her side burning as if she'd been stabbed by a hot Treble. Slumping against the desk while keeping an eye on Pattie, she lifted her hand to find it covered in blood. "I think I need a medpac."

"Iso, comm the police. No, first get a medpac," Emily yelled, pointing the blaster at Pattie in case she woke up.

"No, first get something we can tie Pattie's hands with. She's clearly lost it and probably will go crazy again when she comes to." Alex stared at her bloody hand. "I can't believe she shot me or was going to shoot you."

"Me either. I mean, I know she never liked me much, but I thought she liked you."

"I've called the police and brought a tie and the medpac," Isobelle said as she hurried into the lab.

"I wonder what she meant when she said, 'We have a plan'?" Alex asked weakly as Isobelle ripped her shirt open and slapped the medpac to her side.

"Look at that," Emily said, motioning to a tattoo on Pattie's upper thigh. When she'd fainted, her skirt had lifted to expose it.

"It's the same symbol that was on the flag the police found in Hawaii," Alex said, peering closer at the circle with the line drawn through it. "At the time, I thought the symbol was a lousy drawing of Jupiter."

"I think the circle could be the solar system," Emily said, looking closer.

"Something that Solars group might use," Alex said, turning to look at her cousin.

"She cleared out her office, everything, but this," Erik told Linc as he walked into his office, tossing the device stolen from his safe onto his desk. After Ron had informed him that she'd left the hotel, and that she hadn't even tried to defend herself, Erik went to her office to look around. In the bottom drawer, wedged in the back, he discovered the device they'd planted in his safe. She'd removed her personal belongings—her ratty orange shoes, the weird lizard paperweight—but left everything else behind.

"Have you talked to Dwayne?" Linc asked.

"No, but I left him a message to let me know if we can press charges," Erik said, throwing himself into one of the guest chairs and rubbing his eyes. After what amounted to a short nap last night and the early morning wake-up, along with the fast, hard pace he'd been maintaining to open the hotel and win the network contract, he was fried.

"Here's a nice, hot, double espresso." Linc handed his friend a steaming cup, worried at the weary look on his friend's face.

"You need a vacation. Heck, we all need a vacation. Dwayne can sort this out. What do you say? Maybe get some surfing in? Dusty called and said the waves are hitting North Shore."

"I don't know." Erik wasn't feeling any interest or enthusiasm for one of his favorite sports. "Let's talk—"

"Excuse me, General Watson is on the comm. He wants to talk to you both," Jenny said over the comm.

"Switch him over. I hope the rest of the day doesn't get worse," Erik muttered.

"Gentlemen, good morning. I'm not going to draw this out, so congratulations. Space Force is awarding Xtra the contract. eXo by far outdid the rest of the teams. Well? Aren't you going to say something?"

"Yes, sir. Of course, sir. Thank you, sir. I think Erik and I are in shock, but we are very grateful and thrilled. Yes, thrilled. We thought we had the best solution and hoped to win the contract, but—" Linc started babbling.

"Yes, yes, I get it. Well boys, there's a lot of work to be done.

You'll be getting the contract by end of day today. Have your counsel look it over. We expect an acceptance, that is, if you accept—"

"Yes, of course we accept," Erik said.

"Good. We'll expect to receive your acceptance within the week. I suggest you take a week off after that, except for sending that acceptance. We'll be ramping up quickly and there will be little time, if any time, for R&R. You'll be working with Al and Lee."

"The Al and Lee?" Erik asked.

"Yes, and they don't let grass grow under their feet. I'll have my folks coordinate with your admin to schedule a meeting with them."

"We get to work with them directly?" Linc asked, flabbergasted. "As in in-person?"

"Yes, son, as in face-to-face in person. They're revealing their identities in an interview with some reporter that's being released, I think, right now. Not so fast, young man," the General added when Linc leapt up, obviously wanting to see the interview. "The police should be showing up."

That would explain the red flashing lights on his and Linc's comms, Erik thought. "What did Alex do?"

"Alex?" the General asked and then laughed. "Son, if you think Alex would even consider doing something illegal, then you don't know her at all. No, I'm talking about Sally Greyheart. Confidentially, and I mean that this is to be kept confidential for now, we're arresting her for industrial espionage.

"We found she's the one who sabotaged the other teams and tried to sabotage Xtra, too. Anyway, we contacted your head of security, who said she would contact your on-site security to work with the police and escort them to her office. Gotta go. We'll be looking for that acceptance letter. In the meantime, congratulations," the General said as he disconnected.

"We won," Linc said, a huge grin on his face. "We won the contract. We did it!"

Erik was struggling to process all the information that the General had just dumped on them, especially after the previous night and what felt like a soul-crushing morning. Just then the comm started ringing.

"Sorry to interrupt," Jenny said. "Debbie insists she speak to you immediately."

"Put her on main display," Erik said. "Did Ron or Debbie tell you the police are coming?"

"Yes, they should be here in about five minutes."

"Do you know where Sally is?"

"Yes, she's at her desk."

"Tell Ron to do whatever he can to keep her there," Erik said, trying to grasp the fact that they had two thieves in their midst. "While we're talking to Debbie, please track down an interview with an Al and Lee that's supposed to be airing now. We'll want to watch it as soon as we're done with Debbie."

"And tell Dwayne to keep his eyes out for a Space Force communication—you, too—we won the contract," Linc said, still grinning, before turning to Debbie on the comm.

"Good morning," Debbie, Xtra's head of security, said. "First, I heard congratulations are in order regarding the Space Force contract. I hope you get out and celebrate some. Second, and just as important, Ron jumped the gun. He was wrong. Alex Addington was not the thief. Sally Greyheart is. I had my guys analyze the recording further. It was a very sophisticated job. We almost missed her fingerprints.

"For some reason Sally set up Alex," Debbie continued. "And that's not all she's been doing. Space Force alerted me about twenty minutes ago that the police would be arriving at the hotel to arrest her for industrial espionage. Apparently, she was the one responsible for taking down several teams competing for the contract and trying to eliminate us, too. At least that's what I'm hearing. I've already alerted Ron.

"Before you jump all over Ron, I already have. I've got to run. I told Space Force I'd give them the evidence we have on Sally. It seems not only did she set up Alex, she's also the one who hacked the website earlier. She tried to route it to Alex's comm, but there's no way Alex could have done it. She was at a party on Venus, and remember that solar storm? Comms were down all over, so she couldn't have hacked anything from there. We also found Sally's ID buried in one of the strings."

Alex was innocent? Sally set her up? Erik felt he'd been hammered by a Quina shark. He'd had her thrown out of the hotel without even giving her a chance to defend herself. He'd watched her leave the hotel on the vid, head held high, shoulders back. She looked beautiful even with her hair mussed. And he'd thrown her out.

"Erik, Erik, you gotta look at this," Linc interrupted Erik's thoughts.

Erik looked up and saw Alex and Emily on the display, with a familiar-looking reporter seated across from them. It looked like they were in their living room. A banner headline scrolled across the bottom: "Al and Lee's Identities Uncovered!" Erik wondered why the reporter was talking to Alex and Emily.

Linc pushed the button to restart the vid.

"You've been in hiding since you were children. People thought the famous Al and Lee were men. Why are you revealing yourselves now?" the reporter asked.

"We're tired of hiding," Alex said, the camera zooming in on her face, explaining her uncle and father's reasoning back then.

"Then it seemed smart to keep undercover, if you will, when we lost our husbands," Emily added.

"There was so much publicity at the time, "Alex said, clearly uncomfortable in the limelight. "It would have turned into an even bigger circus."

As Erik and Linc watched the rest of the interview, incredulous looks on their faces, the women explained further why they'd hidden and what they were planning for the future for Seed and themselves. Erik was reeling. Alex was Al? The famous reclusive inventor? The incredibly brilliant Al? Suddenly he remembered the paper she'd handed him with those corrections. When Jim returned after being sick, he denied having anything to do with them. The team never pursued it because they were up against a deadline, figuring it didn't really matter.

"You also have some sad news you wanted to share," Tracy said.

"Yes, Walter Dees, our uncle, has passed. Right now we ask for privacy. We'll make another announcement later regarding his death," Alex said.

"Emily is Lee?" Linc asked, equally as dumbstruck when the interview ended. "Walter is dead? Sally's the thief?"

"I have to go talk to her. I need to apologize."

"Heck, bro, you need to get down on your knees and prostrate yourself. I wonder if she can sue us?"

"Forget worrying about that. I wonder if she'll ever talk to me again." Erik looked at his tracking app to see if he could find her. Relieved, he saw she was at her house. "I'm going next door to see if she'll see me."

"I'll deal with Sally," Linc said as Erik left.

When the interview ended, Daniel threw his glass at the display, cracking the screen and shattering the glass. Damn it. He'd been so close. Now that Alex and Emily did that interview, he had no pull over her. The little bitch. She knew exactly what she was doing when he spoke to her at Pierre's. If only those morons had managed to grab her. And now Xtra had won the contract. He'd have to start over again, he thought, rubbing his hand over his face.

At least Sally and Gary had taken the fall. They couldn't pin anything on him, either. They never saw his face or heard his real voice. And Pattie? He wondered about her, but she'd never known he was the one calling the shots. It seemed like she was already going off the deep end. Maybe he'd push her a bit more.

Pattie was counting on Rictor winning the contract, just like him. But he had other cards to play. The contract wasn't his only ace. Pattie, though, thought she'd be named president. *What a joke*, he thought as he got up and walked out of his office, the whiskey still dripping from the cracked display.

"What the hell," Steven shouted, pacing across the Family Room. "Alex is Al, and that white trash is Lee? They must have been laughing all this time. And Walter's dead? That means those two have been running Ola this past month? And you," he turned suddenly to Richard, pointing an accusatory finger at him. "You said you talk to them all the time. You had no idea?"

"No, I didn't." Richard felt like he'd entered a new universe. He couldn't believe what he'd witnessed, so much so that he'd had to watch the interview a second time. His parents had burst into the Family Room just as it was ending. He'd never seen his father so angry. Meanwhile, his mother just beelined to the bar. Richard was angry, too. He'd thought that even though no one else had treated Alex or Emily particularly well, he'd made an effort.

"Those ungrateful bitches," Marie said, already halfway through her third drink. "After we've been so kind to them all these years."

"If that was kind," Richard muttered.

"What was that?" Marie slurred.

"We could have been nicer," Richard said, amazed she'd heard him. "That's all. We could have been nicer."

"She could have shared Ola's information with us. We would have won the contract. What the hell?" Steven said. "What am I going to tell Anwai?"

"What's Anwai have to do with this?"

"Remember that solar job we had on the moon that didn't pan out? I sold some shares to Anwai to cover our losses."

"Oh, tell him the truth, Steven." Marie refilled her glass. "You sold half of the company."

"You didn't have the right to do that," Richard said, rapidly trying to think back if he'd missed something. "Pattie and I hold thirty percent each."

"You thought you owned that much."

"What's Anwai expecting since we lost the contract?" Richard asked, feeling as if his head was going to blow.

"I'm not sure. Maybe we can offer up your sister as collateral. She needs to get married, and his son needs a wife now that he's divorced again."

"I've heard strange things about him." Richard thought of some of the rumors he'd heard. He wasn't close to his sister, but Peter Jr. was weird.

"Pattie can deal with that. We'll have him sign a prenup. Where is your sister anyway?"

"What're you going to do about Erik? Since Xtra won the contract, we'll be working with him and Linc," Emily said to Alex who was slumped at the kitchen table drinking a large iced cinnamon Certe that Isobelle had made her, the level-five medpac glued to her side.

Good thing they had the pac in the house, Alex thought, not liking even the idea of a trip to Emergency. When their friend Tracy had seen it in the bathroom cabinet during her last visit, she'd teased them about it being overkill. Admittedly, most household medpacs only rated up to a three, but theirs wasn't like most households. Tracy had rapidly changed her tune when she insisted they let her try the new skyjets they'd been testing and ended up cutting her leg. The next morning the wicked cut had almost completely disappeared.

"Remind me to never get involved with anyone again," Alex said, looking across the table at her cousin. She would not be bitter, she told herself. She'd had a nice night of hot sex, to put it mildly, and worse things had happened than the walk of shame she'd had to endure—even if Mr. White had broadcast her picture to the neighborhood. When she had to work with Erik on the new network, she could remain cool and professional.

Now that she knew Sally had framed her, she could better understand Erik's reaction. "Better understand" being the operative words. Forgetting, however, was a different matter. Besides, when he finds out about her being Al, he probably won't be interested. She'd discovered many men felt threatened by smart women.

"Iso told me Erik just commed," Emily said, looking at her friend. "He wants to talk to you."

"That's nice," Alex commented pleasantly, sitting back. "He can blow smoke up his tush." The medpac had started to kick in. She still had work to do, but she was bone tired, the pac sapping the little energy she had left. Medpacs were great, but the more severe the damage, the more of a body's energy they siphoned to heal it.

"He also forwarded the vid that showed you raiding his safe. You should look at it. That Sally woman did an impressive job framing you."

"You looked at it?"

"Yes, it shows a female hand opening the safe. Wanna watch it?"

"Not right now." She would look at it later, when she felt better.

"It doesn't look exactly like your hand, but I know you. The hand had a ring almost exactly like yours. I can see why they thought it was you."

"Yeah, possibly, but he didn't even give me a chance to defend myself," Alex said, turning her ring around and around her finger. "He had Ron kick me out. They even locked the gate."

"I'm not saying you should forgive him. I'm just telling you what I saw in the vid. Also, the General wants to have a meeting. He didn't want to talk on the comm about what they've discovered."

As Alex headed to her room, she thought about the vid. Furious—at the men who killed her uncle, the thugs who'd beat her up, heck, everyone who had been yanking her around like a puppet. She badly wanted to blast something, at the least, Sally and Pattie. Lucky for them, the police had already picked them up.

She almost felt sorry for Pattie—she was definitely certifiable. Sally, however, was a different story. Not only had she almost ruined Susan's rep, she'd destroyed what could have turned into a real relationship. The only bright spot today was the news from Susan's sister. The doctors had moved her to recovery this morning and cleared her of any brain damage. Alex bet once they released Susan, she would want a piece of Sally, too.

With that thought, Alex decided to head to the side yard. She needed some serious decompression. Since the hotel had locked its gate, she wouldn't have to worry about seeing anyone. After telling Emily she was heading to sit beneath Big Ben, she slipped through their gate into the side yard, the dogs at her side.

Passing the big oaks and sycamores, she avoided crushing the new grass rising from the recent rains. Doves and jays chattering as they searched for seeds and insects created the only break in the silence that began to seep in and soothe her rioting emotions. She was amazed at the punch that pac had delivered, but she also felt as if she'd aged fifty years in the past couple of weeks.

She somewhat understood why Erik had acted how he had, as she carefully bent down to brush away some oak leaves from the base of the giant tree. Heck, she might have done the same in his position.

Wincing, she sank to the ground, Fred nosing her hand in an attempt to comfort her, while Barney sat at her feet. She'd permit herself to wallow in misery today. She was so damned angry she'd been set up —that she hadn't somehow seen it coming. Leaning back against Big Ben, she drifted off, feeling Fred's warmth against her side.

"I should set Fred and Barney on you," Emily told Erik as he walked up to the front door.

"Yes, you probably should," Erik admitted.

"I can't believe you thought Alex was a thief or a spy. Even though that vid did show what looked like her ring," Emily said after explaining what had happened with Pattie.

"I knew she was hiding something," Erik said lamely, realizing Emily wasn't going to let him in the door. "Especially when I found the Marbotabs in her desk. I was finding them all over the place. Places where people had broken into the property, my office.

"Pattie's the one who used those tabs. She probably planted them, or Sally did it for her. Alex hates them."

"I didn't know," he admitted, feeling lower than low.

"So why are you here?" Emily asked, folding her arms across her chest. She was kind of impressed that he admitted he'd messed up, but she wasn't going to say it.

"I want to talk to Alex. Apologize. Is she here?"

"If we let you talk to her, do you promise you will leave her alone if she asks you?" Isobelle asked, appearing behind Emily. "We will know if you do not. And if you break your word, you will be dealing with me. I do not tolerate people who treat anyone in our family badly."

"I promise," Erik said, amazed he could feel even worse and

more guilty than before he arrived. "I won't do anything to hurt Alex."

"Anything more," Emily added, glaring at Erik.

"Anything more," Erik replied.

"She's in the side yard, under the old oak." Emily knew her cousin needed to see Erik and hear him out. Whether or not she forgave him was up to her.

"Pattie shot her."

"What?" Erik said, shocked they'd let Alex wander off, even though it was to the side yard. "And you just let her go?"

"She's okay. We had a level-five pac."

Erik found his pixie asleep against the huge old oak in the side yard, a squirrel chittering on a branch high above. Fred and Barney, alert and lying next to her, glared at Erik, warning him not to disturb their mistress. So much had happened since he'd first found her sleeping under that giant tree. The bruises had faded, but the dark circles had returned, this time thanks to him. He felt bruised himself, having been led down a path where he'd hurt someone he discovered he cared about.

Suddenly, she started moaning and tossing. He didn't want to wake her, but if she really started thrashing, he would. Carefully he sat down next to her, the dogs having decided he wasn't a threat.

Erik realized as he walked over that he really liked Alex—a lot. He respected her, too, and that was before he found out that she was the famous Al. Thinking back, he realized that the signs had been there if he hadn't been so distracted. If he were truly honest with himself, he admitted he'd never had a connection like the one he shared with her. He realized he wanted a relationship with her, something he'd always thought was beyond his reach, like what the lucky ones, such as his sister, had. Something he never thought he'd want or dreamed would be in reach.

Alex was becoming increasingly distressed. She was clearly trapped in a nightmare, which, from the looks of it, seemed like a particularly bad one. Just as Erik decided to wake her, she jolted awake with a gasp. Frantically looking around, her gaze sharpened when she saw Erik.

She wondered how he'd found her and realized Emily must have told him where she was, the traitor. She wondered how that conversation had gone, knowing how protective her friend could be.

"I'm sorry," he said. "I was an ass."

"Yes, you were," Alex said, looking around for a way to gracefully get up and leave.

"I didn't give you a chance."

"No, you didn't," she agreed, settling back against the tree and looking at the man who had hurt her. She realized they'd only known each other two weeks—too short a time for any kind of solid trust to develop. Yet still, it stung. "You threw me out. You locked the gate."

"I was an ass," he repeated, tentatively reaching for her hand. "I almost lost everything because a woman stole from me."

"You thought I was like her," she said, feeling a painful tightness in her throat.

"When I saw your bruises, I first thought you'd been abused. I thought maybe you were still seeing the person who'd done that to you."

"You heard my uncle is dead," Alex said, feeling the pain of his loss again.

"Yes, I'm sorry about that, too."

"What Emily and I didn't say in the interview is that Walter was murdered. We still don't know who did it," Alex added quickly when she saw his shock.

"I went to close up his house after his murder," Alex said, leaning back against the tree and closing her eyes. "Some thugs jumped me. They wanted me to tell them where my uncle kept his files."

"How'd you get away?" Erik asked, reeling from that shocking bit of information. What the hell, he thought, feeling even more guilty for adding to her burden instead of helping her. "I knew something had happened at your uncle's house, but I couldn't tell what."

"The General shut things down tight. If people knew Walter was dead, it would have thrown Seed into a tailspin. The Farout colony was on borrowed time. The network tests had to proceed. As Al and Lee, Emily and I were already planning on running it. If the news about my uncle had gotten out, we would have had to reveal ourselves then. Emily wasn't ready; heck, I wasn't ready either."

"The General could have done something," Erik said, his anger starting to boil. "He left you hanging. And he just let you handle the tests? I suppose Pierre is part of all this mess, too."

"That's not for me to say. What I can say is that the General has always protected us as best he could. He didn't want me going to my uncle's house, but I went anyway. And we had to get Ola to Farout. People could have died. Don't blame him."

"I can't believe you didn't ask me for help."

"How was I supposed to do that?" Alex looked at Erik, who for some reason she'd let hold her hand. "You didn't know me. I didn't know if I could trust you. We still don't know who killed my uncle."

"You think I could have killed him?" Erik asked, appalled that Alex could have thought so poorly of him.

"Well, Iso did say at first there was a high possibility you were the killer."

"You're kidding," Erik exclaimed, incredulous anyone would think that of him. "I'll have to talk to her. I thought she liked me," he added, feeling strangely hurt.

"She does like you. Or at least she did before this morning."

"I deserved that," Erik admitted, feeling even worse about everything.

"She did agree with Emily that the vid was good."

"The ring. It was almost a perfect match to yours," he said wonderingly as he examined the ring on her finger.

"That's what Emily said."

"Sally's under arrest. She's going to jail for a long time. Emily told me about Pattie. That she was the one who sabotaged the other teams," Erik said. "She was working with Gary. He caved this morning to get a reduced sentence."

"Pattie mentioned Gary when she was ranting this morning," Alex said.

"They could have killed us," Erik said, first staring at the ground, then looking up. "I don't mean just you and me, but what we were building together. I told you earlier that I don't do relationships."

"I know. And I get it. I'm not sure I'm built for relationships either," Alex admitted sadly.

"When I thought you'd betrayed me, it felt worse than when that other woman deceived me," Erik added, leaning back against the tree, lacing his fingers with hers. "Then, when I found out that Sally had set you up, I felt numb. Then when Emily told me Pattie almost killed you, I realized I could have lost you forever. I didn't think I was capable of loving someone, and I know it's only been a couple of weeks," he said, playing with her fingers.

"Two."

"It's only been two weeks. I know this is fast, but I'd like to try for a relationship with you, an exclusive one. I know you don't love me, yet," he added, looking at her hopefully, "but I hope you feel something for me, even though I was a complete and utter ass."

"Yes, you were," Alex agreed, deciding if he could be honest, so could she. She realized she also wanted more. She wanted him. She clasped his hand and slowly pulled him close, until she could feel his breath on her lips. She closed the gap just enough to kiss him in answer.

"Why do I always feel like I'm being watched when I'm here?" Erik asked when they surfaced for air minutes later.

"We have very smart animals here in Bel-Air," Alex murmured. That was a secret for another day she decided as she pulled him closer. She didn't want to dwell on any more secrets right now. He got the message.

# About the Author

Jeni Lynn has written for newspapers, magazines, online news channels, and multinational corporations. While she's covered topics ranging from custom doll houses to cybersecurity, interviewing innovators, including NASA scientists and engineers, cemented her craving to write about space and the future. If she'd been better in math, she would have been an astronaut.

Bel-Air Confidential is her first futuristic romance. Waikiki Confidential, which will hopefully be finished soon, will be the second novel in her stand-alone Confidential Series. She lives in Los Angeles with her husband, children, and rescue dogs.

To sign up for her newsletter, the Galactic Gossip, and discover details about the Confidential Series, visit www.jenilynnau thor.com.

instagram.com/jenilynn.author

Made in the USA
Coppell, TX
21 March 2026

74372391R00196